STOLEN THREADWITCH BRIDE

SECOND EDITION – THE AUTHOR'S CUT

BOUND BY A FAE BARGAIN
BOOK ONE

CLARE SAGER

Stolen Threadwitch Bride

This Revised Second Edition Copyright © 2022 by Clare Sager

Original First Edition Copyright © 2021 by Clare Sager

All rights reserved.

No part of this book may be reproduced in any form or by any electronic or mechanical means, including information storage and retrieval systems, without written permission from the author, except for the use of brief quotations in a book review.

*For the ones who make themselves small.
I see you, and you are worth seeing.*

BUTTERFLIES IN A CASE

I smiled like my life depended on it.

It almost did. I wasn't in a fight or threatened by a wild beast, no, but danger nipped at my heels just as surely as any ravenous wolf. And with his greying hair, watery gaze, and oak panelled study, Lord Hawthorne had the power to save me.

Apparently oblivious to his opportunity to become my knight in shining armour, he only watched me pull another sample from my basket. The harsh lines of his face didn't move even as I held up a bodice so intricately embellished, his wife and daughters would've drooled and snatched it from my hands before I could so much as blink.

He cleared his throat and raised grey eyebrows at me.

Damnation, I'd been quiet for too long, just depositing sample after sample on his desk.

My throat tightened, not wanting to release any words.

It's only one person, not a whole room. Just Lord Hawthorne. I'd known him for years—Mama had brought me on visits to Hawthorne House since I was old enough to stand still and hold a tape measure. Once or twice, he'd even managed a stiff smile and told his butler to offer me a sweet.

I could speak in front of him. I *could*. My mouth just needed to remember that.

Cheeks burning, I managed to swallow and suck in a breath, fixing my eyes over his shoulder at the frame on the wall. Behind the glass, dozens of butterflies were pinned to a board, cocoons beside them, stunted. Although their patterns were pretty and the metallic colours glorious, they were sad little specimens, dead and still.

It made my shoulders sink, but the distraction meant I could speak at last. "So you see, ser, your daughter could wear such a bodice made with enchantments to draw attention and—"

"Yes, it is quite spectacular." He dismissed the bodice with a flick of his hand. "As is all your work, Ariadne. However, my daughter doesn't *need* more attention."

The burning crept down my neck. Gods, why had I phrased it like that? With her blond hair and green eyes, his eldest was a renowned local beauty. My work only complemented what was already there. "I'm sorry, ser, I didn't mean to suggest—"

"I know you didn't. We both know she has quite enough attention as it is, and I fear if she has any more I shan't be able to fit her head under my roof. Now, I don't say this because I'm offended—I am not—however I simply do not need a full-time seamstress."

Threadwitch.

A threadwitch, not a seamstress. I didn't have an impressive gift that could summon storms or light candles with a snap of my fingers, but I had magic. I could stitch it into cloth and through beads and create garments no *seamstress* ever could.

However, Lord Hawthorne was not a man you corrected. So I clenched my jaw and bowed my head, letting my hood slip forward to hide my irritation.

"We've dealt with your family for many years, and will continue to do so." His voice gentled, but each syllable still came out with such precision it could've been cut from glass. A true lordly accent. "But I see no need to commit to a contract."

Of course he didn't. A contract wouldn't give *him* a steady income so he could pay his rent each month. And I'd bet he didn't have debts.

Instead, he had a mansion full of tapestries and brocade, with lace doilies on the walnut sideboard and silk carpets that whispered under my feet as I shifted. With my too-dark skin and strange hair barely concealed by my hood, I was a flaw in his perfect dollhouse.

"I will leave it to my lady wife to contact you when she next has need of your services." His thin mouth curved in his attempt at a smile. It didn't meet his pale eyes. "I believe the Hamptons will be holding a ball in the summer—I should imagine the girls will require gowns for the occasion."

In the summer? We were barely past the spring equinox, and I only had enough coin for my next rent payment. What about next month and the month after? And what about the wolf at my heels?

His upholstered chair creaked as he sat back and shuffled through some papers.

I was dismissed.

And I'd failed.

Rose, dear, sweet Rose who for some reason believed in me—she'd organised this meeting, phrased the letter asking for the contract. I'd failed her, too.

My hands shook as I gathered my samples from his desk. What an idiot. I never should've let her talk me into this. Why would he give me a contract? I should've known I wasn't good enough. Otherwise he would've said yes.

I stuffed my work into my basket and bowed my head. "Thank you, ser. I'll—"

"Oh!" He started, looking up from the papers as though he'd forgotten I was there. "Yes, yes, good day, Ariadne." Jowly chin lifting, he shouted, "Belton, get in here!"

I flinched at how loud, how sudden that noise was in the enclosed study.

The door opened and the butler appeared, a short, dour man with no more than three hairs on his head. Without a word or a smile, he ushered me to the tradesman's entrance. I couldn't blame him—I might've been that gloomy if someone spoke to me like that every day.

By the time I emerged and reached the tree-lined

street, my burning face had cooled. I should've argued with him, should've made my case. Lady Hawthorne and their daughters preferred me over the seamstresses of Briarbridge and the contract would've reserved them spots in my schedule throughout the year.

Then again, arguing with Lord Hawthorne was easier said than done. Rose might've managed it, but me? I scoffed and shook my head.

Maybe I could try to bump into Lady Hawthorne. She wouldn't be able to resist the promise of—

"Miss Ariadne." The voice, slippery and slick, slithered through my thoughts and stopped me in my tracks.

Shit. The wolf nipping at my heels.

A Wolf at Her Heels

I sucked in a sharp breath and pushed my feet onwards, but he fell into step beside me.

Sallow-skinned and ash-haired, Skeeves bared his teeth in a dull smile. "How delightful to see you."

It was anything but "delightful" to see him. I bit my tongue against the burning need to tell him to fuck off. "What do you want, Mr Skeeves? Rent isn't due for two weeks." I kept my voice flat and my eyes on the road ahead where a carriage rattled by, pulled by a pair of large, black sabrecats, and all sorts of folk went about their days.

"Now, now, is that any way to talk to such a kind and benevolent landlord?"

Kind and benevolent? This was the man who'd put up our rent when Mama and Papa—and, later, I—were ill with the creeping death. I ground my teeth even as my eyes burned at the crushing weight upon my chest. My clipped pace didn't falter, but my breaths…

They didn't come. My chest, my throat—they were full of thick wadding. It blocked air and words. I couldn't...

Screaming would clear it. Not a scream of fear, but one of pure and pathetic frustration.

But ladies in smart gowns trotted past, arm-in-arm, their gazes darting to me and away. Some were my clients. Others would be, if I could only entice them in.

So, no, I couldn't scream here. Or anywhere.

Hands clenched, I coughed and managed to blast the air from my lungs. No wadding. There never was—it was all in my mind, all the imagined weight of what I owed Skeeves. Then there was the grocer and the gravedigger and the apothecary and...

Stop. Just one long breath in, and I'd be able to deal with the here and now.

And out. There. The past was done and buried, and although the debts were here like a hangover, I couldn't solve them right this second. Right now, I had Skeeves slithering along at my side.

"A 'kind and benevolent landlord' wouldn't have increased our rent in the middle of a plague."

He sighed, and I couldn't bring myself to look at him. If I did, I might stab him in the eye with my embroidery scissors.

And that would be a terrible waste of embroidery scissors.

Those things were expensive.

"Miss Ariadne, are you still going on about that after

all these years? Didn't I give you time to mourn your dear parents before I came for payment?"

"Oh, yes, that was a kindness." I couldn't keep the sarcasm from my voice. Not when he'd delayed collecting because he didn't want to catch the plague himself.

"Besides"—his voice dropped and he appeared at the edge of my hood, bending closer—"I have made you a *very* kind offer."

I veered away, tugging my hood around my face. My skin crawled like it wanted to drag itself right off my bones and far, far away from Skeeves.

His offer would've made worries about my rent a thing of the past, but I would never have been able to look at myself in a mirror again. Or stomach solid food, for that matter.

Once I'd swallowed away the bile burning my throat, I shook my head. "And *you* know I have made it clear that I have no interest in—"

"Ari!"

Rose. Oh, thank the gods.

Ahead, tall and strong, hands on hips, stood the best friend a woman could hope for. The spring sun caught in her strawberry blonde hair. Despite her simple clothes and the repairs I'd done to her trousers a dozen times, for a moment she looked like the warrior queen Boudicca herself.

Shoulders sagging, I didn't even attempt to hide my sigh of relief. "You're going to have to excuse me, Mr Skeeves, I have my next appointment."

"Appointment?" He grunted. "She's just your friend."

"I can have an appointment with a friend." I lifted my head enough to shoot him an edged smile. Much as he repulsed me, he'd made himself familiar enough —*over*familiar enough, in fact, that although I didn't *like* talking to him, I could. "You'll get your rent on time, Mr Skeeves." *And with any luck, I won't see you before then.*

I didn't look back as I hurried to Rose, my friend and saviour.

I grinned up at her as I slipped my arm through hers and steered away from Skeeves. "You have the timing of the gods themselves."

"Aye, I spotted him shadowing you." She shuddered from head to toe, face screwed up so theatrically, I couldn't help but laugh. "Bloody creep."

"Understatement of the century." I squeezed her arm.

My stomach tightened at the thought of telling her I'd failed with Lord Hawthorne. That could wait. A long time, preferably.

"I was looking for you." She directed us towards the market square. "Let's go and see if Annon's come with her papa today."

Rose was my only real friend, but Annon was something close. Her family lived outside of Briarbridge, so we only saw her once a week when they brought their catch to sell. They hadn't come the past fortnight, and I had to admit I missed her. Maybe she'd edged past "something close" and now *was* my friend.

"I hope so—she promised to finish her story about that rugged man from the fishing village." I gave Rose a sidelong look, though a little knot of worry tightened in my chest. It wasn't like Annon's family to skip Briarbridge's market. With any luck, we'd round the corner into the market square and find her.

In the meantime... "I was coming to find you." I dug into my basket. At the bottom, beneath the slippery silks and fine beads, my fingers closed on soft lambswool. "Back before Yule... the Yule before last, in fact"—not fact, a lie—"someone travelling through town commissioned me to make this and paid the deposit, but never picked it up." Also a lie.

One red eyebrow quirked, and I pulled out the folded garment. It wasn't wrapped—I couldn't afford anything to wrap it in.

"Here you go." I held it out to her and shook out the forest green cloak. In my hands, it almost swept the ground, but on Rose it would be the perfect length.

Her eyes widened and a soft breath fell from her lips. She traced the oak leaves I'd embroidered down the front in a dozen shades of green. *Strong as oak*, I'd whispered as I'd sewn those stitches.

I shrugged. "They didn't turn up this Yule, either, so I figure they're never coming for it. But you're around the same height as her, so here you go." Another lie.

"Damn, Ari." She shook her head, fingertips still on the oak leaves. "Even without your magic"—a lady passing widened her eyes and edged away—"you'd still be the best seamstress in town. The only difference between you and Madame Froufrou is the fake Frankish accent and her fancy shop. Sorry"—she raised a hand and stuck her nose in the air—"*atelier.*"

I giggled at Rose's impression, even as something pulled at my gut. Madame Froufrou's workshop and lavish showroom with no fewer than *five* chandeliers was just around the corner. Its huge windows looked out onto the most exclusive shopping street in Briarbridge, and Madame Froufrou greeted her clients with a fine porcelain tea service and tiny pastries.

Unlike me. I lived in one room of our—*my* house and worked in the other.

"Speaking of ateliers." Rose arched her eyebrows.

That pull in my gut turned into a wrench, and I might've winced. She was going to ask about the meeting with Lord Hawthorne. She'd arranged it because she was determined I achieve that stupid, childish dream I'd once had: an atelier of my own.

I cleared my throat and pressed the cloak into her hands. "Her loss is your gain."

Mouth open, ateliers forgotten, she held it to her shoulder. Her wide-eyed gaze slid to me and she nodded. "Thank you."

Stomach eased by the turn in conversation, I couldn't help but smile at her reaction. "I had a feeling it would suit you. What a lucky coincidence." Another lie—maybe the biggest of them.

Hells, it was *all* a pretty lie, but one for a good cause. There had been no phantom customer. I'd made the cloak for her, chosen the colour to complement her strawberry blond hair, whispered warmth into it *for her*.

And after spotting the dagger she'd started wearing on her belt, I'd whispered armour into it, too. The fabric was expensive, but I'd been riding high on my Yule commissions at the time and it would last Rose years.

So, yes, it had been for her from the start.

But Rose was like her mama and papa—too proud and too stubborn to accept a gift, even one she needed. Hence the pretty lie.

We continued around the corner and into the market square as she swirled the cloak around her shoulders. "Oh, yes, *very* dramatic. I *love* it." She grinned and fastened it in place, a swagger to her stride.

"Oh, no." I groaned, rolling my eyes. "I've turned you into..." My step faltered as goosebumps crept across my skin.

Something stirred deep in my gut, stronger than my earlier envy. Something tight like a thread twisted too many times, fighting to spring loose. Something that tasted like tart rhubarb, clear night air, and starlight. What starlight tasted of, I had no idea, but that was the only way I could describe it.

And whatever *it* was, it tugged on me, like someone calling my name.

But when I turned to the centre of the square, there was no starlight, only swirling shadows.

A Man of Smoke & Shadow

I swayed, and Rose took a step in front of me, dagger in hand. Twenty feet away, the darkness deepened and thickened, forming a tall shape.

A man built of smoke and shadow.

But no man had that sort of magic. Because *that* was the taste in my mouth, bright and sweet-sharp: *magic*.

Gut still tight, I gripped Rose's sleeve. This was not the time for heroics. Whoever—*what*ever that was, he had—

With a snap, the smoke sucked together and solidified, leaving a man of flesh and bone, dressed in midnight blue.

Taller than any of the gawping townsfolk nearby, he stole the breath from my lungs.

Because he was handsome... No, *beautiful*. Maybe a little of both—hells, *a lot* of both.

One eyebrow arched as he glanced left and right, and his full lower lip jutted out as though he wasn't impressed by what he saw. The light caressed his high cheekbones and cast shadows beneath his strong jaw and the dimple in his chin. It gleamed through his dark, dark hair, leaving a sheen of blue and violet like a magpie's tail feathers.

That wasn't—I'd never seen hair like that. How did he…?

And then my gaze snagged on his ears.

His *pointed* ears.

Not a man.

A fae.

The ones who stole you in the night. Who took you away to dance and dance and dance until you lost your mind. Who could charm you with a glance into doing whatever they wanted.

Every hair on my body strained to attention.

"Rose." My fingers knotted in her sleeve. A fae. Good gods, *a fae*. All the more reason for her not to wave that damn dagger about. "Do you see—?"

"I see." Her knuckles whitened on the hilt, but she lowered it a few inches.

No one in Briarbridge had seen a fae in a hundred years, not since the last Tithe was taken.

Once, Papa had told me, the fae had come every fifty years to claim an unmarried girl from each town near the border. In payment, they left a chest of riches—fae-worked tools and weapons, magical trinkets, rich metals and jewels and impossible cloth spun from silver and sunlight.

No one could agree on the exact reason. Some said it

was a deal Queen Boudicca had made with the fair folk centuries ago, when they agreed the border and erected the Queen's Wall. It was a way to keep humans safe. Others said the Tithe towns themselves had made the bargain as a way of benefitting from their fae neighbours.

Most likely the real answer was lost to time.

The fae lifted that dimpled chin and cleared his throat, gaze off to one side as though bored of waiting for the sounds of surprise to fade. Silence fell.

"Humans of... whatever this place is called"—his broad shoulders rose, filling the tailored lines of his jacket—"I am here by order of the Night Queen of the Dusk Court." He surveyed us, the wide-eyed humans who'd never seen one of his kind before.

I swore the flicker of a smile crossed his lips.

It was as Mama said—the fae were powerful—*too* powerful. And capricious and dangerous with it. More likely to harm than help.

He looked at us just as Mama had said his kind would, like we were buzzing mosquitoes—short-lived irritants drawn by his magic as surely as the buzzing pests were drawn to warm flesh and the promise of blood.

"A bargain was struck long ago." His gaze swept the crowd again and rested on us, turning my stomach to stone. Rose nudged me behind her, back straightening as though she were my shield.

Wild Hunt take me, but I couldn't help peering around her. My eyes burned from staring at him. The iridescent sheen on his hair was a mystery, a marvel. I hadn't even seen anything like that on a fae-touched human. Admittedly, I hadn't seen many other than me.

I'd watched magpies and ravens in the fields and forest, entranced by the gleam of blue and purple on their feathers. And dozens of times, I'd tried to capture that shifting colour in my sewing. Samples in the bottom of a chest at home were testament to my failure. But somehow magic and nature had created it in this fae.

His gaze was still on us, and a lazy smile tugged at the corner of his mouth as though he found Rose's defence nothing more than amusing.

Except... I shifted and his eyes followed, narrowing a fraction. He wasn't looking at us, but *me*.

Fingers aching where I gripped Rose's sleeve so tightly, I shivered.

Djinn and fae, just the same. Beautiful but deadly. Mama's voice chimed in a distant memory.

I sank into my hood and pulled closer to Rose.

Head tilting, the fae turned and continued surveying the square. The long, elegant sword at his hip caught the light as he moved. He was likely just as dangerous without it. "That bargain has been neglected for many years, but its terms still stand." Any hint of a smile vanished from his face as his brows drew together, leaving his expression stormy and dark. It didn't suit him, not as well as the smirk had. "And this dusk, at your stone circle, I will collect the Tithe."

I gasped, and dozens more did the same. The fae

hadn't claimed the Tithe in a century. Why would they suddenly—?

But he was gone. Motes of black shadow puffed out from the spot where he'd stood, like someone had blown a handful of soot in the air. A second later, that too disappeared.

I sagged against Rose's back, the tight twist in my stomach easing. The tart sweetness on my tongue faded, that sense of someone calling my name going with it.

"Are you all right?" Rose gripped my shoulder, brow creased in concern.

"I'm... I'm fine." I was now he'd gone.

Her lips flattened like she didn't believe me, but she only shook her head. "The Tithe. I can't believe he's claiming it after all these years."

The poor girl he'd take. Plenty would volunteer—more fool them.

Mama had told me how as a teenager in her homeland of Thanatolia, her closest friend disappeared, taken by the djinn. Three days later, Mama had found her wandering on the hillside, clothes torn, face bruised. But worst of all was her mind—shattered beyond repair. She'd stared into the distance, singing strange songs. She hadn't recognised Mama or even her own parents or brothers. All those years later, Mama's eyes had shone with tears as she'd told me.

The fae are the same. They take you and break you without a second thought. Humans are nothing to them. Her words blocked my throat just as surely as her voice filled my head.

No matter how handsome that fae was, he was no person: he was a dangerous monster in a beautiful shell.

Somehow, there were women in Briarbridge who didn't understand that—the richer families especially. They thought they could frolic with the fae and have fun, then get on with their lives. They *thought* old stories of the Tithe meant a marriage on equal terms.

Idiots, the lot of them.

At best, a human would be a fae's passing fancy.

At worst, a pet.

"Ari?" Rose rapped on my forehead as I shuddered. "Are you there?"

I snorted and swatted her away. "I'm here. Just worrying about how I'm going to stop you putting yourself forward because you think it'll be a great adventure."

"Hmm, I don't think being sold off to marry a fae lord sounds like much of an adventure."

"So you're not completely insane then. Good to know."

"Insane? Ouch. What have I ever done that would make you fear for my sanity?"

I tapped the dagger that was now back at her belt. "Wearing this and sneaking off to train with the boys so you can become a guard."

Her gaze darted side to side as though checking no one had heard, but the corner of her mouth rose in a secret smile. "Not insane, just... hopeful. Do you think fae let women train? If they do, it just might be worth putting myself forward with the other unmarried women."

With my chin, I pointed to the centre of the square where there was no sign of the dark-haired fae or his shadows. "Call him back and ask him. He seemed the type who'd *love* to answer all sorts of questions from 'humans of whatever this place is called.'"

As Rose laughed, my mind snagged on her words.

Unmarried women. Lord Hawthorne's daughters were unmarried. The last girl to be taken in the Tithe had been from their family—a great-great-something aunt. They would call it an honour to be chosen. Lady Hawthorne would be desperate for *that*.

And what was desperation for Lady Hawthorne would be an opportunity for me.

Sure enough, when I turned, Lady Hawthorne came sweeping through the crowd in my direction.

THE STONES

Lady Hawthorne cornered me, other wealthy mothers stalking closer, eyeing us.

"My girl needs the best outfit there. You must have something." She threw a sideways glance at one of the other ladies. "Exclusive to her. I'll pay whatever it takes, but none of the other girls wear your clothes."

Her desperation. My opportunity.

I pulled out the bodice I'd shown her husband earlier, and Lady Hawthorne gasped, hand twitching towards it. The nearby ladies straightened, eyes widening, fixed on the garment. Even without anyone wearing it, the call of my gift—*look at me, look at me*—weaved its way through them.

Heart pounding, I named a ridiculous price.

"And," Rose added, "if your daughter's chosen, you give Ari a contract with a monthly fee."

My mouth clamped shut. She must've realised how

my meeting with Lord Hawthorne had gone. Either my wince or the way I'd steered the conversation in the opposite direction—I'd given myself away.

But she was too kind, too sweet to make me say I'd failed. Instead here she was, fighting my corner, saving the day.

That price I'd named would clear my debts, and the monthly fee... With that, bills wouldn't be a worry anymore.

I stared at my shaking hands and waited for the inevitable *no*.

And waited.

And—

"You two drive a hard bargain. Very well, I'll send the money and contract in the morning." Lady Hawthorne nodded and snatched the bodice from me.

The contract, as though there was no doubt the fae would choose her daughter.

"Come along, quickly now," she told the girl, who hurried at her heel, a bounce in her step.

Excited at the thought of the Tithe. Silly girl.

I rubbed my chest. "Did that just...?"

Rose grinned and slid her arm around my shoulder. "We'll get you an atelier, yet."

THE SKY WAS SLIPPING past dusk by the time the circle came into view. No bright sunset colours remained, only violet darkening to indigo. The full disc of the moon sat just above the forest, pale in the gathering gloom. Stars winked into being, brighter and brighter as the sky dimmed.

But our path wasn't dark. Hundreds of glowing motes lit the way to the circle and more gathered around the ancient, craggy stones. Pale lilac and turquoise, white and green, gold and blossom pink. I gripped Rose's arm, gaping at the drifting lights.

"What...? How...?" She shook her head, reaching out as one floated closer to us.

"Fae light."

Like the stories Papa used to tell.

As for *how?* It was the fae who'd come to claim the Tithe. Just like Mama had said—they were powerful creatures. This light show was nothing to him. It tasted only faintly of sweet-sharp rhubarb, unlike when he'd puffed in and out of existence in the market square.

Beneath my hood, the hairs on the back of my neck rose.

The lights were beautiful. But they were also a reminder: he could wink any one of us out of existence on a whim.

"They're sniffing around Albion again," Rose muttered as she swatted a light away. "Annon wasn't at market today." She shot me a dark look. "After the deal with Lady H, I went and checked. The stall was set up, but no sign of her, only her papa."

It was strange enough that they'd skipped the past two weeks, but now he'd come alone. Still, what did that have to do with fae?

I tilted my head at Rose. "Maybe she's unwell." Please, gods, say it wasn't a resurgence of the creeping death.

"I don't think so." Rose's expression darkened, her jaw flexing. "Her papa refused to talk about it, but…" She shook her head. "There was something in his expression… Something haunted. And the shadows under his eyes…"

I swallowed, chest twitching a little tighter. On market days, I watched out for a glimpse of Annon's hair, bright like sunlight, because it meant she'd grab lunch with us in the tavern. By the time we finished, my cheeks ached from laughing so much. Maybe it was because she hadn't grown up in Briarbridge, but she treated me like she did everyone else: with friendly warmth.

Rubbing my chest, I touched Rose's sleeve. "You think there's something more sinister going on?"

"I don't know, I just…" She shot me a frown. "Don't you think it strange our friend goes missing right at the same time as a fae lord comes here to claim the Tithe?"

Briarbridge wasn't the only Tithe town, And plenty of stories told of fae whisking humans away, even without any Tithe agreement. It was *possible* the fae's return and Annon's disappearance were connected.

If they'd taken her, we'd never see her again. Chest even tighter, I shook my head. "Shit. I hope you're wrong."

Rose squeezed my hand. "Me too."

There was no sign of the fae when we arrived at the low

hill with the standing stones. Most of the town was already there, some within the wide ring, others gathered outside, peering in, quiet conversation rippling through the air.

Rose's height and sweet smile cut through the crowd as she led the way.

On top of her fears for Annon, her earlier words troubled me: *We'll get you an atelier yet.* The atelier had been a naïve little girl's dream—I didn't want it anymore, not really. Was that why she'd made the appointment with Lord Hawthorne?

My cottage wasn't huge and it could've been brighter and warmer, but it was home. Familiar. A comforting constant, like the blankets on the bed and the rug on the floor. Working there wasn't ideal, but it was where I'd always worked. Just the thought of moving all my equipment and changing everything about my daily routine to include travelling to a separate workshop made me shudder.

But ahead of me, Rose entered the stone circle, her straight back and square shoulders carrying no such concern. She ran towards challenge, grabbed change with both hands and kissed it full on the lips.

As I crossed into the circle, a trickle of energy chased across my skin and every other hair on my body joined those at the nape of my neck, standing at full attention. The flavour here was much stronger, like I'd licked the stars overhead and taken a bite of fresh rhubarb crumble baked by Rose's mama.

My head swam with it and every step was sluggish,

like I'd drunk too much at the tavern and was trying to weave my way home. The stones amplified his magic.

Somehow I kept up with Rose as she nudged through the crowd, glancing over her shoulder to check I was still there.

She stopped just behind Lady Hawthorne, close to the centre. Someone must've sent Lord Hawthorne a message, because he was here with the rest of their daughters. The girls held each other's hands, wide eyes on their eldest sister who now wore the bodice I'd made.

The young women offering themselves stood at the centre of the circle. The eldest Hawthorne girl wasn't the only one who'd altered her appearance—some had pulled their hair down and brushed it, others had changed outfits. One had the back of her skirt caught in her waistband. I couldn't get past Lady Hawthorne to right it, so I called her name and pointed, and she fixed it, blushing and mouthing a *thank you*.

Amongst perhaps fifty women, the Hawthorne girl stood out. Nineteen and slender, she was by far the most beautiful, with or without the bodice.

My magic wasn't the strongest, but even I could appreciate its effect—she looked radiant, as though someone shone a light on her, and when I glanced around the square, every pair of eyes kept flicking her way.

I shot Rose a small smile. The bodice was only a sample of what I could do, but it was *good*.

A thrill rippled through me. The fae *would* choose her.

I'd get my contract.

Skeeves stood on the far side of the gathered women, his mouth open as he leered at them.

No more debt. No more evenings with him on the doorstep reiterating his "very kind offer."

But before I could sigh my relief, tension coiled through me, stealing my breath, and the clear, crisp flavour of night and starlight exploded upon my tongue. There was nothing else in the world but the tightness in my body and that taste.

When I blinked to awareness, I had hold of Rose's arm, barely staying upright.

She squeezed my shoulder. "Are you all—?"

A gasp rippled through the crowd.

At the circle's centre, shadows swirled, pooling and pulling together until there was no darkness, only that same fae man from the market square. It happened quicker this time, his form solid in seconds.

His lazy half-smile from earlier broadened, pressing a dimple into his cheek as he regarded the offerings before him. Because that's all the women were to him—items in a bargain, nothing more than the coins Lady Hawthorne had offered me.

And yet, like a moth fluttering around a flame, I couldn't tear myself away. He was gorgeous, and I plied my trade on beauty, found my inspiration in it, couldn't help being drawn to it.

Handsome, yes, but too powerful, too distant, too otherworldly.

He looked like he was in his early to mid-twenties,

the same as me, but he could've been older than these stones for all I knew. Some stories said fae lived for centuries, others that they were immortal. Whichever was true, he could have no concept of humans as anything more than gnats.

"Fair maidens of Briarbridge." An edge to his smirk suggested more than a touch of sarcasm. "You and I are both subject to the terms of the Tithe. And so I bring an offering in fair exchange." At his side appeared a chest of near-black, gleaming wood, carved with leaves and studded in what might've been brass or gold. It stood as tall as his knees and must've been four feet long. A gilded padlock glinted in the fae light.

While everyone else was distracted by the chest, his shoulders fell and the smirk faded, as though he sighed. A small crease etched between his brows.

Then his black eyes landed on me. His frown vanished behind a tight smirk, and I froze.

He'd caught me staring. Even in the shadow of my hood, he'd *seen*.

And fool that I was, I couldn't look away. If Mama had been here, she'd have cuffed me on the back of the head and rightly so. I knew the danger and yet couldn't help myself. At least there was no risk in looking.

His eyebrows rose before he turned his attention to the gathered women. I sagged like he'd released me from his grip.

The floating lights dimmed, leaving only the women lit. I would've expected him to make an announcement that he was about to choose his bride, but with light at his command, he didn't need to say a word.

A hush descended upon the crowd, so quiet it was like everyone held their breath. The women who offered themselves formed loose rows, smoothing their hair and skirts. A couple pulled their necklines lower.

It was a doomed attempt at gaining attention when the Hawthornes' daughter commanded it. Even the glowing motes pooled around her as if attracted to her beauty. The beads of her bodice twinkled like the stars above.

The fae stalked along the rows, his movements smooth as liquid, solid as stone. *Stalked* was the right word for it, like a sabrecat hunting a hind. He didn't even glance at half the women as he lifted his chin, a thoughtful frown wrinkling his brow. This frown suited him better than the one earlier. The angle of his head made me think of a sabrecat again—sniffing the air, seeking his prey.

When he reached her row, his gaze fixed on the Hawthorne girl and his eyebrows rose as though he'd found just what he was looking for.

A thrill sparked in my veins. It was working.

Rose gripped my hand. The girl's aristocratic beauty, my bodice—they'd done their work. Lady Hawthorne straightened and whispered to her husband. Their other daughters pulled together, one tugging on another's arm.

The fae didn't hurry, though, just passed along the

row, a faint twitch on his mouth, as if he wanted to smirk.

When he stopped before her, the young woman's breasts heaved in the bodice and she lifted her gaze to his. That thoughtful frown was back on his face as his nostrils flared like he was taking in her scent.

So inhuman. I'd heard that fae were wild compared to us, but this… The tailored jacket and exquisitely tousled hair could not disguise his animalistic nature.

It sent a shiver through me, as deep as my bones.

He bent and my breath stopped—he was going to kiss her. He was—

But he turned to her ear and whispered.

My mouth went dry, the ghost of a warm breath in my ear. Callum, my one and only lover, was here somewhere, pregnant wife on his arm, no doubt. Once upon a time, he'd whispered to me like that.

Wild Hunt take me, but some foolish part of me wished it was *my* ear that dark haired fae, for all his inhumanity, murmured in.

It had been too long since I'd had any affection other than Rose's and, much as I loved her, it was *not* the same as a lover's touch. Even with my eyes shut in the deep dark of night, my own touch wasn't the same, however much I pretended.

The girl shook her head and replied, voice too low for me to catch. She couldn't be denying him—that wasn't an option in the Tithe. Once chosen, that was the end of it. The stories were full of doomed attempts to save loved ones who'd been chosen.

Then her head turned in our direction and his gaze followed.

Rose gasped, arm going rigid under my hand. What was happening? Was he choosing one of the other Hawthorne girls?

He stalked this way, something fierce in the set of his brow. A smile spread across his mouth until it revealed pointed canines.

Gods, he really *was* more animal than person.

Surely he wouldn't choose one of the younger sisters.

Lady Hawthorne pushed forward the next eldest of her daughters. The fae dismissed her with a swipe of his finger.

The Hawthornes parted to let him pass.

Because his gaze wasn't on them. Or Lady Hawthorne. It went past them all.

It was on me.

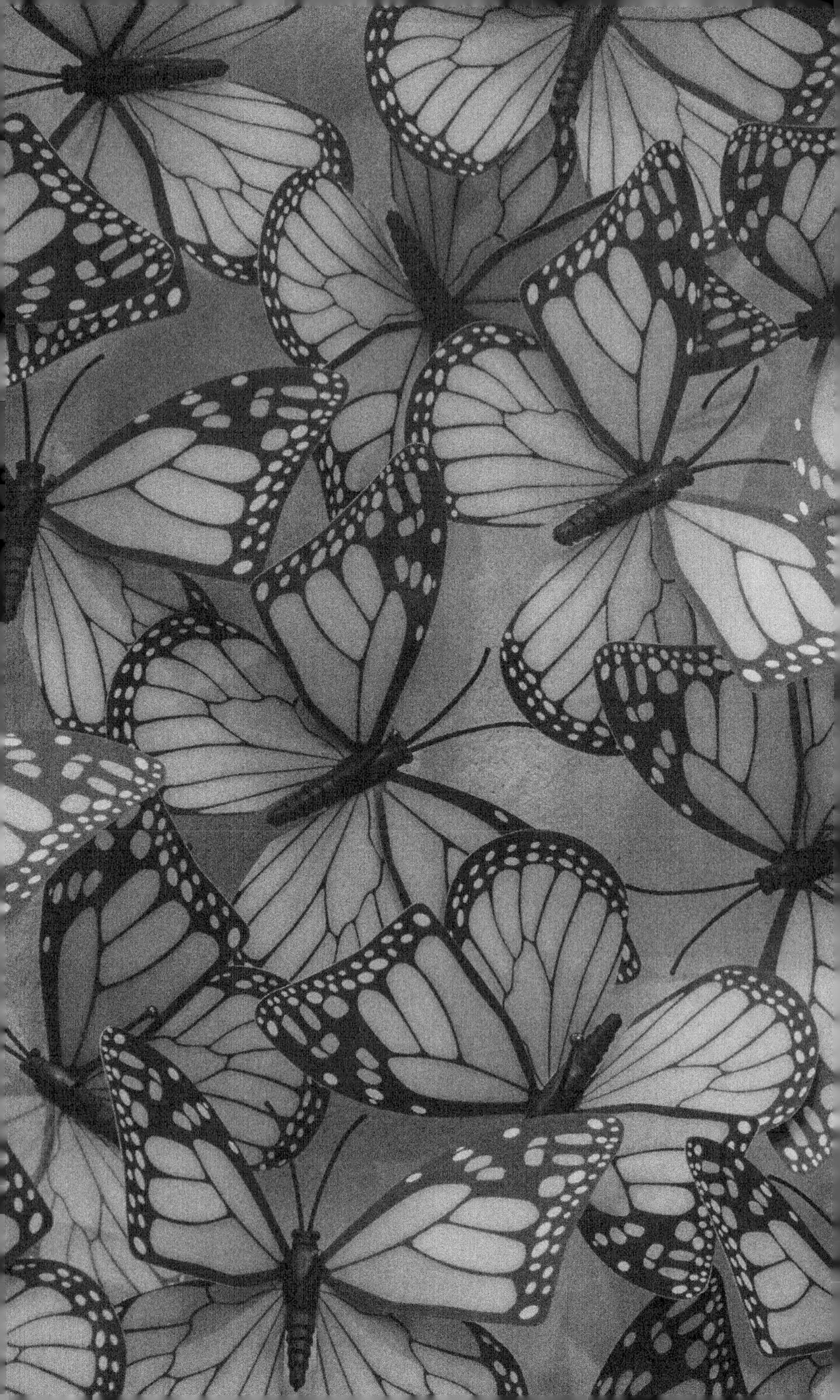

CLAIMED

My heart leapt into my throat like it was trying to escape.

Slowing, he came one step closer. Two.

Every pair of eyes was on me. Grey blotches crowded my vision. Something pressed on my chest. Everyone watching. Even with my hood, I was exposed, and some voice in my head screamed, *Run*.

Lady Hawthorne shot me a look that could've killed. But *his* gaze was far more dangerous.

Three steps. Four.

Rose jerked and might've pulled away if I hadn't been holding her arm so tight.

The fifth step brought him too close, only a foot away, and I had to crane my neck, because my eyes were trapped.

His weren't black like I'd first thought. They were the colour of midnight, perhaps a shade lighter than his jacket, flecked with starlight blue and violet like the glowing motes drifting around us. One caught in his hair, flaring against the iridescent colours before floating away.

Power rolled off him, dark and delicious, flooding my nose and mouth, filling my throat, like I could breathe it instead of air. My face tingled.

Mama used to say power called to power. Perhaps mine, weak as it was, had called to his and that was what this feeling was. Maybe he felt some measure of it and wanted to ask about the bodice, about the magic upon it.

His gaze roved across my face, taking in every shadowed feature at his leisure. He had to be wondering how something so weak could have any magic at all.

I didn't see him move, but I blinked and his hand was at the edge of my hood, pushing it back. I couldn't even stop him.

"Ah." The dimple in his cheek appeared, and his long fingers curled into a loose fist in the air between us. He nodded once, a finality to it that I didn't understand. "You."

I didn't understand that, either, but a collective gasp rushed through the crowd, and Rose gave a low moan. "No." Her hand closed over mine. "*No.*"

He smirked and broke that entrapping eye-contact.

I sucked in a long breath, sagging like he'd released a hold on me. Mama had been right—creatures like him were too much, too powerful. My heart thundered in my ears like I'd sprinted the full length of Briarbridge.

Eyes wide, I threw Rose a questioning glance, but the

look on her face, a glassy stare, one hand over her mouth, stilled the words on my tongue.

The fae lifted his chin. "I claim this woman."

I must've heard wrong. Must've. I blinked at Rose, but her frozen expression remained and now made a horrible kind of sense.

Beyond her, everyone gaped. And well they might be surprised—I was twenty-three and unmarried, just edging into spinsterhood. They had all dismissed me as left on the shelf with my strange hair and lack of dowry.

I had to be in shock, because their stares didn't make me want to run or hide anymore.

The stone circle was still, as though the world waited on my response.

I claim this woman.

I wasn't... Why would he pick me?

That was insane. Impossible. And... and...

I shook my head, casting off the daze. A fae lord was trying to claim me as his bride, to steal away beyond the wall? No. That was ridiculous. "You can't," I whispered. He arched an eyebrow at me, a flicker of amusement on his lips that made me want to punch him in that pretty face. "I didn't put myself—"

"Are you already wed?"

"What? No, I—"

"Then under the terms, you are eligible." He raised one shoulder, dismissing my arguments like they weren't even an inconvenience. Like I was a buzzing mosquito.

Oh, gods. Mama was right. He didn't care what I thought, what I wanted.

I was nothing. Had one of his kind treated Annon like *she* was nothing?

"Say your goodbyes." He took a step back, glancing at the Hawthornes.

If not for the tightness in my throat, I would've laughed: he thought *they* were my family.

Goodbyes, though. Eyes brimming with tears, I tugged at Rose's cloak as though she might have the answer, some way of making this not goodbye.

Because no one came back after they were taken in the Tithe.

No one.

Her shoulders shook as she lifted me into a hug and squeezed the air from my lungs. I clung to the cloak, to her, like she might keep me here.

Beyond her, Lady Hawthorne glared at me, and several other women had joined in. Some watched the fae from beneath lowered lashes, like this was their last chance to catch his attention. Maybe they just enjoyed the view.

They were fools. They thought a bargain like the Tithe would keep them safe from the fae's power. Oh, no, *they* wouldn't be like the men and women lured away to eat and drink and dance beyond the wall. The times those folk did come back—because often they didn't— they were changed. They'd return days, sometimes weeks or months later, feet bleeding from dancing night upon night and hearts sore for a taste they couldn't remember or regain. They were lost to fae madness.

"I'll find you," Rose whispered.

I gasped, pulling away and finding tears on her cheeks. "No." Choking on sobs that I couldn't let out, I gave her a shake. "No, you can't. You mustn't. It's dangerous. It's—"

"We need to leave." The look the fae gave us was unreadable, his expression flat. Bored perhaps?

I gritted my teeth. Of course he was bored—stupid humans' goodbyes or tears didn't mean anything to him. The heat flaring up my back made me square my shoulders. I kissed Rose's cheek and whispered, "Don't come after me. You'll be killed. You understand me? I can't have that on my hands..." Not like Mama and Papa.

She bit her lip, eyes over-bright. I think in that moment, she knew what I thought but had never said: that it was my fault... that I'd failed them.

I swallowed past the sobs clawing their way up my throat. For once, I was thankful for the years of quashing panic on an almost daily basis. "I'll find a way out. I'll make a bargain—Lady Hawthorne said we were good at that. I—I've learned from the best." With a smile firmer than I felt, I nodded, squeezed her hand, and backed away.

The fae gave Rose a long look before turning to me. "Now, human," he said, voice as soft and dark as night, "brace yourself." One side of his mouth rose, and that damn dimple appeared as his gaze trailed to my lips.

Brace yourself? If he thought he could kiss me, he could go and—

His palm slid to my cheek, calluses at the base of his fingers scraping.

Hands fisting, I pulled away, but he was quicker. His arm looped around my waist, clamping me against a body that was all hard, lean lines. Heat rose in my cheeks. Anger—it was the heat of impotent anger, not anything else.

"Hold still." A chuckle laced his words. "I just need skin contact."

For his magic. Even so, he could've asked. He could've taken my hand instead. And he still looked dangerously close to kissing me. "Don't you bloody—"

The tart sweetness of rhubarb cut off my words as shadows gathered around us. That same thread of tension from earlier coiled inside me.

His thumb grazed my lips, then the world disappeared.

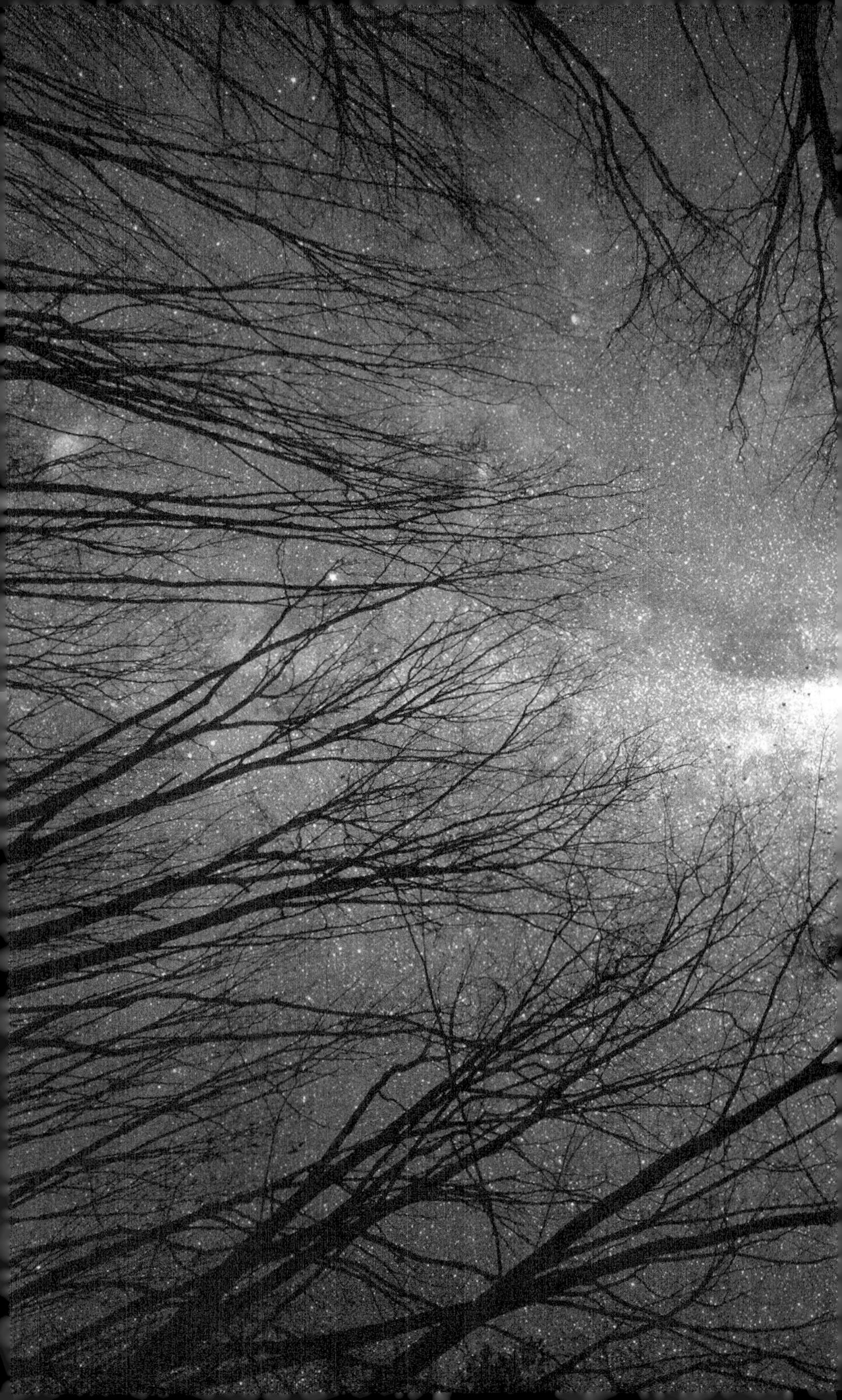

IN FAERIE

Nothing more or less than dust on a breeze, as free as the stars.

Then I was in my body, hanging slack. A strong arm around my waist tethered me to something reassuringly solid, the absolute opposite of those seconds where I'd been scattered fragments. Cold air seared my lungs and tickled my nose.

Eyelids fluttering open, I clung to that solidity.

Midnight eyes swam into view, scanning my face. Shadows caught in a crease between dark eyebrows. A gentle touch stroked my cheek. "Human?"

Gasping, my fingers tightened on—oh, gods, on *him*. Of course.

The fragments of my shattered mind pulled together. The Tithe. The fae man who'd stolen me without even giving his name. That moment of obliterating nothingness had been his magic transporting us here. Wherever 'here' was.

I shoved. He didn't budge an inch away, but he released me, and I stumbled back.

Virgin snow creaked and crunched underfoot. It coated the grove of towering cedars we stood at the edge of. I followed their trunks up, up, up. Gods, they were too tall to gauge. A hundred feet, two hundred, more?

More fae light flecked their branches and danced upon the air. Above, the night sky was even darker than it had been at the stone circle, and the moon hung, heavy and full, somehow larger, surrounded by stars that were brighter than usual.

I worked my tongue around my mouth. Now his power had faded, I could taste clean, fresh air, tinged with resinous cedar and the faintest hint of crisp green apples. Although there was no fruit nearby and they were out of season anyway.

"Are you all right?" His voice made me flinch—I'd been gawping at the trees, the sky. "It can take a few trips to get used to shadowstepping."

I eyed him warily. Beyond him stood a domed tent of deep purple. Tucked at the edge of the cedar grove, two enormous deer, a hart and a hind, sniffed the breeze, nostrils flaring, bridles criss-crossing their faces.

These were no human lands. We were well and truly beyond the wall.

"You're shivering." He turned to the tent. "Come."

Over my shoulder there was nothing but a snow-covered landscape—rocky outcrops, more of those enormous trees, and a range of distant mountains that were little more than grey shadows in the moonlight.

Other than the moon and stars, I recognised none of the features.

I needed to escape, but the ebbing shock and fear left my body heavy. I could bide my time, gather information, and wait for an opportunity to flee. He was right, despite the cloak, my teeth chattered and my fingers were tingling closer to numbness.

Pulling my cloak tight, I followed him to the tent flap. He bent over it, unfastening the ties.

It was cold, but a flush of heat crept through me, tensing my tired muscles.

He had stolen me. Gods knew where I was, how many miles from Rose—from *home*. And he hadn't even given me the chance to pack a bag.

What would happen to my belongings? Papa's books? Mama's sewing tools that had become mine when she'd passed? The little winged sabrecat statuette she'd had since she was a girl; the one she'd carried with her all the way from her homeland to rainy Albion. No more Skeeves, yes, but no more of those things, either.

They were all sitting in my cottage. Another thing I'd never see again.

My pulse sped, pushing the burning flush through my body faster. That fire freed my tongue. What did it matter if I said the things I normally only thought? He'd already taken me from everything I knew. Could it really get worse? I gave him a smile as sharp as my embroidery scissors. "So, the *great fae lord* lives in a tent?"

He exhaled through his nose and those dark eyes slid

to me as he worked on the door. "Only when I have to go and collect such *delightful* humans."

"Then we're travelling back to your home? Where's that? North from here?"

The side of his mouth twitched. "Why? Planning your escape?"

"You kidnapped me without so much as an introduction. Of course I am."

"I don't think kidnapping normally comes with a contract." He pulled aside the flap and motioned for me to enter.

"Well"—I ducked inside—"I didn't sign any—"

My mouth dropped open.

What had looked like a smart, canvas tent of perhaps nine feet across opened into a space four times the size. "What? How?" I gaped at the swathes of fine silk damask draping the ceiling and walls, patterned with shades of blue, silver, and copper. Lanterns hung from the thick timber trusses, gold and silver fae light dancing within. At the centre, a strange fire flickered—it threw warmth onto my face, but didn't singe the silk above, and its flames were the same coral pink as an autumn sunset.

"'How?' You have magic, don't you?" His voice lilted with amusement. "Are you just going to loiter there or can I come in, too? It's damn cold out here."

"Is leaving you out there an option?" But I slipped further inside, my shoes—already dry—sinking into a lush rug that would've put the Hawthornes to shame. An array of chests and low cabinets hugged the edges of the space, none as ostentatious as the one he'd given in 'fair exchange.' These were all elegant, their decoration understated, and I found myself rubbing my fingers together, far more curious about their contents than I'd been about the chest left in Briarbridge.

A couple of low chairs upholstered in gleaming brocade sat by the fire, and to one side, against a wall...

My breath caught.

A bed. *A* bed. Singular.

Eyes wide, I searched left and right, but... no, just the one with a frame of warm reddish-orange wood, piled with furs and woollen blankets.

My stomach dropped. They took women for the Tithe and only women. And they took them to be brides or maybe concubines. *Everyone* knew these things. But... I swallowed, heart kicking up a faster pace. Until I saw that single bed, I hadn't understood, or maybe just hadn't *believed*.

I had been taken in the Tithe. As far as the law was concerned, I was his to do with as he wished. And no one for a hundred miles or more would give a damn.

Even worse, he had the power to enchant *me* into not caring, either.

My pulse thundered in my ears. Being fae-touched, I had a certain magical charm that could make people well-disposed towards me, but only when face to face. Mostly, that meant better deals when I haggled. It also meant I was immune to the charm of other humans who had magic.

But I wasn't foolish enough to imagine it would make me safe from the enchantment of a fae.

A low sigh came as he kicked off his boots. He went to the fire and swept his hand through the air, calling the flames higher. "Here, this will warm you."

With the image of the bed seared into my eyeballs, I edged closer to the strange fire, keeping it between me and him. The law might say I was his, but that didn't mean *I* did.

However, the flames chased away the numbness of my fingers, and soon I was so warm I had to remove my cloak. I slid the crescent moon brooch that had fastened it into my pocket. It had once been my mother's, brought with her from her homeland, but more important at this moment was the pin. Two and a half inches long, it was the closest thing I had to a weapon.

He made no movement towards me, but I kept watch on him through the flames. The orange-pink light edged his strong jaw, the dimple in his chin, the fullness of his lower lip.

The points of his ears.

I forced my eyes away from that strangeness. He wore that thoughtful frown again. Odd how he veered between indolent smirks and this pensive intensity, such opposite expressions with, apparently, no middle ground. Was that a fae thing, the extremes in emotion? Or just a him thing?

As if sensing my scrutiny, his gaze slid to me.

There's only one bed.

I gritted my teeth, but the shiver ran through me anyway. I would not look away. Regardless of any fear or dread or sense of powerlessness, I wouldn't give him the satisfaction of seeing it. I would cling to anger and not back down.

The firelight brought out the motes of starry violet and blue in his eyes and for a long while neither of us spoke.

At last, he lifted his chin. "I'm afraid we'll be roughing it for a few nights."

I snorted. "You call this roughing it?" Good gods, somehow I sounded normal—strong, even.

One eyebrow rising, he glanced at our surroundings as if checking they were as he'd left them. His face screwed up not quite in disgust, but something not far off.

He didn't see the same thing I did. It wasn't that he saw a magical illusion, but rather this tent was as far below his norm as it was above mine. Was this slice of luxury just a rich boy's toy? What did that make me?

Stomach turning, I looked away.

"Are you hungry?"

I shook my head.

"Hmm. I thought humans ate all the time."

I barked a laugh. "You..." I couldn't even fathom how to finish that sentence, so I just huffed. "Only a few times a day."

His lower lip jutted as his brows pulled together into a scowl. "We have a long ride tomorrow. We should sleep."

That wiped the smile off my face. One bed. "I... I thought... Can't you just"—I spread my fingers—"puff us out of here?"

"Puff? *Puff?*" Exhaling through his nose, he shook his head. "Stars above, humans know nothing." My jaw twitched tighter, but he went on, "It's called shadow-stepping. And..." He cleared his throat. "We're riding. It will give you a chance to acclimatise to Elfhame."

Elfhame—that was their name for this land. I knew it from stories, of course, but we called it Alba. Yet another item in a long list of differences.

And, gods, *riding*. I didn't know *how*, and it sounded horribly like giving an animal the chance to run off with me, out of control. I shuddered.

"Are you still cold?"

Did he see every flicker of movement? "No. I'm just tired." Next to the fire's warmth my eyelids had grown as heavy as the rest of my body, begging me to just close them and sleep.

But that one bed... He didn't only mean sleep, did he?

"There are clothes for you in that chest. I believe it includes a nightgown."

If it was some lacy negligee, I would throw it on that damn fire and see if it burned. I certainly wasn't going to wear it. But when I opened the chest, a nightgown of butter-soft cotton lawn lay folded at the top. Shielded by a set of cobalt blue drapes, I found a dressing screen to change behind.

Tugging off my clothes after a long day—it was so normal when everything else over the past few hours had been anything but. My eyes stung as I pulled the nightgown over my head.

Rose. She'd cried saying goodbye. I'd somehow

managed to resist, but now... Would I never see her again?

I gritted my teeth and swallowed back the threat of tears. No. I would find a way.

Not while wearing a nightgown, though. Not tonight.

Fine flounces decorated its off-the-shoulder neckline, the elbow-length sleeves, and the hem, which skimmed my feet. Considering he hadn't known who he'd bring back from Briarbridge, it fit remarkably well and—I smoothed the flowing fabric down my wide hips—it was much prettier than any nightgown I owned.

Which suddenly mattered, because someone was going to see me wear it.

And, gods, I didn't even know his name. Not that it mattered, since he seemed content to call me "human" and *had stolen me*.

Every time I caught myself looking at those deep eyes or his sensuous lips, I had to remember that.

I hid the brooch in my fist.

When I emerged from behind the screen, shoulders set, the fire had dimmed to embers and he was already in bed.

My skin prickled with goosebumps that were nothing to do with the fading fire and cooling air.

One step, then another, I approached the bed. This was inevitable. I couldn't run out into the night, not with that snow and no idea where I was. There were warm clothes in the chest—they would play a part in my escape. But I needed a road and a plan. I rubbed my gritty eyes; I also needed sleep.

For tonight, at least, I was stuck here.

Still, I shuddered and squeezed the brooch, its rounded edges biting into my palm.

He lay with his back to me, broad shoulders peeking out from under the blankets. The soft glow of the fae lights softened the lines of his muscles, but they were still painfully obvious.

As was the fact he was on *this* side of the bed, meaning I'd need to climb over him.

"Can you—uh—move over?"

"I can." He didn't bother to look at me. "But I won't. You're sleeping here." He patted the empty side of the mattress. "That way, if you do something foolish like try to run away, I'll wake up."

Wild Hunt damn him. Maybe later I *would* punch him in his pretty face and pretend I was asleep and having a terrible nightmare. Suddenly I saw the appeal of learning to fight as Rose had.

"It was only a joke. I'd be stupid to try to escape when I don't even know where I am."

"You would."

He didn't move.

Grumbling, I went to the foot of the bed and climbed around him. My knees sank into the mattress. Wild Hunt, not only was his tent bigger than my cottage, but his camp bed was more comfortable than anything I'd ever slept on.

I refused to look at him or think about how hard it

was to breathe as I lay at the very edge of the bed and pulled the blankets up to my neck. I was as far from him as possible, but when the fae lights lowered, my heart pounded against my ribcage.

Despite the weariness in my bones, every muscle in my body pulled taut. My hand trembled as I fiddled with the brooch. It felt like an age before I managed to unclasp it and stick the pin between my middle and ring fingers, forming a spiked fist.

Yes, he was impossibly handsome, and looking at him did strange things to my stomach. But when he touched me, it wouldn't be my choice. *Nothing* about this was my choice.

"You can relax." His murmur was soft, but it still made me flinch. I snuck a glance at him. His eyes were shut, his face relaxed. "I have no interest in forcing myself upon you, human"—he gave a half-smile—"however pretty you may be."

That did strange things to my stomach, like a pathetic, fluttering bird was trapped inside. Still, my limbs and throat loosened.

Unless that was what he wanted—my guard lowered. But he *was* fae and the stories all agreed on one thing about the fair folk. "And your kind can't lie?"

"No, not exactly. I can omit details or be vague, but I can't outright say something I know is untrue." He made a low sound, not quite a chuckle, and it thrummed through the mattress into my back. "We've turned deceit without lies into something of an art form."

In the quiet, I turned that over in my head as well as

everything else he'd said. "I have no interest in forcing myself upon you"—that had to be true. I closed the brooch and slid it under the pillow.

And "however pretty you may be"—did that mean he thought—?

"Hmm. You know, all the humans of your town look the same."

My breath caught when I found his eyes on me. In the low light they were black and unfathomable. Did we all look the same to his kind? Then again, could I tell the difference between one ewe and another on the hills around Briarbridge?

His dark brows drew together as his gaze drifted over my hair. "Except for you."

Cheeks burning, I scowled at the ceiling. So *that* was what he meant. Like I needed the reminder.

Growing up in sleepy little Briarbridge, the fawn brown of my skin, like Mama's, had marked me as foreign, which was enough to be teased and for some to treat our family differently. But I'd had Mama and Papa, Rose, a handful of friends, and, later, Callum. With them, it hadn't mattered what anyone else thought, because they loved me.

Then, when I was seventeen, my gift had awoken and my hair had leeched of colour.

I wasn't the only fae-touched person in town, but what was a reason to celebrate them was an extra layer of otherness in me. All the more reason to keep me at a distance. With a fae mark as obvious as my white hair, it wasn't as though I could hide it.

It didn't bother Rose. Kind, fierce Rose who spent her childhood bloodying the noses of anyone who dared to hurt me. Callum, though? It had bothered him.

I sighed, the weight of it all pushing the air from my lungs. Here I was in the fae lands and I still stood out for all the wrong reasons. "Yes, I look different from them."

Another low noise from him, one I couldn't decipher. "No, you misunderstand. It's not that you are different: it's that they are all the same."

He was mocking me. I turned, expecting to find that stupid smirk on his lips, but his eyes were shut, the lines of his face soft.

Maybe that was worse.

Shivering, I pulled the blankets tighter.

For a long while, there was only the sound of our breathing, his much slower and deeper than mine. He must've fallen asleep.

Although I wasn't stupid enough to run away right now, I would have to at some point, and it was worth testing how heavily he slept.

Breath held, I eased upright.

"Don't," he growled.

With a sigh, I flopped back on the mattress. I wriggled onto my side, teetering at the edge of the bed, and cocooned myself in the blankets. It *was* comfortable. And I *was* tired. Maybe I could sleep tonight, so I'd be well-rested and ready for any opportunity to escape tomorrow.

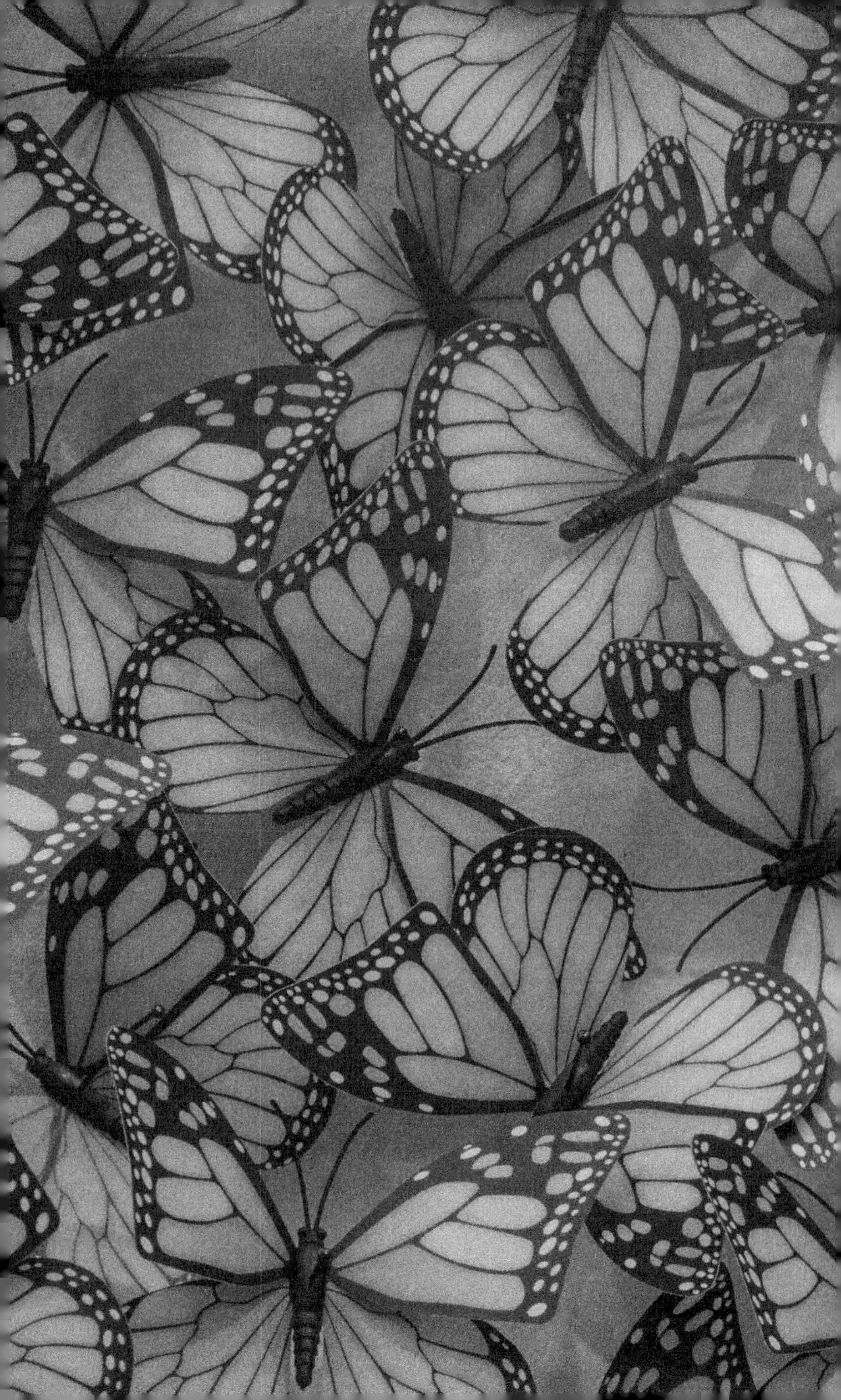

THE THREADWITCH'S APPROVAL

He was already up and the fire burning by the time I woke. I hadn't even heard him leaving the bed, never mind moving around the tent.

From the chest of clothes, I picked warm, fine-knit leggings, a shirt that skimmed my thighs, two pairs of socks, and a fitted woollen coat, all in white. If I managed to get away today, it would help me blend into the snowy landscape. Although, my grumbling stomach reminded me I needed food as well as warm clothing.

When I emerged from behind the screen, he looked up from the bag he was rifling through and cast a slow gaze over me. Shadows hung beneath his eyes as though he hadn't slept. Even so, the corner of his mouth lifted, and he nodded in approval. "Now you look even more like starlight."

I came up short, blinking at him. This had to be some sort of ploy. He'd said he didn't want to force himself on me, but maybe he thought he could charm me instead.

"Flattery will get you nowhere, fae. You don't need to make up idle compliments—"

"Can't lie, remember?" Eyebrows raised, he canted his head. He shrugged and set a pair of grey, fur-lined boots by the tent flap. "These should fit."

Maybe looking like starlight wasn't a compliment—who even knew what the fae liked? By their reckoning, he could be considered horrifically ugly.

Still, as much as I was pissed off about being stolen and stuck here with a creature that could destroy me with a flick of his fancy sword, I had manners. "Thanks," I muttered, re-braiding my hair over my left shoulder.

He gave a single nod and busied himself with another bag. Was I meant to help pack up or...?

I tensed when he approached, but he only held out a plate of bread, crumbly cheese, and some sort of chutney. Maybe this was how they got you. I didn't eat anything last night so I was safe so far, but there were stories of humans being stuck in faerie because they ate the food and—

"Are you going to eat it or just look at it? I heard your stomach, so I know you're hungry."

I pursed my lips, mouth watering.

"It isn't poisoned. It contains no potions or evil magic." He rolled his eyes as though that were a ridiculous idea. "It won't lock you here—the Tithe already did that." His mouth curved in a sharp smile that didn't meet his eyes or the dimple in his cheek. "But if that isn't clear enough, *human*, let me clarify so it gets into your silver-haired head: nothing about this food will harm you—body, mind, or soul. Now, eat."

And he couldn't lie, so...

"Fine." I took the plate. "*Thank* you."

At the first mouthful, I moaned. The bread was still warm, so soft and fresh it didn't need butter. I hated to admit it, but it was even better than the stuff Rose's parents baked. For the next bite, I scooped up chutney and cheese and was overwhelmed by the exquisite sweetness, laced with warm spices, all cut through by the cheese's sharp saltiness.

I'd thought it a simple plate of food—bread, cheese, and chutney were nothing special after all—but the flavours and textures complemented each other perfectly. The spices were so balanced and complex, they created a symphony on my tongue.

It was the best meal I'd ever eaten, and I sighed when it was finished.

Was this why people pined away when they returned from faerie?

I needed to get home. I couldn't *want* to stay here. The food may not be poisoned, but it was a trap nonetheless.

When he took my plate and placed it in a cabinet, apparently unconcerned that it was dirty, he declared we were ready and led the way outside. I tugged on my boots and stomped after.

My steps softened when I emerged into the crisp day. The snow glittered like a jewelled gown I'd made last year for Lady Hawthorne's Yule celebrations. The cedars' high branches spread overhead, a dark contrast with the bright snow and crystal icicles. Beyond them, a clear sky had already moved past dawn into rich cerulean blue. A jagged line of silver and white marked the distant mountains I'd spotted last night.

This place was cold and harsh, but damn, was it beautiful.

The fae didn't so much as glance at the magnificent landscape. He was busy looking at the tent. Did he expect me to help take it down? How did a person even begin to take apart a magical tent that was bigger on the inside than the outside? And how was he going to carry this all away when he didn't even have a wagon?

Before I could ask, he lifted one hand and bent the little finger to his palm. His ring finger went next, then the middle.

Breath steaming, I couldn't help but watch each movement. A prickle crept across my cheek where his calluses had brushed yesterday.

Once his hand formed a fist, the tent moved. Like a piece of paper, one side folded in on itself, then another, one corner, then the next. Corner after corner, inwards, inwards, inwards, until there was only a square of folded canvas no larger than a dinner plate sitting in the centre of flattened snow. No sign remained of the chests, the bed, the rug, or the fire. It was all...

I shook my head and threw him a wide-eyed look, but he merely retrieved the folded tent. Then, with a soft word I didn't recognise, he called the deer to him.

The tent disappeared into a saddlebag and from

another, he produced a pale grey cloak. He shook it out. Fine silver thread picked out a design of snowflakes and stars running down the front. "Does this meet the threadwitch's approval?" One eyebrow and one side of his mouth rose. The dimple in his cheek mocked me.

I gritted my teeth, both at the mockery and the sense I was being dressed up like some pampered pet with a diamond collar. I'd seen fluffy dogs like that in paintings at Hawthorne House. Was that how he saw me? His human pet to show off to other fae when they came to visit or did whatever the hells fae did.

My throat tightened and that familiar wadding filled half my chest.

Gods, I didn't even know what fae did. Or his name. And he hadn't asked mine. No way was I going to volunteer it when he hadn't offered first. He held the power here, but that didn't mean I was going to give him more.

He sighed. "It isn't poisoned, cursed, or in any way harmful to human or fae. But it is warm, and I'd prefer it if you didn't freeze to death. You humans are so delicate."

That cut through my threatening panic and heated my veins. "Maybe I should show you just how delicate I am." I gave him a sharp-edged smile, and never before had I missed my embroidery scissors so much. Hurting him would be fair game, if I somehow managed it—he was fae, armed, and considerably stronger than me. Plus, *kidnapping*.

His brows shot up and that mocking smirk became a grin that showed his sharp canines.

I flinched, the heat of my anger quenched. What was

I doing challenging him? Had I forgotten what he was—what he was capable of? He could squash me like a bug under his shoe.

If I couldn't be nice, I should try to be polite. That, at least, would give him no reason to destroy me. "The cloak actually looks well-made." I shrugged, begrudging the fact it was true. "The embroidery is excellent."

Coming far too close, he swept it around my shoulders. A glint flashed in his eyes as he pulled the collar together at my throat. "Good enough to make you moan like breakfast did?"

Face burning, I snatched the collar from him and fastened it. "Piss off, fae."

He laughed as he turned and readied the stag with blankets and a saddle. "Touché. Consider me mortally wounded with your iron-tipped retort." So he couldn't lie, but sarcasm was allowed.

If only I did have some iron on me—that would shut him up.

Beyond him, the stag towered over us. Each antler was almost as long as I was tall. The doe wasn't much smaller. When he smoothed a blanket over her flanks, I shuffled and crossed my arms. I couldn't get on that thing. I'd never ridden a sabrecat, let alone a deer.

As he buckled the saddle in place, I cleared my throat. "I—I can't ride." I kept my eyes on the deer's hooves.

He gave a soft grunt of surprise. "Then you'll have to ride with me." The next thing I knew, his hands were on my waist. He hoisted me into the air like I weighed nothing, and I barely had time to yelp and swing one leg over the stag's back. Then I was sitting on it, holding the front of the saddle for dear life. The ground was a long way down. If I fell from here, I'd break my neck.

A moment later, the fae was behind me, chest at my back, muscular thighs around my hips.

Stiffening, I gripped the saddle tighter. My pulse thudded at my throat, my temples, deep in my belly. No wonder so many of the romance books Rose and I loved involved the couple being forced to share a mount at some point. This had us very... *close.*

His arms came around me as he took the reins. "Hmm." The sound reverberated through me, and I couldn't help but gasp. "Just..." With one large hand he held my hip and shifted me to one side, something commanding in the manoeuvre. "That's better," he murmured in my right ear, and his breath was just as warm as I'd imagined when he'd whispered to the Hawthorne girl.

Damn me for putting on so many layers, because I was burning.

And once the stag started moving, it only got worse. The gait had the fae's hips rolling in time, brushing my backside, while I craned forward, trying to avoid contact as much as possible.

"You're going to want to relax. Sitting like that will destroy your back after an hour." His arm looped around my waist, and he tugged me closer. "By the end of the day, your whole body will hurt so badly, you'll wish you were dead."

For one second I stayed there, soaking up the warm

solidity. Lords and Ladies, it would've been easy to enjoy the feel of him, like it had been easy to enjoy that exquisite breakfast.

But he'd stolen me. He was fae. He was *dangerous*.

Teeth gritted, I pulled away. "Who's to say I don't already wish that?"

He huffed a laugh that tickled my ear. "Suit yourself. But I won't be massaging your aching muscles when we stop tonight."

I rolled my eyes. "Thank the gods."

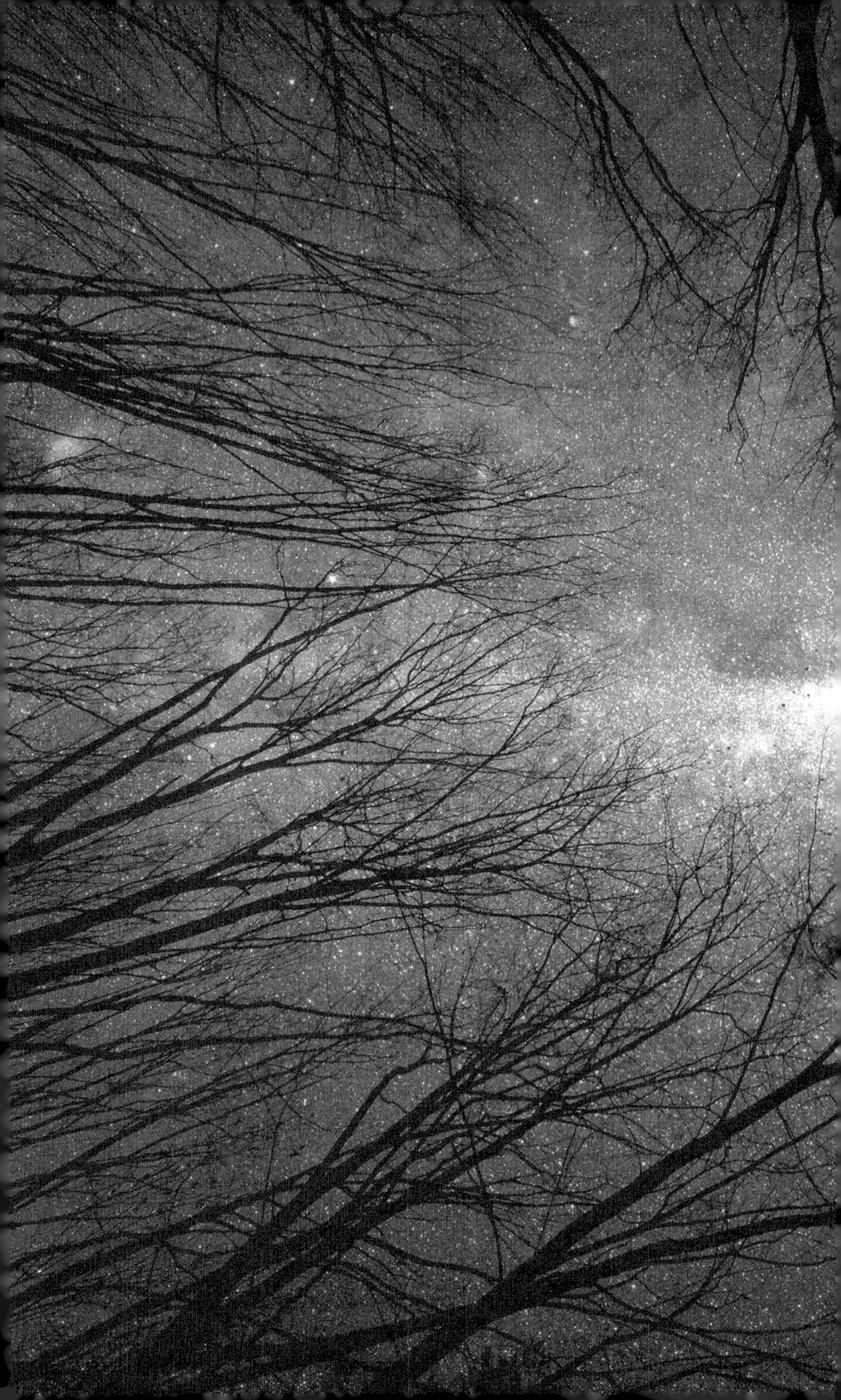

Welcome & Unwelcome

I lasted half an hour. After that, my back hurt so much, I had to lean against him.

To his credit, he said nothing.

We ate lunch in the saddle, and by midafternoon thick clouds blanketed the sky, grey and flat. "Feels like snow." I shivered at the drop in temperature.

He just pulled his cloak around me. This time, I didn't fight it. With both of us in the soft wool, we soon generated so much warmth that the cold air on my face was welcome and refreshing.

However, the heat brought an *un*welcome side-effect. It unleashed his scent—tart rhubarb mingled with something woody and smoky. It crept over me, invading each steaming breath.

I hated myself for liking it.

But soon it wasn't a problem as huge flakes of snow fell, catching on the deer's fur and blankets, flecking the fae's cloak, and freezing my nose until I couldn't smell anything. Fingers numb, I had to release the front of the saddle and tuck my hands inside the shared cloak.

He shifted the reins to one hand and closed the other over mine. I could've pulled away—his hold was only loose—but he was warm and my stubbornness had already given me a stiff back and aching shoulders today. I didn't want to add frostbite to the list.

When I checked over my shoulder, he was staring ahead, perfect, straight nose tipped with pink. That little sign of something like humanity made me smile.

His gaze shot to me. He frowned, but the midnight blue of his eyes was bright in the grey light, less severe, less unfathomable. "*What?*"

Snow flecked his hair and melted. A drop of water snaked onto his temple and down his cheek.

I followed it until it disappeared into his dark stubble. "Just surprised to see you're affected by the cold."

"I'm a living creature just like you."

Not *quite* like me. I grunted, and we rode on.

We passed gates and stone walls that barely peeked out of the white blanket. There must've been some magic to the deer, because they only left shallow hoof prints, rather than sinking to their knees.

More enormous trees speared the grey sky, giving some shelter from the rising wind. Beneath them grew hellebore with flowers as big as my fists. The ones in the woods outside Briarbridge were two inches across at most.

Between the plants and the deer, it was as though the earth here was so rich, everything grew larger.

By the time we stopped in the last dregs of daylight, a bitter wind nipped at our faces and ruffled his hair. I hadn't seen a single road. Either the fae didn't have them or he preferred a cross-country route. So much for scoping out my escape.

To make matters worse, once I was off the stag, I could only whimper and hobble my way into the freshly erected tent. My back, my hips, my thighs, and bum—every movement revealed some new agony.

Apparently, the fae didn't have a death wish, because he made no comment.

I threw myself face-first onto the bed and screwed my eyes shut, backside throbbing in time with my heartbeat. He was torturing me. How many of those stupid girls who'd offered themselves had expected to be subjected to this kind of pain?

"Never mind acclimatising," I said into the blankets. "Why don't you just puff us to your faerie house or wherever the hells you live?"

"There are... certain limitations." His words came out clipped, and when I pushed myself off the bed, uttering a few choice curses, he was kicking his boots off with a ferocity I hadn't seen in him before. The knot in his jaw. The deep *V* of his brows. The fact he hadn't even corrected me for saying "puff." His irritation was undeniable.

So, he got to take me from my home, the only place I knew, without even a bag of belongings and that was fine. But the moment I suggested we use the easy method to travel, suddenly *he* was pissed off? Teeth gritted, I flung the cloak from my shoulders and yanked off the fur-lined boots.

I stomped and grumbled my way through the tent, hissing at each groan of my muscles as I put away my outerwear. Without so much as looking at him, I threw myself into one of the chairs, regretting it as burning pain shot through my backside.

But when he offered it, I ate another plate of delicious food. Hot stew this time. Gods knew where it came from, but it was full of lamb and so tasty it brought tears to my eyes.

Once I'd finished, I flung my spoon in the bowl, fresh heat surging through me. How dare he? How dare he steal me and then have a life that was so much more comfortable than mine that he called this "roughing it?" How dare he kidnap me? And how dare he then have the gall to be annoyed when I asked one simple question?

Grinding my teeth, I glared into the fire. If I thought it would burn, I'd have tried to push him in it.

Except, no, when I shoved him yesterday, he hadn't budged an inch. I couldn't even do that.

A sigh blasted from him. "Did it cross your mind that I'm not exactly thrilled at the prospect of you trailing me around for the rest of your days?"

I bristled, muscles crying out. The rest of *my* days. Because he might well live forever and I was a gnat.

"I didn't want this. I was ordered by my queen to call in the Tithe." He scoffed, a sneer wrinkling his nose. "What use have I for a mere human?"

"Ah." *A mere human.* Worth nothing, not even a name. I smiled, the tightness in my cheeks baring my teeth. "And there it is. What you really think. I knew it. Mama was right."

"I've tried to look after you—"

"Look after me?" I snorted, but something like a growl came out with it. "I'm not a pet, whatever your demented kind might think. But I'm terribly sorry to be *such* a burden to the great fae lord."

With a low sound, he looked away and shook his head. I wasn't worth arguing with.

The quiet stretched on for long minutes until I creaked to my feet and chucked my plate into the cabinet he'd used this morning. Still nothing from him. Behind the screen, I changed into my nightgown.

Mere human.

Fine. I'd be the "mere human" who escaped him. His queen would *love* that.

When I emerged, he sat staring into the fire, the shadows under his eyes darker than they'd been this morning. I paused, gut twisting.

With a deep sigh, he raked a hand through his hair. The way his shoulders sank, I'd have said he was tired. Did fae *get* tired?

I huffed. I shouldn't even care.

As I folded my clothes and replaced them in the chest, which he'd explained would return them clean and fresh in the morning, he cleared his throat. "You should have some of this." He lifted a green bottle from beside his chair. I looked at it, not at him. I couldn't stand to meet his gaze right now. "It'll help with the soreness."

I closed the chest and said nothing.

"It's elderberry wine. No poison, curses, magic, etcetera. No harm to you other than the usual effects of alcohol."

I had to lean on the chest to stand and my thighs still screamed at the strain. Why the hells did people *choose* to ride if it felt like this?

"Admittedly," he went on when I didn't respond, "I believe it's stronger than you might be used to." Sure enough, his long legs stretched out before him, loose, and a rosy glow that was nothing to do with the fire painted his cheeks.

If I didn't reply, he was going to keep going, wasn't he? "No, thank you," I bit out. "Good night."

I slipped into bed, taking the far side. But I didn't shuffle right to the edge this time. What did it matter if I ended up close to him? I'd already spent the whole day cradled between his thighs.

Groaning, I sank into the mattress. The covers weren't quite over my shoulders, but I couldn't bring myself to move.

In every possible way, I was stuck here. My body was too stiff and sore to even consider escaping tonight.

I must've fallen asleep within moments, because the next thing I knew, it was dark. The blankets were tucked around me, and a presence that had grown familiar over the course of the day lay inches from my back, radiating warmth.

In those first days I'd spent alone, after Mama and Papa had gone, Rose had stayed with me. We'd shared a bed and she'd been a warm, steady presence.

Rose. A soft whimper came from my throat.

I *would* see her again. I wouldn't let some outdated bargain that I hadn't even been party to keep me from the person I cared for most. Certainly, no fae lord, however handsome, was going to stop me.

I clung to that thought and the comforting fire of righteous anger, but sleep was a strong tide. It tugged on my eyelids, pulled on my grip.

I'll come back to you, Rose. I'll come and...

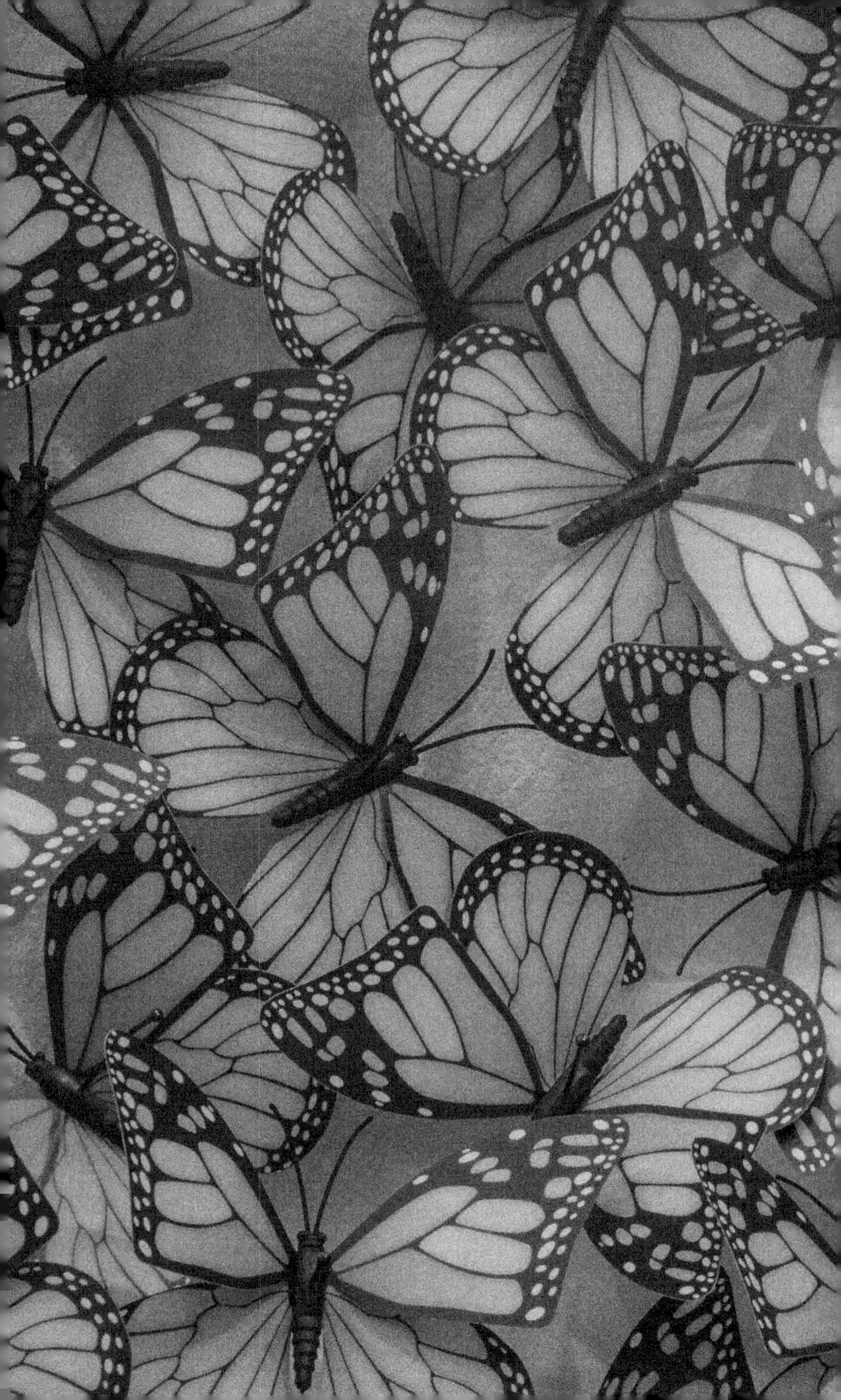

ICE SPRITES & FAERIE FLIGHT

The next day went much like the first and the one after that was the same. We rode. The landscape spread before us, beautiful under a clear sky. I took mental note of landmarks. A craggy rock that looked like a fist. A grove of particularly tall cedars whose branches arched overhead like the vaults beneath Briarbridge's town hall. An icy river that we followed for half a day.

No roads, though.

But we were getting further and further from the border, from human lands. I might have to chance fleeing even without a clear route. If I kept travelling south, with the sun passing left to right, I'd eventually find Albion. That might be enough.

Once we reached his home, I'd be a prisoner forever. Since he woke every time I so much as rolled over in bed, that was looking more and more likely.

Even as I scowled and plotted, I couldn't help but

marvel at Elfhame. My brain buzzed with a hundred new colour schemes and textures I wanted to capture with thread and lace and beads. If I studied this place hard enough, it could keep me inspired for the rest of my life.

I would be some mad threadwitch sewing creations from my time in the fae realm. That's the story everyone would tell about me. I wouldn't mind it.

On the fourth day, the snow had mostly cleared, but we rode past shards of ice that jutted from the ground, taller than the stag. One side of each stood smooth, the other was barbed with tiny, horizontal icicles.

I must've stared, because he spoke up for the first time in hours. "Ice sprites have been through here. They sculpt the snow and ice into these shapes. Unless you fall on one of their creations, they're harmless enough."

I made a sound of acknowledgement and we rode on.

Later, as the sun set and painted the sky the brightest shade of magenta I'd ever seen, lights winked into being around us. Unlike the drifting fae lights at the stone circle, these were pale blue and darted through the air.

One zipped past at arm's length with a whirr of fluttering wings. I jerked upright. They were *creatures*, not idle sparks of magic.

He grunted, the sound vibrating into my back.

"What are they?" I looked up at him. He didn't seem tired as he had at the end of that first day, but he'd grown quiet and sullen. Or maybe *I* had and he was only mirroring me.

"These are faeries." His brows knitted together in a scowl. "Distant—*very* distant cousins."

"And let me guess—you disapprove?"

I gasped as one buzzed closer, a hand's breadth from our noses. I got the impression of a face sharp as a blade and slender limbs. Its dragonfly wings moved so quickly, they were a blur. Otherwise, it almost looked like a tiny human.

"How can you disapprove of that?" I chuckled and reached for the little creature. "It's beautiful."

"*They* are a menace." Scowl deepening, he swatted the thing away before I touched its dainty feet. I huffed at his interference. "They bite, and because they're dirty little bastards, it gets infected."

Grimacing, I rubbed my nose where it had been so close to the danger of a faerie bite.

When the sky flared gold and orange, we stopped in the sheltered hollow between a copse of oaks and a craggy outcrop. He dismounted and lifted me from the stag. I landed pressed against him, his hands on my waist, mine on his chest. Even though I was on the ground and he could let go, his fingers tightened on my flesh and... and I didn't step away.

Much as he was fae, he *was* attractive. Every line on his face came straight from a painting. There was a certain roguish charm to his smirk—when it wasn't infuriating. The strength of his broad shoulders held an undeniable appeal that made my pulse speed.

Under my palms, his solid chest rose and fell in deep breaths, and his fingers splayed at my back as though he wished to explore. Warmth—not the heat of anger, something *different*—flushed through my body. What did *that* mean?

Pupils wide, his eyes searched mine, questioning, perhaps. It twisted through me like that coiling tension when he'd first appeared at the market square.

Swallowing, I tore myself away, and he cleared his throat before busying himself setting up camp.

I stroked the hind's velvety nose while I waited for my heartbeat to calm the hells down. He could've set me on the floor a foot from himself and turned to get on with the tent. Even if bringing me down flush against him had been an accident, he could've stepped away at once. He definitely could've released my waist after a second.

But he hadn't.

And the way his grip had flexed and spread...

Was *he* attracted to *me*, the "mere human?"

He'd called me pretty the first night. At least, I thought he had—I couldn't work out a lie in his statement, though he'd said his people were masters at deception without lies. Callum used to call me beautiful, and although my altered hair colour had scared him away, it hadn't changed my appearance much. Rose thought it was my power that had put him off; I was still "pretty as a picture" so she liked to say.

My chest tightened. *Rose.*

How far was I from her? How many miles between me and the one person in the world I loved—the closest thing I had to family? My fingers itched to sew, and my ears ached to hear one of her lewd jokes.

Wrapping my arms around the hind's neck, I buried my face in her coarse fur. I would get home. I *would*.

If the fae suffered the same affliction as I did and was attracted to me, despite himself, maybe I could use that to my advantage.

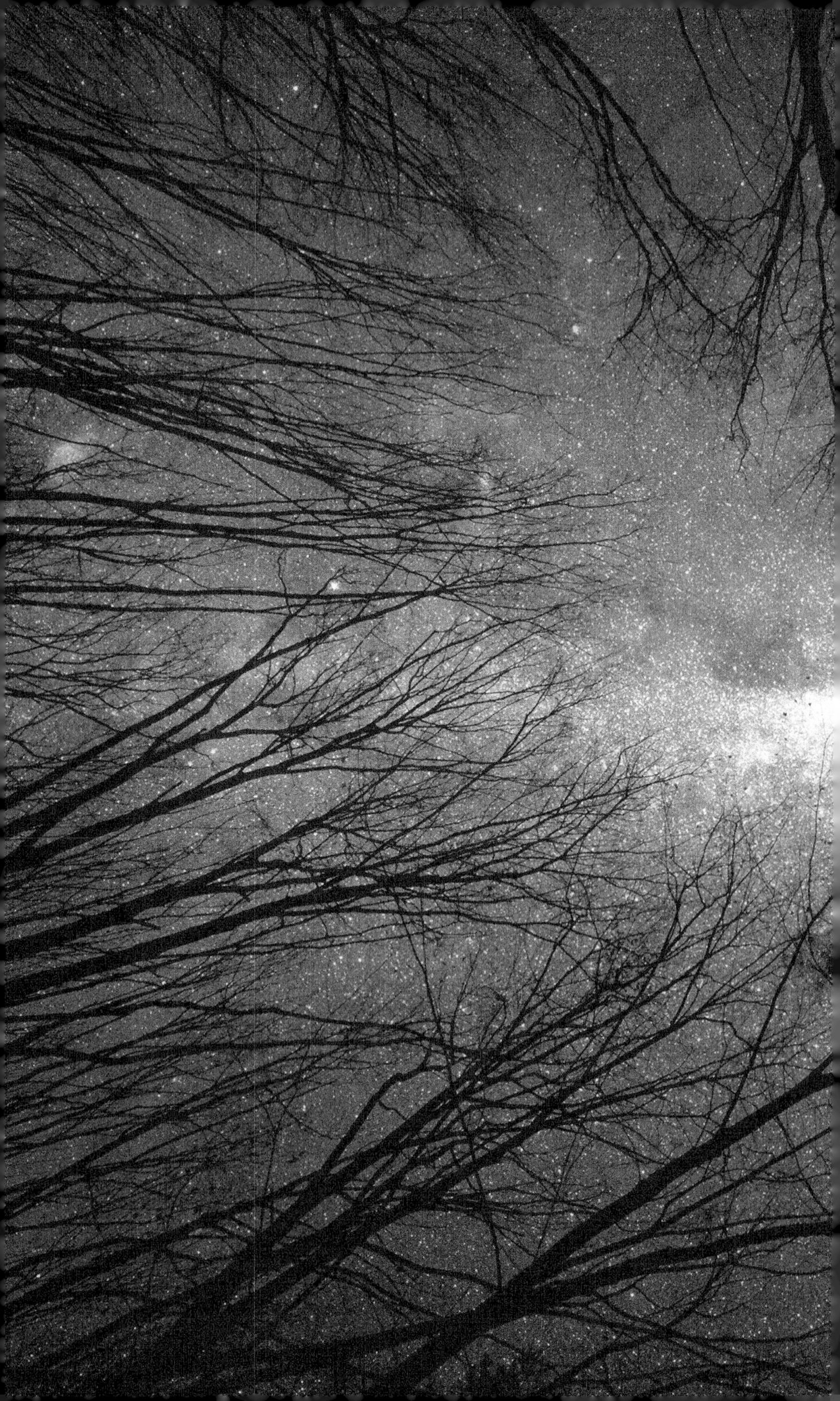

FAE WINE

While the fae put our dinner plates in the cupboard that returned them clean, I dragged one chair closer to the other. I would've brought out the wine as well, but if he caught me going through the chests, he'd realise I was up to no good.

Instead, I threw off my coat, unfastened the top buttons of my shirt, and sat. I would have to make the drink seem like his idea.

When he turned from the cabinet, his brows shot up. He cocked his head, no doubt wondering why I'd deigned to come closer.

I'd planned to give him a fake smile, but the surprise on his face brought out a genuine one. "I want to talk to you. Will you sit?"

Eyes narrowed, he sauntered closer. Damn, could fae sense traps? It wasn't as though I planned to hurt him, just... escape.

"*You*, talk to *me*?" The mocking smirk returned in full force, dimpling his cheek. "I'd forgotten what your voice sounded like. Indeed, I was beginning to wonder if I'd imagined you having one."

He wasn't going to make this easy on me, was he? I rolled my eyes and patted the arm of his chair. "You're such an effusive conversationalist, I couldn't get a word in edgeways."

Chuckling, he sat. "Fair point."

I leant towards him and stretched my legs until my feet were only a few inches from his.

The movement caught his attention and his gaze travelled down my thighs and calves. My skintight leggings didn't leave much to the imagination, showing off my curves.

I managed to swallow back the sudden thick feeling in my throat before speaking, voice low. "I realised I haven't been the best company... or very fair to you." When his eyes met mine, I lowered my chin so I had to look up through my lashes.

Although the hair on my head was white, I still had dark eyebrows and lashes, and the latter were thick and long like Mama's had been. Fluttering them had earned me and Rose free drinks on more than one occasion, despite my foreignness. There was something to be said for fae charm.

"I didn't want to be taken, no, but"—I gave a sigh timed for maximum effect—"you said yourself that you were ordered by none other than your *queen* to call in the Tithe. It was wrong of me to blame you." The words scratched my throat, too close to "sorry." Even if this was a necessary lie, I couldn't bring myself to apologise to him. Instead, I smiled.

"It's..." His broad chest rose and fell as his eyes closed for a beat. "This situation isn't what either of us want."

Saddled with a "mere human." No, he'd already made it clear how much he *didn't* want that.

I tilted my head in understanding. "Exactly. But we can try to make the best of it, can't we? So, I'd like to propose a fresh start." I raised my brows in question.

He held my gaze a long while. The fire sparked in his eyes, bringing out the flecks of pale violet and periwinkle blue. I couldn't look away, but I also couldn't remain still under that scrutiny and fidgeted to hide the shiver running through me.

At last, his mouth curved in a gentle smile, not even remotely mocking. Hells, if I hadn't known better, I might've called it "shy" but I didn't think him capable of "shy."

"I would like that." His voice was low and earnest as he inclined his head.

Gods, was that guilt twisting in my stomach?

I stamped it down. There was no space for guilt tonight. He was a deadly fae. He had stolen me. I was his prisoner. Remember. Remember. Remember.

He stood. "Let's drink to that."

Perfect. Just like it was his idea. I grinned. "Let's."

While he fetched glasses and a bottle, I undid another button, cleavage now on ample display.

I let him fill my glass, clinked mine with his, and held his gaze over the rim as I took my first sip.

My body seized at the liquid flame running down my throat, sweet and sharp as pure pleasure. Sunshine and rich, dark fruit coated my tongue, mellowing to an aftertaste of black cherries.

I gave a shaky exhale as the tent spun. My muscles hadn't ached as much today, getting used to riding long hours, but that dull pain dimmed from just one sip.

"My gods."

His eyes lit as he gave a slow smile. "I *told* you."

I chuckled, no act behind it. "I didn't believe you. But..." My head shake was the only way to finish that sentence. I needed to be careful—this fae wine was even more potent than I'd expected.

We chatted, and I pretended to sip my drink.

While I'd had one lover, Rose was only too happy to regale me with stories of her conquests, and I'd been fascinated to hear them. One thing I'd learned from her tales was that people liked to talk about themselves, and it turned out, the same was true of fae.

I asked him about his people, about their customs, about his home, topping up his glass as he answered. Some of it was as I'd heard in the stories, but other aspects made my eyebrows rise. They respected contracts to the letter, much like bargains, but it even extended to marriage promises. To separate a married or an engaged couple against their will was a grave sin.

Was he telling me this to pave the way for our inevitable marriage? Throat tight, stomach churning, I bent over and pretended to pick up my glass, but he'd left his on the floor, almost empty, so I took that and left him my untouched drink.

Our marriage *wasn't* inevitable. I was going to escape. Tonight.

When I straightened, I managed a smile and changed the subject. He told me about their upcoming Calan Mai festivities, which didn't sound so different from ours. Had fae inspired humans or the other way around?

More importantly, why wasn't he drunk yet?

Our chatter stretched on, each minute painful, making my plan seem more and more flawed. Maybe fae didn't get drunk. Maybe elderberry wine, while strong, wasn't strong enough. I shifted in my seat, limbs at once heavy and restless.

A frown twitched between his brows. "Are you uncomfortable? Here."

Before I could stop him, he was on his feet, crossing the room. He produced a blue velvet cushion from one of the chests and returned. Standing over me, he paused and glanced from me to the back of the chair as though unsure whether he should hand over the cushion or put it in place himself.

Eyebrows rising, he tilted his head, putting the decision in my hands.

I was meant to be flirting with him, making him believe I'd given in so he'd drop his guard. That woman would choose the latter.

With a coy smile, I lowered my gaze and leant forward.

He slid the cushion behind my back, bringing his cheek inches from mine. The drink had already made my face hot, and now it made my pulse pound quick and hard. I'd barely taken three sips, but it seemed that was enough… too much, even. His proximity stilled me, so I could only watch from the corner of my eye, barely breathing as he patted the cushion.

Once he was done, his gaze drifted to mine. Firelight danced in his midnight eyes, stilling my lungs entirely. Even with my skin too hot, the warmth of his cheek reached mine, teasing, tempting.

Too close. We were far, far too close. If we both turned our heads, our mouths would touch. Which I didn't want, but no one had told my lips that, because they tingled.

When he straightened, his chest moved faster, deeper than a moment earlier.

I tore my attention away, pushing it to the fire instead. "Thank you," I muttered, leaning against the cushion. Another pang of guilt twisted through my stomach. It had been thoughtful of him to fetch the cushion—and as much as I hated to admit it, this wasn't the first time. The well-matched clothes, the cloak, wrapping my cold hands in his, the offer of wine when I'd been so sore.

Then again, he had to look after his "mere human," didn't he?

They weren't thoughtful, kind actions—he was just keeping me alive. If he considered me a person, rather than a pet, he would've told me his name and asked mine.

No, he didn't deserve my guilt.

So I topped up his glass and pretended to do the same to mine, and I smiled like my life depended on it.

Because once again, it did.

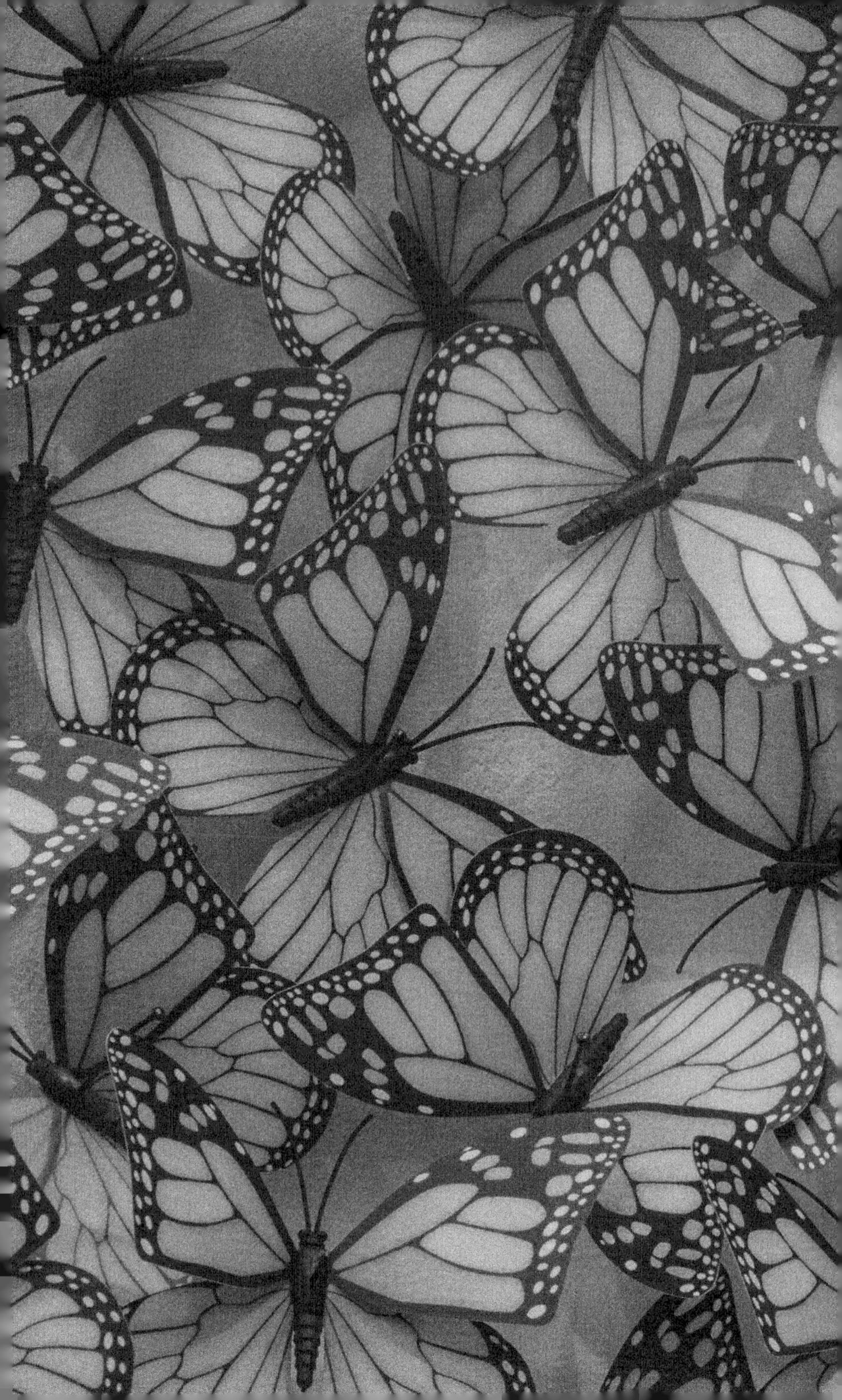

FREE AT LAST

After maybe another hour of flirtation, his eyelids began to droop. I lowered my voice, making it soothing as I asked him about "the wondrous magic of the fae." Somehow I managed to say the phrase without gagging.

His words lost their edges as he spoke about the land itself carrying thick veins of magic that tasted of—

"Of apples." I leant closer, gripping the arm of my chair.

His eyes widened. "That's right. You can taste that?"

"I noticed it when I first arrived. I wondered where it was coming from."

"Hmm." Although his eyelids were heavy, he watched me a long while. "Most fae can taste magic. Not all. I've heard of some fae-touched humans who can, too." He stroked his lower lip. "The one who granted your gift must've liked you a lot to give you so much power."

I grunted what was almost a laugh.

The fae-blooded got their magic from having an ancestor of the fair folk. They were stronger than people like me.

Us fae-touched had been blessed by one of the fae at some point in our lives. Some had let a pedlar into their homes and treated them well, only to find no sign of them come morning. Years later, when their young child grew up and their magic awoke, they realised the pedlar had been a fae and they'd passed a test.

Others, like me, had no idea what fae had blessed us or what we'd done to please them. Was it just a whim? Approval of our work? After all, many gifted folk were skilled artisans or gardeners.

Then again, it could be down to some unwitting kindness like leaving out milk and a thimble of honey on a night where some fae creature had needed exactly that.

Whatever the reason behind my magic, it was *not* strong. He was mocking me.

"Power? I can sew clothes that make people quiet or pretty or warm—things like that. But my gift is so weak, I can't even use it on myself."

And I hadn't been able to save them. My eyes stung as I stared into the fire and willed it to burn away the threatening tears.

"Hmm." A rustle of clothing signalled him moving, but it wasn't safe for me to look away. "Tasting magic comes with the most powerful gifts. Are you sure you haven't—?"

"I'm sure," I snapped. I had *tried*. Everything I knew,

everything I'd read, everything I could imagine. *Everything*. And it had failed. The only physical remnant of the creeping death were pale scars on my neck and chest, but I didn't need him prodding them.

My outburst had silenced him and that quiet stretched on for long minutes. Damn it, I was meant to be putting him at ease, a sweet, compliant prisoner. I'd just undone all my work.

But when I turned, his grip on the glass was slack and his chin rested on his chest.

Holding my breath, I craned around to check his face. His dark lashes shadowed his cheeks. Asleep. Question was, had I plied him with enough drink that he'd stay that way?

I eased to my feet, never taking my eyes off him. He didn't stir. I rescued the teetering glass from his loose fingers. Still nothing.

Despite the fuzziness of alcohol, my muscles sparked. I'd done it.

It took no time to re-button my shirt and pull on my coat and boots. I had no belongings to gather—my brooch was on the cloak, which I also fastened in place. There were water canteens with the stag's saddlebags, but when I tried the cabinet the fae usually pulled food from, it was empty. There had to be some knack to it. No matter. At most meals, I'd snuck food into my pockets and now had a small stash of bread, cheese, and apples. Supplemented by nettles and other foraged plants, it would be enough to keep me going.

I'd gone hungry before. I could do it again.

Within a couple of minutes, I was ready and he hadn't moved, save for the slow rise and fall of his chest.

Wearing a grin of victory, I crept out into the night.

THE WANING MOON was bright enough to see by as I took a saddlebag from the stand beside the sleeping deer. Food stashed inside, I slung it over my shoulder. Although I managed to stay on the stag's back when I had the fae holding me in place, I wasn't foolish enough to think that meant I could ride. No, this escape would be on foot.

The clear sky left the air frigid on my face and in my lungs, and I tucked my hands into my sleeves to keep them warm.

But I was free.

Moonlight outlined the world with silver and blackest shadow as I turned back the way we'd come. The ground was dry, so hopefully I wouldn't leave footprints for him to follow. A river ran nearby—the deer had stopped to drink on our approach. I could use that to cover my tracks.

Breath steaming, I walked downhill, eyes fixed south. After five minutes, the tent was out of sight. Another ten had me warmed by the swift pace, and I found myself smiling.

The tightness that had filled my chest for days—such a constant, I'd stopped noticing it—disappeared. Free and with some measure of control over my life once more.

There was no sign of faeries—perhaps they only came out in the evening. No drifting fae light, either.

Clack, clack.

I froze. Breath held, ears straining, I cocked my head. Nothing.

I turned slowly, searching in all directions but found no movement. The wind tapping distant branches, maybe. Shaking my head, I set off again.

I made it a dozen paces.

Clack, clack, clack-clack.

Shit. That was no branch. It was a hollow sound, like stone striking stone, and it came from a rocky outcrop behind and to my left.

Ice crept down my spine, but I forced myself to turn. Shadows writhed between the stones. Something gleaming. Claw or blade, I didn't know, but it had to be a weapon.

I veered right, pace picking up to not quite a run. Maybe whatever it was hadn't seen me yet.

C-c-c-clack-clack.

Closer.

My heart roared, and every hair on my body rose. A tickle at the back of my neck whispered that something was watching me—I had to turn.

Movement and moonlight on pale flesh.

I ran.

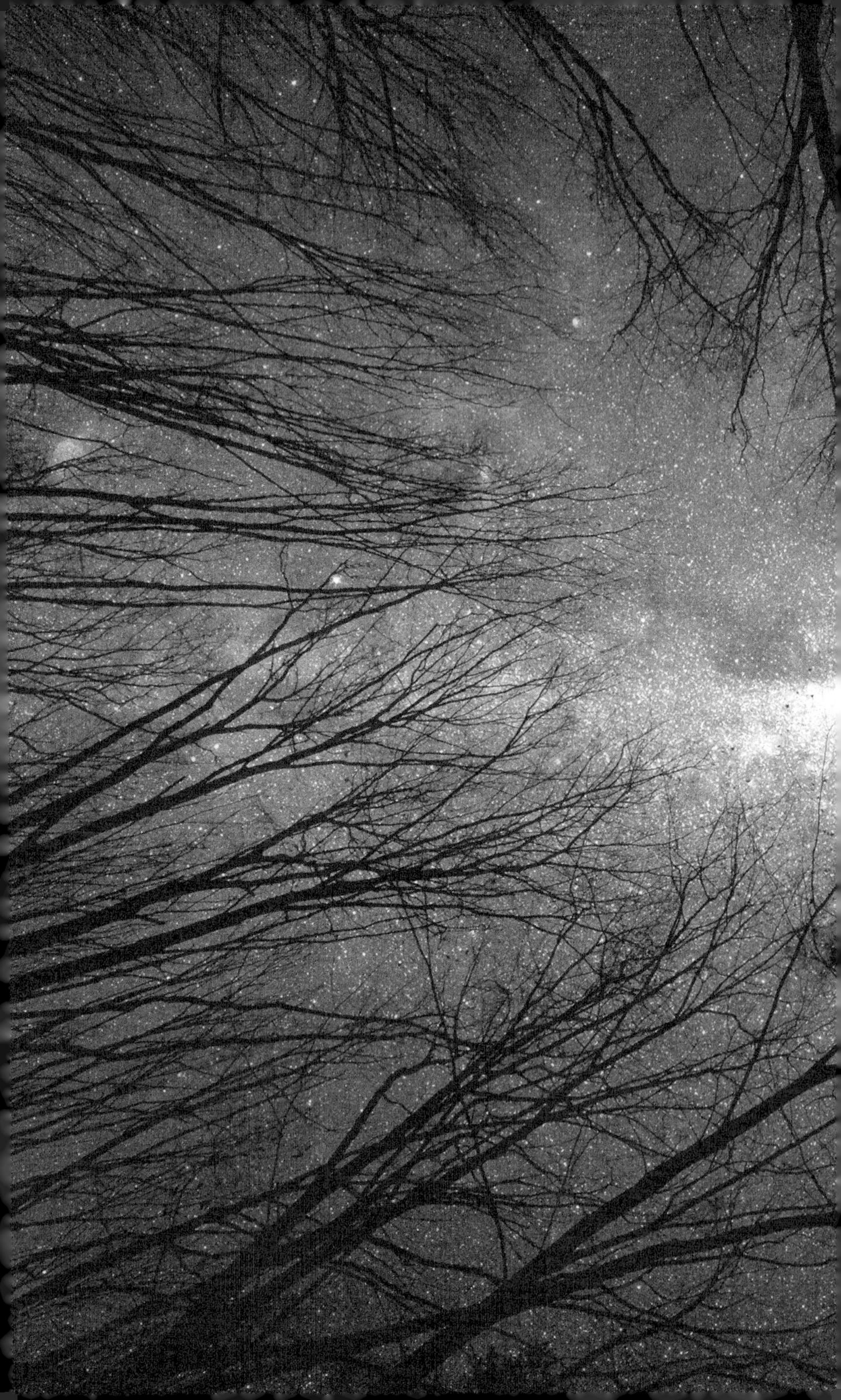

BY THE RIVERSIDE

As if triggered by my burst of speed, the thing leapt and clouds bloomed across the sky. Legs pumping, breaths gasping, I didn't dare look back—I'd seen enough—but its landing trembled through the earth.

It had to be bigger than the stag, with sinewy long limbs and dirty greyish flesh. Shadows streamed at its feet and from its back in a mane. Its gnarled hands tapered into claws that looked like shards of bone.

But the thing that was seared into my mind as I ran and ran and ran, eyes stinging with unshed tears, was its face.

Long and narrow, like someone had stretched a wolf's head, it had a maw the colour of dried blood, full of cracked, yellowed teeth. And where should have been a huge pair of glinting eyes was nothing.

Maybe I could get to the river. Gods knew what this thing was, but in some stories, certain fae beasts couldn't cross running water. I had no weapons. My magic was useless. There was no other option.

Sprinting, heart roaring, I spared a glance back.

The thing ran, swallowing up the ground, using its knuckles to leap over a fallen tree. Its stomach was a hollow below emaciated ribs, but lean muscle clad its thighs and arms. With such an unbalanced body, it shouldn't have been able to move, but move it did.

The ground trembled with each step. Its presence thrummed through the land's magic and jangled on my nerves. That apple-flavoured power was such a constant here, I'd stopped being aware of it. But I could shift my attention and feel it, like shifting my focus from the reflection on a window to the world beyond it. And this thing rocked it, like an angry hornet buzzing in a spider's web.

My breaths were whimpering gasps. That thing could rip me to shreds, body and soul.

Thirty feet away, moonlight gleamed on running water. If I could reach it...

The thunderous steps came closer. A waft of dry, old death tainted the air. I was too slow, too—

Ahead, the thing loomed out of the darkness.

A scream ripped through me, then the world tumbled —dirt and stone and grass rattling my joints, slamming into my cheek, my hips, my knees and elbows. I tried to catch myself, stop my fall, but the ground was too steep and some desperate part of myself said I could fall quicker than I could run.

Then there was no ground, just air, but only for a

split second before icy water closed over my head. It was in my mouth and my eyes, gurgling in my ears.

I flailed and kicked, seeking air and solid ground, lungs burning. Time was meaningless and I turned, weightless, airless.

Somehow, I found my feet and my head broke the surface. I sucked greedy breaths, head spinning. The frigid river only came to my waist, and I waded to the far shore. No sign of the creature yet, but it couldn't be far.

Please, gods, say it couldn't cross running water.

And how the hells had it loomed in front of me when I'd heard it's steps at my back?

Shivering and dripping, I staggered onto the bank. I looked up and froze.

Something darker than shadows looked back, churning in cavernous, empty sockets.

It could cross the river.

I was dead.

Didn't mean I'd go easily, though. Because all the fears I lived with, they were always for what *might* happen, what *could* be. This *was* happening. There was no room for anxiety about possibilities, only action, however final.

The thing regarded me, head cocking, but it didn't approach. Maybe it could magic itself across water but didn't like to touch it. I had no idea, but grasping at possible rules felt less helpless.

I backed away and my foot nudged something solid —a branch. That would do.

Armed with that, I bared my teeth at the thing.

Clack, clack, clack-clack.

Not from it; from behind. I glanced over my shoulder.

Another pair of empty eyes stared back.

Shit. There were two of them.

I was definitely dead.

My face and hands tingled, partly from the cold, partly from the energy pumping through my veins as if my heart agreed I wasn't going down without a fight.

Something pale emerged from the shadows. Another of the creatures. Good gods, how many were there? On the bank behind, two more crept from between river-worn boulders. Five in total.

I pulled the branch over my shoulder, ready to swing. Backing away, I splashed up to my shins in the water and tried to keep all the creatures in view.

But I wasn't a fighter. That was Rose.

I was a threadwitch. Although I liked walking through the hills and forests near Briarbridge, I spent most of my time on my backside sewing pretty spells into pretty clothes for people with more money than me.

Those white-fleshed thighs tensed and the thing in front of me sank, ready to leap. A low whine sounded behind me. They were coordinating their attack. Great.

As my arms coiled, a cool clarity came over me. Just one good hit. If I could get that in, I'd die happy.

Hells, I'd settle for a bad hit.

Its head twitched, and those bone-claws clacked together in a rapid chatter like it was excited. The others echoed that dry sound, so like a death rattle it shook my knees.

Timing—it would all be about timing. Too soon, I'd miss. Too late and there'd be no chance.

With the stink of rot, its mouth opened, wider, wider, wider, until those yellow teeth surrounded an eternal void.

I gripped my makeshift club so hard, my arms shook.

The air exploded.

Black dust sucked into solidity behind the thing. Iridescent metal flashed and sliced, then it and the darkness vanished, so quick I'd have missed it if I'd blinked.

Shrieks pierced my ears from all directions, and the thing fell.

What was...?

Had I just been saved from this monster by another far worse?

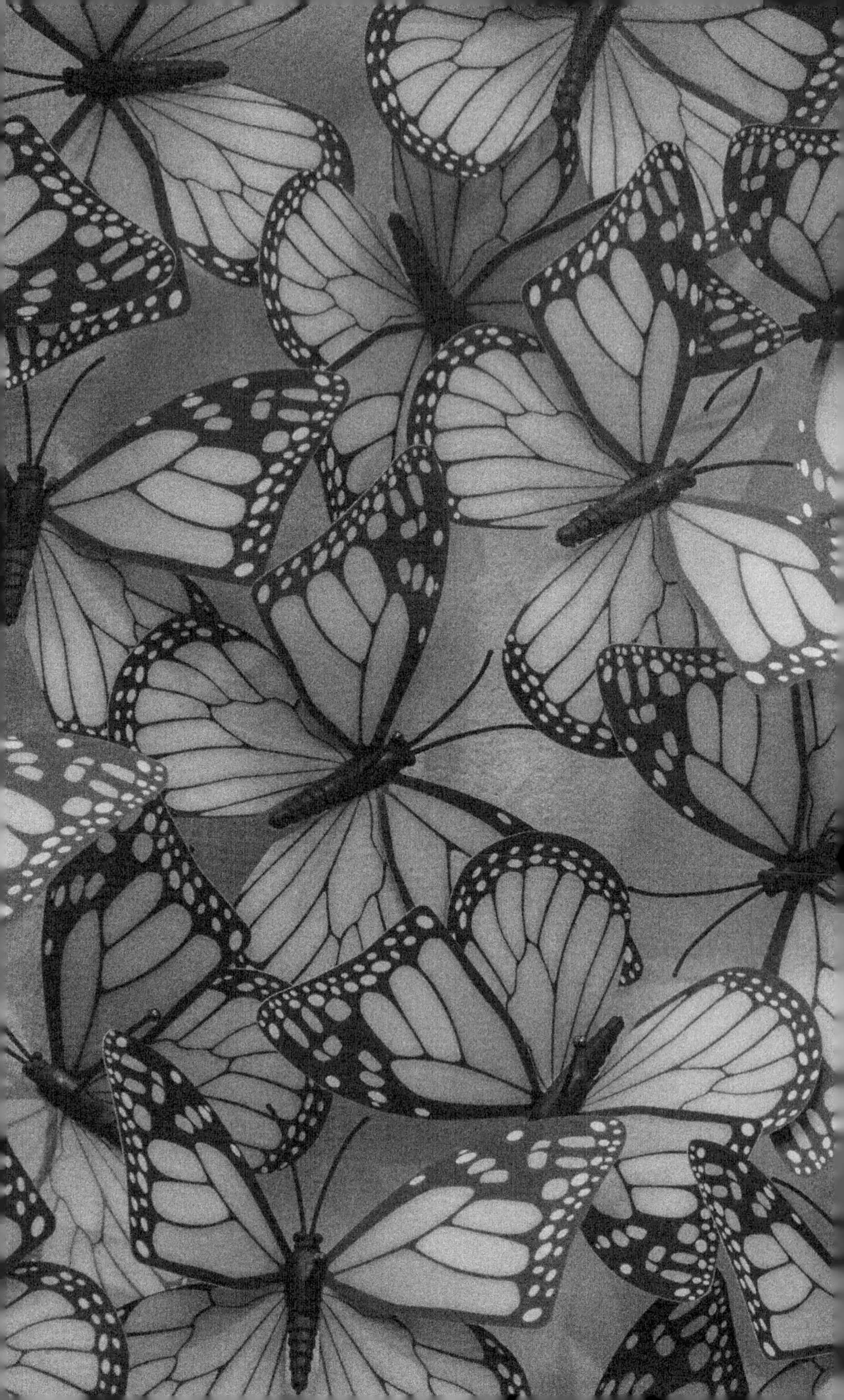

A Monster Far Worse

There was no sign of this other monster, but a splash sounded from behind. Panting, I turned.

One of the pale creatures had reached the water. Claws scraping together, the thing crouched, waiting, watching. Its mouth opened and closed, teeth chopping together.

It lunged.

I screamed. I swung. I missed.

Blood surged through me, hot and loud, and I swiped again and again and again.

I didn't connect, but my wild flailing made the thing pause. It only had to wait for me to tire myself out.

Some distance beyond it, the air snapped and darkness sucked together behind one of its companions. Something that wasn't steel erupted from that creature's chest. The shadows were gone before it hit the ground.

Would it be better to let this thing kill me rather than whatever was powerful enough to face them alone?

My swipes must've slowed as I was distracted, because the thing before me leapt, maw open, tongue tasting the air.

With a cry, I splashed to one side and swung. The impact jolted up my arms.

I'd hit it.

I'd hit it!

A sound came out of me and gods knew whether it was a laugh or a sob.

The thing hunched low, lifting a hand before its empty eyes. One of its claws was broken, the wicked-sharp tip stood between us, embedded in my club.

On the shore behind it, its companion disappeared in a black haze.

But it didn't spare a glance for its friends or the beast that hunted them. The utter void of its gaze was fixed on me, so empty it could swallow me up. Black tongue sliding from its maw, it hissed.

I'd pissed it off. Oh, gods. *Why* had I done that? My knees trembled.

Its attention shifted past me and its claws *clack-clack-clacked.*

There was another beast still behind me. A chill swept from my numb toes through my whole body, closing over my head like I'd fallen in the river all over again.

The instant I turned to look, this one would be on me.

Above, a shriek split the air, growing louder. Even the creature in front of me froze, cocked its head and looked up. I dared a glance over my shoulder. The other creature also scanned the sky.

And burst in a crunch of broken bones and flesh.

The thing hunting them—hunting *me*, whatever it was, had dropped one of the beasts from a great height and...

My stomach lurched, and I threw up in the water, throat burning with bile and soured wine.

The remaining creature tensed, its pale flesh reflecting in the shattered ripples. Its grotesque head swung side to side, but there was no sign of movement beyond us. None of its companions remained.

Face tingling, I coiled my aching arms for another strike, either for this thing or the hunter that had come for it. One or the other would kill me.

It lunged.

I swiped, stumbling backwards with a hoarse cry. My heel caught, pain jarring in my ankle, and I fell on my backside, up to my chest in water.

Somehow, I kept hold of the club. Not that it would do much against that reddish mouth, so wide, so full of teeth, bearing down on me.

Grey spots burst across my vision. This was it. The last moment of my life, and it tasted of festering meat.

Darkness blotted out the pale flesh, standing between me and the creature.

Tall. Broad.

Something sweet hovered at the edge of that rotten death stench.

The moon emerged from behind the clouds and gleamed on hair that wasn't quite black or blue or violet.

It was *him*.

Back to me, his balance shifted from one foot to the other, a perfect, smooth motion, all power and precision that revealed a flash of his glimmering blade.

The creature's head, shoulder, and arm dropped into the water. The rest of its body splashed in the other direction.

I gaped as the ripples stilled around its hulking mass.

He'd killed them.

All of them. And it had taken less than a minute.

I'd been starting to think the stories about fae power were all exaggeration, but here he was standing over a pack of dead monsters.

He turned and surveyed me, chest heaving, a muscle in his jaw flexing. The shadows were back beneath his eyes.

I was alive. Somehow, I'd bumbled my way through surviving while he'd taken care of the creatures. I trembled as various parts of my body started throbbing. Each breath sawed through me, harsh and tight.

"Are you hurt?" His gaze lingered on my cheek where I'd smacked it on the ground during my fall down the bank.

Bruises, maybe a couple of scrapes, but they didn't count. I'd been able to move enough to try and hit the things with my makeshift club, so nothing serious. I shook my head, not even able to consider speaking as I sucked in shallow gasp after gasp.

My chest. Too full. Too tight. I couldn't breathe. A corner of me understood. *You're panicking.* But my lungs didn't believe that, they filled with wadding, couldn't breathe, couldn't...

He offered his hand.

Joints locked as though the river's chill had settled in my bones, I couldn't release the branch. Without a word, he pried it from my grasp, pulled out the bone claw, and threw the branch aside.

Scrapes and scratches covered the backs of my hands, and they shook and shook, but he took them and pulled me to my feet.

The world tilted, and I must've swayed because he caught my shoulders. The wadding crept up to my throat and if I hadn't been shaking so badly, I'd have tried to claw it out.

His fingers bit into me, stilling the world, cutting through the panic, letting me take a single breath. "What the hells were you thinking, going out into the wilds alone at night?"

I blinked, shook my head. It was such a ridiculous question, I scoffed. "Escaping you, of course."

"This is not a joke, human. You could've been killed."

"I did notice." Despite the throbbing ache in my limbs, fresh fire unfurled in my veins. And I could *breathe*. When had that happened? When I'd scoffed? "Those things could've attacked us in the tent. They weren't far—"

"No, they couldn't." He bit out each word. "My tent is warded, keeping the campsite safe. Stars above, did you think I'd let us stay out at night without it? Do you take me for a total fool?"

I snorted, the sound as bitter as the bile that had burned my throat when I'd thrown up. "I don't think you want me to answer that. Perhaps, if you'd warned me about the dangers or deigned to explain that your tent protected us from more than the weather, I wouldn't have taken my chances out—"

"This is Elfhame. Did you think it was all pretty faeries and shiny unicorns who—?"

"Stop damn well interrupting me." I tried to shake him off, but his grip was too strong. Or was I too weak? "And stop treating me like *I'm* the fool because *you* have chosen not to educate me. I shouldn't be surprised. After all, why would anyone educate their pet?"

The fire shook through me, pressing at the back of my eyes, raising my voice, scorching my flesh. Because that's what I would be now—his pet. My escape attempt had failed spectacularly, and no way would I get another chance. He'd fallen for my trick once. He wouldn't again.

I was trapped with him. I'd be forced to marry him. I'd never get to see Rose again. I'd be his diamond-collared dog, put on display and cooed over. No life of my own. No anything.

I'd been so close to paying off my debts and living without the wolves at my heels.

"You ruined it all." I glared at him, even as my sight blurred.

Mouth downturned, he squeezed his eyes shut. "I rescued you from a dull life where—"

"You stole me!"

A low sound reverberated in his chest, not quite a growl. "I didn't steal you. A bargain was made before you or I were born. If you have a problem with it, take it up with our ancestors."

I bared my teeth. "You coward."

His lip curled, more animal than human. "What did you—?"

"I called you a bloody coward. There might've been a bargain, but *you* chose to enact it. You chose to take me away. And yet here you are, hiding behind a deal someone else made. So, yes, I call you a coward."

His eyes bulged in an incredulous stare. But a moment later, it faded as his mouth drew into a cold smirk. "Oh, yes. I am *terribly* sorry for stealing you away from your life. I'm sure you were awfully busy waiting to die of some disease or in childbirth."

Because my life meant nothing to him.

"You arrogant prick. That night"—I jabbed his chest with the tip of one finger, as though I could point through him into the past—"was going to be my chance. You were meant to pick the Hawthorne girl and leave me the hells alone so I could get a contract and clear my debts! Then I could work my fingers to the bone to earn an atelier with glass windows and a marble counter and half a dozen mirrors and a chandelier and customers who treated me with respect and paid what I was worth and... and..." I clutched my chest, eyes burning.

I didn't want that anymore. It was an old dream from *before*, one Rose was clinging onto for me. I just wanted my life, my home, the things and people I knew around me, and to be free of those crippling debts.

Not that he understood. What did some fae lord know of debt or work? He only stared, brows rising, mouth open.

"But you ruined it." Although my voice cracked, I didn't stop. I couldn't. "And I don't even know your bloody name, and you haven't asked mine." His eyebrows rose higher. "Because what's the point in knowing a *mere human's* name when they'll be dead in the blink of an eye?"

He winced and hung his head. "Lysander."

I jolted. "What?"

"My name. It's Lysander." Head still bowed, he lifted his gaze from the ground and met mine. "My friends call me Ly."

I blinked at him—at *Lysander*, whose brows rose in a silent question. There was something hopeful in their angle, even though his shoulders curled in, so unlike his usual confident stance.

Lysander. His name, he'd given it to me at last. Not his True Name, of course, but I couldn't blame him for not handing me that power over him. If I had one, I'd never tell a soul.

Maybe I shouldn't blame him for everything else, either. My debts certainly weren't his fault. Neither was my broken dream—the creeping death had killed that off.

As for the Tithe, he'd been ordered to collect it. If I disobeyed a direct order from the Queen, I'd be executed, and most likely, the fae court was the same. Maybe that didn't make him a coward.

And was that remorse in his hunched posture?

My rage deflated with my next exhale. Limbs sagging, weariness washed over me, giving way to a bone-deep cold.

"Ariadne. Ari for short." I managed a smile, nowhere near the sharp, vicious one I'd given him earlier. "I suppose even fae have names for their pets, and I'd rather you use mine than make one up for me."

"You're not my pet." His voice was soft, and he returned my half-smile. "But you are freezing. Come, let's get back to camp."

Back to camp where I was a prisoner. But it was safer than out here. And now I had his name... Maybe that meant things would be different. Besides, arguing required energy I didn't have, as my shaking knees reminded me. I took a stumbling step and hissed at pain shooting through my ankle.

"And you *are* injured." Without hesitation, he scooped me up, one arm behind my knees, the other around my back.

I gave a feeble attempt at pushing him away, but gave up and leant my head on his shoulder—it was that or let it hang back uncomfortably. "You're just taking advantage of the fact I'm too tired to argue."

He huffed through his nose, dark eyes on our route as he set off. "Maybe."

My boots dripped. They were ruined. "I'm getting your clothes all wet."

"Eh." I bobbed in his arms as he shrugged. "I could do with a bath."

By the time we reached camp, my teeth were chattering. The tent's magic dried us off as we entered, but my toes were still numb and I couldn't stop shivering. The fire slumbered, one orange-pink ember glowing.

When he put me down, I edged close to it, hugging myself, but barely any warmth rose off that dim glow. Instead of coming and waving life into it, he—Lysander turned down the blankets on the bed.

"Won't this warm us up more quickly?"

His mouth twisted and he avoided my gaze. "I... I can't."

Lords and Ladies, he was *embarrassed*. Like the night I'd asked him to puff—shadowstep us back instead of riding. I'd thought it anger, but...

He cleared his throat softly, shoulders rounding. "There are—"

"Certain limitations." Like he'd said that night. And those shadows under his eyes, just like when he'd brought us back here. Was he tired—his magic depleted? How many jumps had he made tonight? Maybe fae weren't the endless sources of magic we thought.

"Come on, then," I murmured. "We'll have to warm up the old-fashioned way."

His head snapped up, eyes bulging.

Oh, gods. I hadn't thought through the double meaning. "Not *that* old-fashioned way." I chuckled, neck hot. "Just"—I waved at the bed—"under the covers. Close... together."

I quickly changed behind the screen. My fingers were too stiff and my hands shook too much. I wasn't about to ask him to come and help me undress, so I ended up ripping off two buttons and tugging the shirt over my head.

When I emerged, the fae lights were at their dimmest and he sat at the end of the bed, shirtless.

I'd slept next to him for four nights now, but either I was asleep when he undressed or he was already under the covers once I'd finished changing, so I'd never seen...

Well.

All *that*.

Shadow and light carved his shoulders, his chest, the ripples of his stomach, hard and well-muscled. My eyebrows rose at the dark hair over his chest and the fine line disappearing into a pair of short, lightweight breeches he'd changed into. For some reason, I'd expected a fae man to be smooth.

Not that I'd thought about how he would look undressed.

When my gaze eventually reached his face, he regarded me with his customary smirk.

I snapped my mouth shut. I'd been staring. And he knew it. Bastard. He had no business looking so... so...

Arms folded, I crossed the floor and slid into bed, not having to climb around him for a change.

"Now"—the mattress dipped as he sat next to me, his smirk widening—"did your new friends scare you out of making any more escape attempts or am I going to have to tie you to the bed?"

My stomach flipped and the heat from my neck crept up to my cheeks and down, much lower. It took a couple of attempts to swallow because my mouth was so dry. I shook my head.

"Which are you saying no to, Ariadne?" Something in his gaze warmed as he drew out the syllables in my name as if tasting them.

"No tying up necessary." My voice came out breathy.

Sighing, he lay on his side and pulled the blankets over us. "I haven't forgotten you can lie. If you try again, I won't hesitate. For your own safety, yes, but also to save me from Her Majesty's wrath." A grimace interrupted the cockiness of his smirk. "Come here, then." He lifted the covers, creating a cave between them and his chest. "If you get on your side and put your back—"

"I know how to lie with someone."

"Oh, *really*? And here I was thinking you an innocent maiden." One dark eyebrow arched.

"Too late for that, I'm afraid. Do you want to swap me for another Briarbridge girl?"

His brows relaxed and that warmth returned—something in his eyes I couldn't place shifted. "Never."

And he couldn't lie.

Goosebumps prickled across my flesh. Clearing my throat, I twisted onto my side and shuffled back, tensed for the moment my body would meet his.

Gods, why had I suggested this? But the icy touch of my shaking fingers on my thighs reminded me—oh, yes, *that*.

"Stars above, you'll have died of cold before you get

over here." He huffed, then slid an arm around my waist, making me gasp. In one commanding movement, he tugged me against the cradle of his body.

He was warm and solid at my back, my thighs. Even his knees tucked up behind mine, and he caught my near-numb feet between his calves. "You appear to have brought ice blocks to bed."

I couldn't help but giggle at that and it pushed the tension out of my body, leaving every part of me heavy and aching. "You insisted on warming me up. You should've realised what you were getting into before you offered."

"Hmm." The sound rumbled through me. "I'm not sure turning down the blankets is insisting. In fact, I believe *you* were the one who suggested it."

"I only said what you were thinking."

"Maybe." A chuckle laced that word. He squeezed me closer, bringing my backside against... well, against a part of him that it would be dangerous to dwell upon. And yet, I couldn't help but notice how he bulged against me. Despite the cold, he wasn't small.

I held still and tried to remind my breaths to stay slow and deep.

"Stars above, you really are freezing. Where are your hands?"

"They're almost as cold as my feet. Don't say I didn't warn you." I touched his forearm.

He sucked in a sharp breath. "You weren't exaggerating. Put them under the pillow." He shifted, and when I obeyed, his other hand was there, closing around my fingers. "There. Perhaps a little slower than some methods"—his huffed laugh tickled the back of my neck, sending a different kind of shiver through me—"but you'll soon warm up."

Already the numbness of my toes was giving way to a painful tingling, so that was true. But I was much too aware of his every movement and each point of contact between us, there was no way I'd fall asleep like this.

I blinked into the darkness. "What were those things?"

"Do you really want to know?"

I shifted against him and peered over my shoulder, even though all I could see were the dimmest outlines of his cheekbone and nose. "Yes. I was almost eaten by five of the things, I don't think knowing what they are is going to make my inevitable nightmares any worse."

"Fair point." His arm tightened around me again, and I took that as a silent instruction to ease back into position.

Sinking into the mattress, I blinked, once, twice, then let my eyelids stay shut. Those things were horrors, but they were outside, and this place was warm and dark and maybe even safe. "So what were they?"

"Young sluagh: the unforgiven dead, wings not yet grown."

Fresh cold shivered through me, warring with his heat, making my tired muscles all the heavier. "So they can fly? Great. Whose wonderful idea was that?" My voice was distant, like something just heard on a breeze.

"I did warn you. They don't get wings until they've eaten three dozen souls."

Like mine. I'd been right to not only fear for my mortal body. I shuddered, which brought me harder against him. Which wasn't as terrible as I might've insisted a few nights ago. "Good to know."

A faint laugh against my back, my neck. "Stay with me and you'll be safe from sluagh and hags and all my other murderous cousins." His hand tucked under my waist, locking me in place. "Sweet dreams, Ari."

But I'd slipped somewhere between the rhythmic press of his chest on my back and the softness of the mattress, and was too exhausted to wish him a good night or argue at being pinned against him so thoroughly.

I sank and sank until there was nothing.

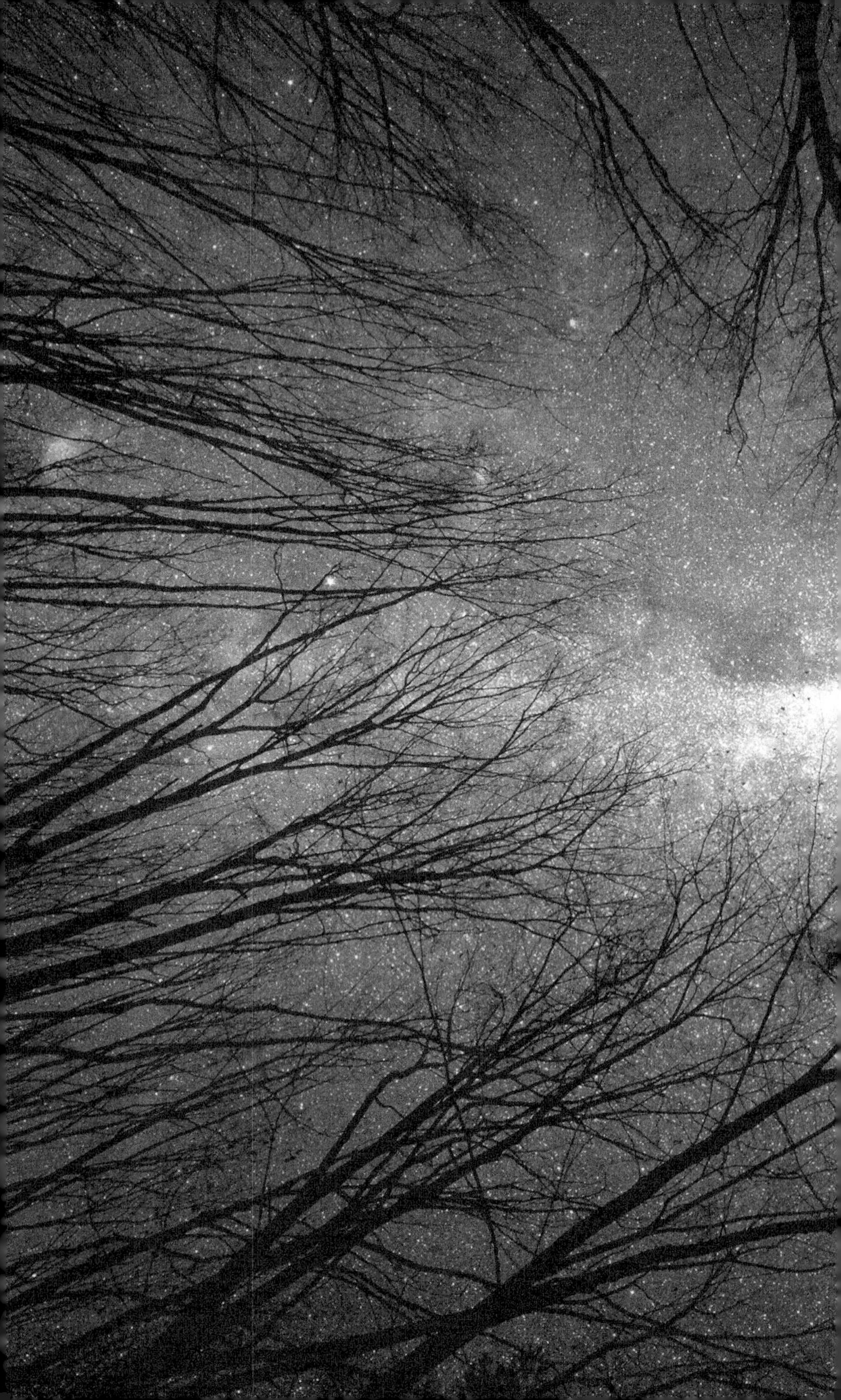

OF BEES & HELLHOUNDS

The next day we rode in near silence. His humour, my exhaustion, and the proximity of his body had all distracted me last night, but now in the harsh light of a new day, I cringed. I'd shared too much. I'd spilled my guts, my hopes and dreams, into a great, ugly pile in front of someone who didn't care. He hadn't been unkind, no, but what was the pain of a human who'd lost everything to a fae like him? It left my skin raw, exposed to every probing look.

So I kept quiet.

By lunchtime, we reached a land where spring was further along with tulips covering the hillsides and new leaves dappling the sky. We removed our cloaks, soaking in the warmth.

When the sun dipped towards midafternoon, we crested a hill and below us, golden light glinted off the windows of a pale grey house.

My mouth dropped open at the size of it—four

storeys tall at its highest point, with square turrets at each corner. Not a house, a *mansion*.

As we approached, we passed more trees and a herd of deer who watched us with only passing interest. We reached the edge of a more formal garden space and ahead figures moved amongst the lush plants.

People.

Apart from Rose, I'd almost forgotten other people existed. We'd travelled for so many days without seeing another soul, it had seemed like Lysander and I were the only ones left in the world.

But the figures stooping over beehives grew larger and more solid as we drew closer.

Throat clenching, I pulled my hood up.

"You can leave it down, you know." His voice was soft in my ear.

I shook my head and gripped the front of the saddle. They would stare at me for my hair or for being human or both.

He squeezed my hip, which didn't feel as strange as his touch had a few days ago. He said nothing more until we reached the two fae, whom he greeted as Sallis and Hobb.

Sallis had skin the colour of fresh, spring leaves and hair that constantly moved on a breeze even though there was none. Hobb was tall, with black eyes, antlers, and bark-like skin over their hands. They smiled and greeted Lysander by name, all the while throwing me questioning glances. He introduced me but gave no explanation, not mentioning how I'd been bargained in the Tithe or that I was to be his new bride.

By the time we reached the imposing front doors of his home and met what must've been a butler, I understood his comment about the people of Briarbridge being all the same.

While we referred to "the fae" as though they were one group, all the fae I'd seen so far appeared vastly different from each other. Although the butler, Boyd, looked like Lysander in some respects—handsome and human-like, with pointed ears and sharp canines—his complexion was paler, and he had russet hair and golden eyes.

I also understood what Lysander meant by "roughing it." He lived in a mansion that put Hawthorne House to shame.

As I tried not to stare at the large entrance hall, a huge white hound came barrelling through the front door.

Long-limbed and well-muscled, it was clearly a hunting dog. But my gaze snagged on its ears and paws, the tip of its tail and its wide eyes. They all flickered with crimson flame.

White for death. Red for danger. For blood.

I froze. A hellhound. One of the dogs that ran with the Wild Hunt.

"Stars above." Lysander darted in to intercept before the beast reached me.

But he didn't draw his sword.

Barely breathing, I managed to blink. Good gods, he

was stroking it. He scratched behind its ears, and the thing's tongue lolled out like it enjoyed the attention.

"Ariadne"—Lysander crouched by the hellhound whose back reached my chest—"meet Fluffy."

Meet Fluffy. That meant... "It's yours? And... *Fluffy?*"

"Hmm." He shrugged and looped an arm around the dog's neck, the casual affection softening the fear in my chest. "No one *owns* a hellhound. She... *chose* me, let's say. It's a long story." He grinned up at me, face and eyes lit. "You're perfectly safe."

And he couldn't lie.

Plus, he was *grinning*. No teasing, no sarcasm, no arrogance, just genuine happiness to be reunited with Fluffy. That was almost as shocking as the fact he had a hellhound as a pet.

"See, she's a big softie." He scrubbed the top of her head, and she panted, sharp teeth gleaming. "You'll keep Ariadne safe, won't you?"

Apart from the fae flames, she looked a lot like a normal dog, albeit a massive one. She certainly didn't resemble a demonic creature on the hunt. Compared to the sluagh, she was almost... *cute.*

If I could smack one of those monsters with a branch, I could pet a hellhound... especially if I told myself she was just a dog.

I swallowed and held out my hand, arm tense, ready to snatch it away.

But Fluffy—he hadn't even addressed how ridiculous a name that was for a hellhound—she inched closer. She sniffed the air, her breath hot and tickling on my knuckles. With a huff, she nudged my fingers.

I gasped at the touch of her pink nose and pulled away, but Lysander only smiled.

"She wants you to stroke her."

Looking up at me with wide, flickering eyes, the dog sat.

His eyebrows shot up. "Well." He blinked from me to the dog and back again. "She likes you. A lot." The faint crease of a frown formed between his brow for a moment before he smiled again.

He could tell that from her sitting?

But here I was in the middle of Elfhame, should I really be surprised by anything?

Breath held, I reached out again, slowly, slowly, and Fluffy lifted her head in anticipation.

Her fur was silky—so soft, I sighed. And no heat rose from her fiery ears as I scratched behind them like Lysander had.

"There." Smiling, he rose. "Not everything here is dangerous, see?"

He left me with a willowy maid, Sylvanna, and touched my shoulder, promising to see me at dinner, then left to take care of some business.

Sylvie, as she insisted I call her, looked like she'd been carved from pale, sun-bleached wood. With Fluffy trailing us, she showed me to a room four times the size of my cottage. I barely took in the big bed and large windows before she led me through another door to a private bathroom with tiles that looked like fish scales. My own *bathroom*.

The tent really was "roughing it."

She ran me a bath, and I perched on the edge of the sink just to watch the steaming water gush into the tub.

Running hot water. How was that possible? Lysander would say *magic*.

I bathed in water scented with jasmine and honeysuckle that reminded me of Mama and made my chest ache. The wardrobe was fully stocked with an array of gowns, jackets, shirts, and even breeches. I chose a simple lilac dress with gauzy sleeves, and a lightweight cloak with a hood, then Sylvie showed me around the house.

She kept a running commentary about each room, what it was used for, and the objects within, unfazed by the fact I barely spoke in return. I was too busy alternating between staring at everything and trying to remember the way we'd come. Although she spoke continuously, her voice was musical and gentle, lulling, and I let my hood fall. It was too warm for a cloak, anyway.

There was a library, a solarium, an orangery, a massive formal dining room, at least two drawing rooms.

So many rooms and corridors, I was guaranteed to get lost.

Perhaps Lysander was trying to ease me into marrying him with all this luxury.

Through glazed doors at the back of the house, Sylvie showed me to a planted terrace with a statue of a woman who seemed to be missing water pouring from her hands. As I'd seen on the ride, the flowers here were brighter and taller, the leaves glossier. And *the scent...* It surrounded me, infused me, green and floral, resinous and sweet, full of woody notes and layer upon layer of complexity, making my head swim.

We descended wide stone steps and Sylvie started to the left, but I paused. A huge yew tree stood in a prominent spot, right in front of the terrace. But strips of craggy bark hung from its branches as if it were shedding, and light timber showed where boughs had broken. What should've been rich, dark needles upon the tree, instead crumbled underfoot, turning to dust. Something sour settled on my tongue, at odds with the glorious scent of the gardens.

Shoulders hunching, Sylvie stopped and waited for me to catch up.

"What's wrong with that tree?" I glanced over my shoulder, the image of it making my heart sink. It was like seeing a once-great sabrecat injured and sickly.

In the couple of hours I'd spent with Sylvie, I'd already come to like her for her easy demeanour, absent of the deference I'd seen in my clients' servants. She had such a ready smile that I didn't mind her sharp teeth—or maybe I'd grown used to Lysander's.

There was no sign of any of that now—her full lips pressed together and her gaze fixed on the path. "It's ill. The stables are just ahead." That was all she said and such sorrow deadened her eyes, I couldn't bring myself to probe further.

To one side of the main house were stables for the deer with open doorways that allowed them to come and go, as well as other outbuildings. It constituted a village in its own right. She mentioned there was also a lake, but it was too far to go on foot before dinner, and she promised we'd go another day.

When we returned to the house, Sylvie took me through a different door, away from the diseased yew tree, but the image of its broken form and dull leaves haunted me the rest of the afternoon.

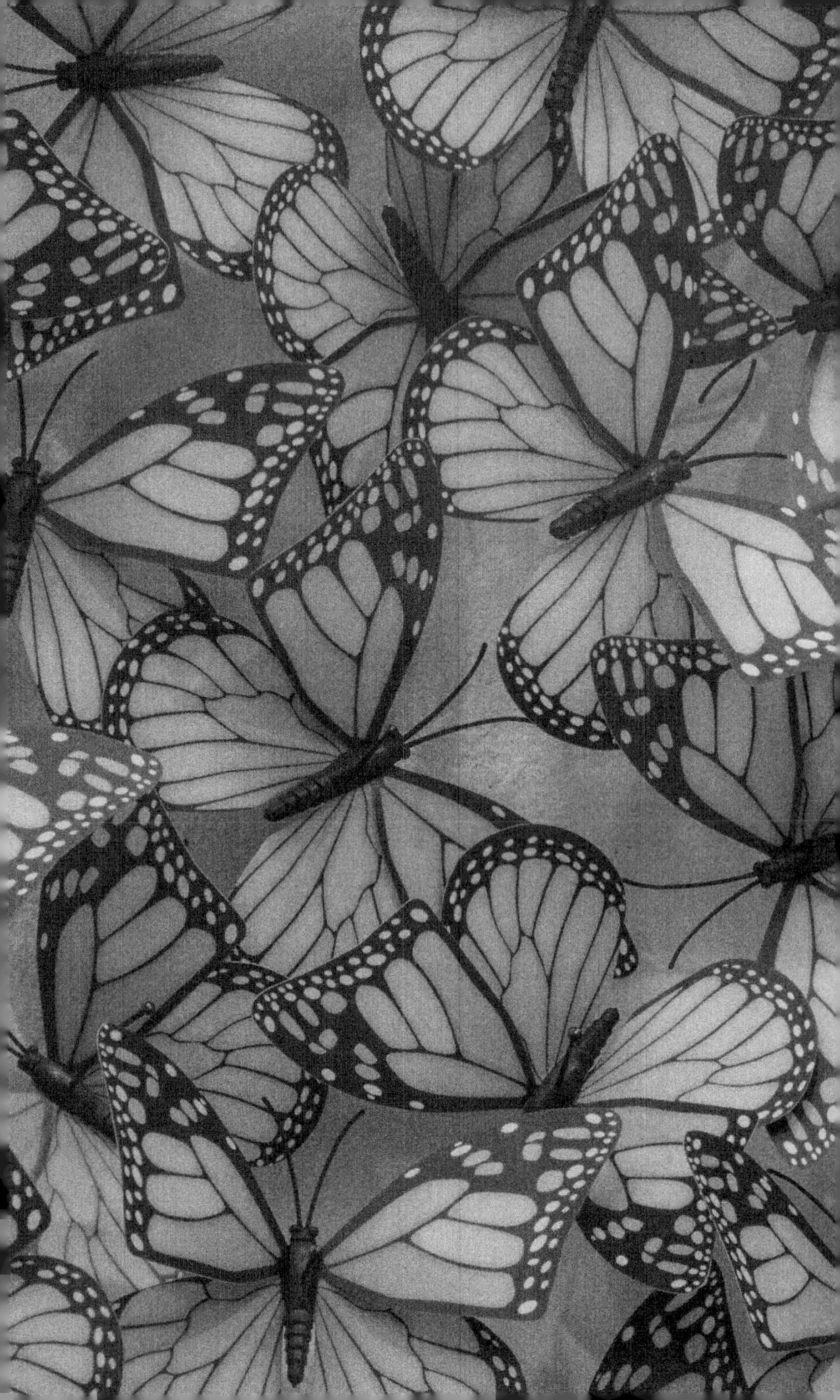

THE BARGAIN

Dinner was... not what I'd expected. When Sylvie had shown me around the grand house with its formal dining room, I expected to sit at one end of the table, with Lysander at the other, and a retinue of servants fussing around us. Rose had told me that was what the Hawthornes and the rest of the nobility did. But not fae lords, apparently... or at least not *this* fae lord.

Because after seeing the house, there was no doubt—Lysander was a lord.

Instead, Sylvie collected me as the sun set and showed me to a cosy room with a round, well-worn table, an assortment of mismatched chairs, and the largest wine glasses I'd ever seen. They were as big as my head and of such fine glass, a wrong look might break them.

One door led to the kitchen, judging by the clatter and savoury smells coming through whenever it opened.

The gardeners and butler I'd met earlier were already here, and Sylvie ushered me to a seat across from them. She took the chair to my right and settled into a conversation with the butler, Boyd, in a language I didn't understand.

I was eating with the servants. Thank the gods. This was far better than the idea of that stuffy dining table. Lysander would eat alone, it seemed. That suited me fine.

A short fae, the same height as me, bustled in, her apron and flour-dusted hair suggesting she was the cook. When her hazel eyes fixed on me, her pointed face broke into a warm smile. "Ah, and here she is—Ariadne, isn't it?"

Everyone turned to me and my tongue withered. Chest tightening, I nodded.

"Such a pretty girl." She patted my cheek, the gesture so like my mother's whenever she'd say goodbye, it made my eyes sting. "My name's Hylder, but most call me Hil. Any time you're hungry, you let me know. Now, you make sure you're comfortable and dinner will be right out. You must be famished after your journey."

With that she bustled back into the kitchen and the attention on me faded. I rubbed my chest and sank into the chair as the separate conversations resumed.

"Where is that boy?" Hil huffed, shaking her head as she returned carrying a great tureen. Apparently her carrying it was all for show, because the moment it touched the table, a dozen more bowls and platters appeared, tinting the air with sweet magic. "Late for his own dinner."

I glanced around, searching for a kitchen lad with short trousers and mucky knees, like Rose's youngest brothers.

"Not late, Hil, just in time." From the doorway behind me came a deep voice, one I'd grown used to over the past few days. It must've been the familiarity in the midst of all this strangeness that sent a thrill through my veins. "Ah, Ariadne"—his fingertips grazed my shoulder—"I see Sylvie remembered to fetch you."

I had to swallow before I could look up at him. It was just as well I prepared myself, because he stood there freshly-shaven and clean of the travel grime that had clung to us both. Just like that first time I'd seen him, it stole my breath. He'd combed his hair, but the lengths on top still flopped onto his forehead, brushing his dark eyebrows. He still wore midnight blue, but just a shirt and breeches, the soft linen of the former draping over the muscles of his shoulders and chest in a way that invited my gaze to linger.

The others were already piling their plates with food as he slid into the seat next to me and opened his mouth as if to speak.

"Oh, it *is* good to have you back"—Hil threw me a glance—"my *lord*."

Lysander snorted. "I think that pretence is like locking the stable door after the stag has bolted." He gestured to the table, then threw me a conspiratorial half-smile. "I'd wager Ari's already worked out we don't operate like that. What gave it away, the table or—?"

"No one bowed when we arrived," I murmured, lifting one shoulder. Of course the dining arrangements shouldn't have been a surprise.

"Ah." He nodded slowly, and offered me a dish of golden roast potatoes before he took any for himself. "We're all the caretakers of this land, it's just my job is a little more..."

"Fancy," Sylvie said in a stage whisper.

I bit back a laugh as I loaded my plate, determined to try a little of everything.

He cleared his throat. "Tied to its magic, I was going to say. Whereas Sylvie's job is to keep me humble." He shot her a sidelong look. "She's very good at it."

Lysander, *humble*? I ducked my head to hide my raised eyebrow.

Sylvie gave a mock bow, canines showing. "Glad to be of service, *sire*."

Chuckles rippled through the group, and conversation turned to gossip, with Sylvie and Hil filling Lysander in on what he'd missed in his time away.

I ate yet more obscenely delicious food while he listened, nodding and exclaiming and offering a soft laugh in all the right places. Every so often, he'd turn to me and explain who so-and-so was and what history there was between them and such-and-such that made this latest occurrence so amusing for Sylvie and Hil.

The food and drink ran as freely as the conversation, and my head buzzed with the chaos of it all. Under the table, my leg bounced. I usually ate alone in my cottage. Once a fortnight, I had dinner with Rose and her family and this was achingly like that—full of laughter and inside jokes, with plenty of gentle mockery.

Rose was the eldest of thirteen and the locals joked that they were "a baker's dozen." Although there were fewer people here, it felt like more. But I'd known Rose and her siblings all my life, while this was new and strange.

I distracted myself from the noise by building a picture of the tangled web of relationships that connected them all. Hil was like Rose's Mama, warm, checking on everyone, ready with a stern word if the ribbing overstepped a line.

Rose would like Sylvie. She took the part of Lysander's younger sister—teasing and bubbly. On the road, he'd told me he had no siblings, just a couple of cousins. I hadn't asked about his parents, but I noted their absence. Were they dead or simply away travelling? No one's behaviour gave the impression of an element missing from the group and there were no empty chairs.

Sallis and Hobb were harder to read—quiet and private. Whenever I caught them speaking Albionic, they were discussing plants, soil, and the creepy crawlies that lived amongst them. Although, at one point Sallis teased Hobb for getting their antlers tangled in some branches this morning.

Boyd, who I'd thought was the butler turned out to be Lysander's secretary. He remained silent, and the only time he engaged with me was to watch across the table with fingers steepled.

One-by-one, everyone retired, whether it was to bed or to play games or whatever else fae did, I had no idea. Sylvie checked whether I wanted her to guide me to my room, but Lysander turned the stem of his absurdly large wine glass between finger and thumb and cleared his throat. "I'll show you, Ari. I'd like a word first, if you're not too tired?" The way his head tilted turned it into a question.

"Not as tired as I was last night." I flashed him a grin, less fazed now fewer people remained.

He scoffed, steaming his glass, and took a sip.

Sylvie watched the exchange, then shared a look with Hil, one eyebrow arched. "I *see*."

"Well, we'd better leave them to it." A lilt ran through Hil's words, and she gave me a knowing nod.

My cheeks burned. "Not like that!" But they were already gone, the door clicking shut in their wake. "Oh, gods, they think…"

"I dare say they do." The grin he gave me was wolfish, displaying his sharp canines.

Though I was going to become his bride at some point, so that meant it was only a matter of time before we *did* what they assumed we'd already done. The burning spread across every inch of skin, and I squirmed, pressing my thighs together. "Is this about our marriage?"

He went very still, blinked. "Our…?"

"Marriage. That's why you take women in the Tithe, isn't it?"

"Oh. I see." Clearing his throat, he rubbed his face. "So you think I'm going to make you marry me. And you don't want that, which is why you were determined to escape."

I still am.

"Obviously."

He nodded, resuming the slow turn of his glass. "How about instead of marrying me, you do me a favour? I can't break the Tithe, but I can bend it that much."

A favour? And a chance to avoid a forced marriage? "I thought the fae didn't do favours, only strike bargains?" That was what the stories said.

His eyes glinted as he grinned. "So you *do* know about us."

"*Hmpf.* I know enough to know you're obsessed with deals." I rolled my eyes. "Everything has to be a bargain with your kind."

"My blood is bound in bargains." He no longer grinned. Gaze fixed on the glass, that thoughtful frown pulled his brows together. "We only have our power because my ancestors made a bargain with the land." He gave a short exhale, almost a sigh, like he wasn't happy about the fact. The shadow of sadness upon him made me think of the yew tree outside. "But a bargain can be for a boon, a favour, an object... a promise."

In the stories that rarely went well for humans, but if I could get the terms right... "So what will *our* bargain be?"

"I will never force you to marry me, if you make me a suit to my specifications."

The breath burst from me. "You don't want a wife. You want a threadwitch. That was why you went to the Hawthorne girl..." The way his nostrils had flared that night—he must've scented my magic on her and asked who'd made the bodice.

A tension I didn't realise I'd been carrying ebbed from my shoulders and back. He didn't want me, only my gift. That was safer, but for some reason my heart sank. "What are these specifications?"

"Stealth. I need to go unnoticed."

Go *where*? And didn't he realise he couldn't go anywhere unnoticed? The power rolling off him, the imposing figure, and that face. None of it was subtle.

Still, this was something I could do with my gift. "If you need to sneak somewhere, why don't you just... shadowstep?" I couldn't call it "puffing" anymore, not after he'd used it to save me from the sluagh. I shuddered at the spectre of their empty eyes.

He stiffened. "For a lot of reasons."

"*Certain limitations.*"

He nodded, tension etching his jaw in a harsh line.

"Unseen. Unheard. Unnoticed." I nodded slowly. "I can do that. I need a workroom, though. And materials and tools."

"Anything you need." The way he said it, intense like he didn't only mean equipment, stilled my breath. "Then you agree?"

"I do. Is there some special way of sealing the bargain?"

"Of course." He rose and I followed suit, standing almost toe-to-toe. "Mirror me."

Pulling a footstool from near the fireplace, he bade me stand on it. "To save both our necks. Eye contact is required."

I scoffed from my perch, which placed my eyes level with the dimple of his chin.

"Better." His tone was so low and private, it made me suddenly aware of how alone we were.

It shouldn't have mattered, considering we'd spent days in a tent and on his stag with no company, but in arriving here, something had shifted between us. Proximity on the road had been a necessity thanks to that one bed and my inability to ride. But with dozens of rooms and beds, including one of my own, being this close was now a choice.

He cupped my cheek like he had at Briarbridge's stone circle. The touch tingled down my neck and spine, all the way to my toes.

I had to take a deep breath before I could mirror his movement. Although he'd come to dinner clean shaven, fresh stubble scraped my palm, already growing back.

He lifted his other hand, palm towards me, and I matched the gesture.

"No," he chuckled. "Like this." He closed the gap I'd left and interlaced our fingers. His hand dwarfed mine, but he was gentle. "And now we state our bargain. I'll let you do the honours."

Giving me the power to phrase it as I wished? Or giving me enough rope to hang myself? I took a moment, straightening my thoughts. Minutes ago, I'd expected to battle against a forced marriage and now here I was making a bargain with a fae that would mean he could never make me marry him. But only *him*.

"I will make you a suit of stealth to the specifications we've discussed, and in return you will never make me marry you *or* anyone else."

The edge of his mouth flickered and he bowed his head in approval. "It is so."

The words of sealing, of agreement. I knew them from the stories, used them in my craft. "It is so."

He squeezed my hand, and his shoulders sank as if relieved. "Thank you, Ariadne."

When he released me and stepped away, his absence left my cheek and palms cold.

He cleared his throat and busied himself returning the stool. "I hoped you would say yes, so I set aside a room and procured some equipment. We can order the materials you need tomorrow."

"Show me this room."

"Now? I thought tomorrow—"

"I'll start first thing in the morning. I want to know where I need to go and what I'm working with."

His eyebrows rose and he gave me an appraising look. If not for the fact I was a "mere human" I might've said he was impressed.

He led me through the quiet house. Some light spilled through the windows, but most of the way darkness pooled so thickly, he had to lead me by the hand. It confirmed another thing I'd heard in the stories—the fair folk could see in the dark.

Fae light flared to life as he showed me to what might've normally been a drawing room. But instead of comfortable settees and low side tables, this had been turned into a workroom. A good one, at that.

My eyebrows rose as I took in the full-length windows covering one wall.

"It's north-facing," he said, watching me inspect the space, "so you'll have consistent light, like an artist's studio. I thought you could work standing at that table and use this one when you wish to sit." He indicated a surface near the windows.

The first table was large and waist-high, clear on all sides—it would be perfect for cutting fabric.

One side of his mouth rose as he took in my hand resting on its surface. "I got the correct height, then."

"*You* did all this?"

"Who else?"

"I thought one of the servants..." The different tables for different tasks. The abundance of lamps filled with pure white fae light. The armchair by the fire, ideally placed for cosy hand sewing in the evening. Each detail had been so carefully chosen and placed, I'd assumed it had been done by someone who sewed, Hil perhaps. Lord Hawthorne would never have risked scuffing his shoes shifting furniture, why would a fae lord be different?

And yet, apparently Lysander was.

He raised his eyebrows as if seeking my approval. Surely my opinion didn't matter to him all of a sudden. "Some of the equipment I ordered won't arrive until the morning"—he winced—"but it's a start, and the—"

"It's perfect." And although I could lie while he couldn't, it was the truth.

A slow smile worked its way across his face like sunlight at dawn, lifting his lips, sparking in his eyes, brightening every feature. This was no mocking smirk. It made my heart skip a beat.

He made a low sound, somewhere between relief and pleasure. "Good." A pad of paper appeared in one hand, a silver pen in the other. "Now, tell me what else you need."

We sat up late, and I listed the materials and tools I required. He noted every item, nodding, asking questions for clarity. Not once did he question the cost or why I needed a particular thing.

Despite the weariness in my limbs, when he walked me to my room, my mind raced with excitement to get my hands on needle and thread again. The last time I'd gone so long without sewing had been during the plague when I'd been too ill to know what was happening around me, never mind lift a pair of scissors.

At the door to my chambers, he thanked me again and paused like he might say more, but he only turned and went to the room next to mine, at the end of the corridor. He'd placed me near him. To ensure I didn't escape.

And when I entered my room, there were none of my things. Even the clothes I'd worn when he'd chosen me —*my* clothes—were nowhere to be found.

Because this wasn't *my* room. This wasn't my home. I'd been taken by a fae lord who could kill five sluagh without breaking a sweat. No amount of sewing could save me from that.

However thoughtful he seemed, his strength dwarfed mine. If I angered him, he could destroy me without batting an eyelid.

Damn it, I should've stipulated in our bargain. Idiot.

My chest tightened as I crawled under the covers, fully dressed.

No matter how kind he'd been, I was still at his mercy and vulnerable. I needed to protect myself, and I needed an escape plan.

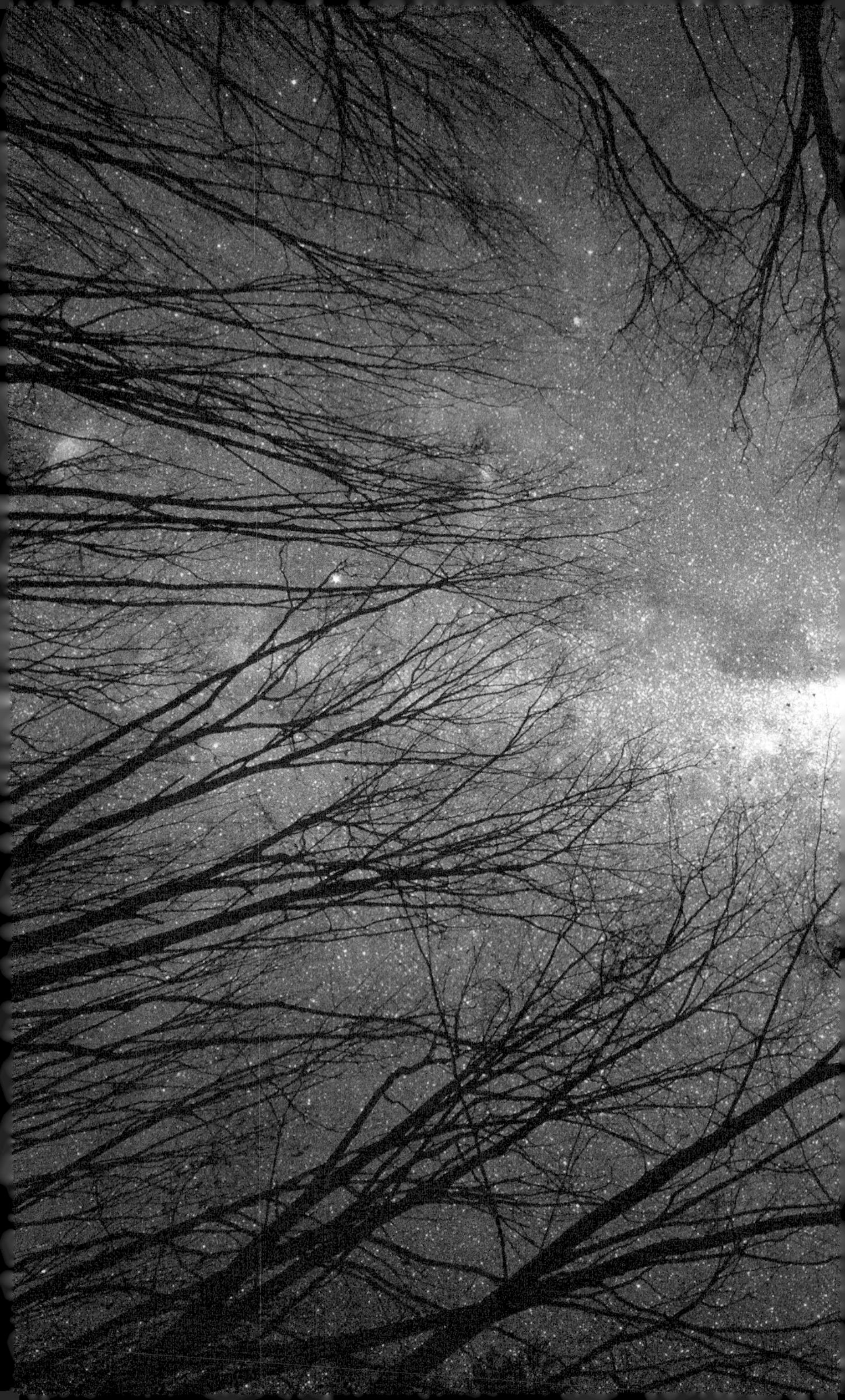

TAKING THE MEASURE

The next morning, I went straight to the workshop. Although it was early, boxes of supplies had already appeared, and I dived in, taking stock. On the low table by the window now stood a cabinet full of little drawers, and I sorted all the different pins and reels of thread into them. In a plain needle book, I arranged needles for darning and beading, appliqué and basting.

Each thing given a home eased the tightness in my chest that had remained all night.

The night after my escape attempt, I'd slept so deeply, I hadn't dreamt. But last night the sluagh had made an appearance in my sleeping world, attacking the sickly yew. Every hack of their bone claws into the tree had cut my heart. I'd shouted at them... and their empty eye sockets had turned on me.

Even in the dream, I'd trembled, realising how stupid I was to try to stop them.

Shuddering, I pressed my hand into the worktop and continued going through the deliveries.

When I opened the velvet-lined box of scissors, an "*oh*" fell from my lips. Each pair sat in a hollow carved to its perfect shape, like Lady Hawthorne's fine silver that I'd caught a glimpse of at a fitting as she'd taken tea.

Thread snips. Pinking shears with scalloped rather than zig-zagged edges. Little embroidery scissors shaped like a stork. Each one was a work of art, and when I tested the tailor's shears, they *snicked* as though they could slice the air itself.

Still, they couldn't kill the fae, not if the stories were to be believed. Even though steel contained iron, there was something about the alloying or the words spoken over the metal by blacksmiths as they worked that made it safe for the fair folk. Iron blocked their magic and poisoned their flesh—there was a reason it had been banned by Queen Elizabeth I and her fae husband.

But iron wasn't the only fae poison. Aconite's other name was *faebane* and the stories said it burned their kind. Its tall purple spires grew in the countryside across Albion. The fae might've largely banished iron from our isles, but an entire plant species was a step too far.

I could only hurt a fae with the scissors, and I didn't even have the strength or skill to manage that in a fair fight. I sighed, touching the rolls of cloth that had appeared overnight—fine wools and linens, silk smoother than anything I'd ever known.

Aconite poisoned with a touch.

The thought came from nowhere, snaking through my mind.

I could make a garment, gloves perhaps, with an aconite-laced lining and spell them so they could only be removed with my permission. They wouldn't be as immediate protection as an iron blade. But as the encounter with the sluagh had reminded me, I was no warrior. If I tricked a fae into putting them on, I could force them to agree to my deal. They got to remove the gloves, and in exchange they couldn't hurt me.

It was better than nothing, which was all the defence I had now.

"Ah, you've found the new deliveries."

I whirled, dropping the duchesse satin I'd been absently rubbing between my fingertips.

He stood in the doorway, morning light kissing his hair and the planes of his face.

My heart pounded my guilt in a beat so loud, he had to hear it. "What're you doing here?"

"I live here?"

"I mean *in this room*."

"Well"—he shrugged—"I assume you need to take my measurements. And... I brought you something."

Eyes wide, I gave the room a meaningful look. "Something *more*?" There was more in this one room than I'd owned in my entire life.

"This is..." He shook his head, stalking closer with one hand behind his back. "I found it amongst my mother's things."

His mother and that phrasing—she had to be gone.

Did that mean his father was too? The back of my throat burned.

Lysander stopped at arm's length and revealed what he'd found. Steel gleamed, and I flinched, but it was no blade. It was a raven, the metal heated to a purple sheen, a black velvet pincushion on its back, feet closed around a metal clamp.

"A sewing bird." I'd lusted after pretty examples in shop windows for years, but always had to make do with a plain clamp to act as a third hand, holding fabric or cord taut as I worked. Smiling, I pinched the back end and its beak opened. "I'm sure this will come in useful."

"It's for you... a gift... to keep. Not just"—he gestured at the room—"to use. I remembered seeing it as a boy, so I knew I had to find it for you."

"I can't accept—"

"You can. I want you to." He gave a single, solid nod. "I'd rather someone use it than it sit in a drawer, lifeless. I can think of no one better than a threadwitch. Mother would've been pleased. She would've liked you, despite herself—despite her ideas about humans." One side of his mouth rose, but sorrow haunted the depths of his eyes, dimming the light flecks.

So that was where he'd got "mere human" from.

Still, my heart ached in response to his sadness, and I couldn't argue. Not when he was being sincere about something so personal. I bowed my head. "Thank you, Ly."

He made a low sound of approval as I clamped the sewing bird to the edge of a table.

I fetched a tape measure and set of steps I'd found beneath the workbench. Shoulders straight, I set to work sizing him, ignoring how the proximity meant I couldn't escape his sweet-smoky scent. I noted each number, professional even when I had to squash against him to reach around his waist and broad chest.

He watched my every move, making me so clumsy I dropped the tape twice and tripped over the steps. Taking a deep breath, I circled to his back although that wasn't next on my list.

It would've been a sin to clothe him in anything less than perfect tailoring, so I would make a full pattern rather than just mirroring the same measurements for left and right.

So I climbed the steps and pulled the tape across his shoulders, one side, then the other. I could always make up for any irregularity with padding.

I needn't have worried.

"You're very... symmetrical," I muttered as I went to the table and the notebook where I'd recorded his measurements.

He looked over his shoulder. "Isn't everyone?"

"No." I added to the list. "Most people have slight differences on left and right. A quarter of an inch here, an eighth there. But you're identical on both sides. Perfect."

He turned and I could practically *feel* the smugness rolling off him.

Oh, gods, why had I said that?

"You think I'm perfect?" Sharp teeth glinted in a self-satisfied grin.

"No. I said your *measurements* are perfectly symmetrical. No one is perfect. If anything, it's a freakish defect."

"Mmm-hmm."

Jaw clenched, I climbed the steps and measured the length of his arm, trying to ignore the fact that smug smile remained as he observed.

"What's that?" He frowned, gaze below my jaw.

I froze. My braid had fallen over my shoulder, exposing the left side of my neck and the silver tracery of scars from the creeping death. An unsightly reminder of my human frailty.

Swallowing, I went to pull my braid back in place, but he caught my wrist.

"No," he murmured, voice softer than I'd ever heard it as he released me. "They're scars, aren't they? What happened?"

Maybe it was just as well if we both remembered what I was and the vast gulf between us. It might stop him flirting and me swooning like a ridiculous girl every time we touched.

"Four years ago, there was a plague. Everyone called it the creeping death, because it spread slowly up the body."

My throat blocked the words for what it had looked like, how it had felt. Black, blistered flesh. Burning like hot coals had been shoved under my skin. The infection had left me thrashing at the faces that appeared in the walls, the gnashing teeth at the top of every bowl and cup. Then it had knocked me out, imprisoning me in feverish nightmares for days.

Closing my eyes, I shook my head. "No one survived once it reached your face." Like Mama and Papa. They'd caught it first and when I'd woken, they were gone—my world with them. "My parents..."

For long seconds, he was silent. "I'm sorry you suffered and lost your family." His brows creased together as his gaze swept down the side of my neck.

I let him look, let him see how close the jagged lines came to my face. "Humans are so delicate." I gave a bitter smile as I repeated his words from our journey.

"No. That's not right." His fingertip landed just below my ear, right where the highest scar reached.

My breath stilled.

He traced the twisting line down, across my hammering pulse to my collarbone where the scars disappeared below the neckline of my dress.

I did not pull away. No one had touched my scars before, but he did it as though they weren't a grotesque reminder of a dark time of terror and death. In Briarbridge, everyone who'd caught the disease and survived hid theirs. There was always this fear in the air, like maybe the disease lived on in our flesh, only dormant for now.

"You have endured"—he stroked that point on my collarbone, and I shivered—"like the Dusk Court's Great Yew."

I tilted my head in question. Speaking might break this spell that had him so quiet and earnest. It might make him stop touching me, and I was a fool, but I liked this business of being touched.

Smiling, his gaze lingered on my throat. "At the palace grow two trees, a yew and an oak, that represent... a lot of things. Centuries ago, the yew was struck by lightning and cleaved in two. The Dawn Court could barely contain their glee, so my parents told me. And yet it survived and both halves grew and *thrived*. It bears the scars of that day but still dwarfs the Dawn Court's oak."

The Dawn Court and the Dusk Court—I didn't understand how that worked. Two courts in one palace. A king and a queen who ruled the same land but weren't married... It was confusing.

But I understood how he saw the yew tree, what he thought of its scars... and perhaps of mine. He made them sound like a sign of strength rather than weakness.

"You, Ariadne, bear the marks of our sacred tree. Your scars are like roots and branches—things of growth and life and sustenance." His fingers slid to the back of my neck, and he rubbed the pad of his thumb over the silvery lines.

Shivers raced through me, not only from his touch, but... those words. They stung my eyes, and I had to swallow before I could look up from his chest.

Our eyes met and we froze. The steps put me almost level with him, and now our lips were only inches apart.

I could've pulled away. I should've. If I told him to release his hold, he would have done so.

I didn't.

His chest heaved and his gaze lowered to my mouth. Gods knew what I was doing, but my chin inched up.

"*Ahem.*" From the door.

I leapt away, and for a heart-wrenching moment, lurched through empty air. But Ly caught me and deposited me safely on the floor beside those damn steps.

"I'm sorry to interrupt," Boyd said from the doorway, not looking remotely sorry as he shot me a look full of daggers. "However, it's nine o'clock—your appointment, Ly."

"Right." He huffed and swept the hair from his forehead. Surely he wasn't ruffled? "Do you have all the measurements you need?"

Clearing my throat, I nodded. "I have enough to get on with."

With a stiff smile, he was gone, leaving me to my work.

A LITTLE LATER, Hil brought me a flaky pastry flavoured with almonds for breakfast, as well as a whole pot of tea and a cup of coffee, because she didn't know which I preferred. I worked all morning, drafting a pattern for a fitted jacket. I flicked through a stack of books while I ate lunch. One included patterns for gloves and bags. I paused over the gloves, mouth too dry to swallow the sandwich that Sylvie had delivered.

I had nothing in the face of their power, but poisoned gloves could be a last resort. They just might save my life.

My hands had ended up in his enough times that it was easy for me to gauge which size to use. Not that I wanted to use them on him, but... Here, he was my greatest danger. And even if another fae posed a threat, with a little luck they'd have hands smaller than Ly's.

I traced the pattern.

All afternoon, I worked on a toile of the jacket, testing the design. I couldn't start on the breeches until I had more measurements. Inside leg—*that* was going to be fun to take. Gods, why had I agreed to this?

I took dinner in the workroom, too. It was quiet where the room off the kitchen was too chaotic.

Hells, I could admit it—my feelings for *him* were too chaotic. Somehow, despite my traitorous chin rising and inviting him to kiss me, I was *relieved* he hadn't reappeared. Avoiding dinner with the others meant I could avoid facing him. And that was almost as much of a relief as bargaining my way out of a forced marriage.

The house was quiet and dark when I emerged, but with lunch, Sylvie had brought a floating fae light that I could direct with a gesture and whose colour and brightness I could change with a word. It was part of another order Ly had made, she'd explained, this one taking a little longer because of its magical nature.

Whatever reason he had for sneaking somewhere, it had to be for something important—he must've spent a small fortune kitting out this workshop. And the sewing bird, the floating light, the books and materials... he'd put a lot of thought into it as well as money.

When I climbed into bed and dimmed the light with a whisper, I lay in the dark, staring up, and my hand crept to my neck. What the hells was wrong with me that I'd let him touch me like that?

Even worse, I'd wanted it.

Groaning, I pulled a pillow over my face. "Oh, shit."

It was simple and horrifying and almost as frightening as his overwhelming power.

I liked him. The fae who'd kidnapped me away was thoughtful and kind and gentle as well as painfully attractive, and I damn well liked him.

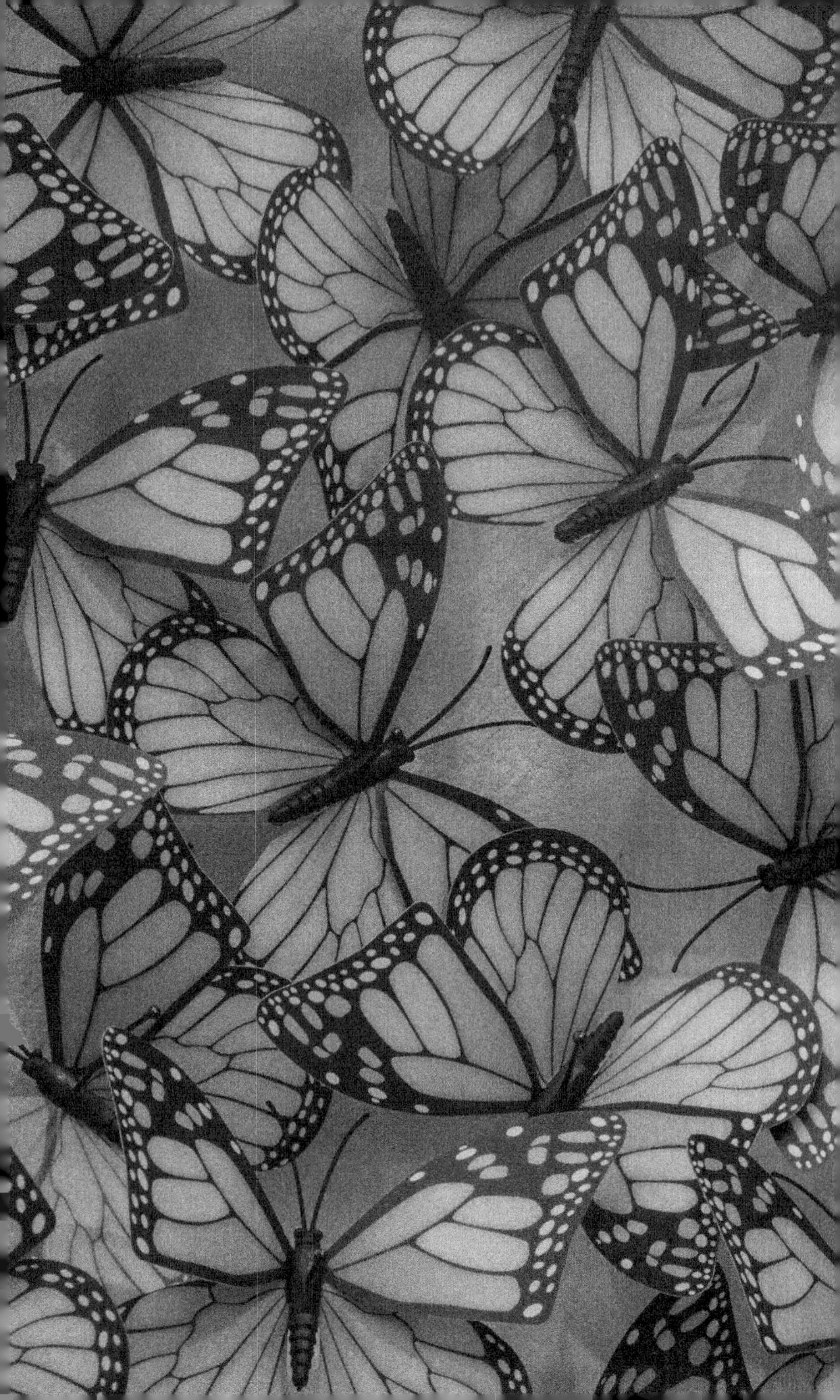

COMPANY

"Do you want some company?" His voice cut through the silence.

I bolted upright, almost jabbing my finger in the process. Thank the gods I was finishing the toile rather than working on the gloves. Clutching my chest, I huffed. "You gave me a bloody heart attack."

Standing in the doorway in darkest indigo with shadows pooled at his feet, he was night. But night didn't give rueful smiles like the one he was wearing. "Not intentional. We're just... naturally very quiet."

We. Fae. Eyes closed, I rubbed the bridge of my nose. I had to remember that. He wasn't a human, he wasn't a person...

Except he was the latter, wasn't he?

Yes, Mama had told me a million times the fae were like the djinn who'd stolen her friend and left her broken. She'd warned me that they were inhuman monsters who wore pretty flesh to tempt us closer and felt nothing but greed and lust.

And yet Ly had shown me it wasn't true. I'd glimpsed grief for his parents, anger at my foolish escape attempt, and kindness with no bargain attached. Yesterday, when he'd said those things about my scars, he'd stood to gain nothing from it. And it wasn't as though he could lie.

"Ari?"

Blinking, I sucked in a breath. "Yes, sorry, I... Heh, well, we'd normally say 'I was off with the faeries,' but I'm already there, aren't I?" I found myself grinning and waving him in.

He chuckled as he approached, and yes, now I paid attention, I realised every footfall was silent.

My eyes narrowed. "How long were you standing there?"

His gaze slid from mine and went to the toile. "A little while. You were so absorbed and... it was pleasant to watch. Did you know you have this little frown when you work?"

My cheeks burned. He'd watched me, and he'd liked doing so. It didn't mean anything. Couldn't. I was, in his words, a "mere human" and why would a fae lord want that when he could have a fae lady who was as beautiful and powerful as he was? My gift was useful to him for now, but I'd be fooling myself if I thought I was powerful enough, pretty enough... *anything* enough for someone like him.

I cleared my throat and returned to stitching. "You're not the first to tell me that." The yawning hole at the centre of my heart expanded as an echo of Papa ruffling my hair ghosted over my scalp. *If the wind changes, you'll stay that way,* he'd warned me.

"Then I'm not the first to observe your skill at work?" His smile was only half-teasing, the other half was gentle, coaxing. It warmed that emptiness in my chest.

I finished basting the seam. "Papa would tell Mama and me stories as we sewed. He knew all the best ones—he'd travelled Europa, even told his tales to kings and queens." He'd had a sonorous, musical voice that had lulled me to another place as my needle rose and fell, as steady and easy as breathing.

"So your mother taught you to sew. Was she a threadwitch, too?"

"A seamstress. She had no magic... but it feels a sin to call her *only* a seamstress."

I shot him a glance, pride for my parents warring with the fear of boasting. But he watched me snip the thread and drop the end in a small bin, apparently content to listen. "Her goldwork was the finest in Europa and won her a position working for the Queen of Frankia. That was how she met Papa."

He'd called it love at first sight, like King Arthur and Queen Guinevere. Mama always laughed and kissed his cheek when he said that. Once I was older, she explained it was *lust* at first sight and later developed into love. That sounded more realistic.

I re-threaded my needle, knotted the end, and worked on the next seam. We stayed in silence like that for several minutes, me working, him watching, our breaths settling into something rhythmic and deep.

"If you wish," he murmured as though not wanting to startle me again, "you can make things for yourself. I don't mean for this space to only be for you to work on our bargain."

That explained the various rolls of different fabric—far more than I'd requested in my shopping list. I nodded in acknowledgement, needle dipping and rising, thread going slack then taut.

"And"—he paused—"and I know you took all your meals in here yesterday. You're not a slave, you know. We abhor—"

"I know. Everyone in Albion knows—it's illegal in our country for a reason." The fae hated slavery, and engaging in it was a surefire way to get yourself damned. Papa had said it was because some unscrupulous craftsfolk, like the cobblers and spinners in the stories, had once set traps to enslave fair folk to work for them tirelessly without pay. "But if I'm not a slave, then what am I?"

I didn't dare look at him. The silence ticked on.

He shifted, sleeve rustling against the table. "I didn't make myself clear when we made our bargain. I'll pay you for your work, a more than fair wage."

I could've laughed. For all the years I'd spent desperate for money, now I was surrounded by wealth and finally understood it wasn't the money itself that I'd needed. It was what it offered.

Options. Opportunities. Freedom.

And here I was with money, but none of those things. Oh, the bitter irony.

In Elfhame, I was property or perhaps a curiosity—the fae lord's pet human. Even if he didn't think that way, everyone else did.

Even if I made all the money I needed or wanted, I'd never get to go where I wished, do what I wanted, move to a bigger city and open my own atelier. Although I'd let go of that dream a long time ago, in Briarbridge I still had the chance to one day change my mind and *try* to pursue it. But here?

For all Lysander's home was beautiful, it was a prison. It could never be my home.

It could never be my *choice*.

Jaw clenched, I stabbed the fabric quicker, harder. "I'd rather have my freedom, thanks." My home, my belongings, my *life*.

"I'm afraid that isn't an option."

"Isn't it? Or are you just not willing to offer it?" I shot him a glare, and his tanned skin paled.

Drawing himself up straight, he took a step away. The stiffness ill-suited him, but so what? Captivity ill-suited me.

"You are bound, Ariadne, just as I am. Under the terms of the Tithe, you must stay with me forever." With a curt nod, he stalked from the room.

Forever. That word lodged in my throat, choking. If not for that, I might've laughed, a bitter, sneering thing.

I'd spent my life thinking I was powerless—to stop my magic awakening, to keep Callum, to save Mama and

Papa, to fight off the wolves at my heels. At least in Briarbridge there had been a *chance*.

But I'd been blind and foolish, because here I was bound to Lysander, and now I truly *was* powerless.

I balled the toile in my fist.

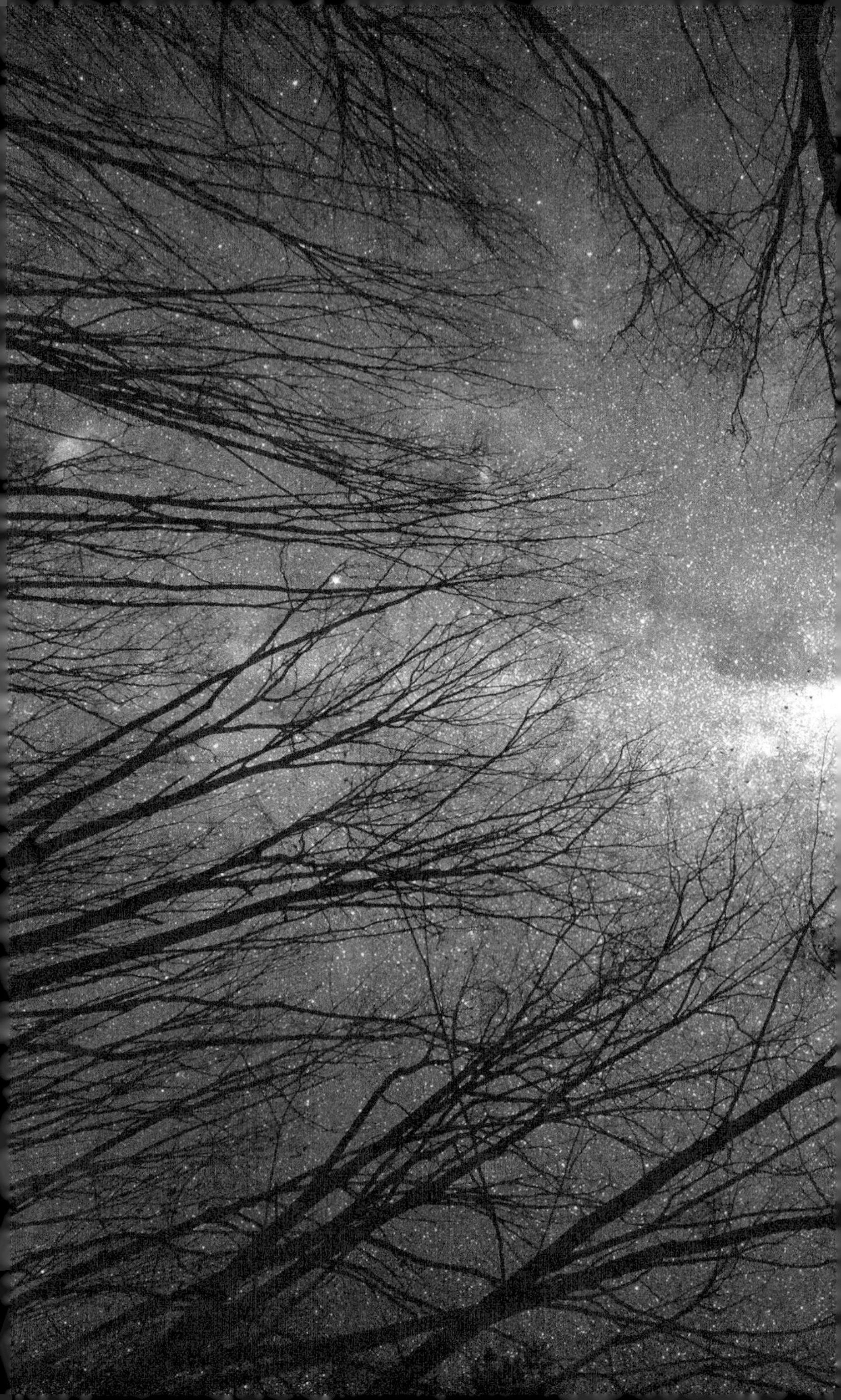

Raspberries & True Names

When I arrived in the workshop the next day, another armchair had appeared by the fireplace, and later that morning he darkened my door. I gave a polite, if cold greeting, and handed him the finished toile to change into behind a screen. It only required pinning over his narrow hips, but otherwise the pattern was there. Silence reigned between us until he left.

Much later in the day, after I'd taken dinner alone, he appeared again.

"I come with entertainment." He waved a book. "Well, a peace offering, really." He raised his eyebrows as if asking whether I'd accept.

I'd cut the gloves and sewn the lining together. They sat at the bottom of the work basket next to the armchairs. My guilty conscience tugged my gaze in that direction, and Ly must've taken it as an invitation, because he took a seat and looked at me expectantly.

He was bound by the Tithe, just as I was. A good night's sleep had lessened my anger somewhat, but it still grated that his side of the Tithe involved his life continuing as normal while mine had changed completely.

Still, that wasn't his fault. So, with a sigh, I took my work to the armchair and flopped into it.

"I'm afraid I'm no storyteller, but I have some good books." He flicked his fingers and a decanter and two glasses appeared on the low table between us. "And if all else fails, you can always drink to distract yourself from my poor diction."

He was going to read to me as I worked. My chest swelled.

The first story was one I'd heard before—*The Maiden of the Tower*. It had been Mama's favourite since it came from her homeland. I didn't mind hearing it again and not only for the reminder of Mama. For all he said he was no storyteller, Ly's deep voice took on that cadence, filling the room and lulling my breaths as I sewed.

A little of my energy sapped into each stitch. "Strength," I whispered into the seams, voice as soft as the thread I drew through the fabric. My magic was in that thread, silver in my mind's eye, part of the dim web that threaded through the world. From me to Lysander, to the sickly yew outside, to the flowers in the gardens, to the ground below the house, to the owls hunting in the gathering darkness. The threads connected all things.

Most of the time I was a fly caught on one bar of that spider's web. But at least working made it feel like I controlled this single strand. It was better than being trapped, waiting for the spider to come and devour me.

Ly had fallen quiet, his story finished, and when I looked up, I found him watching the rise and fall of my hands as I took small, even backstitches through the layers of cloth.

"Raspberries," he murmured with a faint smile.

My magic. It was weak compared to his, but he could still taste it across the few feet separating our armchairs.

Something about that was intimate. Maybe because I'd never known anyone else who could taste magic—at least, none of the other fae-touched in Briarbridge had ever mentioned it. I swallowed and nodded. "I don't really notice it anymore, but yes, I've always thought it tasted like raspberries."

He made a soft sound in his throat and turned the page of the book resting in his lap.

The next story was new to me, about the ancient times when humans and fae lived side-by-side across Albion. A human woman longed for the strength to save her sister from a bargain with a kelpie. Although she was gifted, her magic was too weak to stand against the lake beast.

She asked a local cunning woman what she could do. "Find your True Name, girl," the cunning woman told her, "and all power will be yours. The Lady of the Lake knows all things. Give an offering and declare your truest desire. If you want it with every part of yourself, she will grant you a Name."

So she journeyed across the country to the Lady of

the Lake and declared her wish to save her sister. She gained her True Name and used it to break the wards on the kelpie's stronghold. There, she fought the beast and won, only to discover her sister crying. For, although she thought she'd saved her sister from a terrible fate, her sister had fallen in love with the kelpie and married him.

"The end." Ly closed the book. "Sorry, they're all rather tragic. I'll find something more cheerful next time."

My muscles ached from pouring my strength into my gift, and I'd stopped sewing some time ago, simply watching the pinkish orange flames in the hearth. "Is that true? That the Lady of the Lake can give a human a True Name? I didn't think we had them."

True Names were power. Every faerie had one, and knowing it could grant you power over them. Lysander wasn't his True Name, or else I could've ordered him to take me home.

I'd never heard of a human having one, but the story had made it sound as though knowing her True Name had granted the woman power over *herself.*

"I don't know." He raised a shoulder and drank his whisky. "Perhaps? There's another version of the story where the cunning woman says all humans have True Names, it's just they aren't born knowing them as we are."

"If that was true, why wouldn't everyone just go and ask the Lady of the Lake?"

He scoffed and swirled his drink, offering to top up mine, to which I shook my head. "Well, for one thing there isn't only *one* Lady of the Lake, there are seven of them, sisters. But they're all difficult to find, at least for humans. There are none left south of the wall. Then there's the matter of wanting something so utterly." He paused, glass pressed against his lower lip as he watched the fire. "I'm not sure that's as easy as it sounds. Have you ever wanted something with every fibre of your being and soul?"

To go home. But I'd already made that clear and I didn't want another argument, so I just shrugged.

"Besides"—his mouth quirked—"the whole thing might be nothing more than a story."

But if it wasn't just a story... If I could get my True Name, that power could be enough to break the Tithe. He'd know what I was up to if I asked *where* the Ladies of the Lake were. I'd have to make subtle enquiries. He'd already said I could help myself to the library.

I would start there.

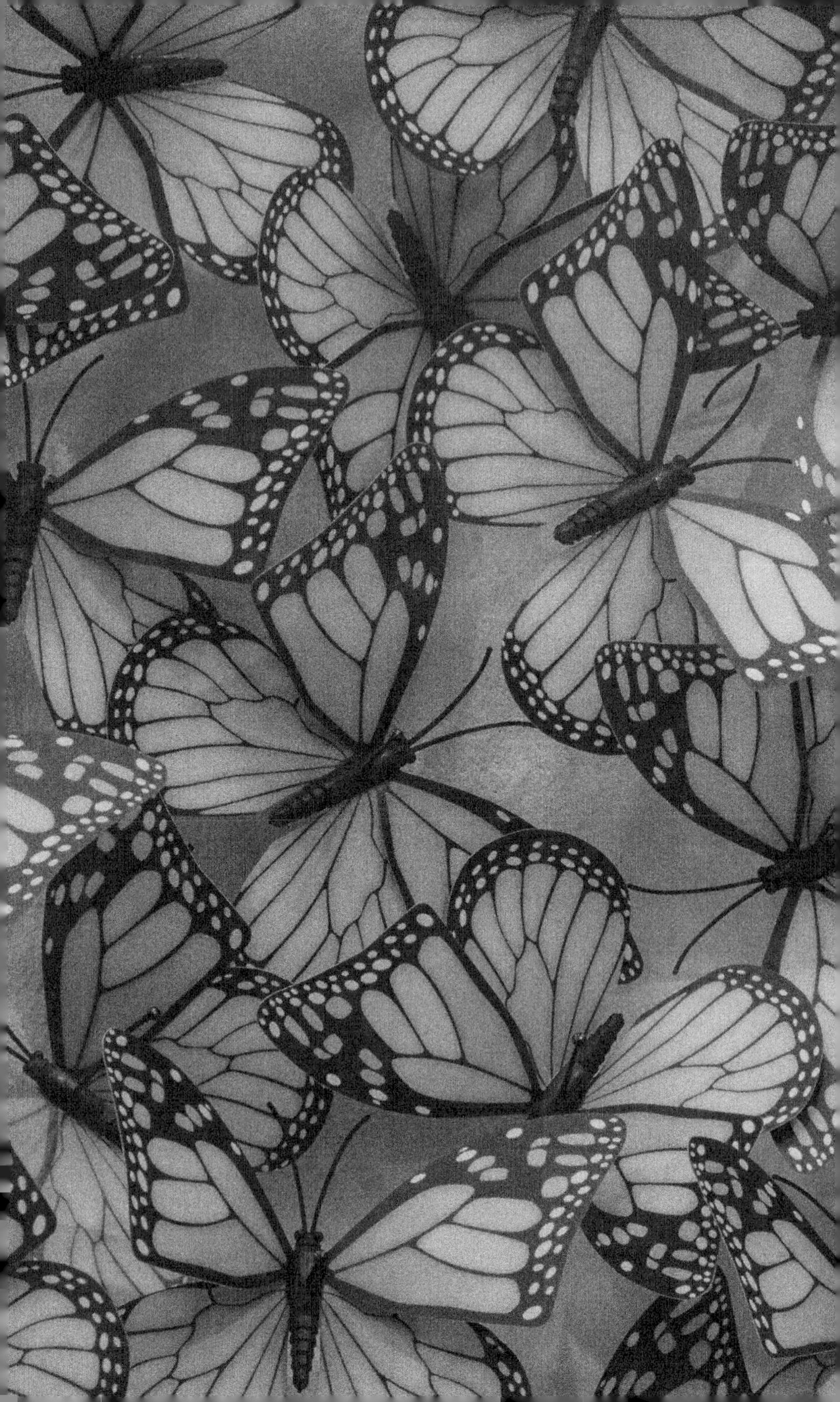

A Boon

The next day, I found nothing in the library, save for a vague explanation: "Knowing another's True Name grants power over them. Knowing your True Name, grants mastery over yourself."

But I did join the others for lunch and dinner. Ly was quiet and stiff, and Sylvie kept throwing him glances, her eyebrows raised as if asking a question. Eventually, once everyone was finished and the plates disappeared from the table with a *pop*, he leant close. "We have guests visiting for Calan Mai."

The festival wasn't for another month or so. It seemed like innocuous news, and yet his hands fisted, knuckles whitening.

Perhaps my presence made that a problem. Did other fae know about the Tithe and were expecting to find him married to the human he'd brought back? Had I made him look weak? "I can... keep out of the way, if that's what you're trying to—"

"No, no." He gave a short, sharp shake of his head. "That's not..." Exhaling through his nose, he stood. "Come."

Sylvie and Hil shared a glance as we left and Boyd pursed his lips. His golden eyes, sharp and cold, made me shiver.

Apparently unaware of Boyd's disapproval, Ly led me back to the workroom. "Some more supplies have arrived."

I frowned as he held the door open for me. "I have everything I need for your suit."

"Yes, but I couldn't resist adding these to the order. They took a little while to source but..." He glanced at me, then away, half a smile on his lips—the smile I might've called shy. "I thought you might enjoy them."

Since I'd left the room just over an hour ago, more rolls of fabric had appeared in the stands, and... I let out a low breath. Where the bookshelves had been empty, they now glinted and glittered with dozens, maybe even a hundred corked jars and phials, each filled with...

I went closer, unable to take my eyes away from the colours. *So many* colours. Crystals and jewels of crimson and scarlet, emerald and olive green, aqua and deep, dark teal, jet-black and slate grey. Chips and flakes of gold, copper, and silver. White moonstone flashed green and blue as the light shifted. Its dark counterpart, labradorite, gleamed with gold, green, and blue iridescence.

An apothecary of embellishment.

"Did you see the drawers?" he asked from the doorway.

A wide set of shallow drawers sat beneath the cutting table and when I opened them, I let out a low sigh.

The finest lace I'd ever seen, some black, some white, some shimmering with metallic thread, some in deep jewel tones. The concoctions I could create with this and the jewels.

Head spinning with possibilities, I wandered to the fabric rolls, but I couldn't touch them.

So much. I covered my mouth and shook my head. *Too* much. It was... I didn't deserve... "What's it all for?" Gods knew why, but my voice cracked.

In silence, he appeared at my side, close enough that I could smell him, feel his warmth. "For you, of course. It's all for you."

Throat tight, I stared at the cloth, but could only see blurred colours. "It's all so beautiful. I've never..." This was so far beyond the supplies I'd ever been able to afford. And the lace—that had to be fae-worked. I'd never seen anything like that, even in Mama's old sample book from when she'd worked at the Frankish Court. "The things I could make." I could create dreams from all this.

"I can't wait to see them." He pushed stray hairs back from my face. "Though nothing in those jars can match your starlight." His soft exhale wasn't quite a laugh. "The first time I saw you, all I could think was that someone had brought the evening star to earth and turned it into flesh and blood."

My lashes fluttered. He couldn't mean that, couldn't...

But that first morning in his tent when I'd emerged wearing all white, he'd said I looked even more like starlight. Cheeks burning, I dared a glance at him.

His attention darted to the fabrics, and he rubbed a sandwashed silk between finger and thumb. "I thought your first creation might be an outfit for Calan Mai. But as you spend all your time sewing, I understand if you'd rather have a seamstress make you something. I can bring one here from the city—"

"No," I choked out. "No, I'll make it." For myself.

All the silk gowns I'd made, all the goldwork embroidery, all the lace and beadwork—and I'd never worn a thread of it. I'd never had anywhere to wear something like that, never mind the money to pay for it. If I managed to escape, I might never have another chance.

He gave a low hum, and when I looked up, he had this private smile that teased the dimple in his cheek.

It tightened something deep in my gut and made my thighs squeeze together.

"I was hoping you'd say that. I also saved this." He pulled a roll from the back that was wrapped in brown paper. "I thought you might like to open it. I doubt you'll have seen it before as it's a well-guarded secret." He deposited it on the nearest table and stood aside, biting his lip.

"Lysander." I sighed as I approached. "This is too much, you shouldn't waste—"

"None of this is a waste." His mouth flattened. "Not a penny of it. And I won't hear a word otherwise, so save your arguments and please open this."

I snorted. "I can't decide if you're arrogant for shutting me down or kind for pleading with me to unwrap this... this... gift."

His teeth flashed as he grinned, all wicked and sharp. "Can't I be both?"

"Apparently so." I smirked back, one eyebrow raised as I peeled back the paper. My mocking expression died the instant I saw what was beneath.

The palest silvery cloth, so lightweight my breaths rippled it, so fine it must've been woven from thread thinner than hair. "What is...?" Almost afraid to touch it, I brushed a single fingertip where it pooled on the table.

"Spidersilk."

"My gods. I've heard of people trying to spin and weave it, but it's so delicate no one's succeeded." I slid my fingers under the edge and lifted a corner. So light, it felt more like a breath on my skin than cloth. But within a second, as if to illustrate my point, it disintegrated. "Oh!" I gasped, heart sinking. "Oh, no, I've—"

"Don't worry." He squeezed my shoulder. "I'm actually impressed—normally when humans touch this stuff, it falls apart instantly."

"Oh." I rubbed my thumb over my fingertips, but there was nothing left. So I could look at this marvel, but I couldn't work it. I was glad to have seen it, but knowing it existed and I couldn't use it was a kind of torture.

Wasn't that the nature of fae madness? Knowing of a thing so wondrous it changed how you saw the world and yet being denied it.

"You don't think I'm going to leave you to only look at it, do you?" The confidence of his grin made me narrow my eyes.

"What do you mean?"

"I mean, I can grant you a boon so you can work it."

A thread of something bright darted through me. "A boon..." Dangerous. Especially when I didn't have much else to lose. I bit my lip. "And what do you want in return? Everything's a bargain—what's my side of this one?" It just might be worth it.

Something flickered at the edge of his mouth, but he only shook his head. "I already have what I want." His voice was low, but it thrummed as though magic ran through it, and the look he gave me... The flecks in his eyes were bright with intensity, the midnight blue glowing like those nights when the moon was full.

My heart tolled in my chest, hard and heavy like when I stood too close to the drums at midsummer. For one fleeting, foolish moment, the way he looked at me said the thing he wanted was me.

But I was a "mere human" and a stupid one if I thought that.

His throat bobbed in a slow swallow, and one shoulder rose as a ghost of his smirk slid in place. "Besides, the way you looked at it with such longing"—he shook his head—"if I don't make it so you can work with the stuff, you'll only try anyway." He held out his hands in the space between us. "Consider this a token in return for 'stealing' you."

"And I don't owe you anything?"

"Nothing."

With a shaky exhale, I placed my hands in his.

"Thank you for letting me do this for you." He lifted my fingers. "Stars above, do you have to be so short?" I caught a glimpse of one long canine as he flashed a grin. Then he had hold of my waist and was placing me on the table like he'd sat me on the stag a so many times before. "That's better."

"I'm so sorry my height is *such* a challenge for you," I muttered, with a mocking scowl. Despite the glibness, my heart wasn't only beating hard, but also fast. The proximity. The gentle waft of his woody, smoky scent cut through with sharp rhubarb. The way he stood between my legs, just pressing against my thigh as he resumed his grip on my hands.

It was suddenly all very dangerous.

Most dangerous, the fact I didn't mind it.

The fae light glistened on his violet-blue-black hair as he bowed his head. Was he going to bite my fingers? Gods knew why, but I didn't pull away even as that thought made my breath hitch.

But no teeth. Instead, his lips brushed over the tip of my index finger in a kiss that was feather light and yet hummed through every part of me: my throat, my chest, my inner thighs, all the way to my toes.

My mouth dropped open with a small "Oh."

A flicker of a smile crossed his mouth before it landed on my next finger. His dark gaze collided with mine as he moved to the next, and heat crept across every inch of my flesh, pooling at my core. With each kiss, that thrumming in my body rose, my nipples tightened, and the dark flavour of night built on my tongue, sparked with starlight and rhubarb.

If he'd asked me to strip bare, to bend over the table and let him fuck me, to marry him, to *anything* at that moment, I'd have agreed in an instant.

But all I could do was stare at his progress, my chest heaving as I tried to contain... everything.

The magic, the thrumming resonance that threatened to shatter me, the burning, burning heat that must've made my cheeks as red as the jewels in their glass phials.

When he reached my thumb, the pad dragged across his lower lip and I couldn't have said whether it was him pressing it against his flesh or if I did.

I didn't care.

By the time he moved to my right hand, starting with the thumb, I was swaying. When he whispered, "It is so," against the very tip of my little finger, I almost swooned as a kick of pure energy throbbed through me.

Chest heaving, cheeks flushed, he caught me. "Are you all right?" He searched my face, concern in his gaze.

"Yes," I breathed. My fingertips tingled. "Just... that was..."

"Sorry, I've never done that before, I didn't realise it would be so"—he swallowed and wet his lips—"heady."

"That's one word for it." I huffed and tried to hop down from the table, but I had to catch myself on the edge, face going numb as the world tipped.

"Hmm"—his grip closed on my shoulders—"maybe not the best idea."

Then the tipping swung even further out of control and when I blinked, I was in his arms, clutching my head.

"I feel drunk." I squeezed my eyes shut, but that did nothing against the spinning.

"Some rest and a sweet drink will restore your energy."

But unlike those nights when Rose and I had flirted our way to too many free drinks, I didn't *feel* tired—something inside me sparked bright and lively. The new magic—his boon.

Still, no one had told my head that, because it lolled forward and back, and my eyelids fluttered and dipped like sleep wanted to claim me anyway.

The next thing I knew, I was being placed in my bed, a dark shape over me. But for some reason it didn't frighten me. The shape resolved into a face... one I knew.

"Lysander," I slurred. I might've smiled.

"It's me." He pulled the blankets over me and brushed hair off my face. He tipped something sweet and floral into my mouth—elderflower cordial. Behind him, the ceiling wheeled round and round and round as I drank.

But I burrowed into the covers and the pillow, the softness so glorious I could've melted into it. There was a distant hum of pleasure. Was that me?

"Sleep now, my evening star."

Then the fae lights faded, the spinning world with it, and I floated away on a cloud of feathers and night.

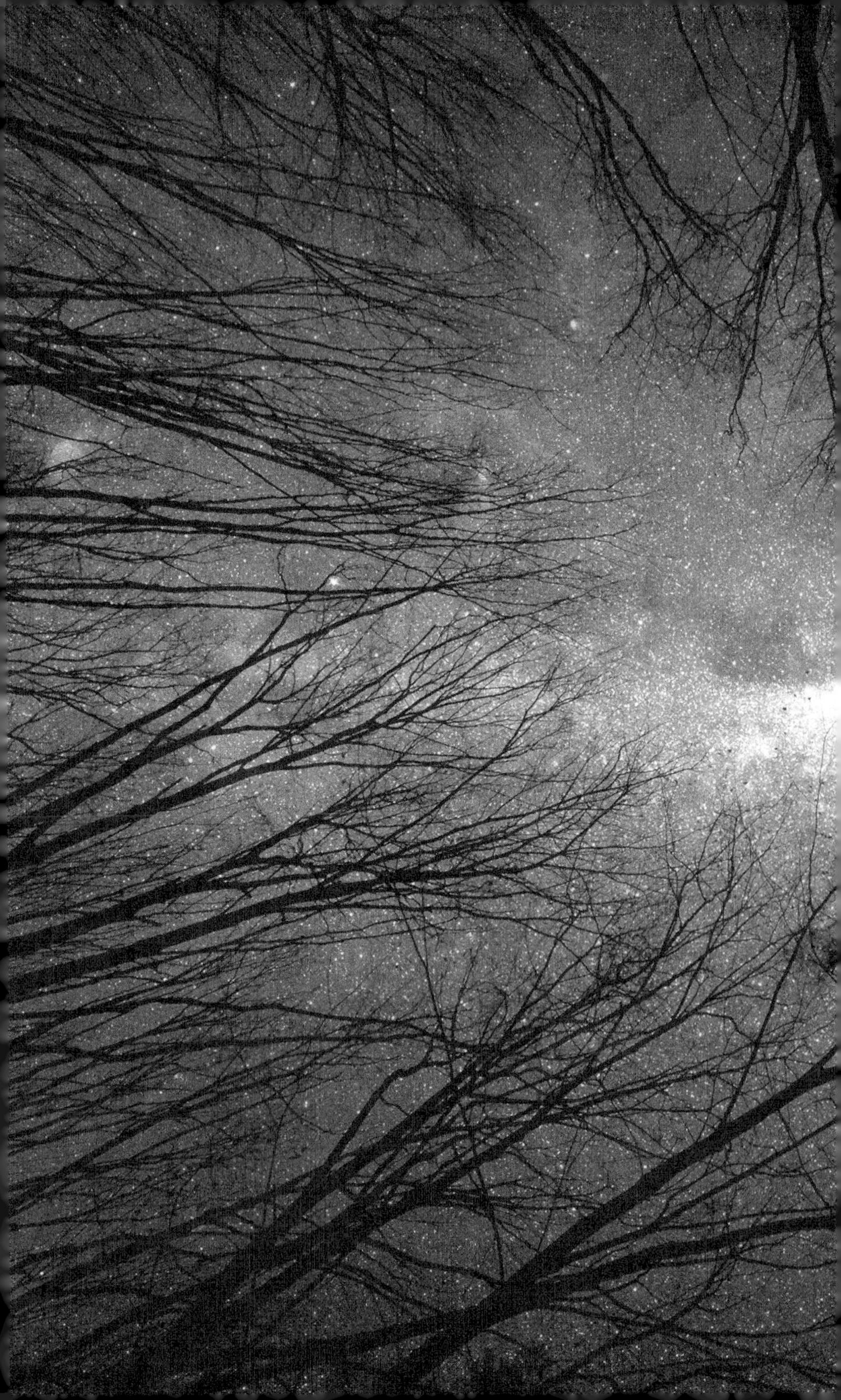

WAR & FASHION

The next day I woke refreshed but ravenous. When I appeared in the little dining room, Hil was only too glad to ply me with pastries and toast loaded with butter and elderberry jam. Once my stomach was satisfied, I thanked her and went to work. Amongst the deliveries, several sketchbooks and drawing implements arrived, and I set to work designing. Ly had told me that if I said *it is so* at the end of sewing my spidersilk gown, it would leave it strengthened and complete, so the delicate fabric wouldn't fall apart as I wore it.

Not long after I started, Sylvie arrived to keep me company and she answered my questions about fae fashions, as well as making some suggestions of her own.

It turned out my assumption that she was a maid had been wildly off the mark. When I asked her exactly what she did, she screwed up her face, the sunlight gleaming on her silvery skin. "I'm a caretaker, I suppose.

Of the house, of its contents... of the wardrobe, especially—both for war and fashion."

"War and fashion?" I raised my eyebrows. No one in Briarbridge would've put those two words in the same sentence. War was important, dangerous, serious. Fashion was a frivolity for women and dandies and other ornamental folk.

"Well"—she grinned—"they're practically the same thing." Her eyes narrowed. "If you're going to stay in faerie for any amount of time, you need to understand. They aren't just clothes. In fae society, appearance is everything. The illusion of power is almost as good as the real thing—hells, it might even be half of it."

My pencil stilled on the page. "I've never heard it put like that before." After all, if they were "just clothes," why didn't men like Lord Hawthorne wear the same as Rose's Papa? Why did he give his wife and daughters the allowance to dress so lavishly? "I think it's the same in Albion, just most men don't like to admit it."

Sylvie nodded, tapping her lip. "And it's not only what you wear. Take Fluffy"—the hellhound lay by the door and looked up from her spot—"when Ly walks into a room with her at his heel, he isn't just a man with a dog. He's the man a hellhound chose. Fluffy is the only hellhound I know of outside the Wild Hunt, and she lends him a whisper of that same mystique."

The dog huffed and returned her head to her paws as if frustrated to find the mention of her name hadn't led to any treats.

When the Wild Hunt's hellhounds caught a scent,

they howled. That sound alone was enough to break the bravest warrior. And if the Wild Hunt caught sight of their quarry, they would pursue them to the ends of the earth.

Fluffy, though?

I cocked my head. "*She* lends him mystique?"

Sylvie chuckled. "Well, when she's putting on the act."

A little while later, around midmorning, she left me to work, and I sketched a few more designs before starting on the long seams of Ly's breeches.

Thread the needle, knot the end, in and out of the fabric, pull taut, in and out again.

The web of magic stretched on and on around me, a complex lattice of interconnection with every line perfectly placed. Here, it was more *solid* than in Briarbridge.

"Silent and unseen," I whispered, intent on that one silver thread I could control. "He is a shadow under starlight." The image of him dressed in shades of midnight, prowling like a hunter, sped my pulse, a dull echo of the resonance that had throbbed through me last night. I tried to ignore it and focus on the task at hand.

My muscles ached the longer I worked as each whisper of magic settled into my stitches and drained my strength.

"Knock, knock."

Blinking up from my work, I found Ly in the doorway, tray in one hand, bottle and glasses in the other, gorgeous as ever.

"Morning." I stretched.

"Not anymore." He grinned as he strode in, placing his load on a side table, safely away from my work. "I thought you must've lost track of time. Everyone else is eating lunch."

"What? No, it can't—"

But the pocket watch dangling in front of my nose agreed with him.

"Huh. Well..." I shook my head and set down my work before scrubbing my dry eyes.

He busied himself, shifting the armchairs so they faced each other with a low table in between.

"You don't need to fuss around me or"—I rubbed the back of my neck—"serve me. That's not... you're a fae lord, you shouldn't be doing this."

He shrugged from where he was crouched, placing plates of cheese, bread, salad, and cold cuts of meat on the table. "To serve is... it means something different to us than it does humans, I think." He patted the chair.

There was a danger of him coming and feeding me if I didn't obey, so I went and sat as directed.

Kneeling at my feet, he looked at me from below dark lashes. If he were a human, I'd have guessed he was a similar age to me, perhaps a little older. As a fae he could've been centuries old for all I knew. But right now, looking up at me with no mockery, no art to his expression, just an openness I hadn't seen before... he seemed so young. Innocent, almost.

"To serve is an honour." He inclined his head, a gesture too close to bowing for my liking.

I squirmed in my seat. I wasn't worthy of being bowed to or served or any such honour.

"Eat up." Rising, he flashed me a grin, none of that innocence left. "You're going to need your energy for this afternoon. I'm teaching you to ride."

I stuffed a slice of honeyed pork in my mouth to stifle a groan. Riding meant letting some creature have control so it could run off with me. Although... I'd let Ly have control on the way here... and technically, he *had* run off with me. Maybe that wasn't such a bad thing. My heart lurched at the thought.

"You can huff all you like," he went on, "but I'm not going to sit in a carriage with you like you're a child, and I can't have you always sitting in front of me whenever we need to ride somewhere." He raised an eyebrow. "However pleasant that might be."

Damn him, but he knew how to distract me. His flirtation didn't mean anything—he joked and laughed with everyone else at meals, just as he did with me—but it was enough to push worries about riding from my mind.

THE DISTRACTION CONTINUED with conversation and food. Age fresh on my mind, I asked and found out that he was twenty-eight years old—an adult by fae reckoning but still young. His parents had died not long after he'd come of age, but he changed the subject after that, and I couldn't bear to prod the sorrow so obvious in his stiff movements.

Instead, since we were on good terms and I felt I could trust his answer, I asked about Annon. He knew nothing about her disappearance, but conceded it could be a fae's doing. For all I knew, she might have returned at the next market day, not missing at all. Still, fears for her snagged in my mind almost as often as thoughts of Rose.

After lunch, he helped me mount the hind and taught me how to sit correctly, how to roll with her gait, and the call to ask her to halt. By the end of the session, my back ached but it wasn't as bad as it had been those first days of our journey.

A hot bath filled with bubbles and herbs Sylvie had left eased the pain. That evening, I ate with everyone and joined in as they spoke about their days. Hil seemed impressed that I was learning to ride—she never had—and Sylvie suggested we could go out together once I was confident. Sallis and Hobb praised my bravery, considering how large the deer were compared to my "minuteness" as they put it. I couldn't help but laugh at that description. Later, Ly read to me in the workshop and escorted me to my room sometime past midnight.

That became a kind of routine. I sewed all morning, working on Ly's suit as well as little gifts for the others. Hobb's was easy to decide on—a kerchief that meant their antlers would never tangle in branches. Sallis had complained they could never get the dirt out of their claws, so I embroidered a cloth that would clean their hands in an instant. For Hil, a rose fashioned from silk that clipped in her hair and would keep flour off it. For Sylvie, I made a bag for collecting herbs and flowers that would keep their scents fresh forever.

Boyd was another matter. He revealed no frustration I could help with... other than by making myself disappear.

In the afternoon, I rode, and after dinner, Ly sat with me. Between the stories, he gave me the space and the quiet to speak. Of small things, silly things, at first, but over time it expanded to life in Briarbridge, tales of Mama, Papa, and Rose.

With halting words, I even told him about the day Rose and I had become friends. I was five and a group of children had cornered me. When I didn't answer their questions about where I was from, what I was doing there, why I looked the way I did, someone picked up a stone. More stones appeared in their little hands, and I curled in a ball, waiting for the first one to land.

I waited and waited, pulse roaring in my ears so loud I couldn't hear their taunts anymore. But nothing hit me.

I flinched at the touch when it came, but it wasn't a stone—it was a gentle hand. And when my gaze followed the pale arm, I found it belonged to a strawberry blond girl. Her knuckles were scuffed, and a trickle of blood ran from her hairline.

That was the first day Rose saved me, and she'd been doing it ever since.

Ly smiled at the story and said he'd like to meet Rose some day. That only made my heart sore.

But our conversations wore on. He would ask me about myself and let me know little snippets about him and his family. As I'd suspected, his mother had told him that my kind were "mere humans." It sounded like it had come from ignorance.

He answered my questions about the Dusk and Dawn Courts, though I still struggled to understand how it worked. When the sun set, the Day King fell into an enchanted sleep and the Night Queen woke. For the hours of darkness and dusk, she ruled and her word was law. But with the rising sun, she fell into her own enchanted sleep, and the Day King rose and ruled.

I'd been riding for a couple of weeks when Sylvie took me towards the edges of the estate. She rode a stag almost as large as Ly's—she was so tall and willowy, her feet would've been close to the ground if she'd ridden my hind.

The sun was warm on my back, not yet too hot, but definitely moving towards Calan Mai and the shift from spring to summer. Our deer walked, ears pricked, hooves rustling through long grass.

"What I can't understand about the King and Queen," I said as Sylvie turned us left, "is how they coordinate. If she sleeps all day and he all night, how do they talk?"

"They don't." Her streaked hair, like woodgrain, gleamed in the sun as she turned to me with a grin. "They're only both awake during an eclipse. The rest of the time"—she shrugged—"well, they have to leave messages for each other or just trust that the other one isn't going to do anything too detrimental. For the most part, the council helps. And, of course, they each have their own spies and courtiers and families loyal to their courts who keep their interests awake even when they are not." She cocked her head, eyebrows rising. "It's worked for thousands of years... mostly."

I snorted and went to ask what *mostly* meant, since it sounded like a story, but as we turned, the path crested a hill and below a great lake glistened in the afternoon sun, stealing my breath.

Sylvie drew her stag to a half beside me. "Do you think you can trot all the way down? Or do you want to try going a bit faster?"

In answer, I clicked my tongue three times, loosened the reins, and my hind sprang into a gallop. The wind swept the hair from my face as her long limbs stretched out beneath us. Sylvie's stag leapt a heartbeat later and together their hooves thundered upon the ground.

It wasn't out of control, it was... free.

My heart soared and I found myself laughing, giddy as I clung to the reins.

We drew to a stop at the lake shore and let our steeds catch their breath. I needed to do the same.

I patted my hind's neck and whispered the words of praise that Ly had taught me.

The lake's peace seeped into me, easing my muscles, loosening every joint. "What a beautiful place."

"I'm sure its Lady thinks so, too." Shielding her eyes, Sylvie squinted out over it. "Just don't go swimming in there unless you have an offering for her."

For three beats, my pulse seemed to pound in slow motion. I blinked from the lake to Sylvie and back again. "Its Lady? As in a Lady of the Lake? One of the sisters?"

"Exactly that." She signalled for her stag to walk on and we passed under the dappled shade of willow and silver birch.

I'd had no luck in the library, but...

Nothing about my pulse was slow anymore.

There was a Lady of the Lake right on the doorstep. I could come and ask her for my True Name. If that gave me power over myself, maybe I could break the Tithe or simply escape, Tithe be damned.

The gloves sat in my work basket, unfinished. I'd worked on them here and there and noted where purple aconite was just coming into flower. But that was more for the sake of completion than out of a desire to use them on Ly.

I liked him and he hadn't really done anything wrong other than find himself on the wrong end of an order from his queen. Much as I chafed against being bound to him or this place, at my lack of freedom, I didn't want to poison him.

But this...

Sylvie gave a running commentary about the trees we passed and the little sprites and other fair folk who lived among them, but I barely heard a word.

My *True Name*.

That was my chance at freedom. My escape from here.

And maybe part of me liked it here. This place was

beautiful, my bed comfortable, and I had every tool and kind of fabric I could ever wish for. And Ly...

But it wasn't my choice. It wasn't my life. I was an item in someone else's bargain, and there had been enough times that I'd had no choice and no power. Never again.

I had no skill with swords, no, but I would fight this.

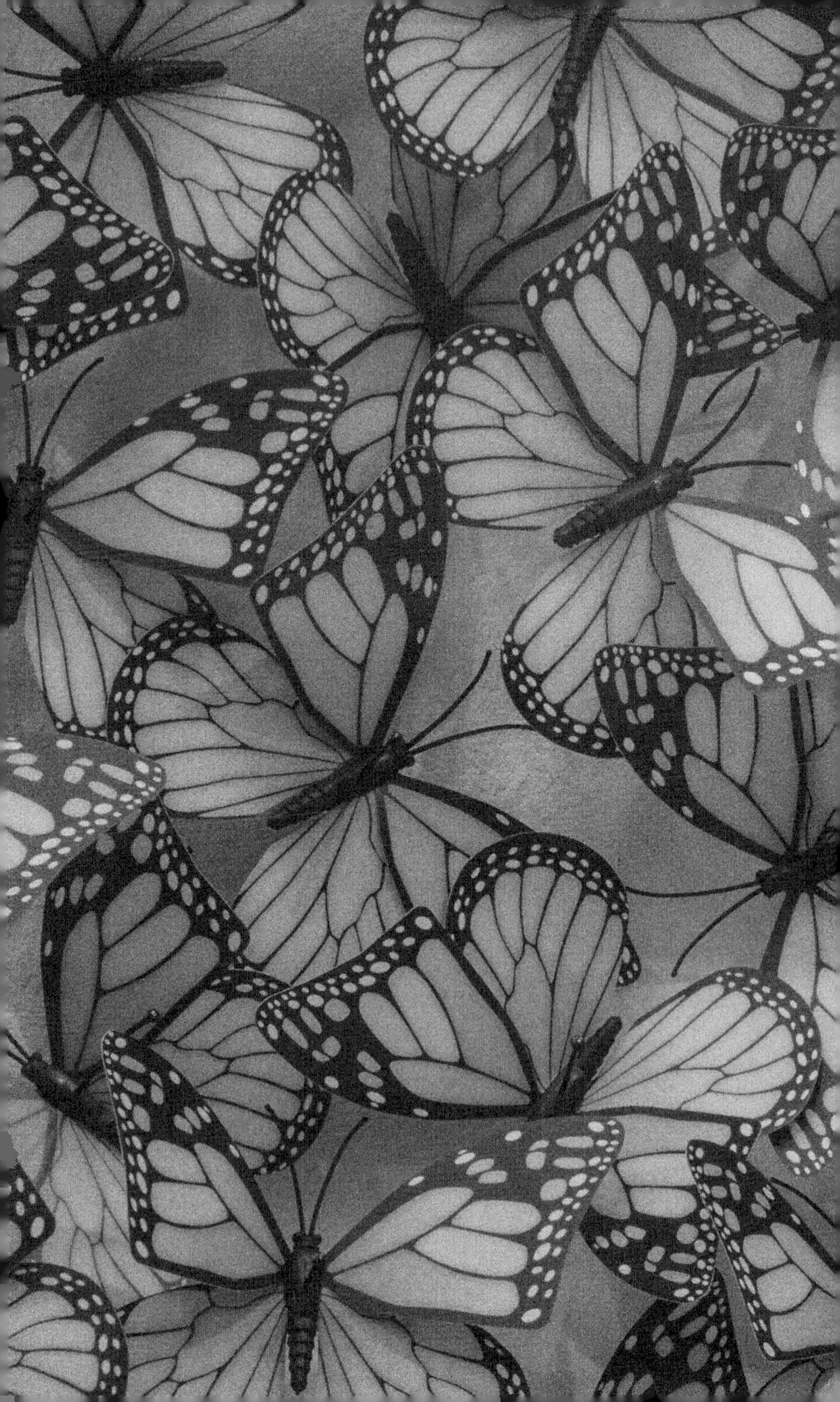

THE LADY OF THE LAKE

It was another couple of weeks before I had the chance to go to the lake alone.

That was a lie.

I had the *chance*, but... I didn't take it until the night Ly failed to appear in the workroom after dinner. For days his laughter had grown rarer and his shoulders tighter. The previous night, his story had petered out and he'd stared into the fire in silence for a good long while.

And that night, I sat there, sewing, glancing towards the door at every sound. But he didn't appear.

Shoulders slumped, I stayed up late, just in case, but... no. The novelty of me had worn off. Or my conversation wasn't entertaining enough. Or he simply had better things to do.

It cut just as surely as any of those scissors and shears in their beautiful velvet-lined box.

When I went to bed, I couldn't sleep. So much had

happened in the past couple of months, I lay there staring at the ceiling, mind whirring. It was silly to care what Ly thought of me. It was stupid to grow attached to this quiet, orderly house. It was madness to befriend Sylvie and Hil, and more tentatively Sallis and Hobb.

And yet here I was. Silly, stupid, and mad.

In a strange way it was comforting that Boyd remained distant, a wrinkle on his nose every time I entered the room. While it wasn't normal—nothing about this was—it was the closest thing to what I'd expected from the fae.

I hadn't seen another human in weeks. I'd written to Rose, but Sylvie and Ly had confirmed it would take some time for the letter to reach her and it was unlikely I'd hear back. It wasn't as though messengers could pass over the border easily. Those miles of snow we'd ridden through—Ly said they were part of the defences to stop humans and fae alike from crossing the wall whenever they wanted.

What if Rose wasn't safe?

"I'll find you," she'd promised. Gods, what if she came after me? I shivered, eyes stinging. Pale flesh and empty eyes and *clack clack clack*. She could use a knife and her fists, but what use were they against just one sluagh, never mind a pack of them?

I wrung my hands, drowning in questions and useless thoughts.

None of this worrying would help anyone and sleep was still a million miles away.

So I crept to the window and peeked out. The sliver

of waning moon was high in the sky, spilling pale light onto the inky world and through the crack in the curtain. It lit the clock on the mantelpiece. Four o'clock.

I'd be up in a few hours and with the moon in this phase there was no danger of the Wild Hunt, even if they did somehow cross Ly's borders. He'd told me how the land was warded so none of the monstrous, dangerous fae could enter without his invitation, the Wild Hunt included.

I dressed in warm, dark wool and took the offering from my underwear drawer. A smooth round rock as big as my palm. I'd covered it in two layers of felt and one of silk taffeta before embroidering into it Frankish knots and warmth. It had to be cold living in a lake and even cold-blooded creatures like adders and grass snakes sought heat, basking in the sun. Surely a Lady of the Lake would be the same.

The creeping was almost over before it began, because the moment I opened my door, I had to stifle a shriek at the huge shape pooled on the floor outside.

But then red glowing eyes opened and a great furry head rose, ears, paws, and tail flickering into life. Fluffy. She sniffed my hand and pushed under it when she found no treats. Apparently a scratch would do.

"Good gods, dog," I whispered, "you scared me half to death." Stroking her soft, warm ears slowed my heart until I was ready to proceed. She followed me all the way —silent, thankfully. If Ly had stationed her at my door to keep me in, she wasn't doing a great job.

I put my boots on at the kitchen door and reached

the stables within a few minutes. As part of my riding lessons, Ly had shown me how to tack up the hind, and she waited patiently for me to do so, apparently unconcerned by the dark.

As we rode for the lake, I kept one eye on the setting moon. In the story, the Lady of the Lake hadn't appeared until the moon was up. As long as it remained in the sky, I had time.

The lower edge of its crescent brushed the forest's highest branches by the time I reached the lake.

What had been slate-blue water in the day now appeared inky black, glinting with ghostly moonlight. The willows' tangled branches dipped in the surface, fracturing it and sending confusing ripples in every direction until it looked like there were faces in the depths, pale and lifeless.

I clung to the hind's reins, the leather biting into my skin. But she wasn't afraid; she stood there, placid, one ear flicking as though bothered by a mite. And Fluffy sat at her side, apparently unconcerned.

So I steeled myself and dismounted. I tethered the hind to a birch a few yards from the water's edge, just in case she did get spooked and tried to run.

"If we're running, we're doing it together." I stroked her nose. "And after tonight, I think you've earned a name. How about Luna?"

She didn't argue, so I patted her neck and approached the lake, Fluffy so close she brushed my leg. Kneeling, I held out the embellished stone and lowered it into the water.

As always, my gift didn't work on me and did nothing to blunt the water's icy edge.

It was cold, colder than the stream the night I'd fled the sluagh, colder than the snow that had fallen on Ly and me on our journey, colder than ice or death or the bitterest winter wind.

Once I'd caught my breath from the shock, I called out: "Lady of the Lake, I call to thee." That was what the woman in the story had said three times, so I did the same.

The third time, a V-shaped wake appeared, cutting through the choppy ripples, coming this way.

I bit my lip, fighting every instinct to run as my heart threatened to explode and my insides turned liquid.

Fluffy gave a soft whine, ears flattening, but she stayed at my side.

A pale shape rose from the lake, water sloshing off it... off *her*, I realised, catching a glimpse of long hair the colour of bone and sheer cloth clinging to small breasts.

As slender and willowy as Sylvie, she stood before me. But where Sylvie was silvery sun-bleached wood, the Lady of the Lake was sun-bleached bone. Wide cheekbones, full lips, and angled eyes the colour of algae—she was beautiful.

Her slender fingers ended in long, pointed nails the same colour as her flesh, making me shiver with the memory of the sluagh. But she didn't clack them together, instead her fingers bent and straightened in constant, elegant motion, like she was testing the air, feeling how it was different from the wet world she inhabited.

"Even in my reckoning of years, it has been a long while since one of your kind called on me." Her voice was a ripple of water, a breath of wind, the plop of a kingfisher diving for prey. "Do you have an offering?" Eyes bright with anticipation, her mouth stretched wider, wider, wider into a smile that revealed many sharp teeth.

Every hair on my body rose, and I dragged in breath after breath before I could speak. "I... I do." I lifted the rock, an icy drip sliding down my arm.

Her pale brows rose as she cocked her head and surveyed my gift. "And what is this?"

"It—it is warmth, my lady." All the stories said the fae were sticklers for manners, and although I'd been living amongst them for a while now, the Lady of the Lake was another creature altogether, as different from Lysander as he was from me. "I made it for you, decorated it, whispered magic into it so that you might have a little heat in your great home."

"It is cold in my home. Always cold and dark." She reached out.

My stomach, my heart, every single internal organ lurched into my throat. Only the gods knew how I didn't flinch, but she paused with rippling fingers inches from my offering.

Oh gods, what if she didn't take it? What if I'd offended her by highlighting the bleak cold of her lake?

Every single story agreed—offending the fae was a terrible, *terrible* idea.

Teeth. So many sharp teeth. And her eyes—they hadn't blinked since she'd surfaced.

"I accept your offering, little minnow." She snatched the embellished rock from my hand, groaning as she held it to her chest. "Oh, Stars above, it *is* warm." A kind of terrifying serenity settled over her features as she stood there, soaking it in. "It is a good offering. What is it you ask in return?"

With a shaky breath, I bowed my head. "I wish to know my True Name. I've heard tales that your wisdom means you know such things."

A sloshing gurgle came from her throat, and it took me a second to realise it was laughter. "I know a great many things. That a queen and not will come from the sea. That a night rider will come from the south and our world will be changed. I can tell you the answer you seek, no flattery required. But only if you can tell me the thing you desire with all of your being."

While sewing the offering, I'd considered this, so my answer was ready. "I want to leave this place and return home to Briarbridge."

She cocked her head and the sharp grin that had remained in the wake of her laughter faded to a soft smile. It reminded me of the smiles Rose and her mother had given me after Mama and Papa had died. "Oh, my sweet little minnow." She shook her head. "That is not true. You are intrigued by Elfhame and wish to see more. And"—one eyebrow arched—"now *that* is interesting." At last she blinked. "You desire the lord of this land."

I choked on a laugh, shaking my head. How could she

know that? I'd only just accepted it myself. And I certainly didn't like him enough to stop wanting to go home. Did I?

"Aren't you going to ask me how he feels about you?"

"You know that?"

"You heard me say I know a great many things, did you not?"

I could only nod.

She tilted her head again. "He feels for you as you do for him. Perhaps even more." Her eyebrows flashed up and down as she grinned and glided away across the water. "Farewell, little minnow. My regards to dear little Lysander." Cradling her stone, she sank beneath the surface.

Once the wake had faded, Fluffy butted my shoulder, and I realised I'd been staring.

Half in a daze, I made my way to Luna and mounted. All the way to the house I warred with myself. On one side of the battle, frustration at my failure to discover my True Name. On the other a wild, bright elation that Ly found me as fascinating as I found him. The Lady of the Lake couldn't lie.

He feels for you as you do for him.

Did that mean he was torn as I was? On the one hand liking and wanting and longing... maybe even *falling*. On the other, mistrust and misgivings about what I was.

By the time I stabled Luna, the sun was peeking over the nearby mountains. I hurried to my room, splashed water on my face, and changed, then headed to the workroom.

Success. No one had missed—

"Where the hells have you been?"

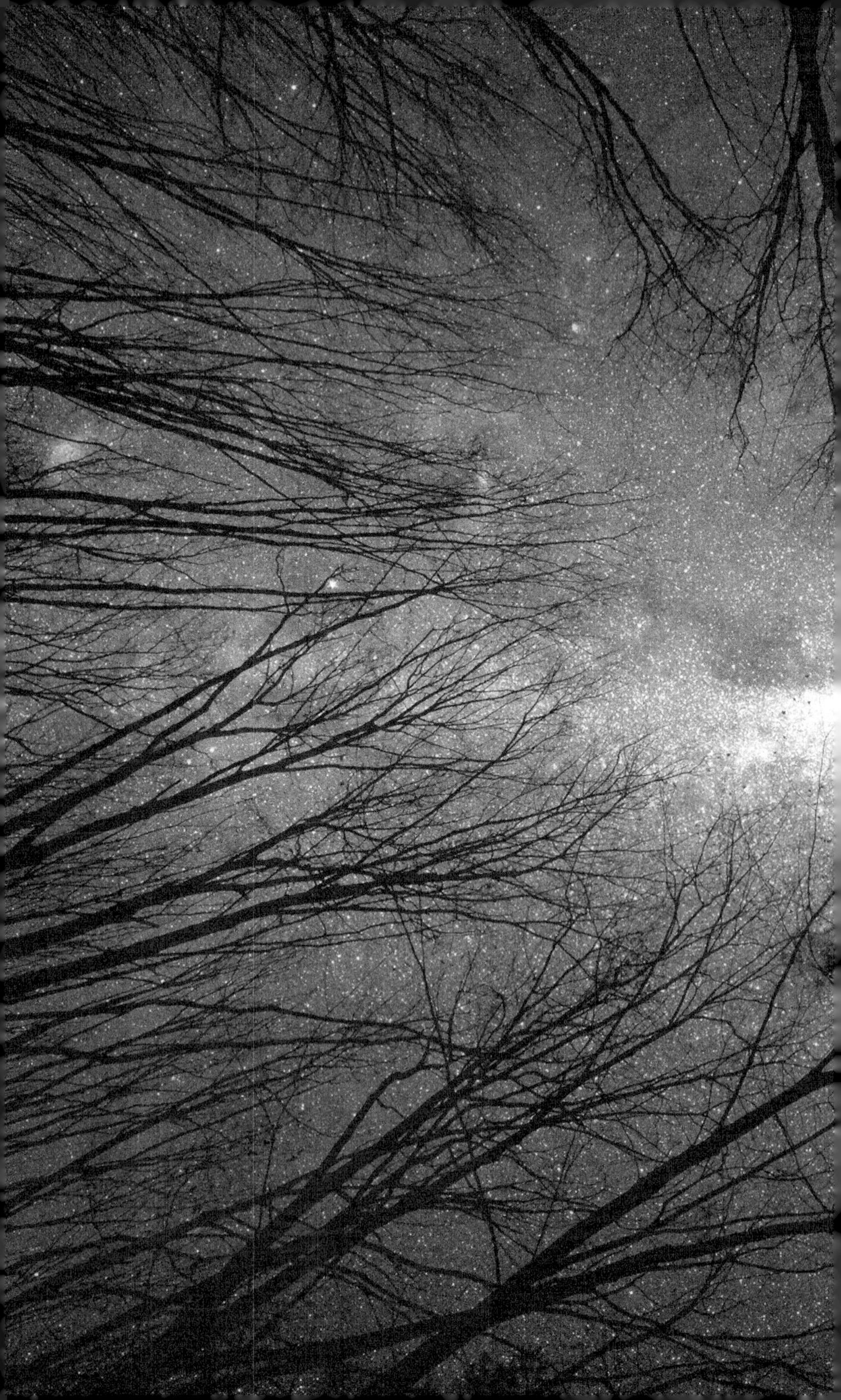

THE YEW

Night darkness pouring off him, Ly stood at the fireplace. The taste of his magic eddied through the room, tart and sweet, dark and bright. A muscle twitched in his jaw and his full lips were pressed together, pale.

My heart thundered. Oh, gods, I *had* been missed.

I pushed out an attempt at a breezy chuckle and shrugged. "Why? I'm not a captive, am I?"

He did *not* laugh. Nostrils flaring, he gave me a look that spelled out exactly how unamused he was.

"I couldn't sleep"—not a lie—"so I went for a ride." Also not a lie. This had to be how the fae deceived. It was easier than it sounded.

"I was looking for you, I need..." He blew out a shaky breath, as if he held himself so tight, he trembled. "I need to talk to you."

So he wasn't angry at me for going out? I bit my lip

against a sigh of relief. Even better, he had no suspicions of where I'd gone or what I'd been doing.

Good for me, and yet something troubled him. I cocked my head at his clenching and unclenching fists. "Ly..." The uncertainty wavered in my voice. "What's wrong?"

He shook his head. "Come with me." Back ramrod straight, he led the way, turning towards the back of the house.

The yew tree. I couldn't have explained how I knew, but I had no doubt of the path we'd take.

Sure enough, we left the house, passed the fountain, and descended the stone steps, star-specked darkness rolling from his heels until we reached the yew's hollow carcass.

Again, that sour note tainted the air, like there was something rotten in the web of magic surrounding us.

If the Dusk Court's Great Yew had been struck by lightning and yet survived—*thrived*, even, what had happened to this tree to bring it so close to death?

Ly stood at my side, attention on the dry branches spreading from the cracked trunk. Even in profile, I could tell how deep the creases were between his eyebrows. He pouted, lips pressed together as though after bringing me out here, he didn't want to speak after all.

My throat tightened at the sorrow etched in his features. It pierced something inside me, so sharp, it broke through all my frustrations—at being an object in a bargain, at my powerlessness, at failing to learn my True Name.

"Ly?" I took his hand, squeezed it.

He let out a long breath, head bowing, eyes closing. "I need you to pay complete attention to what I'm about to tell you, Ariadne. *Please.*"

Not just sorrow, there was *desperation* in that tone. Nodding, I went to release my hold, but his fingers interlaced with mine.

He feels for you as you do for him.

I wasn't sure what I felt for him, exactly. It wasn't how I *should* feel about a kidnapper. That complication aside, perhaps it meant I could comfort him, as he had me when he'd seen my scars. So I tightened my grip and tucked close against his arm, lending him *my* warmth for once.

"This tree is the mark of my family's bargain with the land. It binds our magic, our power."

My blood is bound in bargains. We only have our power because my ancestors made a bargain with the land.

And if it was in this state...

"It is the natural way of living things to die and for new life to take its place." His thumb rubbed over mine. "These trees—each caretaker family, each lord and lady, has one, like the Great Yew and the Great Oak at the palace—they don't escape that cycle. They too must die. But before they do, they produce a seed from which they will renew." His shoulders rose and fell, curling in.

"And you need the yew's seed?" I scanned its branches but spotted no red berries amongst the few remaining leaves.

"We had one, but it was taken. Without it, the land

will fade and die. I'm meant to be its caretaker. I've poured in what strength I can, but..."

Was that why he'd looked so tired after using his magic to shadowstep? Why he hadn't been able to summon a fire the night he'd fought the sluagh? The fight was my fault. My stomach twisted, guilt adding to the sour taste in the air.

"Mother gave all her power to keep it alive as long as she could."

All her power? Fae-touched humans who tried to use more magic energy than they had wasted away. We could die or become unseeing, broken creatures, empty and un-alive. I didn't know which was worse. Did the same happen to fae?

The knot of his throat bobbed as he swallowed. "She gave her life."

So that was how she'd died, saving the yew, her land... maybe even her son, if his life was bound to the family's magic. And if Ly couldn't get the seed back, it would've been for nothing. A deep, cold sorrow burrowed into my chest.

He turned to me, then, and the full force of the anguish on his face struck me. "Ari..." He shook his head, clutching my hand in the space between us, like I was reaching out to save him. "That's why I need your help. The suit..."

"That's why you need to be stealthy, to steal it back." Good gods, he was relying on me—on my gift, weak as it was.

"It took me a while—*too long* to discover who'd taken

it. And our spies"—he smiled, but there was no warmth or humour to it—"they've told us where it is and that it's warded against shadowstepping."

The thief knew him well enough to know his ability. "Someone wants to keep you away."

"Exactly. And that someone, he..." Ly huffed and shook his head. "That's why I brought you here. I wasn't going to tell you—I thought the less you knew, the better. And before, I didn't trust you to keep it to yourself—you could've told him what I was planning and have him kill me so you'd be free."

I winced, but I couldn't blame him for thinking that of me. Hadn't I started a pair of poisoned gloves to hurt him and force a bargain? But why did *I* need to know about this thief? Was it Boyd? Those sneers, were they because he knew I was helping Ly get the seed back?

"But I realised that was selfish of me and you need to be forewarned about him." His eyes locked with mine, a flicker of something in their depths, something I hadn't seen in the weeks I'd known him.

Fear.

The back of my neck prickled. What the hells could frighten a fae lord who'd faced and destroyed five sluagh without breaking a sweat?

He licked his lips. "Especially when you're about to face him."

I flinched and searched over my shoulder. "What?"

"Not right now. At the celebrations tomorrow." He tugged on my hand. "He's our neighbour, someone who's been a friend for years, centuries—he knew my parents long before I was born." A bitter laugh edged his outward breath. "We *thought* he was a friend, anyway. But he wants these lands for himself or our power or…" He shrugged. "*Something*. Enough that he'd do this. He doesn't know I've discovered his treachery, so I must wear the mask of the smiling friend."

That cold sorrow burrowed deeper, reaching my belly. Someone had deliberately done this, risking the land and all the life on it, and had played at friendship all this time. All for personal gain. I gritted my teeth. "Hence the Calan Mai invitation."

"He will be here that night and I… I fear he'll be much too keen to meet you."

I swayed backwards. "Me? How does he even—?"

"News travels quickly in a land where little changes one decade to the next. And Her Majesty ordering me to take the Tithe was big news."

A touch of his usual smirk edged his lips and I couldn't help but return it.

"So everyone wants to see your pet human?"

His face screwed up in a grimace. "No, not… You're not my pet, Ari—"

"*I* know that." And it was only when I said it that I realised I *believed* him. A trickle of warmth pressed at the cold inside me. "But do your neighbours?"

"Knowing Goren, possibly. But whether or not he views you as a *pet*, he's dangerous. I need you to understand that."

Lords and Ladies, if Ly considered Goren dangerous…

I shivered at the prospect. "If you're worried for my safety, I'll just keep out of sight."

"That won't work." One side of his mouth twitched, a shadow of his usual dimple making an appearance. "I'm afraid you'll have to show that pretty face of yours. If you don't appear or you leave too early, it will only rouse suspicion. He'll wonder what I'm hiding." His hands squeezed around mine, solid and warm. "And with his gifts... as soon as he sees me, he'll know how I feel."

Ba-DUM. My heart leapt to my throat. How he felt *about me*?

He half-closed his eyes, giving me a heavy look. "He'll know," he murmured, voice deepening, "*you* are the route to hurt me. I couldn't save my parents from him—I didn't even *know* he was my enemy, and our power was already dwindling..." He shook his head, swallowing.

He *did* blame himself, and gods did I know how that felt. A weight I could never shake. An empty pocket at the centre of my heart. A tinge of guilt that tainted every memory, just as this dying tree tainted the magic here. "Oh, Ly." My eyes stung for him and for me, for his parents and for mine.

Eyes bright he gave such a slight nod, I wasn't sure he knew he'd done it. But it said he understood and he knew I did, too.

"Ari." His voice rasped on my name. He paused, nostrils flaring, jaw tightening. "Please, keep close to me or Sylvie that night. Be careful of anything he says or asks you. Offer him every politeness, but nothing more. If he asks you to dance, make an excuse—use your exquisite lies on him, he won't expect it. Do anything you can to avoid being alone with him." He leant closer and cupped my cheek. "I'm begging you."

A fae lord, begging me for something. I might've laughed but for the intensity of him, the vulnerability, the woody notes of his cologne. It was a wonder he hadn't commented on the pounding of my pulse as it throbbed through me. He had to be able to hear it.

"Ly"—I pressed my cheek against his hand, not shying away as I had that first night we'd met—"I'll be safe. I trust you to—"

A streak of white barrelled into us, and it was only Ly's reflexes bringing his arms around my waist that stopped me hitting the floor.

"Fluffy!" He huffed, the breath fanning my face. "Damn dog." His scowl turned from the panting, prancing dog to me and softened.

I was pressed against his chest, hands at his shoulders, not an inch between us. My feet weren't on the floor and from this height, I only needed to angle my head a fraction and our lips would be touching.

He must've realised the same thing, because his gaze flicked down to my mouth. And maybe the Lady of the Lake was right, because his arm tightened around my waist as though he wanted, somehow, to bring me even closer.

Did it matter that he was fae? Did it matter that I wasn't here by choice? Because right now, he was just as warm and alive and tempting as any human man had ever been—much, *much* more tempting, in fact.

And he was far more beautiful, far more handsome, and had treated me with more thought and kindness than anyone outside my family, apart from Rose.

I might not deserve it, I might not be powerful enough or pretty enough or any of that, but I wanted it.

Good gods, I wanted it.

I'd gone to the Lady of the Lake this morning because his absence last night had hurt me, had left my heart hollow and whispering his name with each beat.

Because somehow I'd spent these past weeks falling and right now, in his arms, flush against him, I was still falling.

I tilted my head.

His lowered.

Only our breaths separated us, growing thinner by the second.

Woof! Woof! Fluffy's red tongue lolled as she stared up at us, fiery eyes even brighter than usual.

"Not now, dog," Ly growled, the sound rumbling into my chest, into my bones.

But beyond the dog, movement made me twitch.

Sylvie and Boyd coming down the steps, right this way.

We leapt apart. If, somehow, their fae ears *didn't* pick up my thundering heartbeat, my burning cheeks would surely give me away.

But Sylvie only asked if I wanted to go for a ride with her this afternoon, and Boyd muttered that there was some business requiring Ly's attention.

I cleared my throat and Ly gave me a little nod, an

uncertain smile at the edge of his mouth, and then we parted ways. Boyd shot me a look, eyes narrowed, before he left.

All the way back to the workshop, Sylvie told me in great detail about a book she was reading, a romance with rather steamy scenes, but I couldn't blush any harder than I already was.

We'd been so close to kissing and I had absolutely played a part in that—a *willing* part. I regretted getting caught by Sylvie and Boyd, but did I regret tilting my head, inviting that almost-kiss?

I searched inside for the slightest pang that said some part of me didn't want it or was glad it hadn't happened.

There was none.

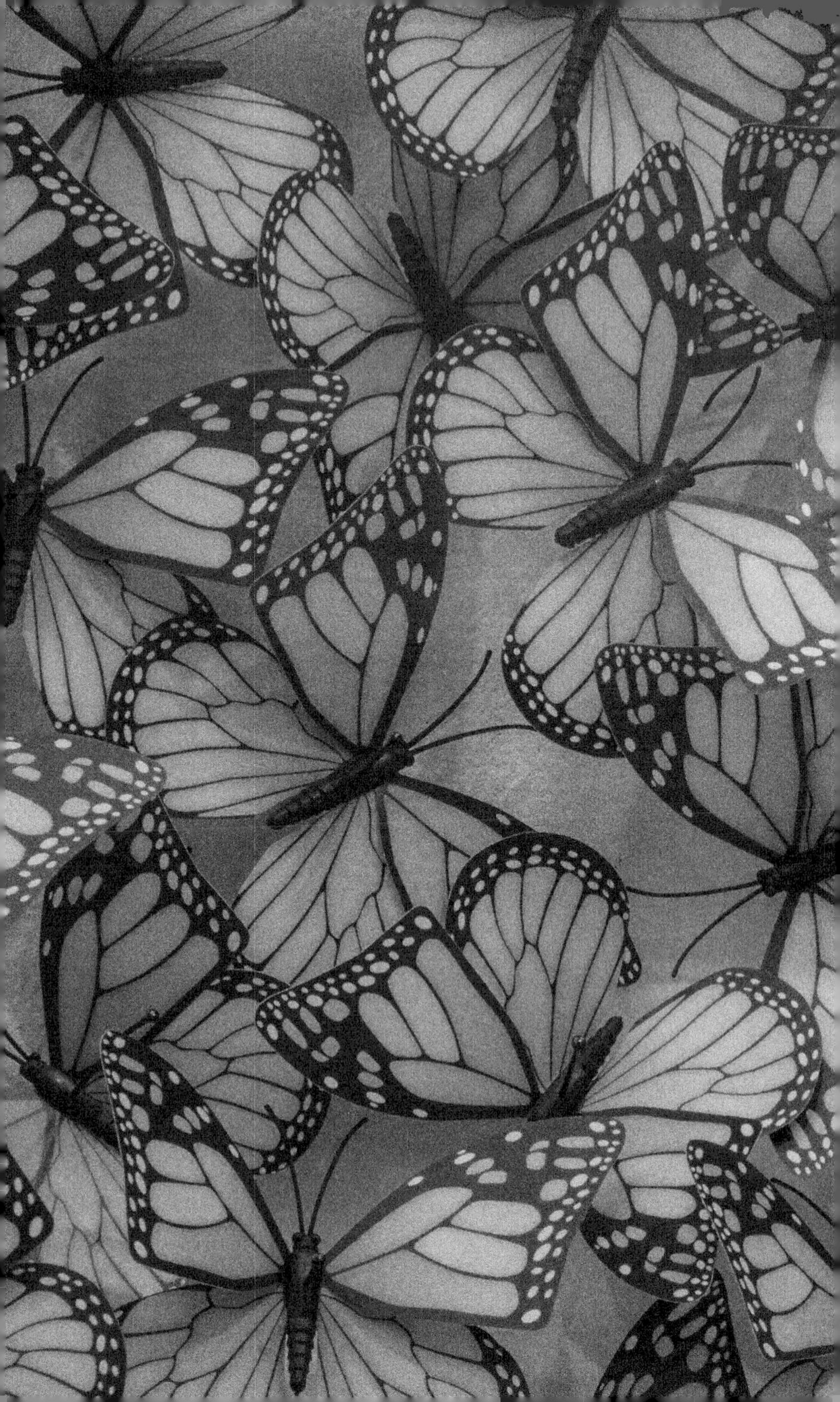

TO BE SEEN

The next day, Ly didn't come to breakfast and I found out from Hil that he'd already been and gone. I barely had time for a twinge of concern and to wonder if he was avoiding me before Sylvie bounded in, chattering about tonight's feast. Her enthusiasm was infectious, despite the tight fist low in my gut reminding me of the danger Goren posed.

I took my time bathing, washing my hair, laying out my gown and the shoes Sylvie had presented to me a week ago. Fluttering excitement and anxiety battered against that tight fist of fear, chipping away at it and leaving me restless.

After lunch (still no sign of Lysander), Sylvie appeared in my room, bringing a chest of *stuff*. Apparently, she'd decided it would be fun to get ready together, and I didn't have the heart to turn her down. Her ready smiles and gentle chatter eased my nerves.

"You know..." She eyed the dark grey gown. "Ly asked

me to help you get ready for tonight—make sure you'd be dressed to navigate fae society, but"—with a grin, she shrugged—"I'd say you don't need my help."

"Of course, the keeper of the wardrobe at work." I flashed her half a smile, but it soon turned into a wince at the tiny, shimmering moonstones scattered all over the spidersilk. At the slit up the leg. At the low back draped with threaded labradorite, moonstone, and crystal. It was a beautiful gown, the best I'd ever made, but...

What had seemed a wonderful idea in a sketch, in the abstract was now far too real as I faced the prospect of actually wearing it. That fluttering excitement gathered around my heart, making my chest sore and tight. "It's not... too much?"

"No, no, *no*." She flashed her eyebrows at me. "This is Calan Mai *and* the new moon. On such a dark night, you should shine all the brighter. And I know you will."

Not too glittering for the fae. Of course not. But... it was too glittering for me. I'd never worn anything like this, so revealing or so expensive. And yet...

No one here had to know that. I could be... someone else for tonight. Someone bold.

The night I'd faced the sluagh, I could so easily have died. If Ly had woken a minute later because of the elderberry wine. If he hadn't woken at all. If I'd fallen at the feet of one of those creatures rather than rolling down the riverbank. If... if... if...

And if I had, I would have died having achieved and changed nothing in the world. I'd have died clinging on to the way things were—running back to that tiny cottage in a horrible town full of people who either feared me or sneered at me.

This change hadn't been my choice, no. But life here... it wasn't so bad. I'd grown used to this new routine in this new place. And although I ached to see Rose, I had new people in my life—new friends.

That was what the Lady of the Lake had seen. She knew my heart better than I did.

Tonight, I could try to embrace this new life. I could try on this gown *and* what it would be like to be less afraid.

Sylvie believed I could do it.

And I was so damn tired of being afraid.

I huffed out a breath, and touched Sylvie's arm. "Thank you. Sincerely. I've made dozens of gowns for grand parties but I've never been to a single one. Part of me is scared of so many eyes on me..." Though none of the fae had stared at me like the people of Briarbridge— it was as Ly had said, it wasn't that I was different, just they were all the same. "But another part, maybe a bigger part, is scared that I'll fade into the background. I've spent my life trying to do that, and..." I clutched my chest where my heart thudded, too loud and too fast. "And I've had enough. Tonight, I want someone to see me."

A slow, gentle smile curved Sylvie's mouth and she pulled me into a hug. "Oh, Ari." She squeezed, her warmth suffusing me. "*There* you are. I knew it was in there somewhere." She pulled back, smile broad and bright as she stroked my hair.

"Knew *what* was?" I blinked up at her, eyes stinging.

"The courage to stand up and be seen. When you arrived, it was like you wanted to disappear. But now... it's like you've escaped whatever was hounding you. It's like watching the first spring flowers blooming."

My chest ached. Sylvie understood something I hadn't. All those years of words muttered behind hands, of stares, of quiet shunning... Every time attention had fallen on me, I'd flinched, sure it would be accompanied by some cruel comment or sneer. But here... the past couple of months, the only sneers I'd seen were Boyd's and he was hardly around. Plus, I suspected they weren't at my difference, but at my weakness relative to him and Ly and every other fae. After all, hadn't I feared and hated them for their strength?

It wasn't only being seen, but finding my voice. Anger at being taken and the desperation to get home had made me start speaking to Ly, saying things I would've only ever *thought* in Briarbridge. But something else had kept me doing so. The comfort I'd found here with him and Sylvie and Hil. Even Sallis and Hobb were easy company, undemanding and gentle.

In my time here I'd spoken more than I had in the past year, and nothing terrible had happened because of it. I made a soft sound, not quite a laugh.

"And as for being seen by someone..." Sylvie cocked her head, a glint in her eye. "I know someone who already does see you. And whatever you wear tonight, I know he'll like what he sees."

I drew a sharp breath. "I didn't say I wanted him to..." My throat was too tight to finish the sentence.

"You didn't need to." She led me to the dressing table and sat me down. "Ly has... had a difficult time over the past several years. He told you about the yew, right?"

I nodded as she combed my hair.

"And about his parents?"

"I know how his mother passed, but..." I frowned. "He spoke like the yew was involved with both their deaths." Asking him yesterday, with how upset and earnest he'd been, hadn't felt right.

"That boy!" She sighed and rolled her eyes, the comb not missing a beat. "He's only told you half the story, but..." Sylvie's hands fell still and she met my gaze in the mirror. "When his mother poured too much of herself into the tree and... faded away. Ly's father followed at once. They were a pair, bonded, and... one couldn't survive without the other."

My eyes burned. A bonded pair. Sylvie had recommended a romance book from the library where the fae couple bonded in that way. They'd tied their magic together, forming a connection that went deeper than just marriage. Their very lives were shared. Ly's parents must've carried out the same ritual.

For Ly to lose both his parents at once...

And to blame himself for not realising Goren's treachery...

A deep ache settled in my chest, my gut, the back of my throat. I knew all too well what it was to fail like that. My gift, although rare and useful to people like Lady

Hawthorne, had been no help in saving Mama and Papa from the creeping death.

In my lap, I pressed my hands together, but it wasn't the same... not when I wanted to take his hands, squeeze them, tell him I understood.

"He blames himself, doesn't he?" I asked at last, voice coming out as a rasp.

Sylvie's eyes were bright as she nodded. "I think so. He's lost a lot—his social standing, his family's power, a place at court..."

My eyebrows shot up. "He should be at court? With the Night Queen?"

"His family has a position in the Dusk Court, always have. But he can only leave his lands for, at most, two weeks at a time and that requires preparation. Otherwise the wards will fail, leaving us open to the Wild Hunt and other, worse creatures."

"Worse than...?"

"Believe me, there are far, *far* worse." Her shudder rippled along my hair as she gathered and combed it. "So he can't take his place at the Queen's side, or he'll leave us vulnerable. And he'd never do that." Frowning, she picked up Mama's brooch from the dressing table. "I thought you could wear this in your hair. Ly said it was special to you."

That ache dragged on me. Even here, in the middle of faerie, I had this reminder of Mama. And Ly, despite all the cares on his shoulders, he'd noticed and had thought to tell Sylvie. I nodded. "It is."

"He's been through a lot, and all of it because of

Goren." Her lips pressed together, paled. "To think, he has to welcome the man into his own home." She bared her teeth, canines gleaming. With a sharp shake of her head, she exhaled. "But the point I was trying to make..." She smoothed my hair behind my right ear and over my left shoulder. "It changed him. I haven't seen him laugh or smile in years—not properly. Bitter chuckles and sardonic smirks don't count."

"He does love to smirk, doesn't he?"

She grinned at me in the mirror, sliding the brooch into my hair and securing it with tiny pins that disappeared. "He *does*. But he's been different since he came back from the Tithe. I've seen him smile, heard him laugh... And all of it with you."

I swallowed against the sudden tightness in my throat. "He's relieved that he'll get the seed back soon, with a little help from my gift."

Sylvie snorted and rolled her eyes. "That *could* be it. But it isn't. You've brought him hope and not only for the yew tree." She passed her fingers over the brooch and a trace of something sweet crossed my tongue as tiny motes of white light appeared around Mama's crescent moon.

I gasped and stared in the mirror. My movements sent the lights dancing and winking like miniature stars.

Sylvie's hands landed on my shoulders, and she held my gaze in the mirror. "Tonight, Ari, you are going to shine."

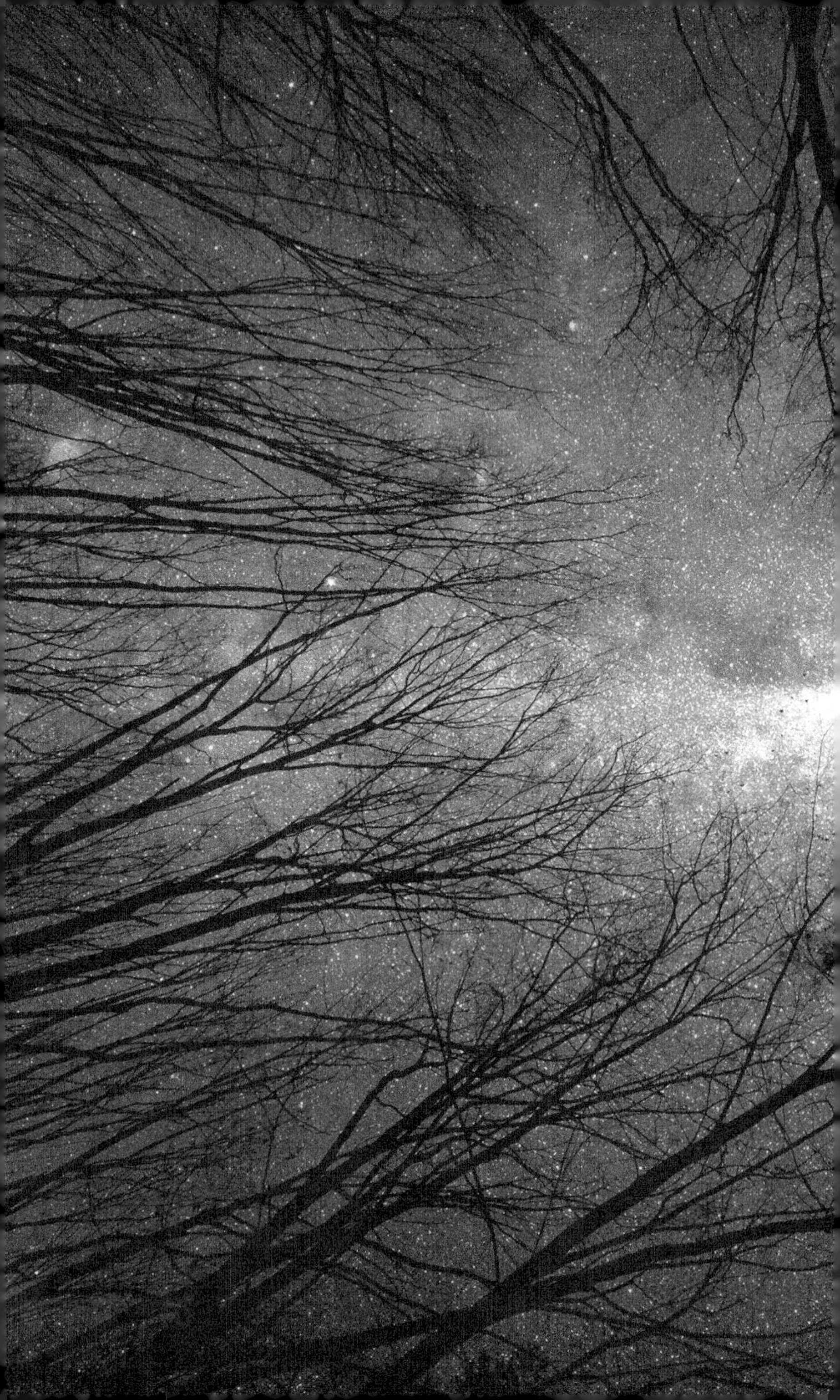

THE FAWN

Music drifted from the open doorway, a haunting sound of chimes and fiddles, with some sort of pipe floating between the notes. It was the kind of tune that could tempt a mortal to follow to the very ends of the earth. Suddenly, a lot of the old stories made sense.

My heart threatened to break out of my ribcage, its beat echoed in my throat, my wrists, my thighs, at odds with the music's steady rhythm. At least my gown's low back and slitted skirt helped cool my burning flesh.

Gods, why had I thought I could do this?

Sylvie waited at my side, for once not saying a word.

I clenched my fists as my muscles begged me to turn and run back to my room.

No. I'd made my decision. I wasn't going to hide away for the rest of my life... or at least not for tonight.

Ly needed me. If I hid, Goren would suspect.

I wasn't here for me, but for him. Somehow, that lie made it easier.

Head up, shoulders back, I would make my entrance like Lady Hawthorne… or, hells, like the Queen herself. I would look like a trophy, let Goren think I was nothing more than that, and help Ly keep his secret. I would not be the weak link in his plan.

Sylvie gave me a gentle smile and offered her elbow.

"Right. Let's do this." I took her arm and I was ready, or as ready as I'd ever be.

Together, we entered.

Around two dozen fae waited within the formal dining room, gathered in small groups, chatting and laughing, eyes glinting in the floating lights.

Too many pairs of eyes, all of them gradually turning to me. My pulse spiked.

Not them, not them. Look at something else.

Spring flowers covered the hearth, the windowsills, the chandeliers, and framed each door leading out to the terrace, their heady fragrance breaking over me in a wave of hyacinth and narcissi.

Even with all those people watching me, I didn't miss a step, because no sooner had I registered the decor than my eyes locked with Lysander's. He stood near the terrace doors, a glass halfway to his parted lips as though he'd been about to take a sip.

At his side, Hil raised her eyebrows before following his gaze to me.

No surprise, he wore his customary midnight blue, though the fabric glistened in the candlelight, showing off the shape of his chest below the jacket. A chest that had been pressed against my back for an entire night.

I bit my lip, and as if that woke him, a slow smile lifted his mouth, revealing the dimple in his cheek.

Sparks of energy rushed through me, as quick as a spider scuttling along its web. Although the sight of him made me jittery, it was nothing like the suffocating fear all those other stares brought. This was... exciting, energising, intoxicating.

Somehow, despite my burning face and inability to look away, my feet were still moving, crossing the floor, until I stood before him.

I inclined my head. "Calan Mai blessings."

"We are blessed indeed," he murmured, still holding me with his gaze, like I was something precious.

On the edge of my vision, Hil giggled behind her hand. "Moon and Stars above, don't you look like a gift from the gods themselves?" She nudged Ly. "Doesn't she look pretty?"

He brushed off his arm, shooting Hil a frown. "Ari, you—"

"Tell her, then." She nudged him again.

A muscle in his jaw feathering, he huffed through his nose. "That's what I was *trying* to do."

"Oh, Sylvie," Hil went on, "doesn't Ari look lovely?" Eyes bright, nose pink, she patted my cheek. A broad smile emphasised her pointed chin.

Ly edged closer. "Ari, you—"

"Sylvie!" Two identical fae appeared at the edge of our group, making me flinch. They had skin the same colour as mine, a rich fawn brown, and hair that matched. Maybe it was that little piece of familiarity that eased my shoulders.

Without a word, Ly slid into the spot next to me and offered his arm and a lopsided smile that might've been an apology. Face warming, I slid my hand into the crook of his elbow, and he made the introductions.

Thankfully, they seemed more interested in catching up with Sylvie and Hil and only asked me a couple of polite questions.

Young fae from local villages served drinks and trays filled with Hil's glorious cooking. Tarts of sweet chutney and sharp cheese. Bite-sized flaky pies, some filled with venison and gravy, others with pork and quail's eggs. Plenty of cakes flavoured with everything from honey to lemon, to cinnamon and mace, as well as pastries and tiny biscuits that melted in my mouth.

Several of the fae serving us had rosy cheeks and ears, as though they'd helped themselves to a glass or two of sparkling elderflower wine.

Ly scooped one of the weaker drinks from a tray for me and pointed out which were safer. Still, I sipped slowly. A little wine helped my courage, but too much and I'd end up on the floor—probably face-first.

Another fae approached and Ly introduced us. Not Goren. Relief loosened my muscles. Maybe he wasn't coming.

After a few mini pies, several cakes, and just the one drink, Boyd appeared at the edge of the group and jerked his chin at Ly.

With a low sigh, Ly pulled from my grip. "Sorry," he muttered. "Will you be all right? I promise I'll be back as soon as I can."

I lifted one shoulder. "You have guests to look after." And tonight I was being someone bold. "I'll be fine." I'd already managed to speak to three strangers, and Sylvie had faith in me. I nodded in reassurance, and he slipped away with a glance over his shoulder.

When the next server came past, I took another glass, but squinting at it, I wasn't sure if it was of the drinks Ly had called safe. I clutched it to give my hands something to do, though it was a poor replacement for his arm. It was almost easy to chat with Sylvie and a soft-spoken fae who reminded me of a sparrow with her flecked hair and skin and flighty demeanour.

Four strangers. I *could* do this.

But as the conversation wore on, more fae congregated on us, just a couple at a time, all keen for an introduction. Although they weren't Goren, they brought noise and questions and inquisitive eyes that looked to me even when I wasn't speaking. I backed into a corner.

Person-by-person, my pulse sped. They blocked out my view of the rest of the room, pressing in, making the air too hot. Air I couldn't take in. My lungs filled with the old, familiar wadding, and my face tingled.

It had been a while, but I'd dealt with this for years. Fanning myself, I counted in a long breath and muttered, "Excuse me."

One benefit of being so short, especially compared to most fae, was that I could slip through the crowd, and within moments I opened one of the glazed terrace doors and crept outside.

The cool night air quenched the panic, and I sucked in its freshness. Out here, dim fae light flickered and drifted along, illuminating the honeysuckle that climbed up the house. Its sweet fragrance tickled my nose and tugged me home. The honeysuckle that grew over Rose's doorway wouldn't bloom for another month yet.

I rubbed my aching chest and fled the reminder.

Out here my only company were the fountain and floating lights, the latter becoming scarcer the further I went from the house. No eyes on me. No crowd. No—

"Ah, this must be *the human*."

I whirled, heart leaping to my throat. I hadn't even heard—

Of course I hadn't. Fae. Silent and standing before me.

This one was as tall and broad as Ly and almost as handsome, but he was Ly's opposite in every other way. Long hair the colour of sunlight spilled past his shoulders. His blue eyes, illuminated by a passing light, were the match for any clear, summer sky.

His cool gaze trailed over me from head to toe, unhurried and unashamed. "Lysander has been holding out on me." A predatory grin showed his teeth.

I swallowed as though that could stop my heart from jumping out of my mouth. He didn't mean my gift, did he? Surely he couldn't know about that just from looking at me.

With the same feline grace I'd admired in Ly, he prowled closer, only stopping once he was a foot away.

I wanted to back away, told my feet to do so, but my muscles refused to obey.

"He didn't tell me you were such a beauty." He held his hand out to me, palm-up. "And what is this beauty's name?"

The way he'd looked me up and down and stood too close—my skin crawled and I'd sooner peel it off than touch him. I managed a step back, but my heels scraped something hard. The fountain.

"Now, now," he cooed, "don't be afraid." He closed the fractional distance I'd opened between us. "I only asked your name, little fawn."

Danger. My nerves shrieked it, my bones screamed it. But like a fawn before the huntsman, there was nothing I could do.

He scented the air, eyes growing hooded. "So exquisite, so fresh and new... and *gifted*." Cocking his head, he edged closer still, and I leant away, the backs of my legs against the fountain. "Ah, but I haven't introduced myself, have I?"

He didn't need to. I realised who he was a frantic heartbeat before he said it.

"Goren, at your eternal service." He nodded, holding me pinned with his gaze as much as with his proximity.

Shit. Of course it was Goren. And somehow I was alone with him.

I needed to get inside. Away. Anywhere that wasn't here.

I bowed my head and ducked to the left, but he was *there*. Fae speed. I was no match for that.

"Such a well behaved little creature. Head down. Knows her place. Quite tame."

Beyond my sweaty palms and racing heart, something burned through me. Anger? Shame? Maybe both.

Tame. I'd give him fucking *tame*!

Was that how it seemed when I kept quiet?

Gods, it was. All those times I avoided attention, that was the picture I'd painted of myself.

I'd been a good girl, meek and submissive so the people of Briarbridge wouldn't have any reason to be cruel or isolate me further. It was meant to be a defence, but it hadn't worked, had it? I'd just become what they wanted—*a well-behaved little creature* who sold them her gift and otherwise kept quiet.

Teeth gritted, I trembled with the effort of containing myself—from fleeing or snapping, I had no idea. Anger had made the words burst out of me with Ly, and I think he *liked* that spark. But Goren? What might he do if I was anything but a weak, meek human?

"I saw you with my *dear* Sylvanna, who was a vision as ever." A cruel smile revealed his long canines. "But next to her trim little body, all I could wonder was where Lysander had been hiding you." He made a low sound in his throat as his blue eyes trailed from my face to my throat, to my breasts, pausing there.

I'd noticed fae women were willowy and slim, but I'd never been so conscious of my curves before. There was no way of backing off any further without ending up in the fountain and something told me he would take that as an invitation.

With a *tsk*, he shook his head. "I'm offended he didn't bring you to visit me. I could look after you very well indeed, if you'd only let me."

He shifted, reaching for my hip, and I flinched away as best I could, but there was nowhere to go and—

"Goren."

The air whooshed out of me.

I knew that voice—would know it anywhere. My throat ached.

Ly stepped out from behind Goren. "How... *interesting* to see you out here." The coldness. I'd never heard *that* in him before.

Goren didn't move, although his hand had paused an inch from my hip. "I was just getting acquainted with this little delight."

An icy smile creaked onto Ly's face. His dimple didn't appear. "By the terms of the Tithe, that 'little delight' is *my* human."

My human. I stiffened. He told me he didn't... No, wait. *By the terms of the Tithe*. That wasn't a lie. The Tithe said I was his, even if he didn't agree with it. And the tone of his voice... He was playing a part: the lord who could tell Goren to leave me alone, rather than Ly, the man I'd come to know over the past couple of months.

Creases forming between his brows, Goren straightened and backed away two steps. "My deepest apologies, I didn't realise." His sky blue eyes left me at last as he raised his eyebrows at Ly. "There has been no wedding, so I thought perhaps you were content to merely *play* with her and would like to share your toys."

Ly's cheek twitched. "Not tonight."

Which could also mean not ever.

Deceit without lies.

"Hmm." Goren flicked me another glance before backing off. "I see you're still breaking her in. As flighty as a fawn, this one. But"—he licked his lips and smirked at Ly in a way that made me shudder—"her fear is quite delicious. Do let me know when you've tamed her and want to share." With that, he slipped into the darkness and a moment later, his silhouette appeared against the glazed doors and he went inside.

I sagged against the fountain, clutching my chest, heart throbbing against my fingers.

"Ari, I am *so* sorry. Did he—?"

"Didn't touch me." I shook my head, catching my breath.

He offered his arm. I clung to it and led him away from the house, my nervous energy demanding movement.

"I'm sorry I called you 'my human.'" His hand closed over the back of mine. "I had to use terms he'd understand." Jaw clenched, he shook his head. "If he tried to take you away, law and tradition would be on my side, and it would be seen as a terrible affront to the Queen. It was the only thing I could think of to get him to leave you alone." He shot me a look, all tight and pinched. "I don't think of you as—"

"I know." I huffed a laugh, the cool night air a balm

against the anger, the shame, the fear. "I knew exactly what you were doing."

By the time we reached the balustrade at the edge of the terrace, I could stop.

The dying yew was hidden in the darkness. That was a small mercy. The sight of it would only have rekindled my rage, knowing Goren was responsible.

Wild Hunt, I would sew Ly the best damn outfit I'd ever made and help him steal back that seed.

Taking another cleansing breath, muscles eased by that vow and perhaps by Ly's presence, I leant on the balustrade.

In the quiet, I couldn't miss Ly's gasp. He was finally getting a view of the back of my gown—of *my* back.

Long seconds passed.

"Why, Ariadne," he said at last, voice low, lilting, "you appear to have forgotten half your dress."

I chuckled, straightening. "I didn't have the fae down as being prudes about modest clothing." I turned to tease him some more, but the breath caught in my throat.

Because he was only inches away.

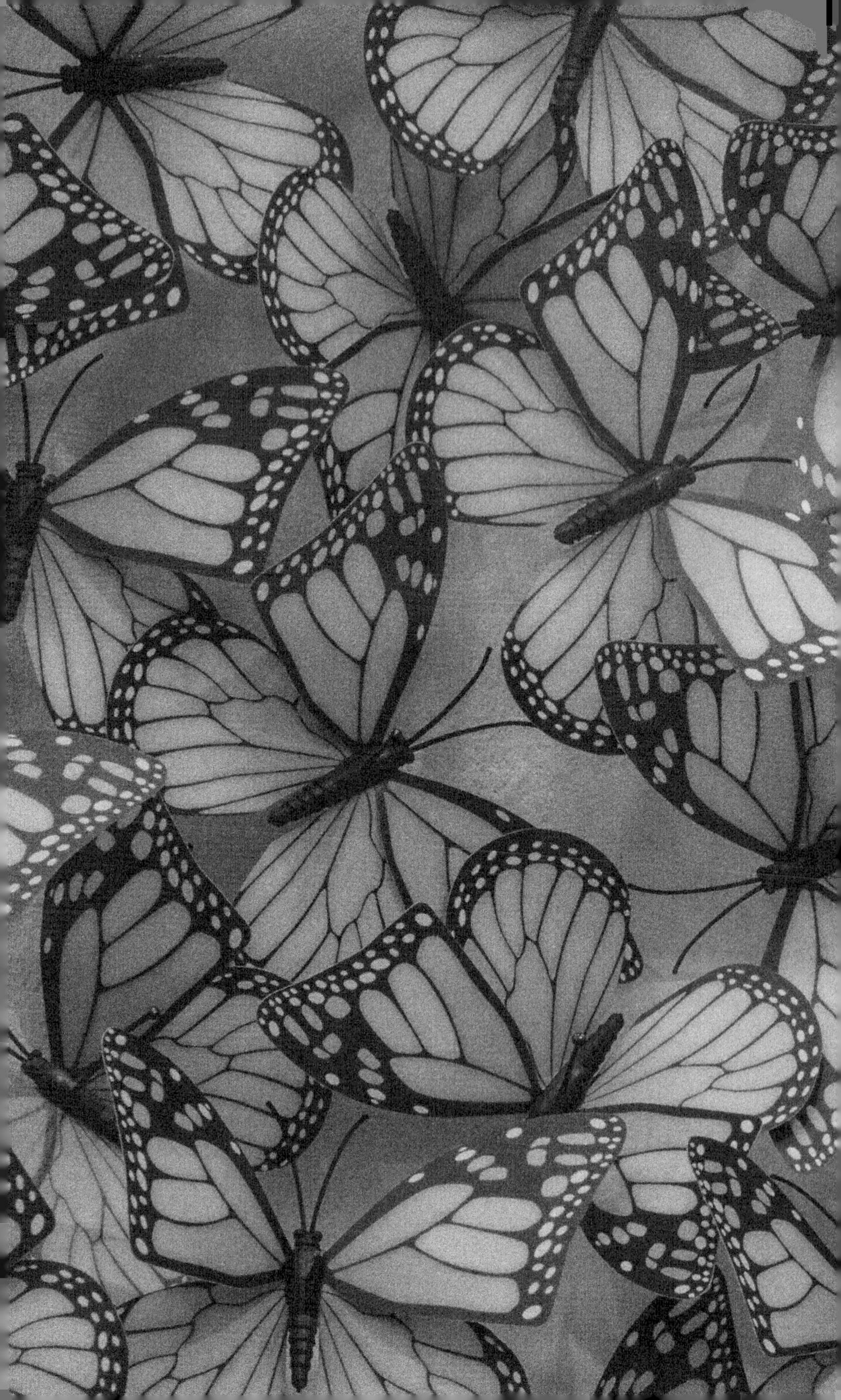

EVENING STAR

My grin faded and fresh warmth broke over me. Not anger or shame this time, far from either.

It took three breaths before I could lift my gaze to his.

Even in this dim light, it bored into mine. The shadows carved his face into dark planes, the darkest beneath his jaw, his eyebrows, his cheekbones, in the dimple of his chin.

Somehow, I was reaching up, though I didn't recall telling my hand to move. His chest stilled. My fingertips slid up his jawline, stubble abrading my sensitive skin. When my thumb stroked his cheekbone, tracing those shadows that so loved him, he pressed into the touch.

"Ariadne," he murmured. The word fanned the inside of my wrist, making me shiver.

"You've charmed me, Ly, and I'm not sure I care."

He made a sound that wasn't quite a scoff. "You're

gifted; I couldn't use fae charm on you even if I wanted to."

So I *was* immune to fae charm.

Everything I felt about him and every ounce of want—it was all real. Just me and him, no magical interference.

All I could do in answer was lift my chin, repeating yesterday's invitation.

Good gods, if he didn't take it, I would die of embarrassment, but the Lady of the Lake had said…

I swallowed as his gaze caressed every inch of my face.

If he liked me, I didn't understand *why*, but maybe I didn't need to. Did it matter what insanity had us both in his grip?

He was not what I'd expected from a fae lord. Perhaps I wasn't what he'd expected from a human woman.

His hands slid around my waist, gentler than all those times he'd lifted me on and off the stag. But after that gentleness came a commanding grasp that pulled me against every solid plane of him.

My body thrummed with anticipation as he bent closer, closer, closer.

He brushed his lips against mine. It was barely a graze, but it set them tingling. One side of his mouth rose as though he knew the effect he had on me. His nose nudged mine, followed by another graze.

For all that he seemed content to take his time kissing me, his hands told a different story. His fingers splayed across the small of my back, bare skin upon bare skin. The other hand slid beneath the jewelled strands draped across the back of my gown, as though they were an obstacle between him and his prize.

I rose onto my tiptoes, sinking my fingers into his hair, thumb skimming the edge of his ear.

"Don't," he gasped, shuddering. His throat rose and fell in a slow swallow. "Don't do that." His voice came out raw.

I tried to pull away, but he kept hold of me against him. "Sorry, did that hurt? I didn't mean to—"

He exhaled a soft laugh. "Not *hurt*, quite the opposite." His teeth flashed in the gloom and I could only hope that same darkness hid my blush.

"Oh."

"Oh, indeed." His low rumble of laughter reverberated into me and I hung my head.

The damn stories hadn't *warned* me a fae's ears were sensitive.

With a gentle grip on my chin, he coaxed me into meeting his gaze. His laughter had faded and that intense look from earlier had returned. "I've wanted this—*you* for weeks, Ari. By no means am I going to rush this." His chest heaved against mine. "We were interrupted earlier when I tried to tell you..." He shook his head, thumb tracing a tiny circle on my chin. "The evening star is the most beautiful, the most precious, the most special star in the sky to us folk of the Dusk Court." As he spoke, he bent closer, until his lips were an inch from mine. "But you put even her to shame."

His fingers slid into my hair, and he closed that last inch.

True to his word, he didn't rush. He made a slow exploration of my lips, kiss after kiss after kiss, until I didn't know where one ended and the next began.

I clung to his jacket, sure he was the only thing keeping me upright, as I tested and tasted each touch, the fire in my flesh stoking hotter.

Then it wasn't slow anymore. It was deep and dark and sensuous, his heat matching mine. I might've whimpered as he used that hand buried in my hair to angle me for better access, tongue delving, stroking, coaxing. My body throbbed and ached in want, pulse pounding at my throat and thighs.

He broke away, just a fraction of an inch. The breaths coming from him were as ragged as my own. "Are all humans so damn short?" He grinned as he lifted me onto the balustrade, putting us almost level.

"Are all fae so damn tall?" I narrowed my eyes at him, but couldn't keep the answering grin from my face.

He shook his head, expression straightening. "You are perfect as you are, Ari. What I wouldn't give to call you mine, to make myself yours."

The words, all of them, fluttered in my belly. Frightening. Exciting.

Wasn't I being brave tonight? Bold Ariadne wouldn't remain silent, she would reply. So I would.

"Isn't that what this is?" I lifted my chin, not quite enough to meet his lips again. "Wasn't that what I was inviting when I did this?" My fingers followed that same line of his jaw, harder this time, letting the stubble scrape my fingertips so they tingled.

Despite the cool night air, his skin was much warmer this time.

He closed his eyes, pressing against my hand. "I think I've found a new light in the night sky," he murmured before piercing me with his gaze again. "My evening star."

My heart skipped a beat at that. I'd always hated anyone calling me "my" anything, but "my evening star" from him? I shivered, grip tightening on his jacket.

A smile flickered across his face, and he grazed one canine across my lower lip, the touch so light it made my breath hitch.

Then his mouth covered mine in a kiss that was anything but exploratory. This claimed me and yet as I pulled him close, letting him stand between my thighs, this was also a kiss that gave.

Every teasing touch, every long look, every *almost* moment there had been between us: he gave me what it had promised in that kiss, in the press of his hard body against mine, in the hand at my back making the jewels jangle in a sound that merged with the distant music indoors.

I arched and wrapped my legs around him, wanting, greedy, aching, and he pressed against me, hard upon the softness at the apex of my thighs. I was liquid fire in his hold.

"*Ahem.*"

I jerked away, a gasp jolting through me.

Ly straightened, still holding my back so I didn't topple over the balustrade.

"It's time for the run." Boyd's voice, even more clipped and cool than usual.

Goosebumps crept up my left leg, reminding me it was bare, thanks to the slit in my skirt and where Ly was flush against me.

"Very good." He bit his lip as a grin tugged at it. "We'll be right there."

"Oh, I'm sure you will." Boyd's footsteps faded away.

I gulped down a long breath, trying to calm the frantic pounding of my heart from all we'd done and the sudden interruption.

"Come on, my evening star"—Ly's grin softened to a smile—"we have a Calan Mai game to play."

CALAN MAI

Either excitement or dread trickled down my back. The forest was warmer, damper than the terrace, and in its fae light flecked darkness, I was alone. Although it was a new moon, Ly's wards kept us safe from the Wild Hunt and other fae dangers.

He wouldn't be able to keep doing that if he didn't get the seed back from Goren. I shivered at the reminder.

As we'd walked here arm in arm, he'd explained their tradition to me. Every Calan Mai, they unleashed a wolpertinger with silver-painted antlers into the forest. The guests separated and fanned out. Whoever caught the fae creature won a boon from the lord of the land—in this case, Ly.

Part of me whispered that I might be able to use that boon to break the Tithe and return to Briarbridge.

Another part of me that had grown louder since speaking to the Lady of the Lake posed the question: did I really want to?

Skirts gripped in one hand, I crept between the trees and winced—both at the question and the sound of my steps as I cracked twigs and rustled through the undergrowth.

Briarbridge and Rose had been the two constants in my life. Constants were comforting and comfortable. They'd helped me get through the death of my parents. I loved Rose, missed her and our weekly visits from Annon. But did I love Briarbridge? Did I really miss anyone else there?

A glimmer of light shone through the trees ahead—perhaps a clearing. Although I was safe from the Wild Hunt, my heart thudded fast and heavy in my chest. Logic and *knowing* were no antidote for instinct, and mine jangled along every nerve, hissing that forests at night were danger incarnate and fae forests, far worse.

So I aimed for that light like a moth throwing itself at a flame.

Ly had promised he would come and find me, but there was no sign of him yet. Still, as I passed between the trees towards the clearing, my eyes strained for a hint of violet-blue gleaming hair.

The Albionic tradition for Calan Mai centred around May crowns woven by young men and gifted to their chosen women, then a run through the forest at night. There was no wolpertinger. We searched for each other.

I'd never taken part, but Rose had told me plenty about the giggles and rustles, the kisses and couplings enjoyed in the darkness. The forest was not a place for society and its rules and its shadows granted permission to cross lines. Many a wedding followed Calan Mai and many a babe was born nine months later in February.

As well as the wolpertinger hunt, did fae do the same? If Ly found me, would we continue what we'd started on the terrace? Maybe it was my turn for a run through the forest at night...

A thrill rippled through me as I stepped out into a small clearing. Starlight added to the dim, drifting fae lights, revealing a blanket of bluebells. In the clear night air wafted the sweet, dark taste of black cherries.

Crack. Behind me.

Although I was safe within these lands, my heart hammered. Was that Ly? Or Sylvie, perhaps? I spun on my heel.

Only shadow upon shadow, leaves and trunks punctuated by fae light. I clutched my chest as if that could slow my heartbeat. It could be the wolpertinger. No, if a fae made a noise walking, it had to be deliberate, which brought me back to my friends, perhaps signalling they were close.

"How dare you?"

Gasping, I spun again, but I couldn't put a direction on the feminine voice. And I couldn't have said whose it was, though something about it was tantalisingly familiar.

Although the night was mild, goosebumps pricked their way up my arms and down my back. "Who's there?"

"How dare you stand here on fae land like you

belong?" It was a whisper on the wind, a dark voice, its tone tugging on recognition.

"Ly?" Maybe he was nearby, searching for me. "Sylvie?"

Cold laughter chimed, tinkling like broken glass, the sound fractured as though it came from everywhere at once. "You call upon the Lord of this land though you are nothing but a mere human."

Ice crept through my veins. Something must've got past Ly's wards.

I tugged on the high neckline of my gown, though it wasn't constricting my throat. A great weight pressed on my chest. I backed away from the trees, finding the centre of the clearing. No signs of movement in the forest and out here, there was only me and my gasping breaths.

"A mere human, pathetic and weak. Already dead." More of that chilling laughter. From... ahead? "You call on him and yet you endanger him."

Yes, definitely ahead. It was as though the sound had consolidated on one spot on the edge of the forest.

My eyes burned. I didn't dare blink.

"You are nothing but a weight around his neck."

Something... a deeper shadow in the darkness moved from behind a trunk.

I couldn't breathe, couldn't move. My mouth was open, but I couldn't even speak.

"You know it's true," it said, a sharp slither of a voice, soft and cruel.

It wasn't wrong.

"You couldn't even help your own family." It hissed a

laugh, though the shadow didn't move. "What use would you be to him?"

My gift... no, it *was* wrong... I was working to help him restore the yew. I didn't have much magic, but I could help him be unseen, unnoticed, a being of pure night.

I clenched my trembling hands into fists and lifted my chin.

"It should've been you." In my ear.

I jerked and turned, the movement taking an age as though the world had turned to tar.

It stood there. My opposite in every way—black hair, pale skin, white eyes... and yet I knew the shape of those large eyes, the full lips that stretched in a sharp smile, even the scars creeping up its neck.

It *was* me.

A changeling. A beast. Some fae creature that had made it past the wards.

I ran.

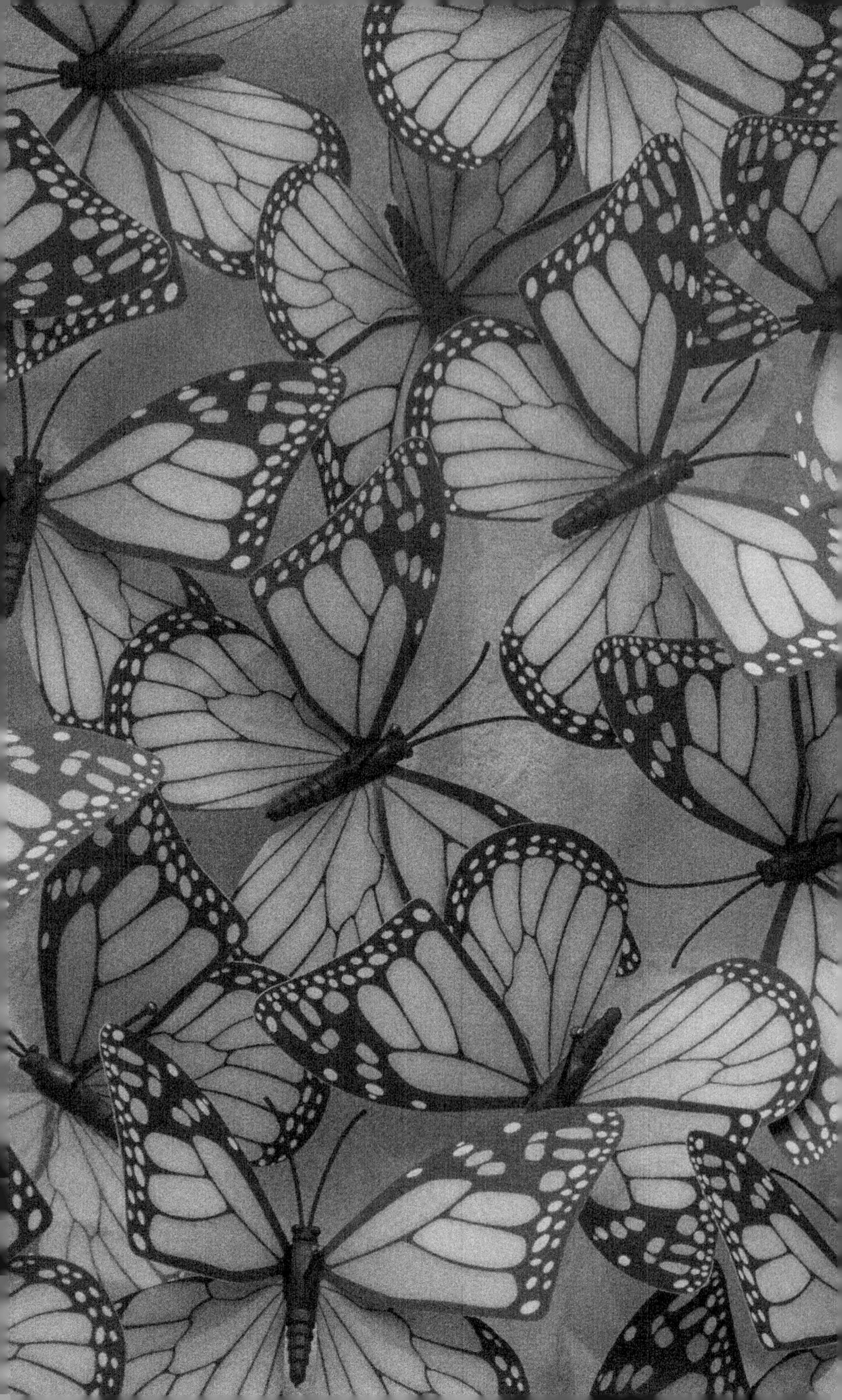

Not Enough

Lungs searing, I didn't know what direction I went, I just ran. I needed to put distance between myself and that thing.

What was it? How did it know things that I'd only ever thought?

Because it was right. I'd failed Mama and Papa. I'd let them die. I'd sewn my gift into their blankets, begging the gods not to take them away. I'd poured every ounce of strength I could into those stitches, and once my magic was used up, I'd bathed their feverish faces and trickled water into their mouths.

And none of it had been enough.

Because I was not enough.

I was weak, so the creeping death had worked its way through my body and pulled me into its fever dream even as I tried to save them, and when I'd woken...

It should've been me.

The tears came.

They burned my cheeks, choking, salting my tongue.

Trees tore at my hair, snagged in my gown, scratched my bare arms. I stumbled over rocks and roots, ducked under branches.

"Silly, silly girl," the changeling's voice whispered in my ear, "run all you like." That tinkling laugh again. "You can't escape yourself."

I lost a shoe, but I didn't miss a step, shoving leaves and twigs out of the way.

Then there were no more leaves or twigs, only the dark sky above.

I stumbled up an incline and fell to my hands and knees, breaths ripping through me.

Once I could hear past my own gasps, I angled my head. Nothing behind me. No whispers.

I dashed away the tears and peered over my shoulder. No sign of the changeling.

Either I'd outrun the thing or it had found someone else to bother.

Thank the gods.

My face tingled as I pushed myself upright, adrenaline still coursing through me as I tore my gaze from the dark forest.

Packed earth stretched left and right, a ditch lining the far side.

A road.

There were no roads on Lysander's land except for the one leading up to the house.

The blank disc of the new moon mocked me.

My blood stilled.

The new moon.

That meant the Wild Hunt were abroad.

And if this wasn't Lysander's land, that meant I'd passed his wards.

A howl split the air and turned my veins to ice.

A dozen more answered.

The ground thrummed.

In the distance, a pale wave with flaming eyes surged along the road.

The Wild Hunt weren't just abroad—they were *here*.

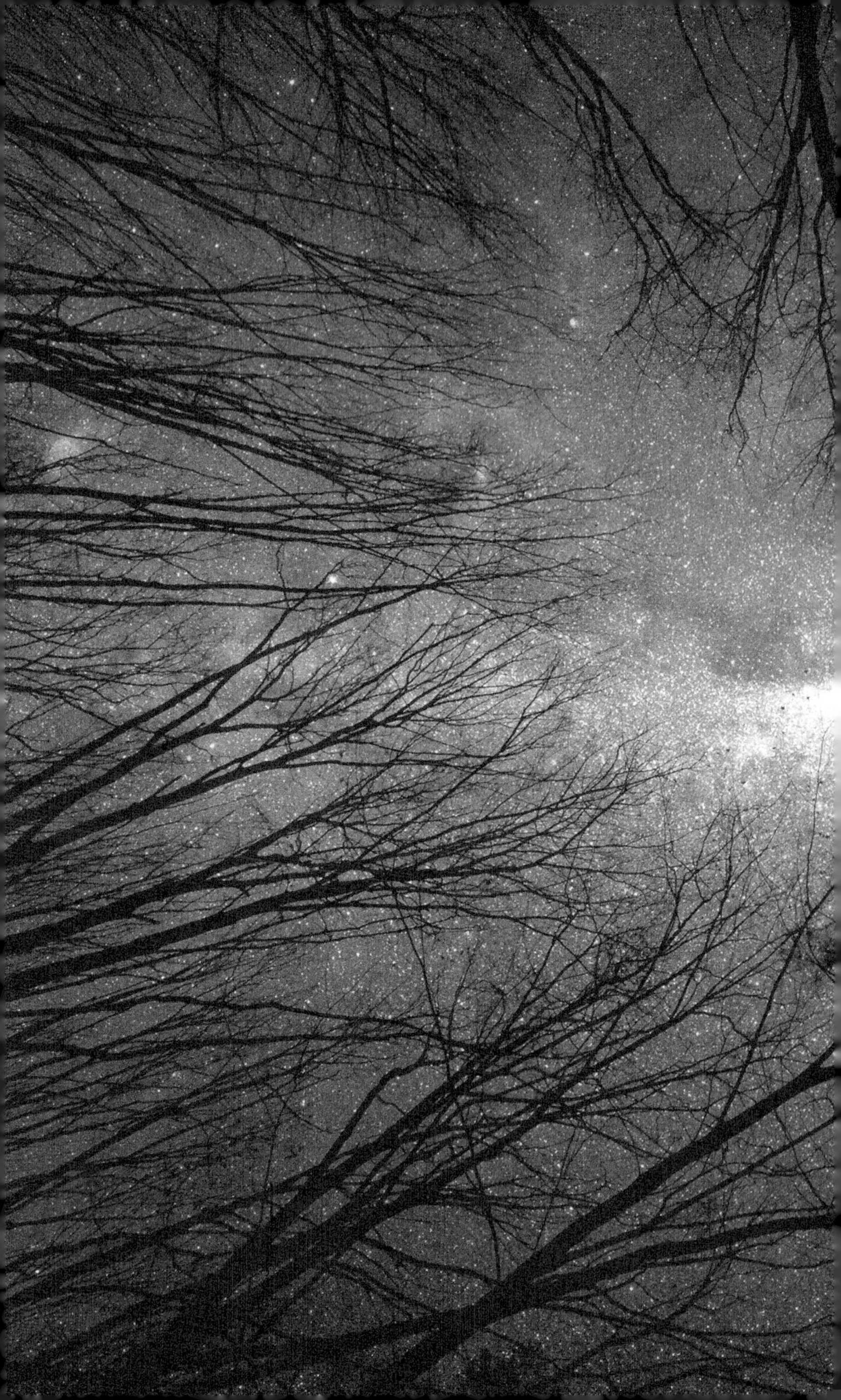

The Wild Hunt

That howl. The hounds had my scent. That surging pale shape—it was the pack, running this way.

Coming for me.

Their baying tore through the night, just like it would tear through me, body and soul, and toss me into the waiting arms of their masters.

Black spots bloomed at the edges of my vision. Even as I stood, frozen, I knew. The changeling had driven me here, like a dog herding sheep.

Would it take my place or just enjoy watching me die? If it shifted and became unAriadne, would anyone know? Would it finish Ly's suit? Would it kiss him like I had earlier? Would it seek him out in the forest tonight and claim him as part of the Calan Mai celebrations?

Its hands, not my hands, on him, on his body, on his cheek, pulling him close for a kiss...

Its clumsy stitches finishing his suit without making him unseen, leaving him vulnerable...

Move.

The word twitched through me, and I staggered down the slope leading back to the forest.

I reached the first tree as the ground rumbled, reverberating through my bones. Hoofbeats. Louder and louder.

I shouldn't look, but...

Beyond the white and crimson hounds rose the silhouettes of thirteen riders. Some rode stags, others horses. Antlers and horned helms blocked out the stars, blacker than night, deeper than the darkness of eyes screwed shut.

Knees quaking, I clutched the tree. Its rough bark scraped my skin, something solid that cut through the terror.

If I ran, their hounds would follow my scent. And if I led them into Ly's estate, that could bring the Wild Hunt's wrath upon him. His wards stopped them setting foot on his land, but what then? Would they wait there? Could they attack his wards? They were powerful, and he had to conserve his strength to keep the yew tree alive until he could retrieve the seed.

You endanger him.

No. The changeling was wrong. I wouldn't bring them to his doorstep.

All these years of hiding, and perhaps the bravest thing I could do tonight was to be seen, even if it meant my death.

I pressed my forehead against the bark and took the longest, deepest breath of my life. I wouldn't let him down.

Shoulders squared, I turned.

They were a hundred yards away, thundering closer.

I took one lurching step towards the road.

Something white burst from the trees ahead. It streaked into the road between me and the hounds. It stopped, lifted its head, and howled right back.

"Fluffy?"

The hounds slowed as though confused.

Flecks of darkness burst into being around me, accompanied by the sweet darkness of starlight and rhubarb. By the time I blinked, Ly blocked my path, face pale, brows drawn together.

His arms came around me and his hand slid against my bare back, blazing hot compared to the chill that had engulfed me since seeing the changeling.

Then we were nothing more than shadows fragmenting on the breeze.

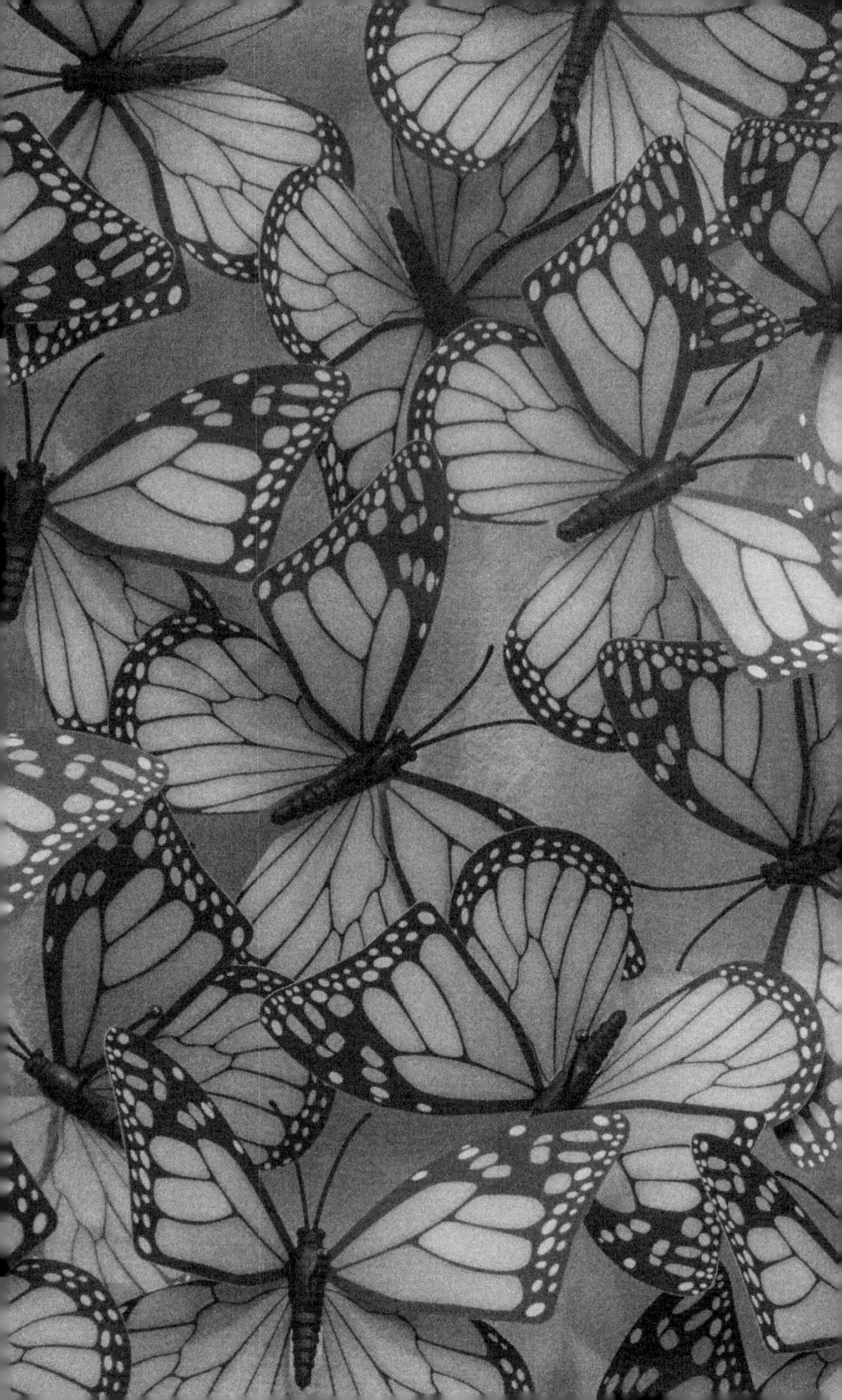

STARRY NIGHT

Sharp and sweet, starlight and night, for a moment that was all I knew. Then there was breath and warmth, arms around me. Solidity. Comfort. A familiarity I'd grown used to, and clung to with shaking hands.

Not just familiarity, *safety*. I leant into him, face buried against his heaving chest, breathing him in as the taste of his magic faded.

He squeezed me against him, though whether he was reassuring me or himself, I couldn't say.

I forced in one long breath and held it for a second. I counted, one, two, three as I blew it all out, even though my lungs fluttered and twitched and screamed at me that I needed to breathe in, in, in.

But that way lay the horrible airless feeling I knew too well.

Another breath. Another.

The tingling faded, that desperate tightness in my chest with it.

"Ari?" Ly rasped, craning back until I met his gaze. I could barely make out the whites of his eyes, the flash of his teeth as he spoke. He didn't release me from his hold. "Are you—?"

"I'm... fine." A shaky breath came out, almost a laugh, almost a sob. I was wobbly, yes, but uninjured. That was some stroke of ridiculous luck.

I'd seen the Wild Hunt. I'd heard their hounds. I'd—

"Fluffy?" I jolted. She'd run out in front of them. "We need to go and—"

"She's safe. She only showed herself, and once we shadowstepped away, she ran. She's faster than the lot of them." A low hum rumbled in his chest and through me. "I think they were confused to see another hellhound."

I sagged against him, the trembling easing every second.

We were... somewhere dark... somewhere that smelled green and woody. A sour note coated my tongue.

"I can't see a thing. Where are we?"

He huffed, blasting my face. "I'm more concerned with what happened." The hand on the small of my back tightened as he pushed hair from my face. "Are you sure you're all right?"

"I... I am." Somehow. "Thanks to you and Fluffy." I grimaced as the sour taste grew stronger. "Wait, are we *inside* the yew?"

That rumble again. "It was the safest place I could

think of. We can stay, but I suspect you dislike the magic here as much as I do."

My stomach knotted, both at the reminder of the yew's sickness, and... "I don't think I can go out there... face... people."

His touch traced my temple, my cheek, the angle of my jaw, easing the tightness in my chest. "You don't have to. Would you prefer indoors or out?"

The cool air, fresh and soothing—yes, I wanted that. "Out."

"Alone or with me?" The tone of his voice stayed neutral like he wasn't trying to lead me one way or the other.

"With you."

In the shadows, he shifted closer, lifting my chin. I tiptoed to him.

"As you wish," he whispered against my lips, before kissing me as the world fell into deeper darkness.

Floating on the breeze, I was nothing. When I gathered into my body, still in his arms, that sensation was strangely calming, as though being nothing for a few seconds was a much-needed break from constant thought and worry and fear.

We were just outside the gardens, far from the house, where fragrant jasmine grew over a wall and grass covered a gentle slope.

"Does this suit my evening star?" He gestured to the ground and a dozen cushions appeared, spread across a velvet blanket the exact deep blue of his eyes.

I screwed up my face, trying not to smile. "Hmm, it'll do."

"Phew." He rolled his eyes before handing me onto the blanket and removing his jacket.

I sank into the cushions and blew a heavy sigh.

Brows drawn together, he lounged beside me more like a sabrecat sunning himself than a person lying in the dark. His gaze skimmed over me and the frown deepened. "Will you tell me what happened?"

I explained about the changeling but not what it had said, only that it frightened me and knew things from my thoughts.

As he listened, his neck corded, and when I told him how it had herded me towards the road, his nostrils flared.

"Goren." He bared his teeth. "He used his gift on you."

Black cherries. That taste I'd caught before seeing the changeling must've been his magic.

"The changeling was in your mind," Ly went on, "put there by *him*." Every word came out harsh, seething with restraint. "He doesn't know what's in your mind, but his gift turns your thoughts and fears against you."

So Goren didn't know those dark things I told myself, the raw places in my heart. I exhaled, rubbing my chest.

Ly's hands flexed, rippling through the muscles and tendons in his forearms. "He could've got you killed—worse, consumed by the Hunt." He blasted out a breath and bolted upright. "I will rip him apart, destroy his fucking soul. I'm going to find him right now and watch his eyes go dark as I crush the life—"

"No." My voice trembled, but my hand on his arm did not. "Remember your plan. If you go after him, you might never get the seed back. Ruining his scheme is the best revenge."

He clenched his jaw but no longer looked like he was about to leap to his feet and hunt down Goren.

"And tonight," I added, "he's your guest—you can't harm him." Goren had an invite, so guest right stood. If Ly could somehow push his body to break that taboo, he'd be damned.

He eased back against the cushions, narrowing his eyes. "When did you get so good at fae intrigue?"

I lifted my chin with fake cockiness. "Too much time around Sylvie." But I couldn't keep it up and the expression broke into a grin. "Really, though, you know I'm right."

"I do," he said on a sigh. He lowered his gaze, lips pressing together. "I'm sorry I left you out there."

"I thought the point was that we ran alone."

"I should've cheated and kept you with me. Especially with him here. You're..." He shook his head. "He knows you matter to me."

I tried to bite back the smile, but... it was too warm and he was too close. And, hells, what did it matter if he knew how much I liked those words?

He had given me a sense of safety, a place to live where I didn't feel judged... somewhere that was starting to feel like home.

I would give him what I could in return. Not because it was an exchange or a bargain, but because I *wanted* to.

Smile fading, jaw clenching, I ran my fingers through his hair. A shiver swept through him, and he looked up, eyebrows rising, hopeful.

"I don't give a damn what he knows." The firmness of my voice caught me by surprise. "I am going to make you the best outfit I've ever sewn." The viciousness in my low tone—that wasn't me. Except... maybe it was. Maybe this was what a brave Ariadne sounded like. "I want you to beat him, and I want him to live to see it. I want you to get your power back."

Eyes closing, he nuzzled my hand. That gesture—I'd have thought it animalistic and frightening a couple of months ago, but now? Now it was him. It was... natural. I stroked the lines of his cheekbones, of his nose, the edge of his lips, locking it all in my heart.

He nipped at my fingertips, a playful grin edging in place. "Then you don't think I'm, and I quote, 'an arrogant prick'?"

"Hmm." I tapped his nose as if telling him off. "One out of two."

He snorted and caught my finger. "I won't ask which one." He kissed the pad, once, twice, three times, expression growing more serious with each. "But I don't care about beating him or getting back my power—not tonight. Let's enjoy the stars."

With that, he rolled onto his back and offered me the crook between his arm and body. I tucked against him, head on his shoulder.

The new moon blotted out a circle of black in the sky, but...

A low breath fell from me, barely getting past the lump forming in my throat. With it so dark, the stars glittered all the brighter, their subtle colours winking silver and white, blue, violet, and gold. A belt of a million flecks of starlight cleaved the sky in two as though someone had flicked paint onto the night's canvas.

So many stars. So many possibilities. Such a vast expanse stretching on and on overhead.

I was a tiny mote of insignificance against that.

Did my actions matter? Could they really have that great an impact on anything? Could Ly's? Could anyone's?

This entire world could vanish or explode tomorrow and it wouldn't make the slightest difference to the stars. They would endure.

Every knotted muscle in my body eased, and I smiled. It didn't matter what I said or did. It didn't matter what anyone else thought of me. Under the infinite stars, I could just *be*.

"I've never seen the sky like this before," I said into the quiet.

He stirred, perhaps looking at me, but my gaze skipped from star to star.

I lifted one shoulder. "The new moon means the Wild Hunt. No one ventures out past dusk on those nights. But this..." My eyes stung, and that lump lodged in my throat. "If more people saw this, I wonder if they'd be easier on themselves... and each other."

He remained silent, and I wondered if he'd fallen asleep, but then his fingers took up a slow circle on my shoulder. "Does this mean you might be easier on yourself?"

I sucked in a breath. Maybe it was the way I worked so feverishly or what I'd said when he'd spotted my scars. It could've been when I'd told him about losing Mama and Papa, or even just the evenings talking between his stories. I hadn't realised, but I'd shown him parts of myself I usually kept hidden.

My eyelids fluttered, trying to ease the stinging of my eyes. "I can't."

"Ah. About that..." He shifted and reached into his breast pocket.

I rolled onto my side, so my hand was on his chest and I could look up at him, but whatever he pulled out was hidden in his palm.

His gaze roved over my face, mouth tugging in not quite a smile. "'I can't.' I see you hesitate and think it. You say it to yourself too often for someone who told a fae lord he's, and again, I quote, 'an arrogant prick.' Or for someone who tricked him into allowing her to escape, albeit temporarily." He arched an eyebrow. "Or for someone who smacked a sluagh with a piece of wood despite a *total* lack of training with any sort of weapon. Or for someone who saw the Wild Hunt and survived. Or..." His voice lowered an octave, making my heart dip. "Or for someone who's so utterly enchanted me.

"Next time anyone, including you, tells you that you can't, I hope this will remind you that you already did."

He opened his hand, revealing a two-inch long pearlescent spur mounted in silver. Its chain clinked softly as he held it out.

I frowned from it to him and back again. "I don't..." But... the length, the slender point. Not a spur, but a *claw*. "*Oh*."

"You took it from the sluagh, so I figure it's yours." He cocked his head. "Polishes up nicely, doesn't it?"

That was one way to put it. Sitting up, I pulled the chain over my head and slid it under my gown. The claw sat between my breasts, cool and smooth. "A reminder," I murmured. It filled my heart with something bright. No, *he* had done that. "Thank you. It's perfect. And..." I bent over him, kissed him—just a light touch, but it brought a low hum from his chest. "And you... thank you for being thoughtful and kind... for encouraging me... for letting me be myself... for liking that..." I shook my head, too many things trying to come out at once.

His hand planed up my back, jingling the jewels draped there. "I like that *very* much indeed."

I felt his words as much as I heard them and it was too much to bear being this far from his lips when they said such things, so I kissed him.

He must've felt the same, because he pulled me to him, crushing, wanting, and he delved, eager to taste every part of my mouth. I stretched along his hard body, its strength making me feel safe in a way I hadn't since my parents had been alive.

I gave myself to that feeling, letting go of fear, falling into him completely.

His hand at my back, his fingers in my hair, the scrape of his stubble—this was better than good. It was a perfectly tailored jacket or a lost glove returned to its partner.

It was right.

We kissed and explored, breaths coming faster, harder. His pulse thrummed against my lips as I tasted the corded lines of his throat, and then, somehow, I was beneath him, whimpering at the pleasure he spiked through me with just a kiss.

I wanted more than just a kiss, though.

I took him between my legs, mere fabric between his hardness and my core, and our movements became more forceful as we pressed together. My body throbbed, pleasure bright in every nerve.

His hand skimmed down my shoulder to my breast, the fine spidersilk doing little to dampen the sensation. His every touch was fire, lighting me up, roaring through me until I trembled beneath him, the want overwhelming.

"Ly," I whispered against his lips, "please." I didn't know how to say what I wanted and my tongue seemed interested only in kissing, not words.

But his dark eyebrows rose and he pulled back an inch. "You want—?"

"Yes." I slid my fingers down the powerful planes of his back, savouring the strong muscles so unlike my own soft body. "I want you." I kissed him, body arching of its own volition. "All of you."

A slow smile dawned on his mouth and he looked at

me like he was replaying my words, committing the moment to memory—us entwined together in the star-studded darkness. After a long while, that smile turned cocky and his hand slid around to my back. "Then I'd better get you up to my room, hadn't I?"

"No." I clutched the front of his shirt. "Here. This. It's perfect."

The cockiness vanished and he sank against me, propped up on his elbows, gaze crossing my face in a way that made me want to run and hide. But I was trapped. Utterly. Willingly. And all I could do was squirm.

"Perfect," he murmured, the word blowing across my lips and leaving them tingling in its wake.

This night. He just meant *this night* was perfect, with the stars and the new moon. Not me. But each coupled beat—*ba-dum*—of my pounding heart said, *A lie. A lie. A lie.*

He feathered a lock of hair from my cheek and pushed it behind my ear, where he paused to trace the rounded line that was so different from his own. All I could do was take shaky breaths and cling to him like the world had dropped away and he was all that remained.

He nudged his nose to mine, all trace of the arrogant lord gone. "It is, isn't it?"

I smiled as I kissed him, opened my mouth to him, let him claim my lips, my tongue, the sensitive roof of my mouth. And when his hands slid to the clasp at the back of my neck that would let my gown fall away like it was nothing more than dreams come dawn, I let him claim that, too.

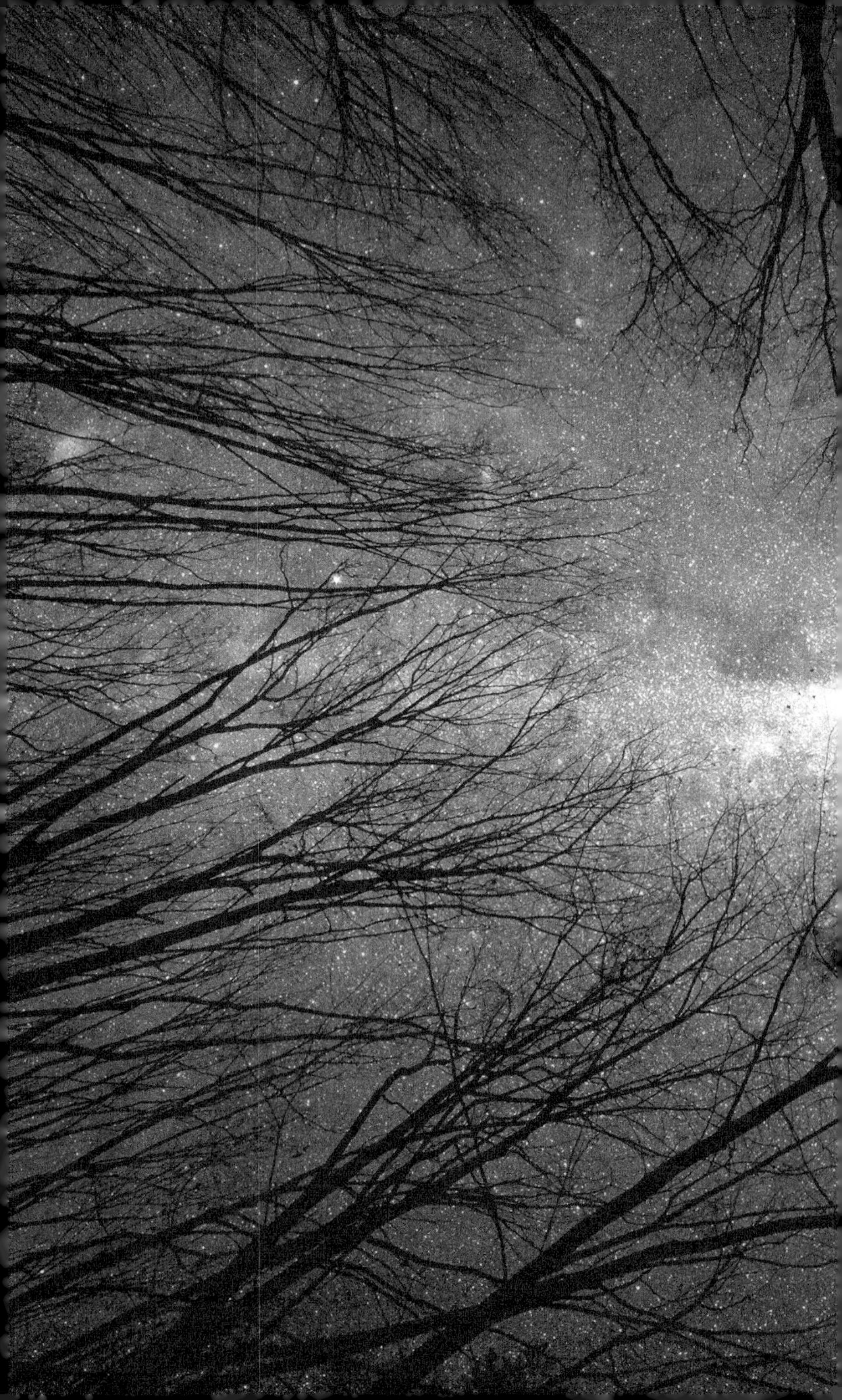

MINE

The clasp clicked in Ly's grip and my breaths heaved, fast but not with panic for once.

He gave a gentle tug, and a low growl came from his throat. "I swear you created this thing to torture me."

I chuckled, the sound throaty and low, so unlike me. Yet I felt more myself than ever. "I thought you liked it."

"Yes, but that's the problem." He glowered at the offending clasp as I angled to one side to give him better access. "I've had to see you wearing it all evening—the tease of your back and leg... and now I can't get the damn thing off. Ah, *there*." His teeth flashed in triumph.

My laughter faded as the shoulder straps slackened. Pulse thundering in every fibre, I stared up at him as his grin disappeared and became something at once gentle and heated.

Lying here, his hardness pressed into my hip. It was sizeable in a way that sent delicious tension coiling within me and gripped my throat with apprehension all at once.

Sylvie had too casually dropped into conversation that fae males took a tincture every month, which meant they couldn't father a child, so I was in no danger of that. But still...

"I..." I swallowed, cheeks so hot, I had to be blushing. "I'm no innocent maiden, but... it's been a long time." Years, in fact. And then... even Callum's kisses had been nothing like *this*.

Ly kissed my throat, my scars. "Then I'll make sure you're ready." He spoke against me, stubble scraping my sensitive flesh, making my breath catch. "And you can tell me at any point to stop."

I exhaled what was almost another laugh. "You haven't even started yet."

"Hmm." The sound rumbled from his lips into the jumping pulse at my throat. "Challenge accepted."

A thrill surged through me. It *had* been a long time and gods damn it, I was ready for this.

Although the back of my gown scooped to just below my waist, the neckline at the front was high, brushing my collarbones, and Ly started there with a feathering kiss. He slid the straps down off my shoulders and followed with his lips, the slick swipe of his tongue, and all the while I barely knew how to breathe, how to do anything more than cling to his shirt.

I gasped as one of his canines scraped my collarbone, and he tugged the gown lower.

He kissed me a hundred times, a thousand. My

shoulders. Down my chest, the tendrils of my scars. Over my heart. Then the straps reached my elbows, trapping my arms at my sides, and he exposed my breasts to the cool night air.

I couldn't contain myself—every part of me was too tight, too hot, too empty, too full.

He flicked me a glance, eyes dark and gleaming, half-lidded. A smile played at the edge of his mouth like he'd uncovered a rare treasure. Not releasing my gaze, he trailed his fingernail along the chain of my necklace, each link clinking as he passed. When he reached the pendant, his touch pressed the cool claw into my flesh.

I can.

He didn't only want me; he *believed* in me.

Chest full and warm, I splayed my fingers over the velvet blanket. If they'd been free, I would've cupped his cheek and kissed him.

Instead I lay there as he held me in his darkly burning gaze.

He stroked one thumb over my nipple and it furled under his touch, shooting pleasure to my very centre.

Biting back a whimper, I gripped the soft velvet, crushing its pile. Good gods, he'd only pulled my gown to my waist but I was already trembling with need. "Please," I managed on a gasp. I just wanted—*needed* him to take me. This was too much to bear.

"I will." His voice came out husky, belying his cocky smirk. "But I promised to make sure you were ready, and ready you will be."

Damn it, why had I told him it had been a while?

A moment later, there were no more thoughts, because he replaced the pad of his thumb with his lips and tugged my nipple into his hot mouth.

Body jolting, arching, I bit back a cry. Wetness pooled between my legs, and every breath tore through me. "I'm ready now." Somehow I said it between gasps.

But he shook his head, still holding me in his lips, sparking more pleasure in my sensitive flesh. Sucking, he pulled away. "Not ready enough. And I can tell you're holding back, keeping quiet."

That and the dangerous flash of teeth should've warned me.

He blew across my glossy, wet nipple and the sudden cold, the not-quite-a-touch sent sparks flying behind my eyelids as I screwed them shut.

I fell against the cushions, biting my lip so hard the skin had to be close to breaking.

"*Tsk tsk*, Ari, that will never do. I want to hear all those glorious sounds you're holding between your teeth."

Panting, I stared at him, but he only smiled and took my other nipple in his mouth in sweet, sweet torture as he pulled my gown lower.

I couldn't keep still, squirming under him as his kisses trailed to my belly, to the top edge of my dress, lingering just above the dark triangle of hair at the apex of my legs.

He huffed a laugh that tickled across my bare flesh, and held my hips still. Despite that commanding gesture, he looked up, now kneeling between my legs, and raised his eyebrows in question.

Yes. Oh, gods, yes. I didn't want him to stop.

Ever.

I might've spent hours making this gown, but he could rip it off me right now for all I cared, as long as it had him inside me sooner.

I nodded harder than I'd ever nodded in my life.

He pressed a single, firm kiss right below my belly button and peeled my dress down, leaving me utterly exposed. It was such a light design, I hadn't worn any underwear, and his eyebrows flashed upwards like he was surprised at the discovery.

Lying there, I tried to catch my breath, and part of me whispered that I should be ashamed to be lying here under the stars, naked and wanton, especially while he was still fully clothed. But I couldn't find an ounce of shame or regret—there was no room in me for that, not when every fibre of my body thrummed with need.

Not when his name was a whisper in my heart.

Hair gleaming violet-blue in the dim light, he set my gown aside and resumed his spot kneeling between my thighs. He drank me up with his gaze, like he was some dark god of night and I was an offering upon his altar.

"Ari," he breathed, hands sliding up my calves, "you are the most beautiful sight I ever beheld."

That warmed me deep inside as his palms planed over my knees and up my thighs, every touch of his skin upon mine at once reverent and blazing.

I knew what came next. He would push my legs

apart, free himself from his breeches, and push inside me. And I was ready for that—*needy* for it.

But instead, he hooked his arms under my thighs and lifted my hips, pulling them over his knees, making me gasp as my necklace fell against my throat.

Staring at his mouth hovering closer to my sensitive flesh, I gripped his solid thighs. "What are you doing?"

His lips grazed my inner thigh, right where a silvery scar threaded, but the corner of his mouth rose. "Making sure you're ready." A frown flickered between his brows. "Have you never tasted a man's cock or had a man taste your sweet pussy, Ariadne?"

My mouth went dry. I managed to swallow. "I've... kissed, tasted, taken a man there." I touched my lips, and Ly's hungry gaze followed the movement of my fingers as though it was the most important thing in the world at that moment. "But I didn't know..." I shook my head. Rose had told me about her conquests but not in so much detail. I'd have remembered if she'd mentioned *this*. "It can be done the other way around?"

He grinned and kissed my thigh again, higher. "Oh, yes. Let me show you."

Gripping my hips, he trailed his way up my thighs with his mouth and tongue. One sharp canine grazed the delicate skin, and I bucked with another gasp.

He fixed me with his dark eyes, expression suddenly serious. "I'll never hurt you, Ari." He squeezed my hip, his other hand trailing up my belly. "This I swear." He palmed one heavy breast, then the other, threatening to pull a moan from my tight throat. A faint smirk gave another flash of his canines. "Unless it's the pleasurable kind of pain."

"Pleasurable pain?" I frowned. "Isn't that a contradiction?"

"You tell me." He pinched my nipple, and I jolted as the pain *and* pleasure darted through me, driving a soft sound of surprise from my mouth.

Catching my breath, I nodded. "I... I see."

"Good." He grinned, cheeks flushing, then resumed his path of kisses along my thigh, up, up, up, until...

His lips landed on my apex, soon followed by his tongue dragging its way right through the centre of me, lighting up my flesh.

"Oh!" I clutched his thighs as though they might keep me tethered to the world.

His eyes on me crinkled like he was smiling as his mouth continued exploring, driving bright, bright joy through my core, radiating out to every part of me.

Sucking, licking, kissing. Between and inside, then around that tight bud of nerves that throbbed harder and harder.

He shifted his grip, fingers digging into my curved hips, holding me steady, then his thumb rested against my back passage. He didn't enter, but it felt forbidden all the same. And... and so sensitive, heightening all that his mouth was doing inside and around my pussy.

Good gods. I was a thread pulled taut, ready to snap. My muscles thrummed, so tight I thought *I* might snap.

I'd spent all these weeks so keenly aware of his every touch and wanting, wanting, wanting. And here he was, lapping me up, tongue delving into me, thumb massaging such a secret part of me, not once releasing me from his gaze.

I covered my mouth as my breaths came in tight little gasps. I couldn't contain it anymore.

His thumb slid higher, to my slick entrance and pressed there as his tongue tormented the bundle of nerves that was so sensitive, so responsive to his touch.

Tighter, the thread of me strained at breaking point.

"Let go, Ari." His murmur fanned my hot flesh, driving fresh spikes of sensation through me.

I pulled my hand from my mouth and instead gripped the spur pendant. *I could.*

Glancing at my fisted hand, he inclined his head. "Let me please you." Then his mouth was back on me, tongue flicking across my bud as his thumb slid into my centre.

I broke, bucking like the snapped end of a thread whipping towards its needle. There was nothing but darkness and the spark of shooting stars and his touch, burning through me. In the distance, there was a low cry.

When I came back to myself and blinked at the sky above, he was still on me, *in* me. A low sound of approval hummed into my core, coiling more delicious tension.

That... I couldn't... What had he *done* to me? I'd never known anything like that, anything so sweet and devastating all at once.

But he wasn't finished.

He replaced his thumb with one finger, two, taking up a steady thrust as his tongue made slow circles. Each stroke tightened me further until I broke apart again under his mouth, around his skilled digits.

Still, he didn't stop.

He sent me over the edge once more before kissing my belly and cupping his hand around my throbbing centre. "Do you think you're ready, my evening star?"

My breaths heaved too much for words, so I nodded hard and hoped he understood the depth of my need. Although he'd given me such pleasure already—more than I'd known in my life—I still ached to have him inside me.

"I think you are, too." With a smile, he set my hips back on the blanket and unbuttoned his shirt.

Kneeling, I tried to help, but my hands shook and were of little help. Still, I revelled in the feel of his hard body and soft skin, the chance to finally touch his muscled stomach and broad chest as I pushed up the hem of his shirt. When I fumbled with the buttons of his breeches, he huffed a soft laugh and captured my fingers before kissing their tips.

"Let me." He grinned and pressed a quick, impulsive kiss to my mouth.

Then he was free, the length of him, the *width*, making my eyes widen. Perhaps it was just as well he'd lavished me with so much attention.

Touch more sure, I ran a finger along the underside of his cock and a low hum rumbled in his chest. Utterly solid beneath soft skin. I smiled and wrapped my hand around him, not able to make fingertips and thumb touch. He twitched as I slid down his length.

"Good gods, Ari, I love your hands." His chest heaved and when I looked up, I found his gaze transfixed by my grip on him. "Always have. But now..." He shook his head and cupped my cheek, pulling me in for a searing kiss as I worked him up and down.

By the time he pulled away, his breaths were as fast as mine and a bead of moisture had formed at his tip, coating my palm.

Hands on my shoulders, he pushed me back as though giving himself space, then shucked off his boots and breeches. His muscles worked and rippled, each movement revealing some new shadowy indent that I couldn't help but touch.

"Ly, you're..." I shook my head.

He threw his breeches to one side and slid his hands around my waist, heavy gaze meeting mine. His thumbs traced idle circles on my hips as though he could map my bones, my being. "*Yours* is what I am."

My heart skipped one beat, maybe two. Under the Tithe I was his, but this... this was him choosing to say he was mine, and he couldn't lie. I had no words for that, didn't even know what to make of it, so I threaded my fingers into his hair and pulled him closer.

With a kiss that I felt right down to the tips of my toes, he lay me back on the blanket and took his weight on his forearms. Then he was at my entrance, pausing as if to check I was still sure.

"Please," I breathed against his lips.

He nodded and, tongue stroking mine, he eased into me.

One inch, two, three...

His neck, his shoulders, his back and arms, every part of him under my hands was solid, thrumming with tension as he entered so slowly, I thought I might die.

My centre throbbed around him, stretching as he pushed. A low groan rumbled from his mouth into mine and I couldn't help but answer with my own.

At last he was done and paused there, filling me completely. I pulled from his lips and took a few deep breaths, easing into the sensation.

His gaze flicked over my face, a frown of concern between his brows. "Are you—?"

"Yes. Gods, yes." I huffed a soft laugh that brought me tighter around him and dissolved into a moan.

"So keen." He smirked and pushed a stay lock of hair from my face before pulling out of me entirely.

The emptiness made me gasp, then a moment later, it was gone as he filled me inch by inch, quicker this time. I choked on a cry, fingers digging into his back of their own accord.

"Stars above," he breathed into my ear, "you feel so good, Ari." He kissed and nipped at my neck as he took another slow draw out. "I could just do this for the rest of time."

I tried to laugh at the ridiculousness of that idea—for one thing, we needed to eat and drink—but he drove back into me then, and I hovered on the edge of oblivion.

His chest heaved against mine, trapping my pendant between us, his hairs tickling my nipples adding more layers to the overwhelming sensations he wrought in me. He withdrew again and gripped my hip before driving in, a little harder, a little faster, somehow deeper.

I moaned, pushing up to take him, to take everything. My thundering pulse throbbed through my body, threatening to drown me in pure pleasure.

With the next thrust, he fastened his mouth over my nipple and I fell.

I cried out, louder than before, unable to help myself, unable to bring myself to care whether anyone could hear, because there was only us, only him inside me, only the drowning ecstasy.

He destroyed and remade every part of me.

When I blinked and knew the rest of the world once more, he was maintaining that steady rhythm into me, a smile on his lips, eyes bright.

"I could watch you fall apart forever." That grip on my hips tightened as he angled them and deepened his claiming of me, stealing the air from my lungs. He kissed me, part sweet, part savage. "I want to make you scream my name, though."

"Scream?" I rarely spoke out loud, never mind anything more, and right now I could barely speak between panted breaths. "I'd never."

"We'll see." His words came out with a growled edge as his muscles solidified under my hands.

Then there were no more words, only his steady drive into me, his hand sliding from my hip over my belly, my breasts. His lips on my throat, my shoulders, my mouth. The softness of his magnificent hair between my fingers, tickling my neck, gleaming in the darkness. My legs wrapping around his hips, accepting him, claiming him for my own.

Good gods, he was mine.

That's what he'd said and now his body was proving the truth of those words, making me his but equally making him *mine*.

Maybe that was what I'd meant with my whispered *please* against his lips when this all began.

With a harsh cry, I splintered into a thousand shooting stars in his night sky.

His groan rumbled into me as he stroked my hair and kissed me. A few strokes later his body jerked. He spilled inside me, marking me as his even in that secret place, bellowing my name into the dark.

Our breaths mingled in the stillness, and I held him close, kissing his hair, the side of his neck, anywhere I could reach, as he buried his face in the crook between my neck and shoulder. For all that he'd been in charge throughout this, right now vulnerability shook through him, and I cradled him in my arms, between my legs.

Somehow, with that *please*, I'd asked for what I wanted for once, and here it was—here *he* was.

I'd asked and received. Thoroughly.

"Ly," I whispered, fingers weaving through his hair, "I... that was... thank you."

With a shaky exhale, he pushed himself up, just enough to meet my gaze. "I'm the one who should be thanking you, my..." His throat bobbed and he shook his head. "You are perfect. All I could want."

My heart did something strange and my mouth

didn't know how to respond, so I let it do something else —something much easier—and I kissed him.

We lay under the stars, naked and sated, entwined. When the cool air finally quenched all the heat he'd raised in me, I shivered, and at once Ly produced a cloth and cleaned between my legs before pulling his jacket around my shoulders and tugging his breeches on. In one swift movement, he took me in his arms and carried me towards the darkened house.

On the way, we kissed and I took advantage of the fact his arms were taken up with carrying me. I explored his chest, his nipples, which hardened under my touch, the lines of his throat and jaw, and finally his ears. By the time we reached his chambers, his pace had gone from leisurely to determined, and his breaths came edged with a growl when he threw me onto the bed.

We didn't sleep for quite some time.

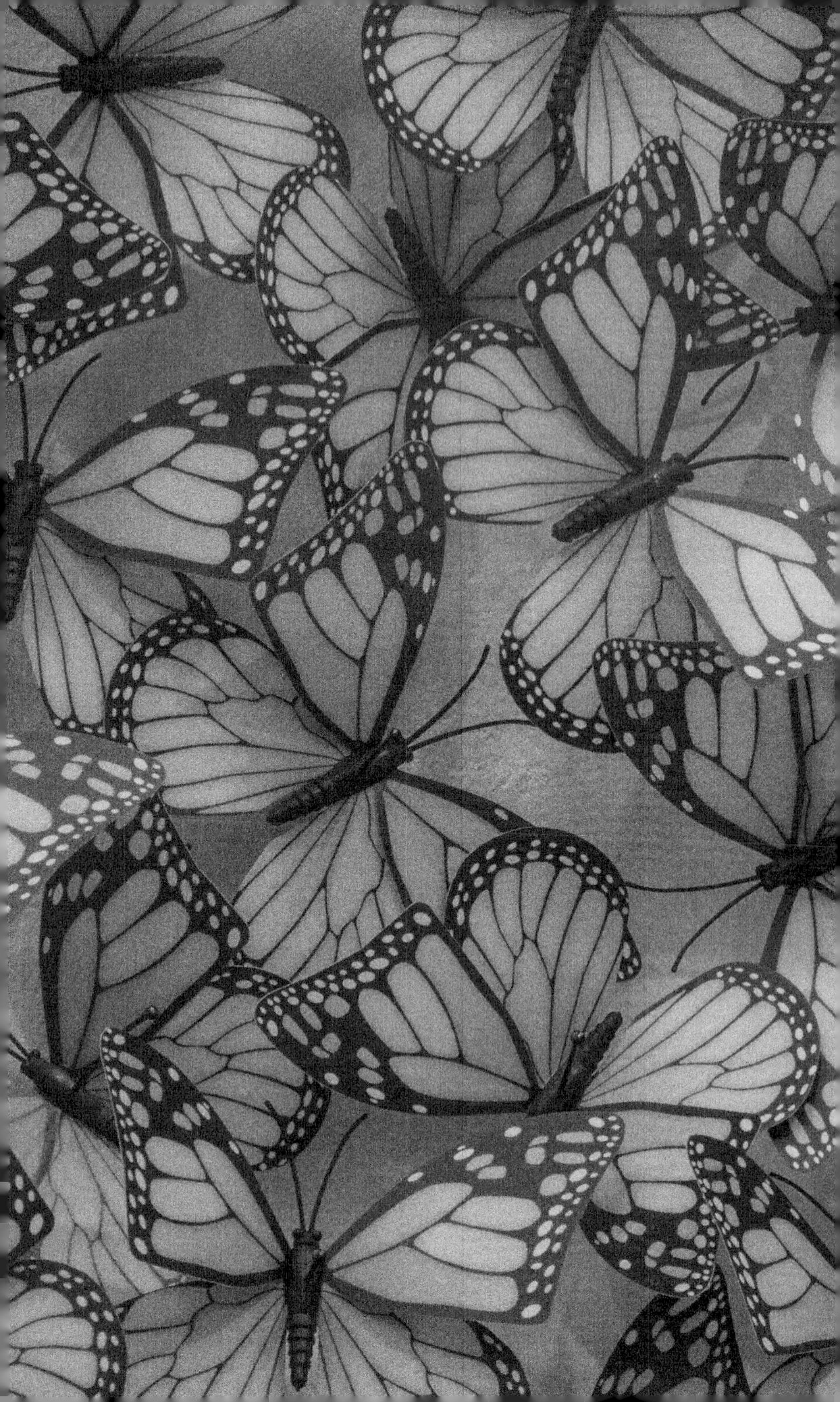

The Morning After the Night Before

Faint sunlight trickled around the edges of the curtains, but I was warm, in a huge bed, and tucked against something solid.

Someone solid.

Ly. Who just might be mine. How had that happened? Some miracle I wasn't about to question. I smiled and wriggled closer, arm draping over his waist.

"Ari?" He spoke against my hair, hand planing up my back. "Does that mean you're awake?"

"No. So tired." My limbs and head were heavy as though all the fear from last night had caught up with me.

"You stay here, then." He kissed the top of my head, my cheek, my other cheek, a slow smile easing into place. His hair was tousled from sleep, his shoulders relaxed, and he had never looked more gorgeous. "I need to go and attend to some business."

I made a soft sound of protest, but he pressed a quick kiss to my lips.

"You see"—he nudged my nose with his—"I have this demanding threadwitch, and I'm scared of what she might do if she runs out of fabric, so I need to work to keep her in supplies."

"I hear she's highly dangerous." My hand went to the pendant he'd given me—the only thing I wore under the sheets. "She smacked one of the sluagh with a piece of wood, don't you know?"

He chuckled and kissed me again, lips lingering even as his feet slid out of the covers. "I'd heard as much. She's positively dangerous." He paused half out of bed, gaze caressing me in a way that made me fidget under the covers. "Or at least she is to me. I think she could get me to do anything she wished."

"Useful to know." I scoffed, even as my eyelids drifted shut in slow, heavy blinks.

With a groan, he dragged himself from the bed, and I forced my eyes to stay open a little longer as the encroaching sun painted his naked body with hazy light. The powerful lines of his arms, the muscles of his back, the trim line of his waist and hips.

I must've fallen asleep, because the next thing I knew, the light at the edges of the curtains was brighter and Ly was gone. When I rose, I found a set of my clothes folded on a chair, so I wouldn't be spotted leaving his room in last night's gown. I wasn't even sure I could put it back on without help. On top was a square of paper.

I'll bring you lunch. Ever yours, L.

The warmth of that note clung to me as I dressed, slipped it in my pocket, and crept out the door.

"So it finally happened." Boyd's low voice drawled.

Gasping, I turned and found him watching me, arms folded. My cheeks burned, but I had a weapon he didn't—I could lie. "I needed to borrow—"

"A bed?" He raised an eyebrow. "Don't insult me with your stories. This was inevitable. Fae men like to enjoy human women. Your curves, your dim little magic, the fact you'll be dead in the blink of an eye." He snorted.

Despite my hot face, a deep cold threaded through my bones and my belly, tying me down.

"Of course he bedded you. You're exotic and unusual. Those soft handfuls of flesh are a fun diversion for any male. You're nothing more than a novelty."

I flinched. It was like I'd been punched in the gut—one of the Briarbridge boys had done that once, when Rose had been busy helping her parents with the bakery. I hadn't been able to breathe then and my lungs refused to cooperate now.

Because Boyd couldn't lie.

Besides, hadn't I thought these things before? Those men and women who returned, longing for something they could never regain, pining and fading away for its lack... They were just playthings to fae lords.

And so was I.

"What's wrong, girl?" He cocked his head, a small,

cruel smile edging his lips, glinting in his golden eyes. "Did you think you might actually hold more interest for him than something new and interesting between the sheets for a few nights?" He laughed, canines gleaming as the sound cut through me. "Humans are even more stupid than I thought."

Arms folding, I hugged myself and something smooth dug in to my breasts. The pendant.

Ly wouldn't have given that to someone who was just a conquest. A meaningless trinket, perhaps, but not this—he'd had it made for me to give a specific message.

Still, my eyes burned as I turned and made for my workroom, muttering, "You're wrong."

He had to be.

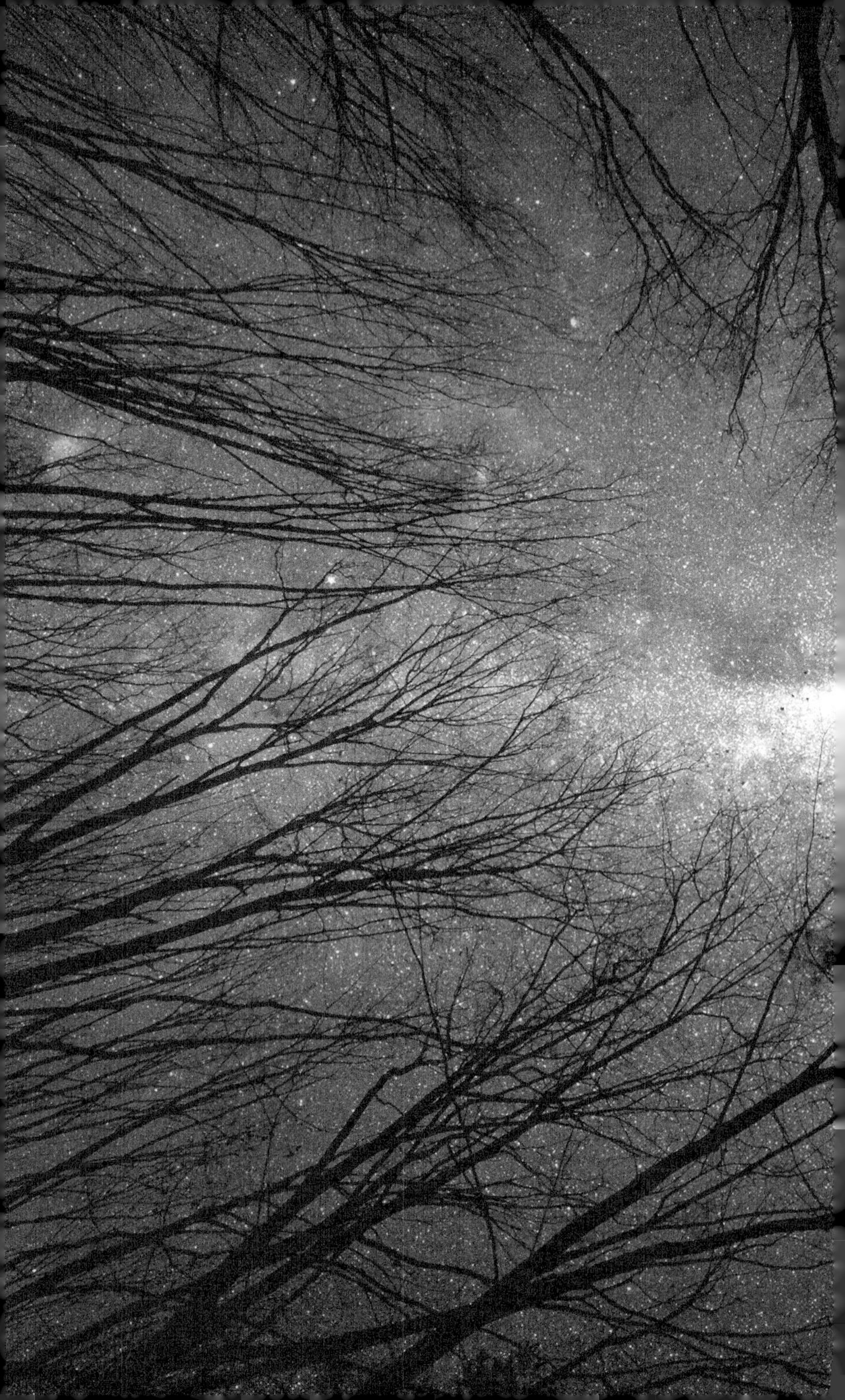

An Invitation

I threw myself into my work, not bothering with breakfast. I needed that dip and pull of needle in cloth to centre me, distract me. The breeches were almost done and just needed hemming after the next fitting. The jacket and shirt waited on buttons, buttonholes, and hems. Sylvie popped in to check how I was but didn't stay long.

The sewing bird sat on the edge of the table and my gaze kept skipping over to its blue-violet steel as I lined up the buttonhole cutter. Like the pendant, Ly wouldn't have given it to me if I was only "a fun diversion." It had belonged to his mother: it meant something to him.

I meant something to him.

Didn't I?

A mere human, pathetic and weak. Already dead.

Gritting my teeth, I smacked the mallet into the buttonhole cutter.

"Imagining that's a sluagh or Goren?"

My heart leapt when I found Ly standing in the doorway. Had he come to tell me what Boyd had said was true or...?

Head tilting, he entered. He held up a tiered cake stand full of sandwiches and sweet treats. "Hil said you didn't appear for breakfast, so I thought you might need an extra large lunch." The smile he gave me, gentle, warm—it wasn't a smile that said Boyd was right.

Still, I couldn't bring myself to go to the table where he deposited the cake stand as a tea set winked into existence. If he had come to let me down gently, going over there would mean this was all over when it had barely started.

"Ari?" A flicker of a frown appeared between his eyebrows, and he stalked closer. "Are you all right?"

"I'm..." I put the mallet and cutter down. "Yes, I'm fine."

"No"—he paused at arm's length—"*regrets* about last night?" His chest rose and didn't fall, and his gaze fixed on my hand resting on the table.

"You think *I*...?" I huffed, shaking my head. "Gods, no. *No*."

He blew out a low sigh and closed the distance between us. "Then..." His hands landed on my shoulders and slid down my arms. "Are you tired? Or...?" He shrugged, eyebrows rising in question.

Why are you acting so strangely? That's what he meant.

I'd let Boyd get to me. And Goren's magic that had made the changeling appear to me. Their words had wormed their way inside my mind.

Wincing, I tugged on Ly's shirt. "Tired and... so much has happened... and I wanted to make progress on this, so you could teach Goren a lesson." Again, that quiet venom sounded in my voice.

Ly nodded at the mallet. "So it *was* him, then?" He grinned, making me ache to kiss the dimple in his cheek. "Well, you're going to need your strength—I had no idea sewing was so energetic."

Before I could laugh, he scooped me over his shoulder.

"Ly! What are you—?"

"Delivering you to your lunch." Under my belly, his shoulder shook with laughter as he gripped me by the backside and crossed to the armchairs.

Cheeks burning, I wriggled. "Firstly, I can walk."

"Yes, but you weren't doing so, were you? You didn't even make it down to the kitchen for breakfast."

"And secondly, I'm sure you don't need to hold my bottom."

"Ah, you've got me there." He gave a squeeze, and my pulse sped. "I don't *need* to, but I *like* to. It's such a lovely bottom—wonderfully round and soft and positively glorious. Besides, your heart rate says you don't mind me doing this *at all*."

One eyebrow raised, grin utterly wicked, he set me on my feet.

"My heart rate is a traitorous fool." I glared up at him. The effect was probably spoilt by my flushed cheeks and breathlessness. "But maybe it has a point." Hands sliding up his chest, I tiptoed to his lips and lost myself there for a while.

Just as a low groan sounded in his throat, and his grip on me tightened, I pulled away and smiled sweetly. "Our sandwiches are drying out."

He made another sound that might've been a growl, but he nodded and waited for me to sit before serving me tea and the little sandwiches Hil had made.

As I picked up the first one, he watched, intent.

"What?" I frowned and swiped at my cheek in case a stray thread was caught on me.

Head tilting, that warmth entered his eyes, and he lifted one shoulder. "I'm just enjoying the fact you don't wear a hood anymore. I like getting to see you."

My cheeks flushed as I touched my hair. I hadn't even thought about my hood in weeks.

"In Briarbridge, I saw how you hid, how you spoke softly, kept small." A frown ghosted between his brows. "I don't think it was something new or something you did because I was there. I think that place kept you that way."

My chest filled, not with suffocating wadding but with something bright and warm, as though his hand rested over my heart. I blew out a shaky breath. "I think you're right."

He bit his lip, but a smile tugged it from between his teeth. "Much as I cursed her when I received the order, I'm glad the Queen made me go to Briarbridge."

So am I. But the words stuck in my throat, so we ate our sandwiches and turned the conversation to lighter subjects. We drank cup after cup of tea, poured from a pot that never ran out, and all the while, he insisted on serving me.

The next tier of the stand contained a dozen varieties of cake, each no larger than a mouthful, and on the top tier were scones with little pots of raspberry and rhubarb jams and clotted cream. Ly called it "afternoon tea" and that tugged on a faint memory. Lady Hawthorne had once asked me to make her a day dress that would impress her guests at afternoon tea.

It looked more like dessert than a meal, but I was *not* about to complain about that.

When I peered at the cakes, trying to choose which to devour first, he craned over the gap between our chairs.

"This is the best." He pointed at one that was flat and round and a vibrant orange-yellow. It had two parts with buttercream and what might've been lemon curd sandwiched in the middle. "It's a macaron. Tastes like sunshine, and I guarantee it'll make you smile."

I raised an eyebrow. "Tastes like sunshine? Is this like your magic tasting of starlight?"

He bit his lip in this way that made me ache to kiss him. "You noticed that, then?"

"Of course I did."

"Well, this is... more of a metaphorical sunshine. It's flavoured with yuzu, this knobbly-looking citrus fruit Sallis and Hobb grow in the orangery. But"—he inhaled and touched his chest, shaking his head—"the flavour always reminds me of the best summer days."

His gaze went distant, like he was drifting off in

memories, and I wanted to know them—*all* of them. My heart stuttered at the realisation.

I wasn't just falling, I'd tumbled all the way down and had landed.

"I've stunned her to silence," he murmured, the dimple making an appearance.

I didn't dare speak. If I did, for all that I could lie, I might blurt the terrifying truth. My pulse roared in my ears, almost as loud as when I'd fled the sluagh or Goren's not-changeling.

"Ari, are you—?"

"*Ahem.*" Boyd.

Of course. Was he destined to appear every time I realised something about my feelings for Ly or our relationship took a new direction?

And was he back to repeat his earlier sentiments? *You're nothing more than a novelty.*

Hands twisting in my lap, I hung my head.

"A message arrived for you." He brought a note to Ly. I didn't look up—couldn't—but I felt his eyes on me, burning with disgust.

Once the door clicked shut, I managed a deep breath, shoving down the shame and the cruel things he'd said.

He was wrong. He was *wrong*.

Ly read the note, eyebrows pulling together, nostrils flaring with each moment.

"What the...?" The paper rustled as he screwed it up. "That... that..." But he didn't complete the sentence, only surged to his feet and paced, chest heaving.

"What is it? Who's it from? What—?"

"Goren." Shaking his head, he turned on his heel and brandished the crumpled note. "He knows about your gift. He's asked to 'borrow' you. '*Borrow*'—he used that word, like you're a carriage or a pen."

My chest tightened. "How does he know? He smelled my magic, but I didn't say anything about what—"

"I know." Eyes closed, he sighed. "Just as I have spies, so does he." He shot a scowl at the wide windows. "He'll have some in the city. They must've told him about the supplies we've ordered and pieced it together from that."

I covered my mouth like that could slow my breaths. Goren wanted me. He'd terrified me with just a spectre conjured in my mind. What was he capable of?

"The audacity of it." Ly bared his teeth, feral ferocity in the lines wrinkling his nose.

"What will you tell him?" If he denied the request, it would make Goren suspicious.

"*Tell him*? I'm damn well telling him *no*." He scoffed as though I were mad for even asking.

"You said I couldn't hide away last night because he'd get suspicious. What will this do?"

Eyes wide, Ly stared at me, muscle in his jaw ticking. Maybe he realised I was right.

"This could be..." My voice quaked so much, I had to stop and swallow. Wild Hunt, was I really about to suggest this? "It could be our chance. If I go, I can make something that will harm him." Like the unfinished gloves sitting at the bottom of the work basket. I bit my lip, stomach turning at the fact I'd even considered poisoning Ly.

"Absolutely not." His hand cut through the air. "It's too dangerous. After what he did on *my* lands... What do you think he'd do to you in his own halls?"

What do you think he'd do to you, a mere human?

I clasped my hands together, some cowardly part of me relieved that I didn't have to go.

And wasn't cowardly right? After all, I was only a human with a scrap of magic. What could I do surrounded by fae that could terrorise me with a thought, kill me with a click of their fingers?

I needed to finish those gloves. They might be my only defence against any fae who were less friendly than Ly and Sylvie.

Shoulders easing, Ly returned to his seat. "I'm sorry, I just..." He shook his head. "That man. The idea of him anywhere near you..." His knuckles paled to white as he gripped the arm of his chair.

He wouldn't need to worry about a fae woman like Sylvie—she'd be strong enough to look after herself.

We resumed lunch in near silence. When we finished, he kissed me goodbye, and I went back to work, slamming the mallet into the buttonhole cutter as my eyes burned.

All the while, my heart clenched like someone squeezed it in their fist.

He had to be regretting this. Regretting me.

Maybe I was a fool to cling on to this idea that there could be an *us*, but cling, I did.

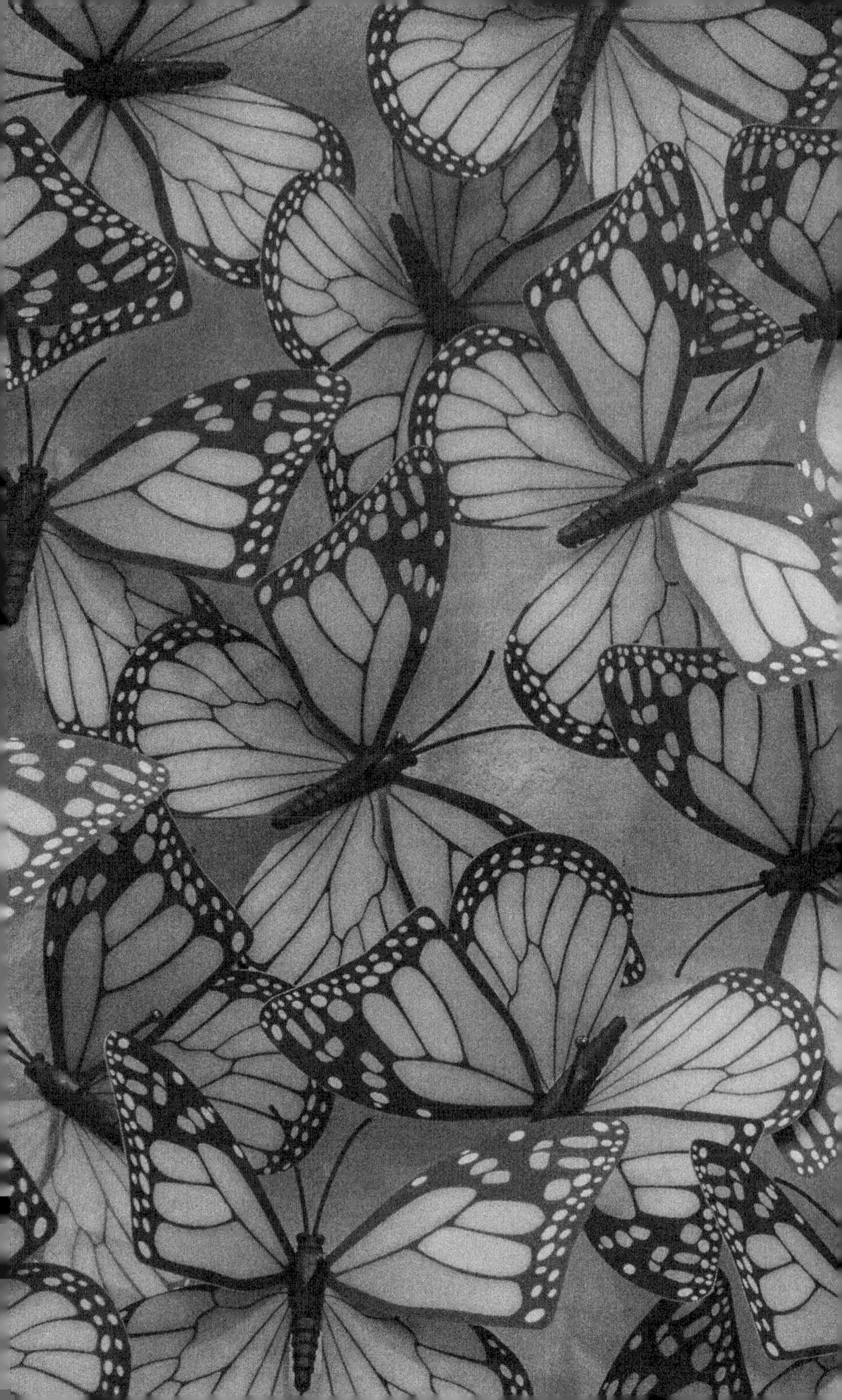

BEAUTIFUL BUT DEADLY

That night I stayed up working, even after Ly went to bed. The work—it was something I knew. It was safe. It was somewhere I belonged. Not fooling myself that I had a place in his bed.

The next few days passed in what had become my usual routine. Sewing in the morning, riding and walking in the afternoon with Ly or both him and Sylvie. When no one was around, I picked up the gloves and worked on those. In the evenings, I sewed and Ly joined me, reading or talking.

All the while, I warned myself it couldn't last. I hadn't been enough to keep Callum, how could I be enough to keep Ly? He was a fae lord, for goodness' sake.

Perhaps it made me a coward, but I still went to his room each night, and in his arms, my fears fell away.

One afternoon, a week after Calan Mai, Ly was busy, so Sylvie and I rode alone. I'd slept poorly, plagued by nightmares that combined the sluagh and Goren's not-changeling. The latter told me I was a fool, a gnat, that it should have been me, before the former sank its claws into my flesh. I woke clutching my chest, and a headache plagued me all morning.

But once we were out in the brisk breeze, the headache faded. I eased into Sylvie's chatter, which was familiar and didn't require too much input from me.

Since we were alone, she filled me in on all that had happened the night of Calan Mai as I'd only heard bits and pieces. She'd caught the wolpertinger but hadn't yet decided what boon to ask Ly for. After, Goren had returned to the house with the other guests, but he'd scowled when neither Lysander nor I appeared and left soon after.

Clouds gathered overhead as we rode through the gardens, but they were as pale as my hair and didn't threaten rain.

Beyond the garden walls, we passed huge spires of purple aconite and my mind turned to the gloves, which only needed the poison adding to their lining before I sewed it to the outer piece. With the warm weather here, they bloomed much earlier than in Albion, where they wouldn't put in an appearance until late summer.

At a natural pause in her tale, I cleared my throat. "Why would you grow faebane if it's poisonous to you?" Unless it wasn't and the stories were wrong. I grimaced. This could destroy my whole plan to have some sort of weapon I could use to keep myself safe.

Sylvie shrugged, her streaked hair gleaming in the

cloud-diffused light. "It's beautiful, isn't it? Such a rich colour—it's even more brilliant in the sunlight."

That was why I'd stared at it as a child and Papa had warned me of its danger as we'd walked along the lanes around Briarbridge. I nodded and steered Luna along the path.

"Its poison doesn't detract from its beauty." Sylvie grinned, raising her eyebrows at me. "As long as I don't touch it, I'm safe."

"True." *Beautiful but deadly*. Just like Mama had said about the fae. My gloves would be the same. I would come tonight and gather the flowers. We were well within Ly's wards, so I'd be safe from any night monsters.

We rode on, and Sylvie continued her story of the feast. Someone I didn't know had disappeared with someone else I didn't know, the implication being that they'd taken advantage of all Calan Mai had to offer.

She gave me a long look as though asking if there was anything I wanted to add.

I liked her. I *trusted* her. Another day, I might've told her like Rose told me about her flings and conquests. But my words were all tangled in my gut, like a thread hopelessly knotted.

Instead I asked her if *she'd* found anyone to disappear with and she scoffed and shook her head. "All the best ones are at court, *alas*!" She gave a dramatic flourish, and it reminded me of Rose so sharply, it stole my breath. "Except for Ly," she hurried to add as we approached the back of the house.

The yew tree creaked and shuddered in the breeze, its colour leached to a warm grey rather than rich, bark-brown. I winced at its deteriorating condition.

"It keeps him here," she went on, frowning at the diseased tree. "Otherwise, he'd be off at court, probably married by now."

My heart twisted. "Oh? Married so young?" I raised my eyebrows, trying to keep my voice light.

"Not that young. He's an adult by our reckoning and a lord. They usually marry by his age. Being stuck here and... not having his full power—it decimated his prospects."

And when he got his power back…

My heart didn't just twist, it shrivelled, leaving my chest empty.

"Not everyone is burdened with an arranged marriage. But, maybe that's not such a bad thing, eh?" She waggled her eyebrows at me. "Almost like the Stars kept him available all these years, waiting for the right woman."

Not me.

Something rushed in my ears like I was underwater. I gripped onto the reins as though they were a lifeline.

"Who'd have thought…" Sylvie went on, but I only picked up odd words. "… the Tithe…"

When Ly got his power back, he would go to court and find himself a bride. Some fae lady, elegant and tall and powerful in her own right. One who could face a room full of people without batting an eyelid. One who didn't flinch at loud noises. One who could've killed the sluagh herself.

Someone who was more than a threadwitch.

Someone who was more than me.

"... such a great match..."

Good gods, I'd been so stupid. Boyd was right. How had I ever dreamed he wasn't? Ly had squeezed my *wonderfully round bottom*. It was just as Boyd had said: *Those soft handfuls of flesh are a fun diversion for any male.*

It wasn't even the first time I'd made this mistake.

When my gift had awoken and my hair had turned white, Callum had kissed me and lured me out to the clearing in the woods where we went for privacy. We'd fucked, though I'd told myself it was making love. I had this foolish, sparkling hope that it meant he still loved me, that he didn't care that I had magic or had changed.

After, he said he'd wanted to see what it was like. He'd wondered whether a fae-touched woman was different, special.

But I wasn't. I was only a freak of nature.

And then he'd left. A week later, he was parading through town with another girl. Two months later, they were married.

And here I was making the same mistake. I'd thought Lysander liked me for my difference, but, no. I was just something to sample, a novelty for him to enjoy before he regained his power and found someone who'd be his forever.

"Ari?"

Eyes burning, I fought to control my breaths.

"*Ari?* Are you all right? What's—?"

"I'm... I don't feel well. Could you take Luna for me? I need to lie down."

Dismounting, I barely registered Sylvie's agreement before I muttered a thank you.

The world blurred as I ran inside, the pressure at the back of my eyes too much to contain, like a river bursting its banks.

What had I been thinking? Lysander had stolen me as part of a contract. And I'd be dead centuries before him. Of course he saw me as just an object, a plaything.

I'd been such a fool. Such a damn fool. Playing at pretty faerie stories and happily ever afters.

I'd been so stupid to think I belonged here... that I could have a life here.

As long as I don't touch it, I'm safe. Just like I should never have touched Lysander. What I felt for him was dangerous, and here I was about to be destroyed by it when he got his power back.

I needed to finish his outfit, get my True Name, and return to Briarbridge.

Even if the people there were horrible, nothing they did could hurt me as much as seeing Lysander marry someone else.

That would be a wound beyond bearing.

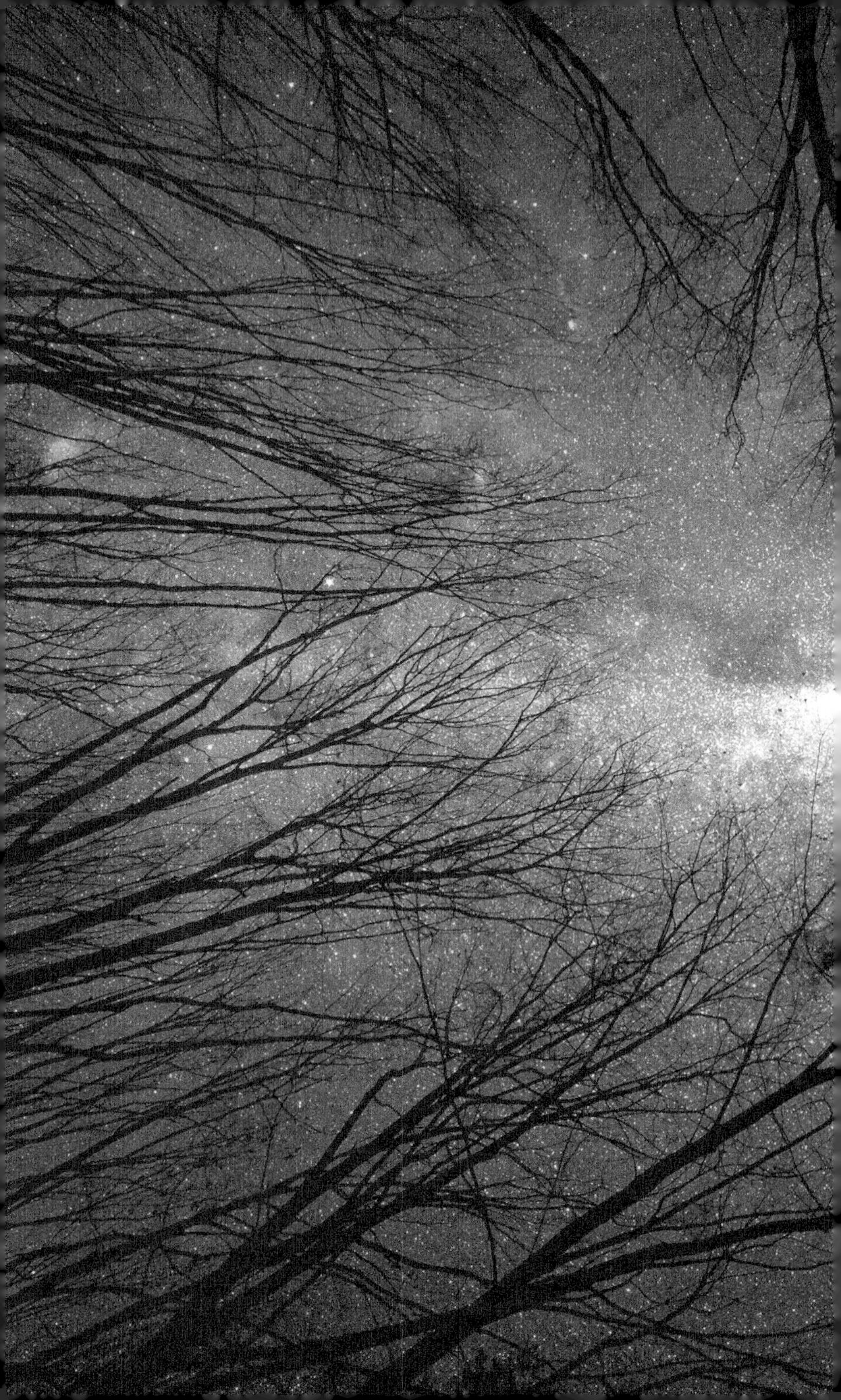

MY NIGHT

When Lysander arrived in the workshop that evening, the suit was ready save for the hems, and I'd started work on another offering for the Lady of the Lake.

"Too busy for dinner?" He grinned as he approached. The shadow of his dimple made the hole where my heart had been ache. "I missed you."

I clutched the folded suit to my chest. Maybe I could stay... maybe I could...

Then he was in arm's reach, and I brandished the suit like a shield. "You need to try this on." I shoved it at him and waved towards the dressing screen.

He didn't bother with it, undressing right before me.

Throat tight, I turned away and tidied. I tidied like my life depended on it. Loose threads in the bin. Needles straightened in their book. Thread snips back in the velvet-lined box with the other scissors and shears.

I'd unclamped the sewing bird earlier, unable to

stand looking at it, but it had left a tiny indentation on the table's edge.

And, of course, my traitorous fingers slid to it.

That little dent against my flesh. It felt more like a brand, one that marked me as the idiot who'd dared to think I could be anything more than a moth drawn to his dark flame.

"Ariadne," he breathed. "My word."

When I turned, that empty spot in my chest spasmed.

Because, good gods, he looked…

He had become the night shadows that poured off his heels when he walked. *He* was the deeper shadow in the darkness. Beautiful and deadly.

The suit was the exact colour of the motes of pure black that he became when he shadowstepped. It moulded to his square shoulders and his broad chest. It tapered to his waist and down his long legs.

Despite the empty ache in my chest, I could admit it. I had outdone myself.

The tailoring was perfect. Each bound buttonhole, even and symmetrical. The magic flowing off him flooded my mouth with raspberry and rhubarb and, as always, starlight and crisp night air.

It wasn't that I'd made his clothes. It was more that he now wore a substance so utterly made of self, he'd become what he was always meant to be.

This was a glimpse of him with his full power.

And it was glorious.

"My night." The words fell from my lips though I

hadn't told any part of me to move. It was truth. For all that I could lie, I couldn't have lied about that.

Here he was, night made flesh. And he would get his power back. No question.

That I could play this tiny part, it was almost enough to close the pit in my chest.

But not quite.

A slow smile revealed his canines again, and before I could stop him, his arms were around me. "Stars above, woman, you are..." He shook his head and twirled me around. "You're incredible."

I sank against his chest, letting myself have this moment before I did what I had to. Gods knew I couldn't say it with the full force of him upon me. I couldn't say anything. So I enjoyed the warmth, the hard lines of his body, the faint smokiness of his cologne that was only detectable at close quarters.

Because I'd never have another chance.

I tapped his arm to get him to put me down. He frowned as he did so, bending to try and meet my eye, but I turned and grabbed the bracelet pincushion and tugged it over my hand. "I need to pin the sleeves and check the fit."

That last part was a lie—the fit couldn't have been more perfect.

"Right." He straightened, but his gaze burned into me as I folded the cuffs to the right length and pinned them.

Every time I opened my mouth to say it, my tongue refused to work.

I couldn't do it. Not with him watching me.

"You need to look ahead or it'll hang unevenly." I circled behind him.

Clutching my chest, I dragged in a long breath. My eyes stung as I stared at his back. "It's over."

His shoulders rose and fell. "Thank the stars above, it soon will be. You've almost finished this suit, and then I'll—"

"I don't mean the suit. Or Goren's deceit. I mean..." Even though my heart was an empty pit, it somehow managed to pound, pressing on my ribcage. "I mean us. What we've been doing."

He whirled, lips parted, eyebrows screwed together. "What?"

I backed out of arm's reach, not because I feared him, but because I knew, if I could reach out and touch him, I would. And then I'd lose my nerve.

But the words were out there now. I'd done the hard part. I just had to get him to believe it.

"I don't want to be your novelty plaything while you wait to marry some fae lady."

He blinked, eyebrows shooting up. "*What?*" Head shaking, he took a step closer, but I kept my distance even as my hands ached to reach out. "You think...? No, *no*, Ari, that's not—"

"You *stole* me, Lysander. I have no choice about being here." Only half-true.

He hadn't stolen me: he'd acted under a bargain he was bound to, whether he liked it or not.

But I'd used the accusation against him enough

times and using it now made it easier to push him away. "Dress it up how you want, but that's what happened. In this country's law, you own me."

That *was* true. All these weeks, the idea of ownership hadn't gone away and had quietly festered inside me. "How can I be anything else? How can I be anything other than, and I quote, a 'mere human'?" I lifted my chin as I threw his own words back at him, although all I wanted to do was crumple to the floor.

Shoulders sinking, he deflated. Even his expression and his gaze dropped. "I... I... Stars above, Ariadne, I'm sorry." He scrubbed his face, a sudden weariness spelling itself out in the slack lines of his body. "I should never have given in to my feelings. Not while you were bound to me."

His words twitched through me, pushing bile to the back of my throat.

He did regret it.

Of course he did. He'd meant this to be a brief fling, a little fun. *I* was the one who'd got the wrong idea and had fallen in love with him.

Because that was the bright feeling I had every time I saw him. *Love.*

And the empty pit in my chest? *That* was where I'd ripped out my own heart so I could do this before he did.

"I'll fix this." He raked a hand through his hair, eyes darting over the floor as though it held the answer.

It couldn't be fixed. But my words were all dried up.

My stupid tears weren't, though. I thought I'd cried them all this afternoon, but fresh ones stung my eyes. I turned my back on him and tidied my perfectly tidy work table so he couldn't see.

"Leave the suit on the side." My voice came out raw like it had been torn from me. "It'll be ready for you tomorrow."

Then he'd be able to go to Goren and get the seed back. Below the terrible, dragging ache in my chest, my stomach tightened at the thought of him in Goren's lair. But he was strong, he would win. The suit would keep him hidden, and he'd get his power back.

Once that was done, I'd go to the Lady of the Lake and get my True Name and the power to break the Tithe.

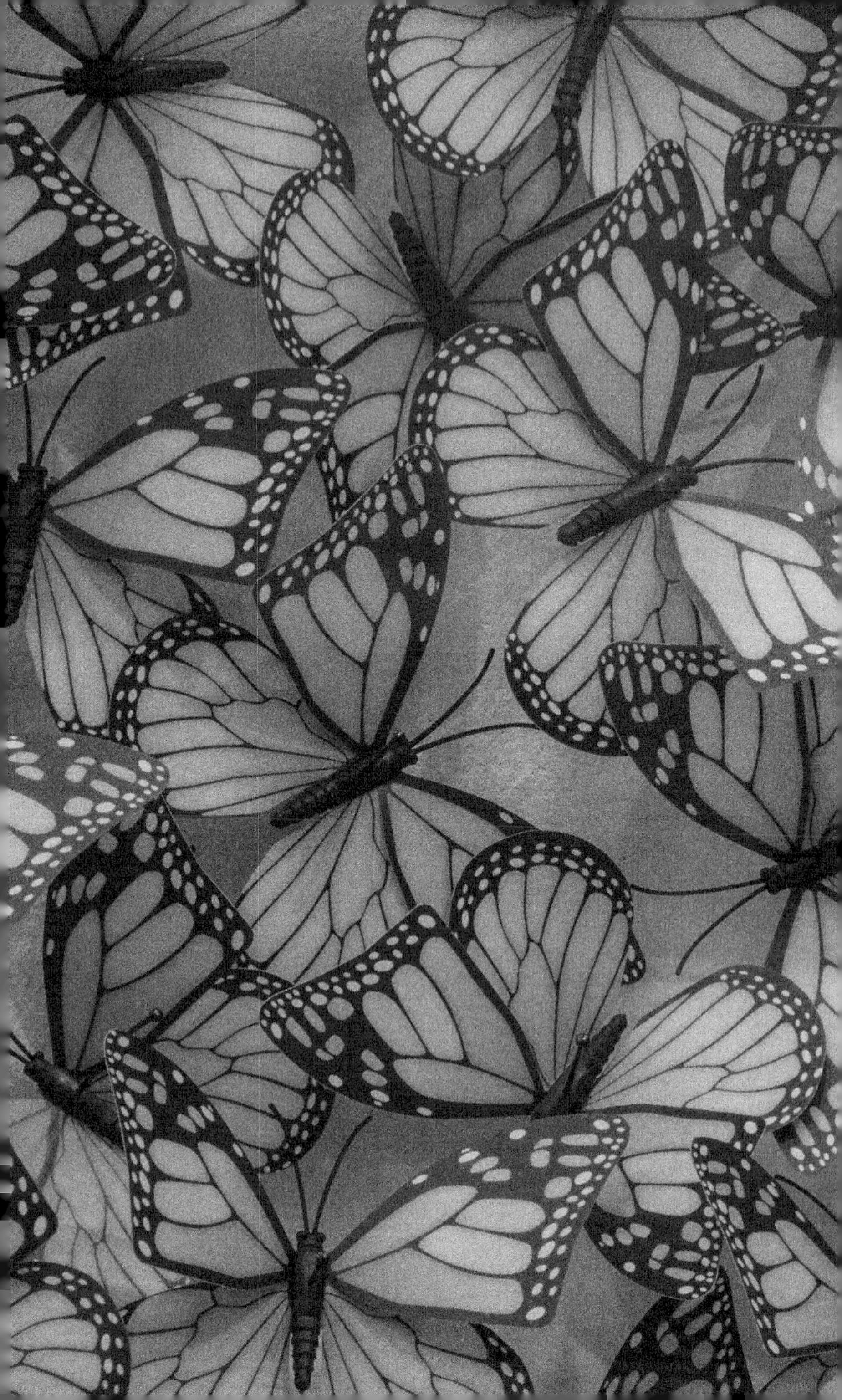

ACONITE & SALT

Tomorrow was here, and I had just one cuff to hem, then the suit would be complete. I'd already whipstitched the raw edge and pressed it under, leaving a crisp fold where I'd marked it at the fitting.

I hadn't seen him since then.

I'd only left this room to sleep late in the night, Fluffy trailing me like a flame-eyed ghost. Despite the heaviness in my gut, the soreness of my eyes, it had taken a long, long time to fall asleep. The stricken look on his face when I'd told him it was over had haunted me. And his words...

Swallowing around the thickness in my throat, I screwed up the cuff. Even now when I was meant to be working, I couldn't escape them.

I should never have given in to my feelings.

It tore my insides open afresh.

I sat that way a long time, but no more tears came. I'd given them all last night.

Today was a time for calm, a time for work.

But maybe not for hemming this cuff quite yet. Once it was done, I'd be a step closer to leaving.

I rubbed my too-tight chest and smoothed the jacket sleeve. I could finish the gloves first. I might need them on the journey home.

The thought of it made my stomach sink. Knowing Lysander, he'd offer to shadowstep me there. With the yew tree restored, he'd be able to take me all the way back to Briarbridge in one jump.

Great.

I grabbed my cloak, boots, and a pair of leather gloves and went into the gardens.

No sooner had I stepped outside than hooves clattered into the stable courtyard. At the edge of the terrace, I craned but couldn't see past the stable blocks. A messenger, perhaps.

With a sigh for the crumbling yew, I trotted down the steps and through the garden, aiming for the aconite I'd spotted just beyond the walls.

The journey home would be so much quicker than the one here. No tent. No shared bed. No running from the sluagh. No Lysander warming me under the covers.

And once I was in Briarbridge, no Lysander at all.

None of his smirks or frowns. None of his flirtation. None of his thoughtfulness.

I dropped to my knees before the aconite. The sun was out today and it set the purple hooded flowers aglow. I couldn't move, couldn't speak, couldn't do anything but kneel and breathe while my eyes filled with more burning tears at the sheer beauty.

So much for giving them all last night.

But these tears weren't just for the aconite's blazing purple or even for Lysander. They were for the land so full of crisp apple-flavoured magic and dangerous wonder. For the food that was the best I'd ever eaten. For the afternoons spent with Sylvie. For the sweet gentleness of Fluffy, my constant shadow. For the solid presence of Luna as I groomed her. For the quiet smiles of Sallis and Hobb. For the kindness of Hil. For the fact that these past couple of months, I'd finally belonged.

And for how much I'd miss it all.

When no more tears came, I scrubbed my face with my sleeves and gathered my gasping breaths.

No more tears. Work.

I tugged on the leather work gloves and pulled nine stalks of aconite, stuffing them into a sack. It was a contact poison, so if I pressed the gloves' lining between the flowers, it should infuse them. Then I could use my gift to lock the poison in place as I stitched the lining to the outer.

With heavy steps, I took the path leading back to the house. Before I reached the terrace, something long and grey blocked the way.

Eyes still sore and blurry, I blinked. A branch from the yew tree. The path had been clear when I'd left—it must've just fallen.

Another step towards death.

I needed to finish that suit, and Lysander needed to get the seed back. He would gain his full power and find a fae bride who'd live a long, long time, just like he would.

He'd be happy.

And I—I could go home and sew and one day help Rose look after her children.

It would be enough. Maybe not for joy, but for a quieter kind of happiness.

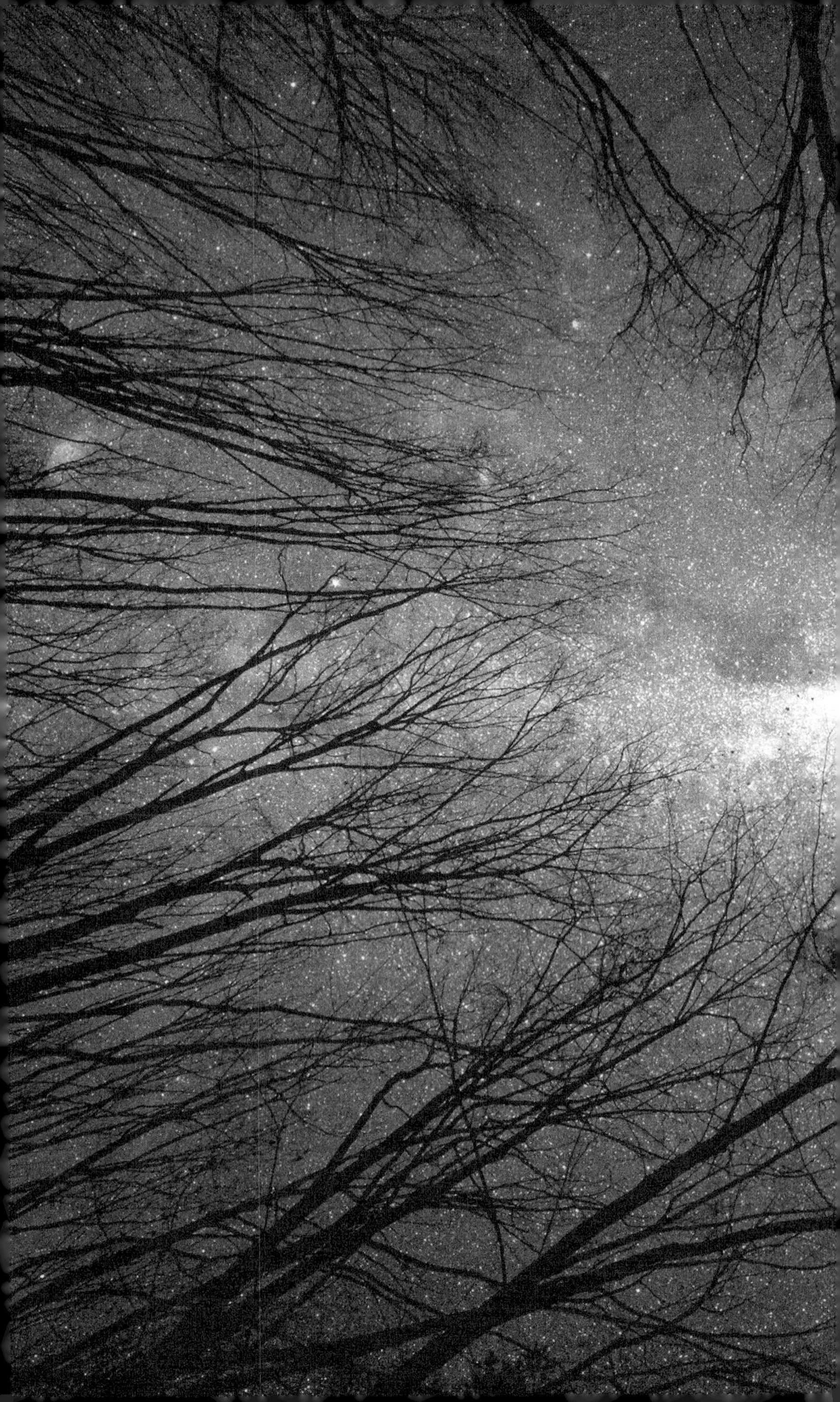

BECOMING

I left the gloves between the aconite to press overnight and finished my offering for the Lady of the Lake. Another stone, covered and embellished. If she touched the stone and asked, light would appear.

When I crept to my room, neck, shoulders, and chest aching, I found three large trunks—the type I'd seen on the back of carriages. Was this Lysander's way of asking me to pack and leave? I couldn't blame him.

But inside, I recognised the brown folded blanket, the clothes beneath. They were mine. Tucked down the side, Mama's mirror. In the next—my sewing tools in the box with a broken hinge. In the last were trinkets and Papa's books.

Everything from the cottage.

The only thing missing was the furniture. I tried to laugh at the fact it had all arrived just as I was so close to leaving, but it came out as a grunt. At least I had my things—familiar scents and textures, the worn handle of the lamp I'd carried to bed every night since I was eight.

The hole in my chest opened to a crater.

Lysander had arranged this. I'd complained that I'd been taken away without my belongings and here they were. He must've had someone pack it all and bring the trunks here on a wagon. Was that the clatter of hooves I'd heard in the stable yard?

So much trouble, just for me.

He meant it as a comfort—yet another thoughtful gesture—but as I sorted through the items, I found my shoulders sinking. I put aside Papa's books, my sewing tools, the little box of Mama's hair combs, and the winged sabrecat statuette that she'd brought from distant Thanatolia.

The rest was junk.

Threadbare clothes and blankets. A cracked mirror that only gave a murky reflection. Chipped plates and blunt cutlery.

Why the hells had I cared about any of this? Why had I wanted it back? Why had I fought to return to it?

Even the smell... it was musty, not a trace of Mama and Papa anymore. How had I ever found it comforting?

That was why I'd cared. I hadn't been clinging to the objects themselves, but to the familiarity. But I'd let familiarity and my own sense of control become too much, too important, and I'd lost myself in their lulling comfort. I'd let them blind me to anything else: to the dream of an atelier and to all I'd found in Elfhame—

Lysander, this home, this life, this odd little family that I'd become a part of.

I hadn't fought *for* that house in Briarbridge, but *against* change.

But the world outside had changed in the short time I'd been in Elfhame—the aconite now blooming, lilac blossom unleashing its heady scent, the lengthening days.

Change was life.

Or life was change.

Either way, the only things that didn't change were the dead. They were perfect glass-encased specimens captured in our memories, like the butterflies and cocoons in Lord Hawthorne's study, never adapting, never growing, never *becoming*.

I wanted to become.

THE NEXT DAY, I couldn't put it off any longer. I finished the cuff of Lysander's suit.

It was two days since I'd ended things, but facing him was still a challenge too far, so I left the suit folded on his desk. I couldn't even write a note. What would I say? Much as I'd realised my mistake in clinging to the past, that didn't change his future with a wife who was his match in power and lifespan or my inability to stay here and witness it.

I'd dreamt of butterflies, and their fluttering shapes clung to my thoughts all day as I busied myself. A thorough tidy of the workroom—fabrics folded and rolled, jars of beads lined up on their shelves, tools cleaned, oiled, and put away. If everything went to plan, I'd never sew in here again.

I'd hidden behind my old life, in a strange way grateful for the debts because they meant I didn't have to face change.

I understood now.

Instead of going back to Briarbridge and the life I'd had, only ever dreaming of more... Instead of waiting for Rose to fall in love, marry, and have babies that I'd play aunt to, I would become. I would live *my* life.

Because it turned out change wasn't as bad as I'd feared—or at least, some changes weren't. I could open my atelier. Lysander had said he'd pay me generously. Depending on his definition of "generous," I could use that to cover my rent and materials. I might even be able to afford to move to Lunden and open there. Mama had sewn for a queen... perhaps I could, too.

With the workroom tidied to within an inch of its life, I started on my room, though there was little in there. Once that was done, I snuck into the kitchen, grateful to find no sign of Lysander.

Hil touched my cheek and asked if I'd been sleeping as she slid a cheese-encrusted pastry onto a plate in front of me. One end, I slipped to Fluffy, my silent shadow, but the rest I savoured, knowing it was one of the last times I'd get to enjoy her cooking.

That sense of finality on my shoulders, I stayed a while, dodging Hil's concerned questions. She must've understood, because after a while, she stopped probing and instead plied me with cakes.

Thoroughly full, there was nothing left to do but wait for moonrise. I lay in bed, reading and snoozing, until the world outside grew dark, and then I crept out.

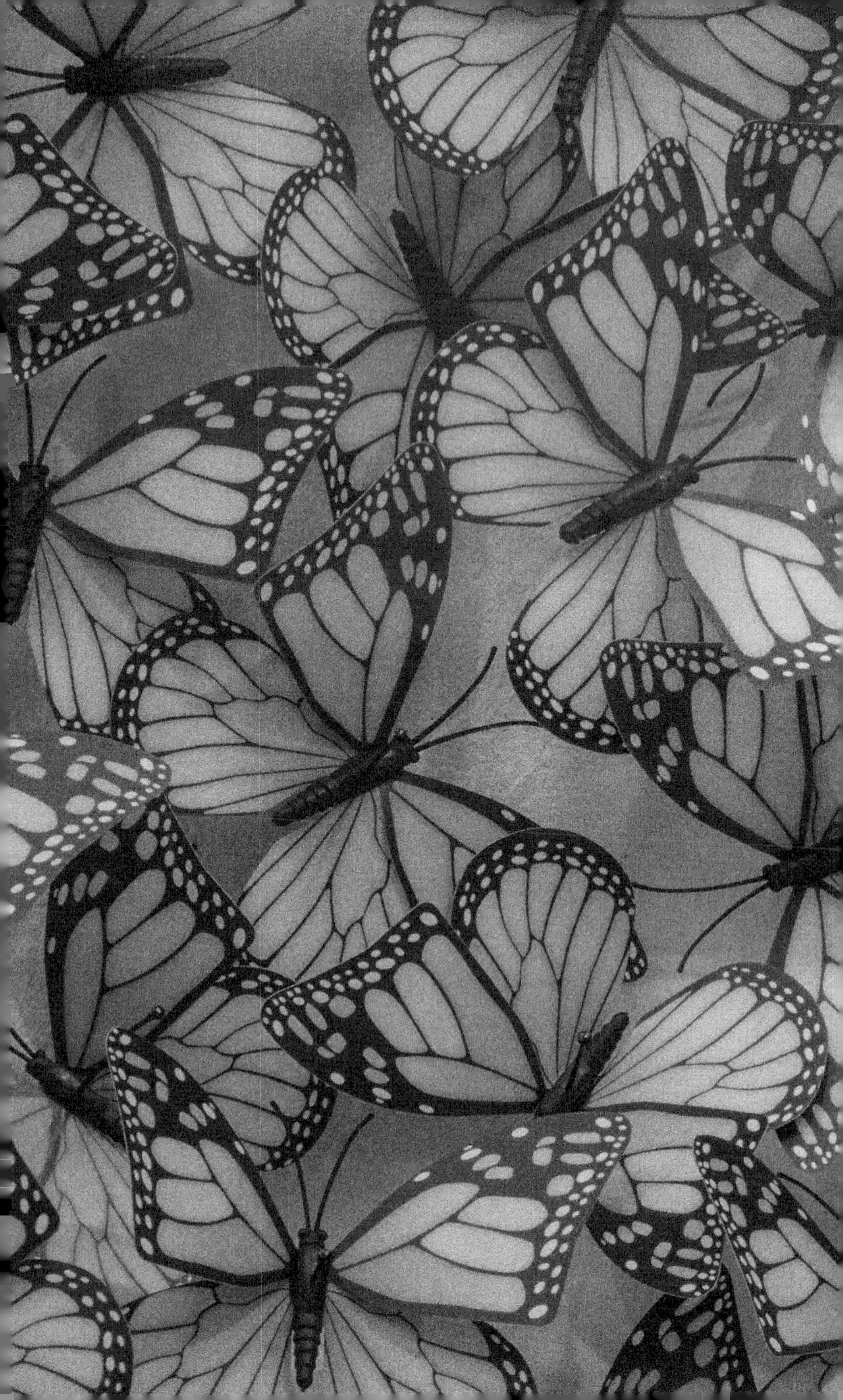

LITTLE MINNOW

This time I wasn't surprised by Fluffy waiting outside my room, and instead of keeping Luna to a steady walk, I urged her into a gallop. The wind pulled my hair free from its ribbon and chilled my cheeks.

And it was glorious.

The lake was just as dark and beautiful as last time. Above, the moon was a little past half full. Its light flashed and flickered on the water's surface as I lowered my offering into its cold grasp and called for the Lady of the Lake.

Her wake rippled this way at once, as though she'd been expecting me, and when she emerged, she was smiling. The brilliant, algae-green eyes glinted, warm. "Little minnow, you bring me a fresh offering."

"I do." As before, I held out the embellished stone. "I bring light. Say the command and it will glow."

She cocked her head, smile softening. "Another

thoughtful offering, little minnow. What is it you ask in return?"

I squared my shoulders and lifted my chin. "The same as last time."

One pale eyebrow rose. "And you've found something you truly want?"

The empty space where my heart had been spasmed, and I clutched my chest as though I could still it. "I want to leave. Staying here is torture." All the reminders of Lysander. The fear of bumping into him at meals or in the gardens. The thought of a future where he'd bring home some fae bride. The thought they'd stay young and beautiful while I aged and died. "Please, I really want to—*need* to go." My words wavered, although I kept my head high.

"Oh." Her shoulders sank and a fine crease formed in the otherwise smooth skin between her eyebrows. "Oh, my, sweet little minnow." Her voice, the rush of water and wind, came out soft as she regarded me a long while.

Please. I want to go. Please.

She inclined her head. "A rose flowers and the east rises." A chill breeze blew in off the lake, raising goosebumps on my arms. "Three and one join for all under the gilded lily. A king's bastard seeks redemption and steals a heart. You see, I know many things, sweet little minnow. And I know you *do* want to go."

The hollow in my chest squeezed, hope flaring inside. I could see Rose and save for my atelier. I could get on with the business of *living*.

"But"—she shook her head and that flare extinguished—"not quite entirely. The hellhound"—her fingers wafted towards Fluffy—"and the friend... Ah, Sylvanna, yes. You don't want to leave them or the one with the cakes and kindness."

Breath huffed from me. I blinked, shook my head. "No. I... I want to go. I do. I *do*."

She gave me a pitying smile and stroked my hair. Her touch was cool and dry, not icy and damp as I'd expected. "Oh, my sweet, you think you do, but..." Her delicate shoulders bobbed. "I see the truth. It's all I may speak. And that wish is not in every scrap and thread of your being."

I sagged, hunching over my hands in my lap. What the hells was I supposed to do? This had been my plan—my *only* plan. I needed to get away from here—away from him. That frayed hole where my heart had been couldn't take staying.

"You know," the Lady of the Lake murmured, "you don't only have to call me to give an offering and ask a question."

Brow pinching into a frown, I narrowed my eyes at her. "What do you mean?"

"I mean, tell me what troubles you."

"Why would you want to listen to my troubles?"

"I grow tired of the company of fish and water sprites." She settled on a half-submerged stone, limbs folding gracefully, and nodded at a dry rock neighbouring it. "I already know your secrets just from looking at you, so it's not as though you have anything to lose by telling me all about that aching heart of yours and the fae lord who contributed to it."

I looked from her to the rock and back again.

She couldn't lie.

So I sat and let Fluffy put her head in my lap, and haltingly at first, I poured out the story.

It looped and stumbled, clumsy, and somehow I started much earlier than I'd intended, back at Mama and Papa's deaths. The Lady of the Lake only nodded and listened.

The moon was past its zenith by the time I talked myself into silence. The lake had gone smooth as glass and reflected the stars and the trees on the far shore. As I took long breaths, throat sore from speaking so much, I realised a weight I'd carried for years had disappeared as if carried away on the water.

"Thank you," I said to her at last.

With a touch and a whisper, she lit the stone I'd made. Its silvery light gleamed on her hair and pale skin. "It's a more than fair exchange." She nodded and glided away towards the lake's centre. "Remember, little minnow, I grow tired of the conversation of fish. You're welcome to keep me company any time the moon is high."

The last thing I saw before she sank beneath the surface was a smile.

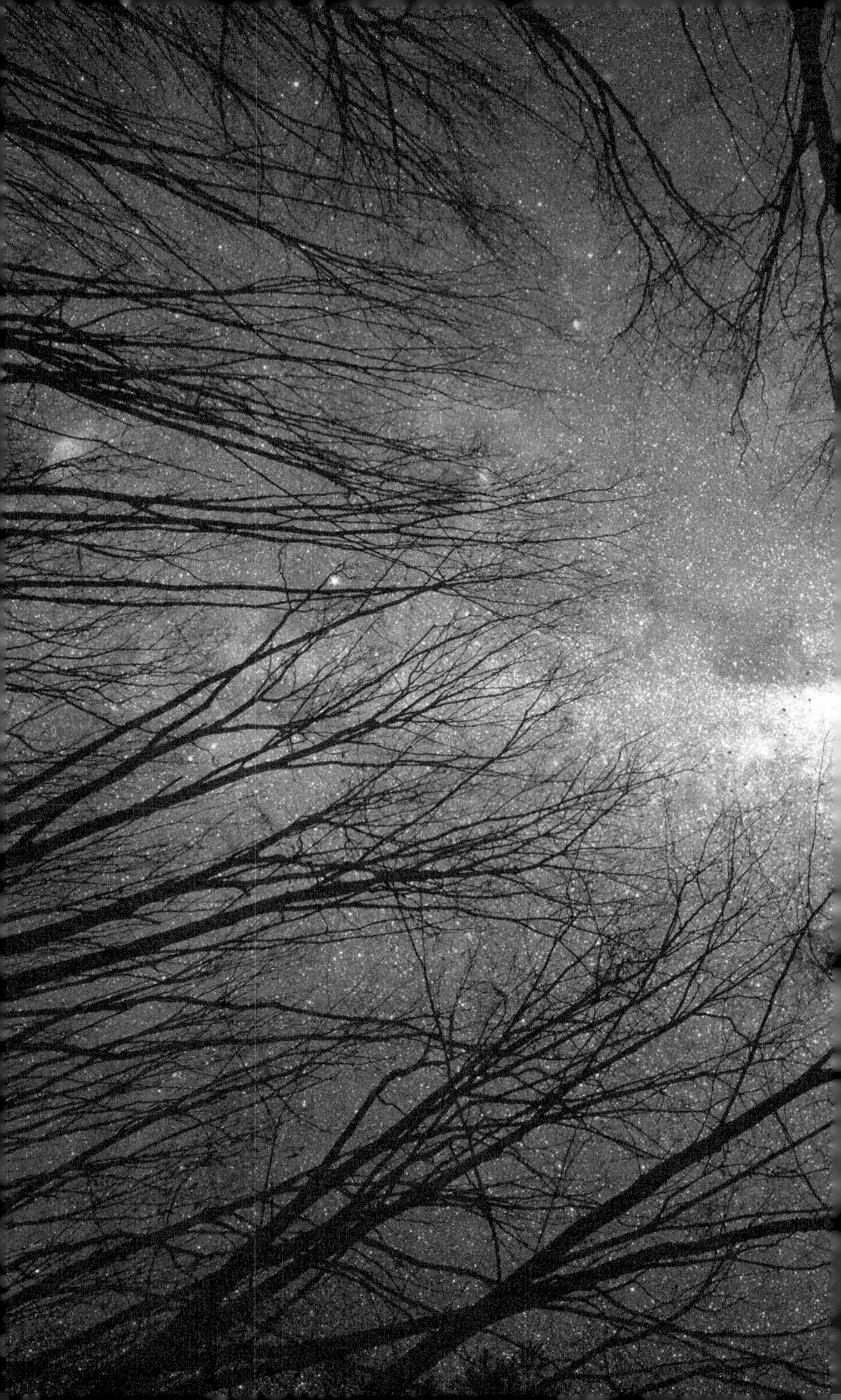

FINAL WISH

I let Luna set her own pace back to the stable yard and removed her tack before leaving her in a stall with fresh food. I might've befriended a Lady of the Lake, but it didn't get me any closer to breaking the Tithe.

"It's your fault," I grumbled at Fluffy, scratching her behind the ears.

Her eyes flared, and her tongue lolled.

I snorted and scratched even harder. "You're not even sorry, are you?"

As I trudged to the house and along the corridor from the back door, Fluffy stuck to my side, ears pricking. "What's—?"

"Where have you been?" Boyd stood in the front entrance, his russet hair in disarray.

Sylvie looked up from the bench beside him, silvery brown face pale.

The one time I did anything brave as a child, I'd

ended up falling out of a tree. My stomach felt exactly like that now, dropping to my feet. Fluffy let out a soft whine.

"What's wrong?" I glanced around the hall. There was no sign of Lysander. It should've been a comfort.

"Don't you worry yourself." Boyd sneered, eyes bright. "You're free to go now. He won't be coming back from there. No one does."

"Leave her alone," Sylvie snapped. "This isn't her fault."

He wheeled on her. "Isn't it?" He jerked his head to me. "How do we know she didn't sabotage that suit? Shut away in that room... All that sewing... Do we really know what she stitched into it?" He huffed, jaw rippling. "I told you humans couldn't be trusted."

I blinked from him to her and back again, lips tingling. "Sabotage..." *He won't be coming back from there.* "Where is Ly?"

Boyd's jaw worked, but he wouldn't even meet my gaze, never mind reply.

Sylvie slouched over her knees, head bowing. "He went after the seed. His stag returned half an hour ago. Goren has him."

A dull roar rose in my ears.

"He left this." All the fight apparently burnt out of him, Boyd held out a sealed letter. "Said to give it to you at midnight if he didn't return."

In Ly's elegant script: *Ariadne*.

I stared at it, the roaring growing louder. If he died,

the Tithe would be void and I'd be free. I could leave. I finally had what I wanted.

But instead of light and free, I was lead.

"At least do him the service of reading it." Boyd's voice wavered. That brightness in his eyes—he was close to tears.

Shaking my head as the world spun slowly, I cracked the seal.

> *My Evening Star,*
>
> *I write this as a "just in case" and hope you'll never get to read it.*
>
> *Much as they pain me, I understand your sentiments and don't wish to cause you any further distress by treating this like a love letter. Perhaps I shouldn't have begun it by calling you that name. I should cross it out.*

He hadn't crossed it out. Hands trembling, I read on.

> *After our conversation in your workroom, I petitioned the Night Queen to free us from the Tithe. I received her refusal this morning. However, there is a freshly-drafted letter to her on my desk.*
>
> *I'm hopeful that, given my sacrifice, she might grant it as my final wish.*

Tears blurred my vision and the roaring grew deafening. No, no "final wishes." That was...

"No." I shook my head. "No. I'm not reading any more of this."

The letter, the insane talk of "final wishes" meant...

This. *This* was the worst thing. Not his desire to marry someone who suited his position and would live longer than sixty or seventy years.

I clutched my chest as it heaved too fast, too shallow.

No. Not that, either. Through my dress, my palm pressed on the solid form of my pendant.

I can.

A breath in. One. Two. Three. Hold. Out. One. Two. Three.

Again. Again.

The roaring faded.

"Ari?" Sylvie stared up at me and shared a glance with Boyd, who frowned.

Even if I couldn't be with him, I couldn't let him...

I gritted my teeth and forced myself to face the word that my mind kept skittering away from.

I couldn't let him *die*.

"We need to go after him." Gods knew how, but—

"I can't." Sylvie hung her head. "If I set foot on Goren's lands, I'll have to marry him, and Ly made me promise never to give him the satisfaction."

My mouth dropped open. "What?" He'd referred to her as "my *dear* Sylvanna" at Calan Mai. "How?"

"A bargain, of course." She flashed a sardonic smile,

bitterness in her eyes. "My parents. Before I was born"—she waved a slender hand—"you can guess the rest."

I exhaled, nodding.

Sylvie explained Hil was sick from the news. No surprise—she was like a mother to the whole household. And Sallis and Hobb were quiet, delicate. I doubted they could harm a fly, never mind Goren.

I gritted my teeth. "Fine. Looks like it's you and me, Boyd."

Lips tightening, he avoided my gaze. "No."

"What do you mean 'no'?" My skin blazed. "Lysander's over there and you don't want to help save him because you don't like me?" I stomped across the hall towards him, and the rage must've shown on my face, because he backed away. "Are you bloody—?"

"I have no magic." The words were barely more than a breath.

I ran them through my head again and again. *I have no magic.* He was fae: he couldn't lie. "You..."

"You heard what I said," he bit out. A muscle in his jaw twitched. "Don't make me say it again."

A fae without magic. I shook my head and rubbed my face like that might make this make sense. "I don't—"

"Stars above, why do you think I can't stand the sight of you?" His eyes were wide and for the first time they were on me without a sneer on his face. "Not only are you a human and can lie and thus can *not* be trusted, but you"—he huffed a humourless laugh—"*you* have magic. *You* have power."

He envied *my* magic. *He* mistrusted *me*. Oh, gods, the irony.

I snorted. "You know all I can do is make clothes, right? And I can't even use my gift on myself. And, as for power, I don't have... Unless..."

The power I'd wanted for myself—to free myself from the Tithe... If it could break a bargain, it could save Ly.

My heart, no longer just a hollow space in my chest, sped. "Is the moon still up?"

Boyd narrowed his eyes and shared another glance with Sylvie. "Er, yes, for another couple of hours."

Sylvie unfolded from the bench, canting her head. "Why?"

I would have to go and face Goren alone. My hands trembled at the prospect, but I gripped the sluagh claw pendant and they steadied. *I can.* "I'm going to get him back, and I'm going to need your help."

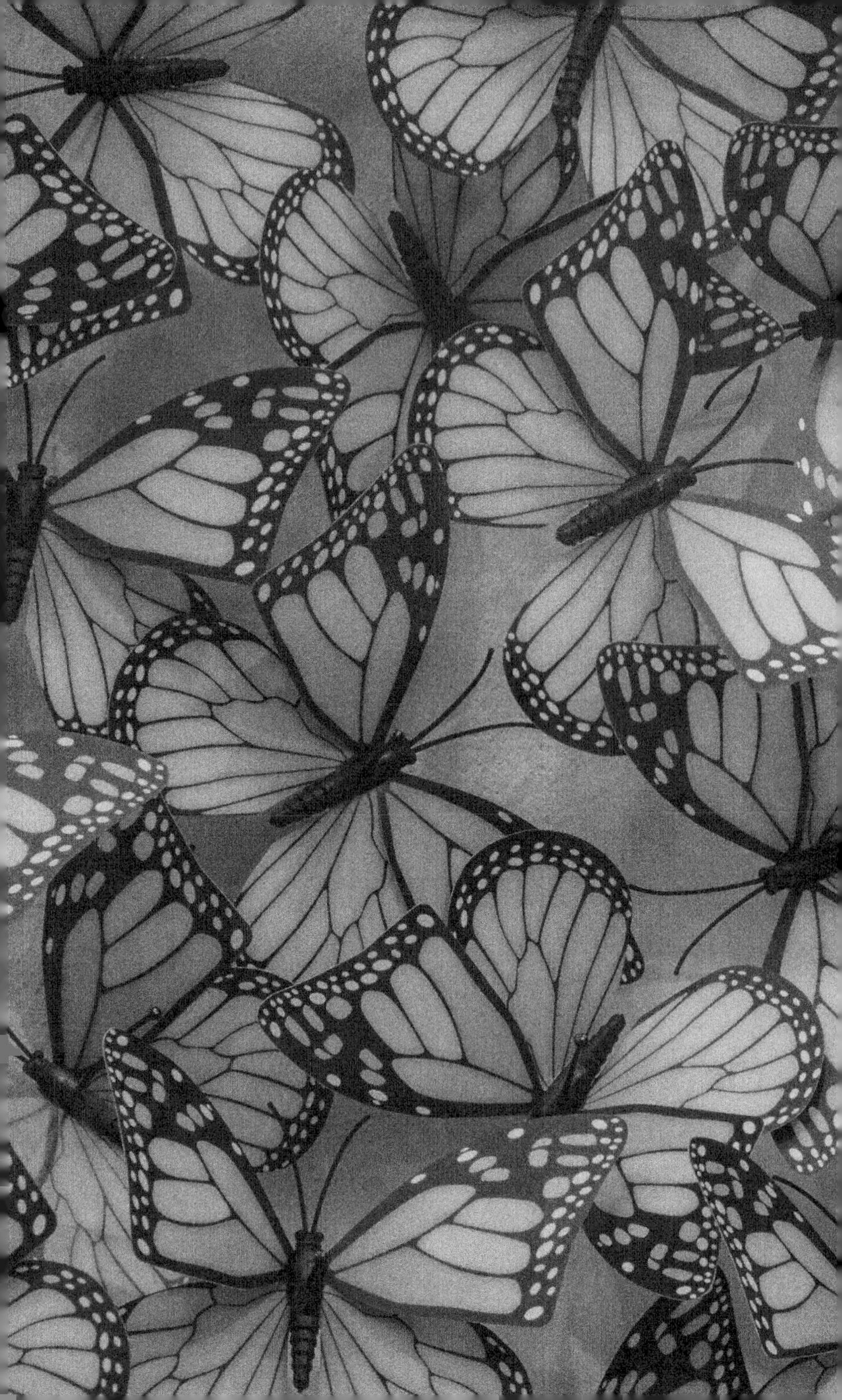

SCARS & STRENGTH

"You did *what*?" Boyd's eyes bulged.

Even Sylvie paled another shade.

I shrugged, unable to help the smile tugging on my lips at the fact I'd done something that shocked these fae. "I only talked to her. She's not so bad."

Sylvie gave a laugh of disbelief. "And you think you can get her to tell you your True Name?"

"Definitely." Not entirely true, but I pushed a broad smile in place like I *was* confident. I squeezed the pendant. *I can*.

She raised her eyebrows at Boyd. He lifted his hands as if to say "What do I know?"

"Well"—she sighed and cast an appraising gaze over me—"if you're going to go after Ly, we're going to need to get you a better outfit."

I gathered my sewing kit and the poisoned gloves while she and Boyd hurried upstairs, saying they'd check on Hil, who was in bed being tended by Sallis and Hobb.

When I arrived in my room, Sylvie had laid out a white gown with silver stars beaded into the hem. I'd spotted it in the wardrobe when I'd first arrived, but there had been no occasion to wear it. Boyd shook out a cloak of midnight velvet that I'd never seen before. Plates of silver curved over the shoulders, like it was armour rather than simply a cloak.

"Where's that from?" I ran a comb through my hair.

"It belonged to Ly's mother." He turned it this way and that, the velvet gleaming in the lamplight as he checked it over.

My throat tightened at his name, like I was the one Goren had captured instead of him. Was he hurt? Boyd had insisted he couldn't be dead or we'd have seen it in the yew, and Sylvie and I would have felt it in the land's magic.

I shifted my focus to see past the world. The web stretched on, from me to Sylvie to the trees and other plants outside, to the deer in the stables, to Hil, Sallis, and Hobb down the corridor. Pale ghosts of threads linked Boyd—I'd never seen anything like that before.

More importantly, no threads sprang loose like they'd just been severed. The yew was intact, albeit sour and sickly. If Goren had killed Ly, the tether between him and this place would've gone slack.

I swallowed past that tightness and raised an eyebrow at Boyd as Sylvie tugged off my boots. "Wouldn't she take offence at a 'mere human' sullying her clothes?"

"To save her son?" Boyd's eyebrows pulled together.

"No *mere human* would even try to do that. And you've faced the Lady of the Lake"—he scoffed—"most fae wouldn't dare." Straightening, he bit his lip. "I was wrong about you."

That shook me more than the offer of the cloak. Tongue too thick to answer, I inclined my head.

"Yes, yes." Sylvie huffed. "It's all very touching, but I need accessories." She waved Boyd off. "Ear clips and a tiara. Go."

"Oh, and the invitation Goren sent," I added.

From the doorway he frowned, but disappeared down the hall. Once he was gone, Sylvie helped me dress, finding white kid ankle boots to go with the gown.

"Don't you think a tiara's a bit much?" I raised my eyebrows at her in the mirror as she pulled my hair back.

A frown etched between her brows where she focused on her work. "You need to look like a queen if you're going to walk in there and demand he frees Ly."

I fought the wince pulling on my face.

I hadn't explained my entire plan to Sylvie and Boyd. They knew I was going to make a bargain. Which was true.

But they didn't know I planned to use poison to extort that bargain. My gift meant once Goren put on the gloves, he wouldn't be able to remove them without my permission. And I'd only give permission if he agreed to let Lysander leave with us, unharmed.

Sylvie and Boyd, though? I couldn't bring myself to tell them I'd made poisoned gloves—not when I'd originally planned to use them on Ly. They thought my True

Name would give me the appearance of power and make Goren listen.

Again, not entirely untrue.

It would give me the confidence to face him and his retinue, and it might make him take me seriously. But much as I wanted my True Name in the hopes of breaking the Tithe, I wasn't foolish enough to think it would allow me to stand against a fae, especially one as powerful as Goren.

Instead, I would rely on lies, poisoned gloves, and guest right.

With a thoughtful hum, Sylvie pulled my hair over my right shoulder. "There."

My scars caught the light, silvery and pale against my skin. "Oh, I wear it over the other—"

"I know." She gave me a gentle smile in the mirror and smoothed my hair as if affirming that it should sit that way. "Let them see your scars. Let them see your strength."

I took a shaky breath, then Boyd was back, and in a flurry of activity, they had a starry tiara on my head and pointed clips over the tips of my ears.

After a final check of my bag, we hurried to the stables and rode for the lake, Fluffy running at my side, Boyd leading Ly's stag. The full skirt of my gown draped over Luna's hindquarters, allowing me to sit astride. Thank the gods, because I didn't need another thing to worry about, like working out how to ride side-saddle.

As Luna's hooves thundered over the ground, my heart pounded in an erratic beat, chest growing tighter and tighter. Biting my lip, I shoved it down and took a long breath.

Sewing kit.

Poisoned gloves.

Goren's invitation.

Sewing kit. Poisoned gloves... I ran through the list over and over like it was a prayer.

I still needed an offering and something I wanted above all else.

For the first... all I had was myself. That would have to do.

As for the latter... the answer was easy.

"Hold on, Ly," I whispered into the wind as we galloped down the hill.

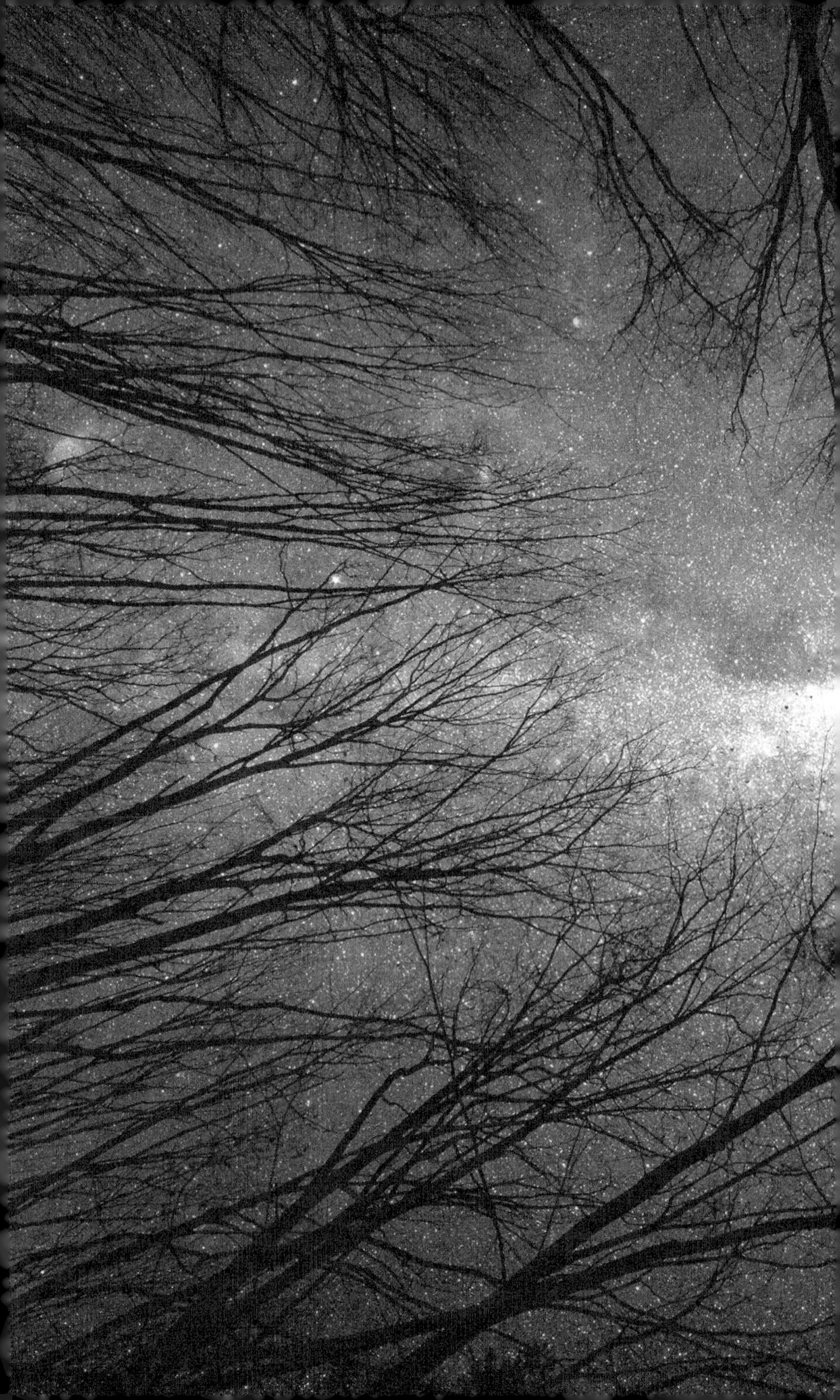

THE OFFERING

The moon brushed the treetops by the time we arrived at the lake. I half fell from Luna's back in my haste, but Sylvie caught me. "Don't worry," she muttered, "I can clean your skirts." She waggled her fingers, suggesting magic, and gave a tense smile.

For the third time, I knelt at the lake's edge.

This had to work.

I lowered my empty hand into the water. "Lady of the Lake, I call to thee." Again. The ripples began when I was only halfway through the third call.

Low gasps came from Boyd and Sylvie as she emerged. She watched me with a delicate frown. "You call upon me again so soon, little minnow?"

"Please. I need my True Name. *Please.*" My voice cracked as though speaking broke the dam holding back feeling and letting me act.

She nodded at my empty palm. "And your offering?"

I shivered but raised my chin. "Myself. It's all I have to give. I only ask that you wait until Ly is home and safe before you take me."

"Ari, no," Sylvie hissed from behind, but I didn't drop the Lady of the Lake's gaze.

Lips parted, showing a hint of those sharp teeth, she took a long breath. "I see. And what is it you desire above all things?"

"I want to save Lysander from Goren." I clenched my jaw to stop the threat of useless tears. "Maybe I'm not enough to do it, even with my True Name, but I don't care. I'll do whatever it takes or die trying."

It was no lie.

"Ah." Her eyebrows rose and she inclined her head. "*There* it is. You do want that, utterly." With the scent of damp earth and deep water, she bent close and whispered in my ear.

My Name.

It thundered in my heart, prickled through every inch of flesh, darted along my veins.

My Name.

It was power. It was truth. It was belonging.

I gaped at her as she pulled away, face inches from mine, and nodded. She knew.

"Tomorrow," I pushed out, voice thrumming. "I'll come then. Your offering."

"Oh, *that*." She grinned, every pointed tooth on display and a sharp pain pricked my scalp. "I decline your offering and instead claim three strands of starlight from that sweet head of yours, little minnow." Between her finger and thumb, the moonlight gleamed on three white hairs. "Now, hurry." Then she was gone.

With a sigh of relief, I rose.

"What have you done?" Sylvie's voice wavered, her face even paler.

"The plan?"

Jaw clenching, Boyd shook his head. "Whatever your stories say, the Ladies of the Lake are not benevolent gift-givers. Why do you think even other fae are wary of them?" He huffed a harsh sigh. "They have their own agendas and now she has your hair. Only the stars know what she's going to do with *that*."

"Perhaps nothing." I shrugged and went to Luna's saddle bags. I was already afraid of what Goren might do to Ly; there was no room in me for any more fear. "That's a worry for another day and, frankly, it's better than her taking all of me."

"Maybe," Sylvie muttered.

Now came the guesswork. I had my True Name, but the story hadn't been clear on how the woman in the story had used it to access her power. I already had my gift, so it stood to reason that should work.

Should.

From the sewing kit, I took thread, needle, and embroidery scissors.

Breaths slowing, I let my focus shift to the web of magic. Still no loose ends pinging back because they'd been cut, but the silver thread I stood on shone bright and brilliant like the moon.

Needle threaded, I found a seam in the skirt of my

gown and turned it over, exposing the neat seam allowance. As I stitched into that excess silk, I whispered my Name.

The web trembled.

Another stitch, another whisper.

It reverberated through me. Pure power.

Another, another, another, the steady pick of stem stitch gradually spelled out my Name.

I finished the final letter, and the web shifted.

Lines radiated from me, spokes spreading out, every one of them glowing silver. Sylvie, Luna, Fluffy, even Boyd—their presence trembled through the threads all the way back to me. Sylvie's was the strongest, Luna's the weakest. Nearby, the Lady of the Lake was a constant thrum.

I wasn't the fly trapped on the web.

I was the spider at its centre.

With a quivering breath, I shifted my focus back to the visible world. I'd done it.

Returning the sewing kit to the saddlebag, I glanced over my shoulder and found Sylvie and Boyd staring at me, eyes wide, mouths open.

"It worked." Sylvie looked me over from head to hem as though seeing me for the first time.

"I'll say," Boyd muttered.

But the moon was sinking behind the trees. The sight dried my mouth. "We don't have time for awe."

I had a fae lord to save.

When I went to mount Luna, Sylvie placed her hand over mine. "No." She shook her head. "You ride the stag."

Swallowing, I eyed Lysander's huge stag. Theoretically it shouldn't be so different from riding Luna, but I shivered all the same. Surely Boyd wouldn't like the idea of me riding the lord of this land's steed like it was my own.

But when I raised my eyebrows at him, he gave a grim nod.

"You ride the stag, Ariadne, because tonight you ride to war."

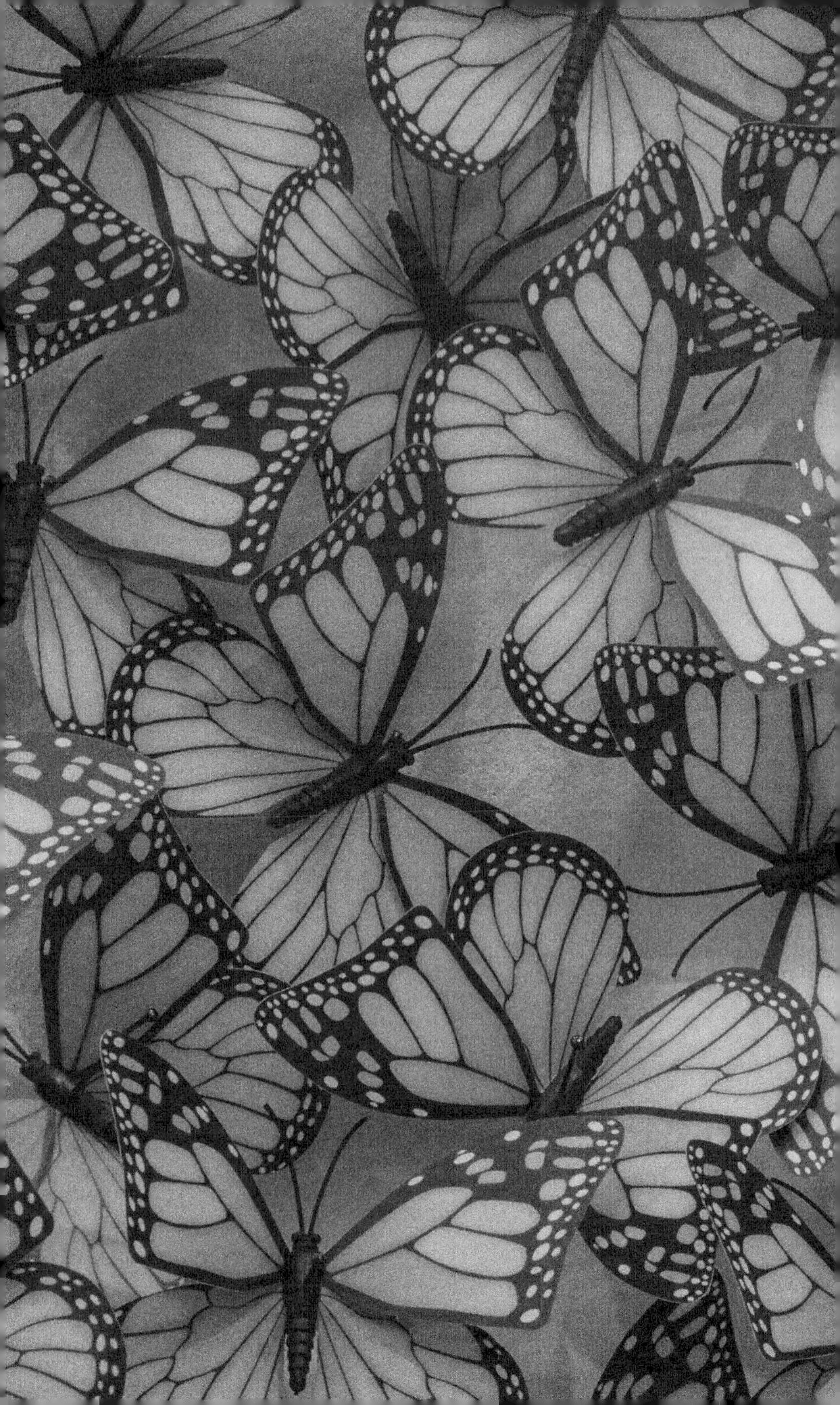

GUEST RIGHT

Sylvie rode as far as the edge of Goren's lands, where she cleaned my boots and the hem of my gown with a touch that tasted of lemonade and mint. With a fierce frown and a kiss on my brow, she wished me luck, and I rode on with Boyd and Fluffy.

We approached a marble-pillared mansion of such a pale sunshine yellow, it practically glowed at the top of its hill. Although it was bright in the darkness, the place made me shudder. I couldn't pinpoint it, but it had an empty quality, and when we reached the drive, the huge double doors opened with an echoing creak.

Boyd pressed his lips together, jaw ticking. "Do you want me to—"

"No." I dismounted and handed him the reins. "Wait here and be ready to leave in an instant." With no magic, he could be in danger within Goren's halls.

Mouth dry, I clutched the invitation and the wrapped

gloves. As long as I came here as a guest, just as Goren had invited, I was safe. Relatively.

I left Fluffy with him. On the ride, Sylvie had explained taking a hellhound into Goren's halls could be construed as an act of aggression and cancel guest right, so I entered alone.

A small, hunched servant with watery eyes led me through the dark corridors towards the sound of a single, distant violin.

Cold settled in my bones, and I had to count my breaths to keep them steady as I passed the dim edges of furniture, shadowy statues, and gaping doorways.

But I let my focus drift past what my eyes could see, and the web, full of silver strands, calmed my nerves. That was *my* magic. I had some power at last.

The sluagh claw pendant bit into my fingers as I squeezed it.

"I can do this," I whispered.

We stopped at a pair of ornate double doors covered in gilded scrollwork with twisted little faces grinning amongst the leaves and vines. As the servant opened them with a gesture, I squared my shoulders.

After the dark corridors, the light within was blinding and before I could see more than that, I caught the shuffle of many people turning.

"Ah, rescue is here." I knew that lilting, mocking voice. It had made me cringe at Calan Mai, but tonight it made my hands clench to fists.

Goren.

"But, what's this?" he went on. "No Sylvanna? Oh, my Stars above—it's the little fawn." He laughed.

From left and right came skittering laughter... booming chortles... cackling shrieks and crows.

At last I could see.

Ahead, on a gilded chair atop a dais, was Goren, his sunlight hair gleaming. He had one leg hooked over the arm of the chair, taking up all the space in the world. Above him, a great sun decorated the sky blue wall, its longest ray pointing down to him. I stood on a strip of golden carpet that led to his feet.

No sign of Ly.

Around me were teeth and claws and bright, sharp eyes. I didn't dare look directly at them. That way lay madness. True Name or not, I would run.

These fae creatures gathered either side of the carpet, below his dais. They took the role of subjects, and he placed himself as their king, sprawled across that ornate chair.

This was a throne room.

Power. *That* was why he'd stolen the yew seed. *That* was the thing he wanted above all else.

That was something I could use.

When the laughter faded, he turned his sky blue eyes to me. They narrowed a touch, and he gave a cold, calculating smile.

Something moved to my right and my spiking heart reminded me of the danger. I held up the letter he'd written to Ly asking to "borrow" me. "You invited me here, and I invoke guest right." My voice rang through the room.

The movement stopped, and I had the faint impression of something large and moss-green pausing on the edge of my vision.

"Not as tame as I thought. And you've learnt some of our ways already." He inclined his head and that moss-green shape receded. "And what brings this guest to my door, I wonder?"

I exhaled but kept my back straight. He'd accepted me as a guest. That meant he couldn't harm me. So far, so good.

Chin high, I approached, each step steady, unhurried, like I imagined a queen would walk. The cloak's plated shoulders made me feel stronger, taller, broader than I was. Still, my heart galloped. "I'm here to make a bargain."

His brows rose, and he sat up, the side of his mouth twitching like he couldn't believe his luck. He was at least a couple of centuries old and with all that practice making bargains, he had to be sure he'd trick me into a bad deal.

"But first"—I stopped a short distance from the steps leading up the dais, out of arm's reach—"I need proof my fiancé is alive."

"Fiancé?" His eyes widened. His smile widened, sharp teeth glinting in the fae light. "You sly old dog, Lysander"—his gaze shifted above my head—"you never told me."

Brow tight, I followed his line of sight up. From the

ceiling, hung a cage and behind its metal bars... Ly.

Every vein, each muscle, all the fibres of my body burned. The bastard had locked Ly in a cage for him and his cronies to laugh at.

Even from here, I could tell those midnight blue eyes smouldered with rage. It was a tangible force filling the room, stoking my own anger.

But when Ly looked down at me, a wrinkle formed between his brows and he shook his head. Something in his shoulders, in his eyes, crumbled.

"Well"—Goren bared his teeth—"are you engaged to this lovely little fawn?"

The breath caught in my throat. *I* could lie and say we were engaged in order to justify demanding a private conversation. But Ly couldn't. When Goren discovered my lie, would that cancel guest right? I hadn't thought to check the particulars in so much detail.

My palms went slick.

Ly cleared his throat. "We made a marriage bargain."

That was no lie. I could've laughed with relief, but I bit my tongue and nodded to Goren.

"Then I cannot deny you an audience." He gestured and the cage lowered.

A cut marred Ly's lip, and shadows pooled beneath his eyes, but otherwise he was the same as always. The bright fae lights brought out the violet-blue sheen on his black hair, and his dark eyes fixed on me.

It hit me like a fist, stealing my breath.

I loved him.

A fae lord about to regain power I couldn't hope to

understand. A man who'd stolen me from a life I *thought* I wanted.

All those things and yet I loved him so much, it pressed on the edges of that empty spot in my chest, threatening to break through it.

But I'd pushed him away. I'd stamped on his emotions because I'd been so ready to believe he couldn't feel for me what I felt for him. Perhaps he didn't. But he *had* written me a letter as one of his final acts before riding here knowing he might die. And he'd tried to release me from the Tithe.

Here he was, the man I loved, so close I could touch him, and yet trapped. The cage was so small, it forced him to hunch over. That cut through my churning thoughts and made me grit my teeth.

His lips parted as he surveyed me, disbelief and fear warring across his face.

I tilted my head and tried for an irreverent smirk like that one he wore so well. "Surprised to see a 'mere human' here to save you?"

"Ari," he whispered, brow creasing. "You're not a mere human, and you never were. I was wrong, just like you've always been wrong about yourself... and about how I see you, how I *feel* about you."

My heart leapt over one beat, two, and it took a second before I could move again. There was too much in those few sentences, and we had too many enemies in this room.

His lips pressed together like he realised the same thing.

"So long as he's in this cage, that isn't proof of anything." I turned to Goren, cursing my wavering voice, though it still echoed around the room. "For all I know, this could be an illusion. I won't bargain with you when for all I know, my fiancé is dead."

He sighed and rolled his eyes. "Oh, yes, and when I let him out, *poof*, you two disappear. I think not."

"My love"—I almost choked on the word to be saying it for the first time like this—"give him your word you won't use your magic to escape." He would be bound by the vow, but if this went according to plan, we wouldn't need his magic to escape.

I *did*, however, need him out of the cage.

His gaze searched mine, and I gave the slightest nod of reassurance.

"I give you my word, I won't use my magic to escape tonight." Meaning that if this failed, he could use it another night.

The fair folk really were better at these slippery truths than I was. I swallowed at what that might mean for the bargain I was about to attempt.

"Fine." Goren huffed behind me.

Something thudded at my feet—a key. As I crouched to take it, my too curious eyes darted to one side.

Claws as long as my hand *tap-tap-tapped* on the floor, edged a little closer, gleamed the crimson of fresh blood.

Ice crept through me, lifting goosebumps on my flesh. Oh dear gods, what where these creatures? What had I walked into thinking that a pretty dress, a scrap of paper, and an embroidered name would keep me safe?

Something pressed on my chest. My breaths went shallow. The hand clasped around the key shook.

I was a human in a room of fae monsters. They'd already captured Ly. What chance did I have?

"Ari." That soft murmur, one I'd heard in the dark of night while surrounded by warm, solid arms.

He was counting on me.

And I'd come here with a plan.

I'd smacked a sluagh with a branch. I'd befriended a Lady of the Lake. I'd learned my True Name.

That power had dulled to a low hum, but it reverberated through my bones still. I wasn't helpless.

One long breath in. Two. Three. I nodded and stood.

When I slid the key into the lock, my hand didn't shake.

I met Ly's gaze and managed a small smile.

A tiny shake of his head. "You shouldn't have come."

"I had to. I failed you. The suit..." Even behind bars, he was magnificent in the outfit I'd made—a caged predator. I turned the key.

He scoffed, every part of it bitter. "No, you were perfect. *I* failed me. He had the place warded with fear and my cries brought the guards running. I... I thought he had you, Ari." His lashes fluttered as he shook his head harder. "He was hurting you, and I was too weak to save you."

My heart squeezed for him. He felt responsible for his parents' deaths, just as I'd blamed myself for mine. And Goren had stoked that past horror into fresh fear, making him believe someone else was about to die and he was powerless to stop it.

When the door swung open, I couldn't help but reach for his cheek. Warm, solid, real. *Alive* and so beautifully vulnerable. Not the untouchable, inhuman creature I'd once thought.

He covered my hand with his and pressed it against his stubbly skin. "He must've been on alert after I turned down the invitation. You were right, I should've pretended. I'm sorry I didn't listen to you."

"I'm the one who needs to apologise, but now maybe isn't—"

"How touching," Goren said in a tone that suggested it wasn't. "Now, I've met your demands, little fawn. What bargain have you come to make?"

"Trust me," I whispered to Ly, thumb grazing his full, soft lips before I drew a long breath and faced Goren.

"I already do." The soft answer came from behind, but it suffused me, a bright spark in my chest that had me standing taller.

It lent a fresh edge to the smile I gave Goren as I lifted my chin, and unwrapped the gloves. Back straight, I squared the pauldrons of my cloak like I really was a queen. "Give me Lysander immediately, safe and unharmed, together with the seed you stole from his family."

Goren's brows rose slowly as I spoke, eyes flicking to the gloves. Maybe he was surprised I knew about the seed. Hopefully, he was impressed I'd phrased my side of the bargain so well.

There couldn't be any way of twisting his way out of that, not when I'd said "immediately, safe and unharmed." Right?

"That's rather a lot you stand to gain from this bargain," he drawled. "What is it I get in return?"

"I will give you these gloves." I held them up so the little gold spangles caught the light.

The fae around me shifted, little rustling sounds, clicks, and chitters signalling their interest.

"I made them for Lysander," I continued, forcing my attention to stay on Goren. "The wearer may kill the Night Queen or the Day King, unseen, undetected, and take her or his power for their own." I hadn't prepared this part of the lie, but seeing his would-be throne room had inspired me. "Why else would Lysander come for the seed if not to regain that power to aid him in pursuing a greater one?"

Goren's eyes widened and fixed on the gloves, a glint of greed in their sky blue depths. "My, my, my, Lysander." Clicking his tongue, he shook his head and grinned, wolfish. "You're far more ambitious than I could ever have imagined. Bravo, old chap."

He'd bought it. Good gods, he'd actually bought my lie, my bargain. My head swam with it—this had to be what power felt like.

"I accept your bargain, fawn." Craning forward, he leant on his knees and jerked his chin at a servant who waited at the foot of the dais. "But since humans are well-known for their pretty little lies, you'll excuse me if I have someone try on the gloves first."

My smile of triumph froze in place. When the servant came for the gloves, he had to pry them from my hands.

Think. Think! There had to be some way out of this. Some lie that would stop them trying on the gloves, some—

"The gloves will bond to the first wearer," I blurted out. "If he tries them on, you won't be able to—"

"Is that so?" Goren arched one eyebrow, eyes narrowing on me. His chin lifted as he sniffed the air. "Because I think... Hmm, is that the scent of deceit or just the faebane you've brought into my house?"

Every possible argument withered on my tongue. He knew. Oh, gods, he *knew*.

"Poisoning your host." He clicked his tongue. "Tell me, Lysander, *is* that a breach of guest right?"

Chitters and howls, gasps and cackling laughter erupted around me.

Each sound turned the blood in my veins to ice.

"I thought so. Seize her."

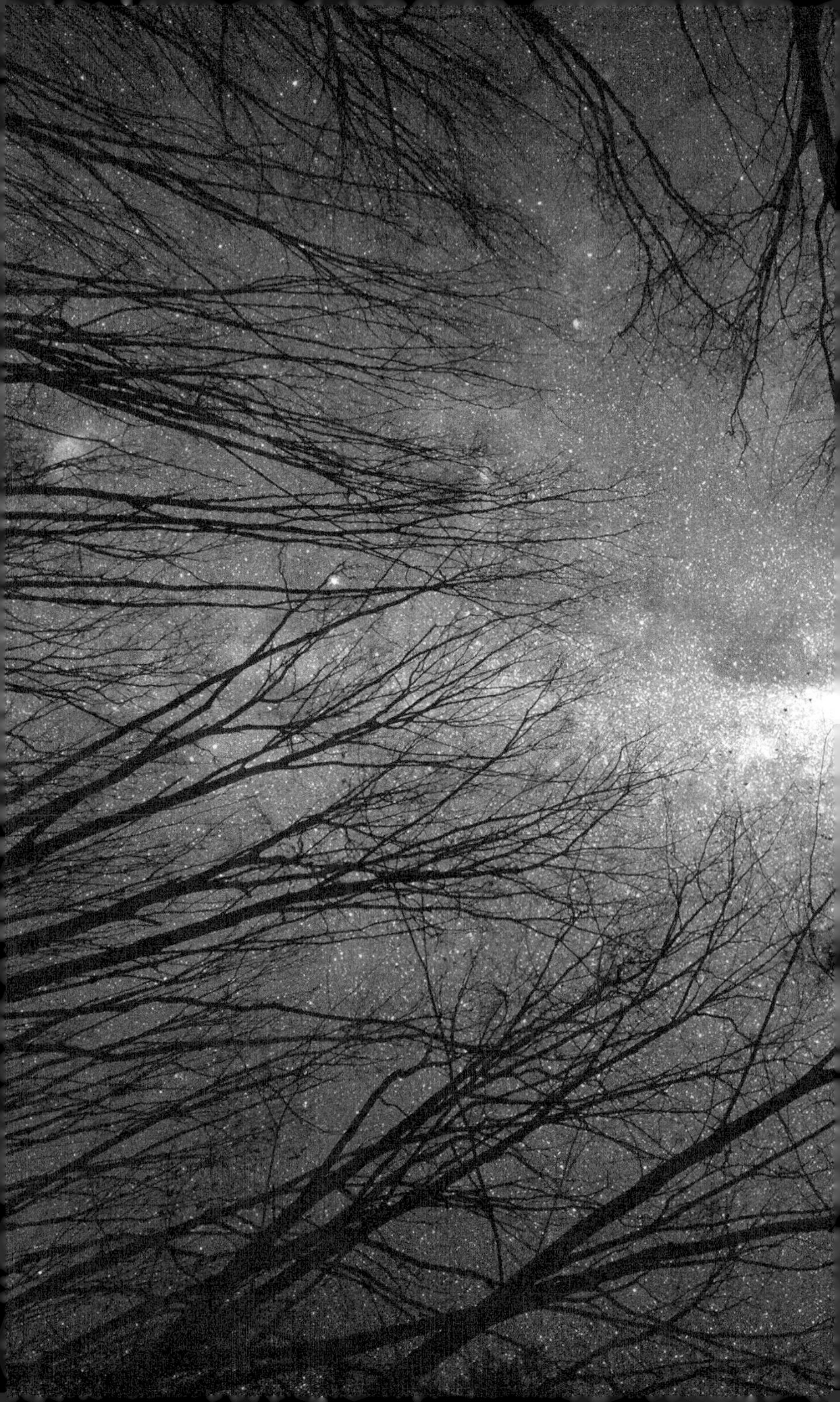

A Tremble in the Web

The roaring in my ears drowned out all thought. Those fae on the edge of my vision closed in. Some were like Ly, *almost* human, but the others...

Claws, teeth, and horns, all in that glossy blood red I'd glimpsed earlier. The creature loomed over me, great wings splaying.

Chest spasming so I couldn't draw breath, I backed away.

A blond fae that could've been Goren's brother circled, eyes cold and fixed beyond me, on Ly. His scabbard was empty but he wielded no sword.

The air hazed with heat, searing my lungs and eyes, and a figure closed in from the right. Instead of skin, this was a man of cracked, black flesh like burnt wood. Beneath his wide-brimmed hat, instead of eyes, two embers smouldered, and a line of red appeared—a burning smile.

The acrid stink of singed hair filled my nose. The hem of my dress smoked. Shit. What *was* he? Fingers pressed to my lips, I jerked away. I almost screamed when I backed into something solid, but there was no air in my lungs to make a sound.

But that something was warm, and through the stink of my burnt hair came the sweet-sharp scent of fresh rhubarb. I sagged. Ly.

"Ari." His hand closed on my shoulder, pulling me against him. "Keep close." Steel thrust past me, glinting in the too-bright fae light as he warded off the red fae, then the burning one.

He must've grabbed the blond fae's sword. Even without magic, he was fast. Thank the gods *and* the Stars above.

Within the protection of his stolen blade, I could breathe at last.

We turned left and right and every time, another of Goren's retinue was too close. Ly's speed with that wicked, curved sword kept them wary, testing, hanging back as they sought an opening.

But I slowed him down and there were too many of them. At some point he would turn too late.

A grunt rumbled from him into my back, and as he whirled us around, he let out a hiss of pain. Blood sizzled on the burning fae's sword and his red smile appeared again like a pit of fire.

Pain lanced through my chest like I was the one he'd cut, but...

"Ly." My voice came out broken. I squeezed the

hand he had around my waist. Over my shoulder, I glimpsed a slash in his jacket and a thin red line beneath.

Another grunt and his grip on me twitched as we turned. The blond fae had a blade now and it glistened red.

They were going to cut him down, slice-by-slice. Even without me slowing him, there were too many of them, and he'd bound his magic with his word. Although it wasn't my fault he'd been caught, that stupid vow absolutely *was*.

Beyond the circling fae, Goren remained on his throne, biting his lip, eyes sparkling with something that looked horribly like pleasure.

A sharp hiss in my ear from Ly tore my chest open. They were going to kill him.

"Please." I whimpered, throat thick and burning. "Stop." The word tasted of raspberries.

The air rippled. The nearest fae, the red one, hesitated mid-step.

Something tugged on me.

A tremble in the web.

I let my focus shift beyond the fae, beyond Goren's throne, beyond the blue and gold walls...

The silver strands stretched in all directions, linking me to every life nearby, including the fae's. Their presence, their movements jangled along the lines straight back to the centre—back to *me*.

My True Name tingled on my tongue and against my leg where I'd embroidered it in my gown. I'd thought it was just that brief moment, that flare of light spreading through the web.

But, no. All of it glowed silver.

They were in *my* web.

Magic thrummed in my veins, buzzed on my lips.

"Stop."

The word thundered through the chamber.

And then, silence.

The red fae stood on one leg, frozen in the act of taking a step closer, their grasping, clawed hand only a foot away.

Behind them, on the throne, Goren's mouth hung open as though he was about to speak. His eyes swivelled side to side, no longer sparkling.

The only movement other than mine was Ly's ragged breathing at my back.

They'd stopped.

"Ari?" Hand on my waist, sword raised, Ly slid into the space next to me. He glared at the red fae and flicked his blade in front of their face.

They didn't even blink.

Ly's stare passed from the red fae to me. "How did you...?" He sucked in his lower lip as if tasting something on it. "Your gift, it's..." He stilled, mouth dropping open.

A slow smile crept over his face, pressing the dimple into his cheek, shining in his eyes with something like wonder.

It was confirmation: I'd done this.

I'd spoken and it was as though a hundred voices had joined mine, and this room full of fae had *obeyed me*.

If I could make them stop...

"Goren," I boomed and his eyes turned to me, although no other part of him moved, "you will bring me Lysander's yew seed."

My energy trickled away with each word, but Goren lurched to his feet. With jerky movements, he pulled a pouch from his inside pocket.

"Bastard," Ly growled as he approached. "The vault was a decoy."

Goren stopped before me, face still frozen in that same cruel smile he'd worn when I'd commanded him to stop, but there was something desperate in his eyes now.

Something afraid.

How appropriate.

I held out my hand and he dropped the pouch into it. Magic tingled up my arms, numbed my palm. This—the seed was even more potent than the power weaving through my words.

"I believe this is yours," I said, voice normal as I handed the pouch to Ly.

He made a low sound as his eyebrows drew together, forming a peak. The shadows below his eyes faded, the cut on his lip too. And the flavour of night and starlight and rhubarb struck me with an intensity that shook my knees.

"Ariadne." His midnight eyes blazed as they turned to me, as though the night sky could burn. "Thank you."

I inclined my head, throat burning at seeing him restored.

But I still had more to do. Who knew how long this

power in my voice would last? Once we left, what was to stop Goren riding to our door and attacking?

I lifted my chin and squared my shoulders and gave him a sharp smile.

"You will let Lysander and me go, immediately, safe and unharmed." My voice shook the floor. Dust hissed from the ceiling. "You and your minions will never bother us again. You will never speak our names again."

As I spoke, my arms grew heavy, like I'd spent hours hefting rolls of fabric. But there was more; I had to ensure Ly's safety from Goren forever in every possible eventuality. There could be no wriggling his way out of this.

"If you find yourself within one hundred yards of either of us, you will turn and walk in the opposite direction." My legs trembled, but my voice did not waver. Darkness threatened at the edge of my vision and grey spots overlaid Goren's frozen face. "You will never lay eyes on us again."

Swaying, I caught my breath. I needed to finish this, seal the spell, but every muscle burned and my face tingled like I hadn't eaten in days.

A warm, familiar touch landed on the small of my back.

I swallowed and nodded a silent *thank you*.

I inhaled once more. "It is so."

The world spun, and a pair of strong arms slid around me.

Then darkness swallowed me up.

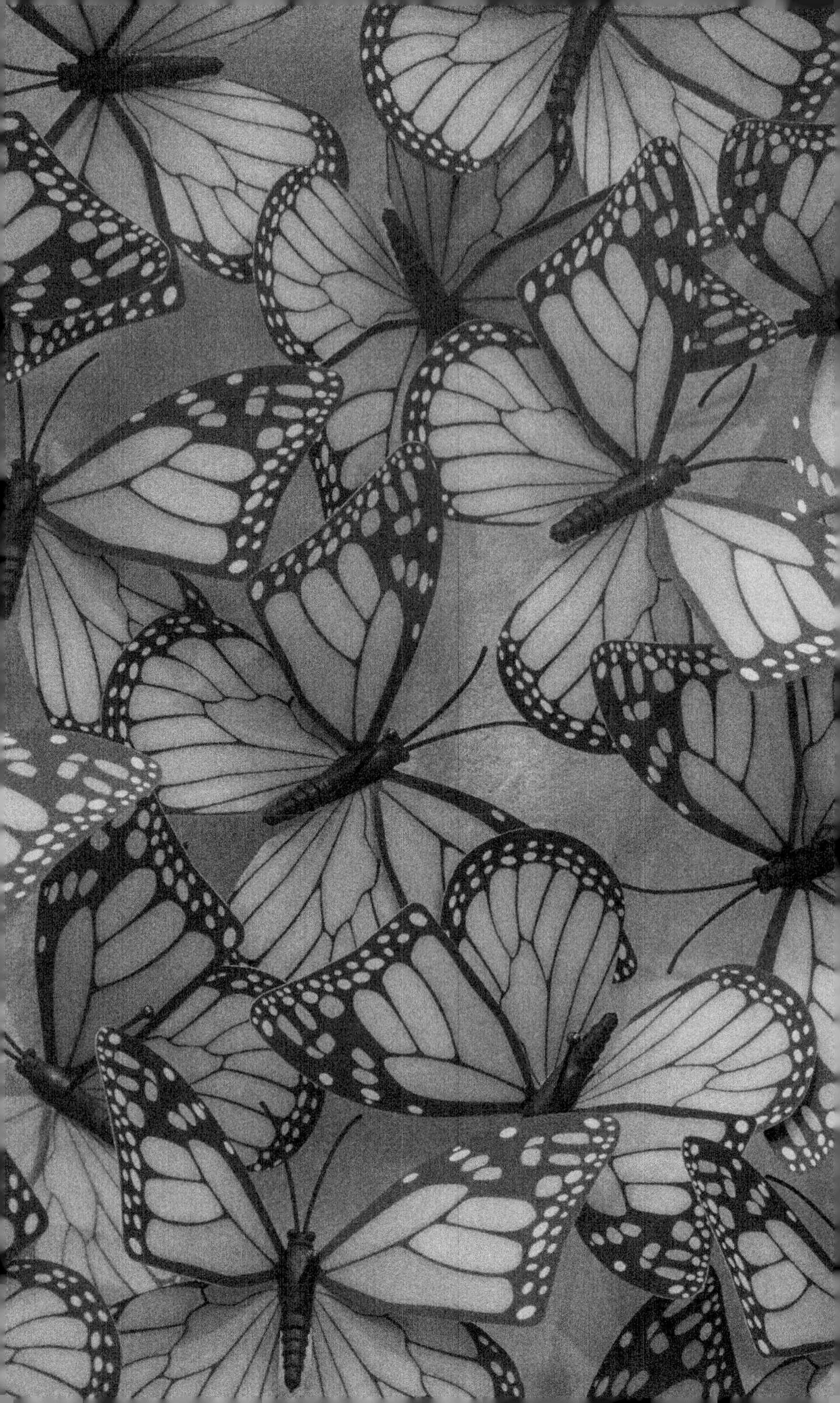

THE HAPPIEST CREATURE IN ALL OF ELFHAME

I didn't dream, didn't feel, didn't think, but eventually I woke. Limbs heavy, I took a deep, sweet breath and stretched across the glorious softness of a thick mattress. I could just go back to sleep, back to—

A low gasp came from somewhere nearby. "Ari?" Ly's voice... and that had to be his hand covering mine.

I dragged myself to full wakefulness. "I'm here." My voice was dreamy and distant.

"Good gods, you *are*." His face swam into view, brows creased in undeniable concern.

"Obviously."

"Ari"—a sternness entered his voice that made me rub my eyes—"you've been unconscious for *three days*. After you used so much magic, I thought..." He shook his head like the end of that sentence was impossible to state.

"Three days?" I blinked and pushed myself upright.

"Three days." He bit out each word. "I thought you weren't coming back. I've been losing my damn mind."

"Huh." I frowned and scrubbed my face, energy creeping back into my muscles, the grittiness from my eyes fading.

Beyond him, moonlight streamed through the windows of my chamber.

The last thing I remembered, it was the middle of the night or maybe the small hours of the morning and...

So much magic. My magic. My words. It flooded back, every moment before the darkness had engulfed me.

Using more magic than you had energy for carried a hefty price—death of the body or mind—and I must've come close to paying it. I gave a shaky exhale, rubbing my chest. "I remember. I remember it all."

The silver web under my control. The fear of him dying. The need to save him.

Why I needed to save him.

He huffed and shook his head, a deep frown forming between his brows. "Why did you come after me? You could've died. That—what you did, it was impressive, incredible, but... you shouldn't have have risked your life like that. Why would you come after—?"

"Because I love you."

His mouth hung open, mid-word.

My heart leapt to my throat. I hadn't meant to say it, but there it was... The words were free, and there was no magic to them, but...

I gulped and suddenly found my clasped hands very interesting. Well, at least I'd admitted it. And there was something else I still needed to admit. "I... I made those gloves for you originally."

There was a beat of silence, like he swallowed or sucked in a breath or somehow mastered his surprise at my admission. "I worked that out."

I waited in case he would say more, but, no, that was it.

"Somewhere along the way"—I picked at a hangnail—"I decided I didn't want to use them and... and I realised I quite liked you—or at least you weren't the arrogant prick I first thought."

"Ouch."

I arched an eyebrow and dared a glance at him.

He cleared his throat and looked away. "But deserved, perhaps."

"And when Boyd told me you'd gone to Goren's and hadn't come back, I was horrified." I rubbed my chest, an aching memory of that moment twisting inside me. "Because somewhere along the way, and I can't tell you where or when, I'd gone from hating you to quite liking you to... loving you." There was again, that dangerous word.

I shook my head and blasted onwards. "I know you don't feel the same. I'm like a gnat to you; I'll be dead in the blink of an eye. Like..." I caught myself before I got Boyd in trouble. "Like some might say, I was just a novelty in the bedroom."

"He said that, did he?" Ly's voice came out in a low rumble like threatening thunder. Maybe Boyd had said the same things to him.

My cheeks burned as though his response had confirmed I'd said all those things out loud. I pulled my knees to my chest.

I shouldn't have admitted all this. I should've kept quiet. I should've...

No. I wanted him to know. Even though he didn't feel the same, I wanted to speak the truth.

To be heard.

"Do you think you're well enough to walk?"

I twitched at the sudden question, the hairpin turn in conversation. "I—uh..." Of course, he felt awkward and wanted to change the subject. I couldn't blame him. Studiously avoiding his gaze, I wriggled my toes. "I think so."

"Get dressed and meet me on the terrace." With that, he rose and stalked out.

I washed, and the air coming through the open window was so mild, I dressed in a light gown of dove grey. Silver threads wove through the cotton lawn, glinting as I moved. I brushed my hair and pulled it over my left shoulder. Then I paused in front of the mirror.

The woman who looked back at me was not Ariadne of Briarbridge.

She was older, her shoulders squarer, her chin lifted higher. The pearlescent pendant hanging between her breasts said she'd cracked the claw from a sluagh and lived to tell the tale. Albeit with some help.

A *lot* of help.

I gave myself a half smile and brushed my hair over

the other shoulder, revealing the scars that disappeared below the dress's scooped neckline.

Moments later, I was hurrying through the corridors and out onto the terrace. At the far end, at the top of the steps, Ly's broad shoulders cut a fine shape against...

A mass of deep green leaves... no, *needles*. They blotted out the stars, held aloft on great branches that spread out like arms welcoming the moon.

Breathless, I drew level with Ly.

"The yew." I shook my head, a thickness in my throat that made my eyes burn. "It's... it's glorious." Fae light drifted around it, clustering amongst its branches as though drawn to its power.

Beneath my feet, the ground hummed with magic. It tasted of elderflowers with no taint of sour rot.

"It is, isn't it?"

When I looked up at him, his gaze wasn't on the tree. Raw and bright, it was on me.

My heartbeat spiked, and I had to knot my fingers together to keep them from him.

"But there's something else I want to show you." He held out his hand in invitation.

With his power restored, he could shadowstep us easily. How far, exactly?

I placed my hand in his and the world dropped away.

Motes of dust and darkness, we fluttered along and a moment later we were indoors, the delicious flavour of rhubarb and starlight teasing my tongue. It only took me a breath to recover this time and I smiled at the fact.

When I turned to see where Ly had brought us, the

smile guttered. A dressing screen of midnight blue covered in silver stars. A low table with two armchairs. A counter of pale marble covered in pretty knick-knacks—fans and bags and little boxes that had me itching to open them and look inside.

As I turned, movement caught my eye. My reflection. A tall, silver mirror stood at one end of the room, the moon's phases moulded into the top edge of its opulent frame.

And at the other end of the room, lace curtains covered large windows and a glazed door that looked out onto a street.

"A shop?" I peered outside, though I didn't recognise the road.

He tilted his head and pressed middle finger to thumb. A door appeared in the back wall, which had looked like nothing more than rich wood panelling. "I may be wrong, but I think this makes it an atelier."

My breath caught, but when he gestured for me to go first, my feet took over and carried me into the back room. The waist-height table, the large windows, the upright, supportive chair at a lower work surface, the shelves and racks ready to hold rolls and lengths of fabric, the armchair...

It was just like my workroom—like the one I'd designed in my sketchbook in idle, dreaming moments. Right down to the frosted skylight in the ceiling, through which the full moon peeked.

I opened my mouth, closed it, but no sound came out.

"I didn't mean to snoop," he said from near the door, watching me, "but some time ago I noticed you'd left your sketchbook open and when I saw this…"

I chewed my lip, mind slow and whirring at once. Was he saying…? Had he done all this for me?

"I consulted with seamstresses and tailors on the details, and I wrote to the Queen's seamstress on a few particulars. But I tried to keep as true to your design as possible." He shook his head, glancing at the shelves. "It isn't finished, of course. But…"

His throat bobbed in a slow swallow and he lifted his chin as his gaze returned to mine. He took a hesitant step towards me. "I realised sooner than you did. But then, I suppose I wasn't the one stolen away from my world and everything I knew." He winced. "In case I haven't said it, I *am* sorry about that, you know. Truly."

And he couldn't lie. But—I rubbed the back of my neck—what had he realised?

"So I had this built as…" He bit his lip and approached.

Oh, gods, this was dangerous. The way he bit his lip begged me to kiss him, and if I did, I would never stop and here he was, coming closer, stopping within arm's reach.

I clasped my hands behind my back.

"I built it as an apology and an explanation. This wasn't how I was planning to unveil it, but I can't have you thinking you're some novelty to me or a 'mere human.' I want you to have something that is yours, not a place you were brought to against your will and not a life you were left with because of circumstance."

"This is for me?" I took in the racks, the chair, a set of tiny drawers ready to house all different findings perfectly organised. So much. "All of this?"

He cocked his head, dimple teasing a shadow in his cheek. "Who else?" He said it like it was obvious.

Pressure built at the back of my eyes. "Ly, you didn't have to..." My voice cracked and I couldn't go on.

"I did. Or, rather, I wanted to—*needed* to. You see, Ari, I want you to be happy."

Just like I wanted him to be happy, even if that meant marrying a fae woman who'd be his match in every way. One he wouldn't lose in forty or fifty years.

He blasted a sigh and winced. "Stars above, I'm saying all of this in the wrong order. I haven't even told you..." Smiling, he took my hands, and I was a fool, because I squeezed his in return. "The Queen has heard what you did for me, and she's freed you from the Tithe."

The thing I'd been working towards for weeks, it should've brought me joy, but it was a lead weight in my belly. If I was released from the Tithe, he would send me back to Briarbridge. I frowned at the workroom—the beautiful workroom. "If I'm going back, why build this?"

His smile faded. "Because you don't have to go back. Not if you don't want to. And this place... now I have my strength back, this place isn't fixed here."

My brows rose. "You can move a whole building?"

He lifted one shoulder and one side of his mouth. "Basically."

Good gods, just how powerful was he?

"What I'm trying to say... badly... is that you have a choice—a few, actually. And in all those options, this is all yours, so please don't think this place is a bribe or dependent on whether you... on what you decide."

My lips twitched to see him stumble over his words, hesitant for a change. Where had the arrogant fae lord gone? "And these choices are?"

"You can live and work here in our capital—there's an apartment above the showroom and I know you'd have customers clamouring to wear your work. If you wish to return to Briarbridge, well, this can all be transferred there. Or somewhere else in Albion, if you prefer. With the wages I owe you, you could buy... hmm, probably a quarter of Lunden, if you really wanted."

"Sorry, *what*?" I spluttered. "A quarter of Lunden? You're exaggerating."

"Can't lie, remember?" He lifted my hands, thumbs grazing my knuckles.

For a second, I thought he was going to kiss them. Hoped he would.

But his chest rose and fell in a heavy breath, and he edged closer still. The scent of him that I'd grown so used to filled me, sweet and sharp, woody and masculine, with that last drift of smokiness that made my breath catch.

I swayed towards him, wanting, wanting, wanting, despite the pretty lie I'd told myself—that I'd be happy without him, that the knowledge of his happiness would be enough.

"There is another option." His voice dropped, rumbling through me. Head bowed, he examined the back of my hands like they were fascinating. "You could come here to work on your amazing creations during the day, and then in the evening, come home to me."

Ba-DUM. My heart, here in my chest, which was full and not an empty, aching pit.

Come home to me.

I'd misheard... misunderstood. My hopes were playing a cruel trick on me. Because he couldn't be saying... "What do you mean?" My voice wavered, every ounce of uncertainty I felt audible in that once sentence.

He looked up through lowered lashes, the flicker of a smile at the edge of his mouth. "I was hoping this might be a wedding gift from me to my bride."

Did that mean...?

Was he...?

A wedding gift.

My pulse rushed in my ears.

I must've been gaping, because his brows shot up and he sucked in a sharp breath.

"Damnation, I didn't actually say it, did I?" Releasing me, he raked his hands through his hair. He cleared his throat and closed his eyes. "Let me do this properly."

He sank to his knees, placing his large hands on my hips. His warmth seeped through the thin cotton lawn of my gown and deep into my flesh, lighting sparks in my body, little motes of pleasure, of what was very nearly happiness.

My mouth went dry. I barely breathed.

"For avoidance of any doubt," he said, eyes locked with mine, "I, Lysander of Elfhame, love you, Ariadne of Briarbridge, with every fibre of my being, with every dark speck of my magic, with every syllable of my True Name."

I swayed, and his fingers pressing into my hips were all that kept me upright.

He loved me. Good gods. Stars above. He *loved* me.

He feels for you as you do for him. Perhaps even more.

That was the thing he'd realised before I did.

His warmth filled my chest, bright like the stars at Calan Mai's new moon when we'd first made love.

That smile flickered on the edge of his lips again, and I ached to kiss him. "And," he went on, "I'd be the happiest creature in all of Elfhame and Albion combined if you would give your wholehearted and willing consent to marry me."

Yes.

Of course, yes. All those rushing beats of my heart shouted it. *Yes-yes. Yes-yes. Yes-yes.*

But... I would die long before him. I'd leave him alone and grieving. But he knew that and yet he was still here, still asking me. And we could have many, *many* years of happiness before that.

If I filled those years with as much joy and laughter and life as possible, they just might last him the centuries to come.

"You have it." I sank to my knees and cupped his face, thumb resting on the dimple in his cheek. "You have me."

He pulled me to him, lips an inch from mine. "And you've always had me."

Then that inch was gone.

His mouth on mine, his hands at my back, in my hair, mine on his cheeks, gliding up into his hair. We melded together. Even our breaths merged as I ran my fingertips over his ears, making him groan against me.

We were one.

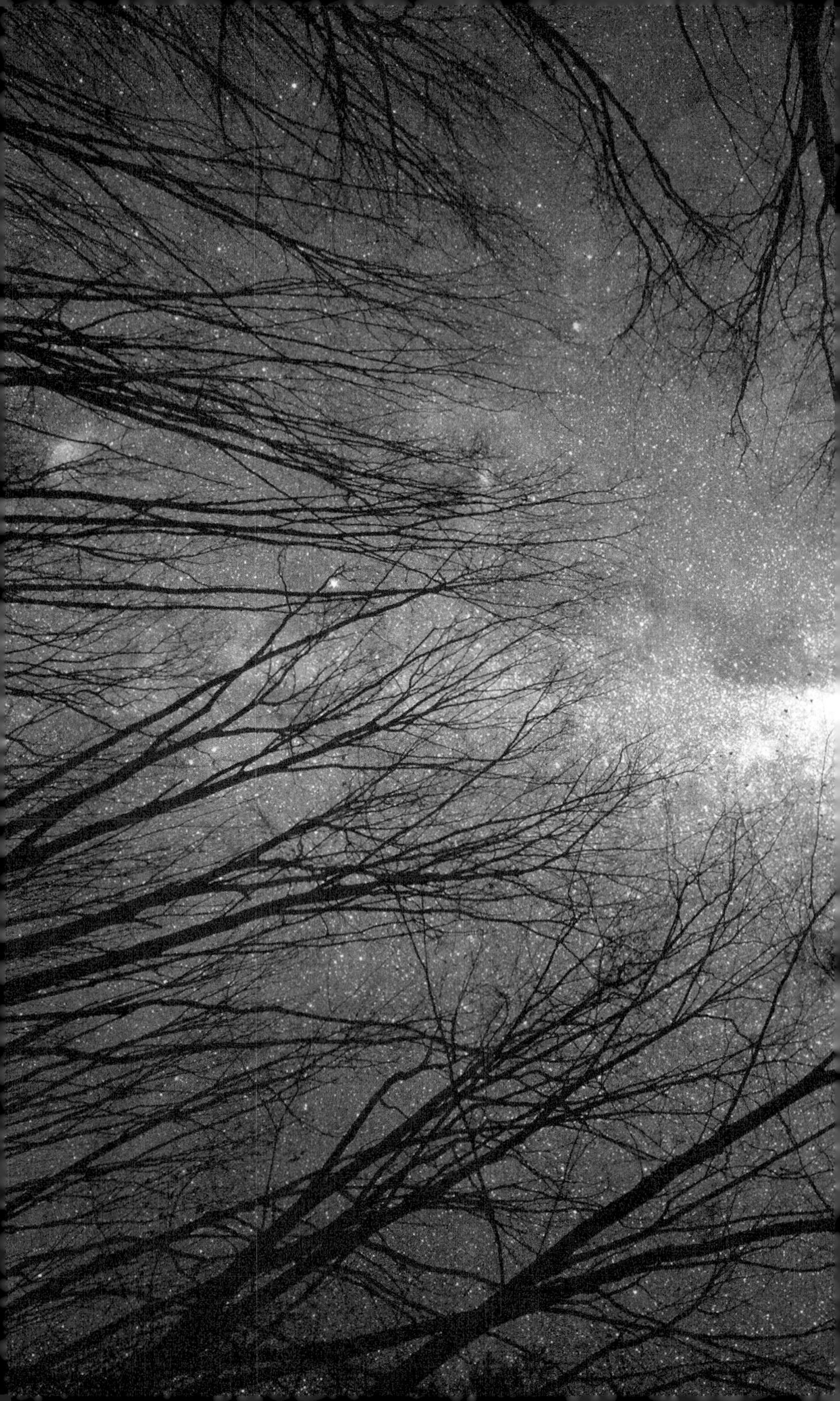

IN THE ATELIER

We were married a month later at dusk on the night of the next full moon. It was a simple ceremony under the boughs of the restored yew tree, with Hil acting as celebrant. Ly was dashing in midnight blue, and I wore a simple off-the-shoulder gown of pale violet, like the flecks in his eyes.

Sillas and Hobb had added the finishing touch to my outfit—early peonies and starry astrantia arranged like a crown. I had to admit Boyd looked handsome in a black suit, though maybe he'd always been handsome and it was his smile rather than the suit that made the difference.

Even Fluffy was dressed for the occasion, with a large satin bow tied around her neck.

"She looks ridiculous," Sylvie said after she'd wrapped Ly and me in tight hugs.

"You do know she's a hellhound with the name

'Fluffy,' right? I think the ridiculousness ship has sailed." I grinned and scratched behind Fluffy's ear. Her tongue lolled, and she half-closed her flaming eyes. "Besides, I think she looks *adorable*."

Sylvie raised an eyebrow at Ly, as if appealing for his agreement.

One hand at my back, he raised the other as if to say *don't drag me into this*. "Come on, let's leave this adorable dog to show off her bow while we go and have supper."

We ate and chatted and laughed, and I had no problem with the noise or everyone speaking at once or that they fell silent and listened when I added to the conversation.

Not that I used my magic to *make* them listen.

In the time since I'd saved Ly from Goren, we'd discussed my gift and what I'd done that night. "I think your power was always in your words," he'd said. "It's just you focused through something familiar—your sewing."

I'd nodded, understanding threading through me. "Because speaking out loud didn't come naturally."

He'd smiled and kissed my brow. "Exactly."

My True Name had only unlocked it.

He'd also told me, gently while stroking my knuckles, that he suspected all those years of being told I was lesser and unworthy, both by others and myself, had stopped my gift from working on myself.

He was not wrong.

My growing confidence, all the things I'd done that had seemed so impossible not that long ago—together, they'd helped unblock me. I'd experimented by trying on Ly's suit jacket, newly repaired, and sneaking past him and Boyd, Sylvie and Hil. Even out in the gardens, Sallis and Hobb and their bees hadn't seen me.

My gift worked on myself.

Still, I'd unpicked my True Name from the gown. It was too risky to leave it written anywhere. Just as it had given me power over myself, it would give someone else power over me if they discovered it.

At the mere thought of my True Name, the silver threads stretched out from me again. Maybe I didn't need it written or sewn anywhere. It would be an adventure to discover the exact nature of my unlocked gift and what I could do with it.

It was an adventure I was excited to take with Ly.

After supper, we danced under the yew tree, fae lights clustering around us like little stars, clinging to my hair and the night shadows that poured from Ly's heels.

The moon was high and bright, as full as my chest, which burst with how rich my life had become and how much I loved the man who spun me, then pulled me close.

I'd been to see the Lady of the Lake a few times since saving Ly and had even invited her to the wedding, but she couldn't leave her watery home. Still, I'd promised to take her a piece of Hil's cake and tell her all about the ceremony tomorrow night.

"Hmm." Ly shifted his hold and pushed a stray hair from my face as we swayed to the slowing music. I shivered at his light touch on my temple. "What's going on in here?"

With a soft snort, I put my hands around the back of his neck. "Nothing. Everything."

The dimple in his cheek flirted with making an appearance. "The usual, then?"

"I'm afraid so. But you're stuck with me now."

His lips grazed mine, as right as the feel of a needle between finger and thumb. "I wouldn't have it any other way. And this whirring mind of yours"—he smoothed my hair like he couldn't help but touch it—"is one of the many, *many* things I love about you."

I couldn't help but give what was probably a very smug grin. He loved me. Even the things I'd always thought unloveable. I stroked the soft hairs at the nape of his neck and let my touch stray closer to his sensitive ears. His shoulders tensed in anticipation as he sucked in a little breath.

"Flatterer." My voice came out husky.

"Truth-teller," he murmured back. With a small, private smile, he lifted me against the hard planes of him and kissed me like we were the only things in all the world.

By the time we pulled apart, our breaths came a little too hard, a little too fast, and the others had disappeared, the music with them.

He nuzzled my jaw, kissed my bare shoulders, made my body quiver. "Should we retire, my love?"

"I haven't given you your gift yet."

"You *are* my gift." He flashed a grin and nipped at my lower lip, forcing a gasp through me.

"And yet, I still have one for you. It's at the atelier so Fluffy can't sniff it out." I'd made a gift for Boyd last week, but Fluffy must've been drawn to the scent of my strengthened magic, because she pulled it out of my work basket and we'd found her knocking it across the floor like a toy.

Ly huffed a short laugh in my ear. "Hmm, it's not a pair of poisoned gloves, is it?"

I narrowed my eyes at him and lightly tugged the short hair at the nape of his neck. "Not *this* time."

He gave a rumbling mock growl but smirked. "Come along, then, I want to get my wife up to bed as soon as possible." His hands planed up my back and it was equal parts the touch and his words that rose heat in me.

We kissed, and in blooming darkness, we stepped to my atelier.

The dizziness faded in an instant, and I led Ly by the hand through the showroom to the workspace.

All the construction was finished now, the equipment and supplies delivered, the last touches put in place. He and Sylvie were helping me plan a grand opening for a week's time. The Night Queen had even agreed to come, a fact that gripped my chest every time I thought of it. But I could breathe past it and Ly had promised not to leave my side all evening.

Besides, I'd survived worse.

And after the grand opening, we would go and visit Rose, which made me both excited and nervous. She still hadn't replied to any of my letters, but despite that and how much I loved her and ached to hear her voice, tell her about all I'd seen and done, and ask about Annon... Well, truthfully, despite all that, I'd embraced being busy with the atelier and wedding in order to put off visiting.

I'd changed so much and so many things had happened since I'd last seen her at the stone circle, I couldn't help but wonder *what if?* She might not like the new me. But Ly was sure she'd love me just as much as she ever had, and part of me knew he was right. Rose was steadfast, as loyal as they came, and she'd be thrilled to see the atelier—my dream made reality at last. Ly had offered to bring her, and knowing her, it was an opportunity she'd leap at.

It was a smart woman who embraced change and made the most of it. I understood that now.

Ly's gift was in a small drawstring bag, which I dropped in his hand after making him close his eyes and wait so he wouldn't see where I'd hidden it. There were bound to be other times I'd want to hide his presents until they were ready to open.

"Hmm." His brows drew together as he smiled. "I taste raspberries. My favourite." Licking his lips, he opened his eyes, and suddenly I was all too keen to get home to bed with my new husband.

I held my breath while he opened the pouch. I'd made the suit, but he'd asked me to, paid me to, and it had been to his specifications. This was the first time I'd made him something as a gift, and it was something I'd invented myself. He might not even like it.

He made a low sound as he pulled out the stone. Like the two I'd given the Lady of the Lake, this one was covered with fabric and embroidered. For Ly, I'd chosen a black silk dupion shot with violet, and into it I'd sewn Frankish knots, ray stitches, and swirling textures in subtle, raven colours. Tiny chips of labradorite twinkled amongst the thread. I'd even found a little, gleaming magpie feather and added that to the embellishments.

Ly turned it over, examining every inch of it. "Ari, it's beautiful."

"I hope you find its contents even more beautiful." I cupped my hand beneath his. "You just have to use the command to access the moving images." I pointed to the word *Night* embroidered on the pouch. If I said it now, I'd trigger the stone and I didn't want to do that when he wasn't ready. It might take a few days before he was used to the idea—it had been so long since he'd seen them.

I had to swallow past a lump in my throat before I could say the next words. "Each stitch contains a memory of your parents."

His mouth dropped open on a soft gasp. Eyes glistening, they turned to the stone and skimmed over it. "But there must be a hundred stitches... more... I..." He shook his head. "How did you...? *How*?"

"With help. Sylvie, Hil, Boyd, Sallis, and Hobb all added their memories and favourite moments. Then I had Sylvie take me to your neighbours and some folk from court to ask them to add to it."

His eyebrows rose. He understood how hard facing strangers had been for me, that it was something I couldn't have even dreamt of a few months ago. Hopefully, it showed just how much he meant to me.

"They all agreed with only token bargains." Little things like asking me to pass Ly their well-wishes. I'd been prepared to offer much more to get those memories. "Your parents were well-loved. I wish I could've known them."

A muscle feathered in his jaw as he nodded and caught my hand. "One day, in the great beyond, where I'll meet yours, too. But perhaps before, you can visit these memories with me?"

"I would love that."

"Ari..." He shook his head and put the stone back in its pouch. "Thank you seems woefully inadequate." He lifted me and rested his forehead against mine. "But woefully inadequate words are all I have. Thank you, Ari. *Thank you*. My love, my evening star, the best bargain I ever made."

We were both smiling as our lips met, but that soon faded as we tangled together and our breaths heaved.

My hand went to his chest, seeking. In my throat, my thighs, my entire body, my pulse pounded. It was an asking call that his heart answered, throbbing against my palm, hard and sure.

With ease, he sat me on the workbench and cupped my head, angling us together. My husband, my love, my night kissed me thoroughly, breathlessly, gloriously, then he made me his and gave every part of himself to me.

AFTER, we lay entwined, and he pulled a blanket from the armchair over us. "Hmm, you know," I murmured, cheek on his chest, hand resting over his heart, "we're going to need another chair in here."

"Oh?" He raised his eyebrows, one hand stroking my hair, drawing the strands between his fingers.

"For when you come and read to me while I work. I can't possibly manage without that."

"*Really*?" He grinned, canines indenting his bottom lip. "Only just married, and here you are, *such* a demanding wife."

Wife. It buzzed through me, warm and sparkling like magic.

"Oh, dear, husband." I shook my head. "Didn't my list of requirements for the workroom give you a clue?"

His chuckle was a rumble under my cheek, against my chest. "I should've known. And yet you're entirely worth it."

That filled me. I was worth it. I was enough—for him *and* for myself. I'd spoken and I'd been heard and seen. I might never like large groups of people or loud noises, but I would not be silent or cowering again.

We fell quiet for a while, just our breaths and his heartbeat in my ear. His heartbeat that would go on so much longer than mine.

"I'll be sad to leave you, you know." I said it so softly, I wasn't sure if he would hear, but he shifted and peered down at me, frowning.

"Why? Where are you going?"

"Not for a long time yet, but... there's no escaping it—I'll go long before you." I couldn't bring myself to say *die*. Not when we were in such a happy place with so much to look forward to for decades yet.

"Ah, you mean the brevity of human existence?"

Despite that happiness, my eyes stung and my vision blurred. I nodded.

"You know you've been living in fae lands and eating fae food for months now? Didn't you pay attention to the stories?"

The threat of tears faded as my eyebrows knotted together. "Wait, what? You said the food was no harm to me!"

"It isn't. But it will lengthen your life, keep you healthy and youthful. And..." He licked his lips as though nervous and traced the edge of my ear. "If you wish, there's an element of marriage—a private ritual. I didn't ask yet because I thought the proposal and the wedding might be too much alongside asking you to—"

"To bond?" Like his parents had.

His chin dipped, the slightest nod. "Although you're human, you're fae-touched and it's magic that allows us to bind ourselves to each other. Your magic will be tied to mine and mine to yours, and that will link our lives. You'll have the same longevity as me. If I go, you go. If you go, so do I."

He wouldn't have to watch me age and die. I wouldn't have to pass on to the next place and leave him behind, wondering if he'd find new happiness or live broken evermore.

Fingertips tracing the edge of my jaw, he tilted my chin and held my gaze, no hint of his dimple or any grin. "But that's only if you want to. And I understand if you don't, there's no—"

"I want it, Ly." I slid against him, kissed away the grim, straight line of his mouth. "I want to spend my life with you, to build our life *together*. Let's make it a long and happy one."

He pulled me close and smiled against my lips before murmuring, "I fully intend to."

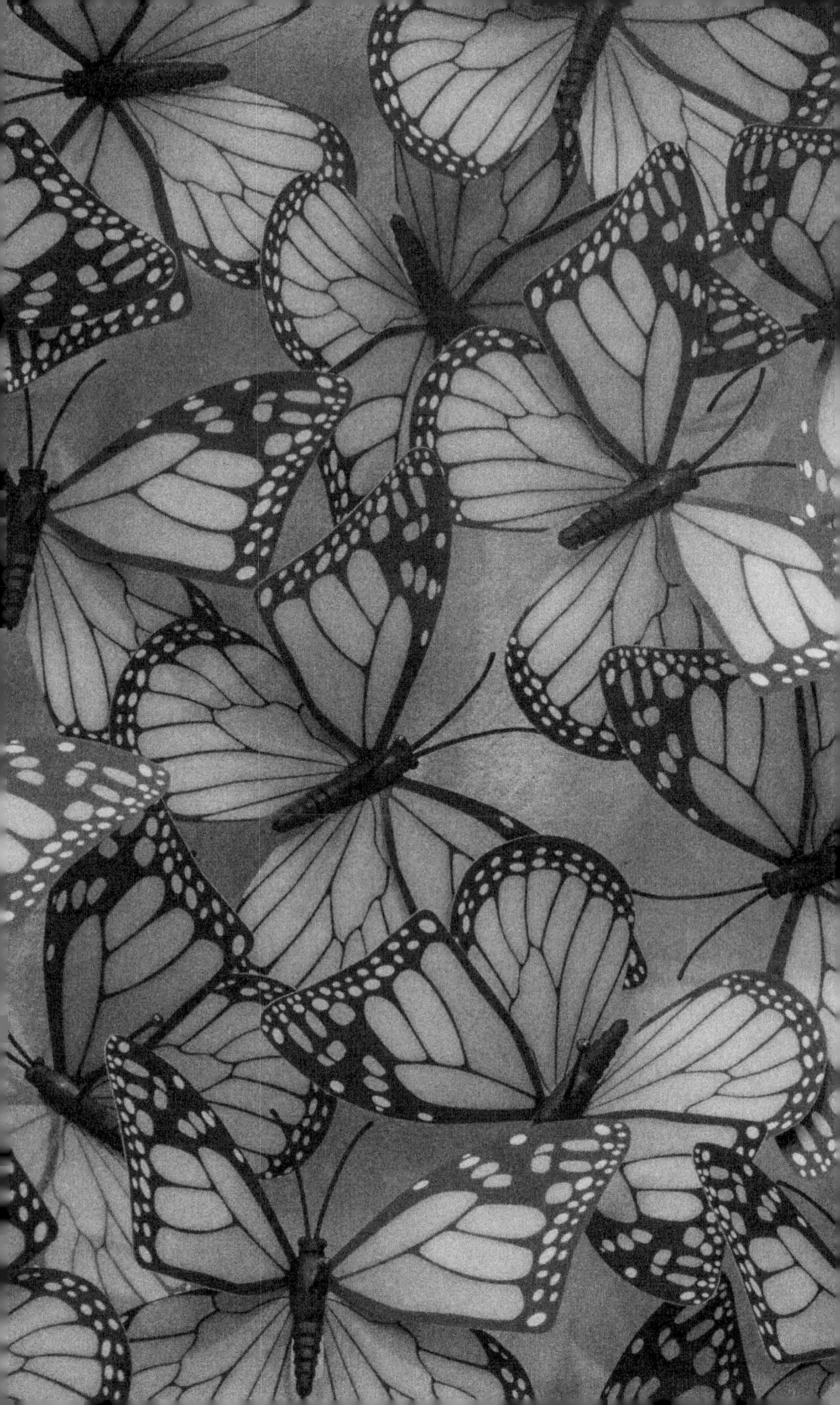

EPILOGUE

Up and down, up and down, I paced. Outside, the sun sat high in the blue sky, and I huffed. Still afternoon. I glowered at the clock on the mantelpiece. *One o'clock*. Dusk was *hours* away, and my skin was too tight, my thighs too tense.

With a sigh, I threw myself onto the bed. This had been my room, but not anymore, though. That was enough to make me smile a little.

Now Lysander and I had *our* room.

We'd married the day before yesterday and tonight we'd complete the bonding ritual.

I hadn't seen Ly since sunset. One part of the ritual he'd left out—one very *frustrating* part—was that we had to be apart from dusk until dusk.

To ensure freely given consent, he'd said.

To ensure I was aching with need, *I* thought.

Not only for his body, although I was keen to feel him all over me, but for his voice, his tender touches for no reason in particular, for his dark eyes glinting above a grin. For his laugh.

It was as Sylvie had said—now the yew was restored, his laughter and smiles came more easily and every one of them was a warm mote in my heart, like embers floating from a bonfire.

"Sulking because you miss your husband?" Sylvie lingered in the doorway, grinning wickedly. "I thought you'd take your chance to escape."

I snorted and threw a pillow at her... or *tried* to—it barely reached halfway to the door. "I don't want that anymore."

Her grin gentled to a sweet smile, though something dimmed in her gaze—a sadness, a longing, perhaps. "I know. I'm glad." Tilting her head, she slunk in. "Thought you might want some help getting ready."

Sitting up, I returned her smile. A little corner of my heart that wasn't full of Ly ached for her, for whatever dimmed her light. "From you? Always."

She ran one of her gloriously scented baths—jasmine and amber today—and stayed with me to chat as I washed my hair. Somehow it reached my waist now, and she explained it was the food, not only keeping me free from disease, but making every part of my body healthy. I had to admit, my skin had never looked so smooth or felt so soft.

After, she coaxed my hair into soft waves using some fae contraption that heated the shape in place. I saw no sign of clips, but she somehow fastened a small stem of white lilacs behind one ear. The sweet floral scent wafted with every movement.

As part of the wedding preparation, she'd helped me pick out a wedding trousseau, since there'd been no time for me to make it—all manner of floaty nightgowns and barely-there undergarments. It was just as well we'd bought such things, because with a smirk, she advised me to wear something I could remove easily.

We picked out a slinky black robe, the silk so slippery it could've been liquid. Tiny, *tiny* black and silver crystals scattered across it, as random as stars, so small, I couldn't see any stitches holding them in place. Perhaps they were fixed with magic.

The effect as I stood before the mirror, turning this way and that, certainly was magical. They only showed when they caught the light, like shooting stars winking in and out of existence.

As she helped me finish getting ready, I tried to coax more information out of her about the ritual. The outcome, I understood. All I knew of *how* was that it involved reaching for our magic while making love, which would weave our gifts together. Other than that...

Sylvie only smiled and shrugged. "It's like a lot of rituals—certain words you have to say, a couple of questions, and the appropriate symbolism."

I frowned and opened my mouth to ask *what symbolism*, but she nodded at the window.

"It's time. Come on." With a tug on my hand, she pulled me from the mirror.

Sure enough, outside the sky was darkening to violet,

which made my heart leap. It had only been a day since I'd seen Ly, but it felt more like a week, especially coming so early in our married life.

She led me to the next door along the hall—to what was now *our* room. Pausing, she took my other hand and squeezed, raising her eyebrows. "Ready?"

Heart skipping, I nodded. "Very."

This time there was no trace of dimness when she smiled, only warmth. "I'm so happy for you, Ari." She kissed my hand, opened the door, and led me inside.

After so many weeks, I knew this room well, but I'd never seen it like this. The curtains were drawn and candles blazed on every surface. In all my months in Elfhame, I'd never seen a single candle. The flickering light made me smile, something homely in it.

Then my seeking gaze reached the bed, its canopy decorated with yew and oak boughs, as well as waxy white lilacs, matching the sprig in my hair.

The delicate, perfumed flavour of elderflowers curled around my tongue—the boughs were from *the* yew tree. That wasn't an offering given lightly, and the idea filled my throat with a lump.

One you're worthy of. That's what Ly would say. Something I wouldn't have believed not so long ago, but... I touched the pendant hanging between my breasts. I could believe it now. Ly was here to offer himself to me in this final, eternal way, and he brought such a precious offering because I *was* enough.

And there he was.

Never mind leaping or skipping, I think my heart stopped.

Standing at the foot of the bed, in low conversation with Boyd, my husband, my beloved, my night. He wore a black shirt of the lightest cotton lawn and plain trousers. The candlelight licked at the contours of his face and brought fire to the violet-blue gleam of his hair.

My thumb rubbed against my fingertips, aching to trace the outlines that I loved so much, that I'd memorised.

Like me, he was barefoot. And that little detail, so comfortable, so intimate, tugged on my chest and the lump in my throat.

Boyd spotted me, eyebrows rising. With a half-smile he nudged Ly and nodded towards us.

Ly turned and his lips parted the moment his gaze landed on me. He drank me in head to toe, and his throat rose and fell in a slow swallow.

That look—it was a wonder it didn't strip the robe from my shoulders. My pulse jumped at my throat, my belly, my inner thighs, and deep, deep within.

Sylvie had advised me well—clothes that were quick to remove.

Somehow, my feet weren't as dumbstruck as the rest of me—a moment later, they'd crossed the room, and Sylvie and I stood before Ly and Boyd.

Biting his lip, Ly gave me a smile, both reassurance and heat in his eyes.

With a fluttering breath out, I smiled back.

"Are we ready?" Boyd raised one eyebrow at Sylvie, as

though realising he wasn't going to get much sense out of Ly or me.

"It certainly looks like it." A chuckle bubbled through Sylvie's words. She cleared her throat and tugged on my hand with both hers, yanking my attention from Ly. No amusement remained on her face.

This was a sacred ritual, one whose effects would last the rest of our lives. Ly had told me it wasn't something taken lightly.

With a long breath, I smoothed my expression, ready to begin.

"Ariadne"—she nodded, holding my gaze—"do you come to the bonding freely, willingly, and wholeheartedly?"

I squeezed her hands and nodded. "Freely, willingly, and wholeheartedly, I *do*."

She released me and we faced the men.

Boyd gripped Ly's shoulder, expression also grave. "Lysander, do you come to the bonding freely, willingly, and wholeheartedly?"

Ly inclined his head. "Freely, willingly, and wholeheartedly, I absolutely do."

"Then, be bonded," Sylvie and Boyd said in unison, placing my hands into Ly's.

I sucked in a soft breath as his warmth suffused me, so missed over this past day and night. He held my gaze, mouth twitching like he was suppressing a smile. His eyes gleamed, as dark and bright as the night sky on a new moon, and he ran his thumbs over my knuckles.

My husband. My love. The man who'd seen me even

when I tried to hide. Who now was choosing to link his life to mine, to bind us forever.

The world blurred and I had to blink away hot, happy tears.

Boyd produced a red cord and gave one end to Sylvie. "Red for your heartsblood." They wrapped the cord around our linked hands. "Spelled silk for your bond." Another wrap. "Unbreakable." Somehow they coordinated and tied a knot. "One for tomorrow." Another knot. "Two for a year and a day."

Ly squeezed my hands, chin dipping in not quite a nod. My heart fluttered like it was trying to break free of my ribcage and reach him.

Sylvie and Boyd tied a third knot. "Three for forever."

They stepped back, Boyd sniffing. Were his eyes overbright?

But Ly tugged me closer with our linked hands and ducked, touching his forehead to mine. "I've missed you," he whispered, immediately followed by, "I love you." As though he didn't know which to say first.

"Me too."

He flashed a grin and nudged his nose to mine. "Which?"

I scoffed softly and angled up to almost meet him. "Both." Then we moved as one, closing the distance with a long, sweet kiss.

Sylvie cleared her throat, and we pulled a couple of inches apart.

"Sorry." Ly huffed. "Thank you both."

I nodded my thanks and blinked from her to Boyd. "Is it... are we done?" I didn't *feel* any different.

"Well, you two have the main—ahem—*body* of the ritual to perform." Sylvie *actually* winked as they started for the door.

Snorting, Boyd clapped her on the shoulder as if congratulating her for such a good pun. "And gods forbid we keep you two apart any longer." They waved from the doorway.

"Have fun." Sylvie grinned, canines glinting.

"Lots and *lots* of fun." Boyd flashed his eyebrows up.

And then they were gone, the door clicking shut, leaving us in silence.

"Ari." Ly grazed his lips over my knuckles, pulling me so close, our bodies pressed together. Head bowed, he examined our linked hands. "Is it silly some part of me feared you might not come?" He bit his lip and looked up at me through dark lashes.

Shy. He was actually shy. And he'd feared I might refuse the bonding.

Not such an arrogant prick *at all*.

My heart warmed like it might be made of the hot chocolate Hil had started brewing in the evenings.

"Oh, Ly." I shook my head and kissed the tip of his thumb. "I'm afraid it's the silliest thing I've ever heard you say." I kissed his fingertips next, each in turn, as he had when he'd given me the boon to work with spider-silk. "But I think you might've just achieved the impossible."

Cheeks pink, he raised his eyebrows. "Oh?"

I started on the little finger of his other hand, holding his gaze as I dipped my head. "Somehow you've made me love you even more."

A foolish kind of smile pulled at his lips. "And all it took was for me to say something silly? I should do more of that, then."

I laughed against his middle finger before moving to the next. "It was vulnerable of you to admit your fear. *That* is what touched me." His next finger pressed into the soft flesh of my lower lip. "And that's what I'm here for, to hear all your fears, your hopes, your dreams... and desires."

When I kissed his thumb, I flicked the pad with my tongue. "I am here for all of you. Just as I don't hide behind a hood, I don't want you to hide any part of yourself from me. No shame, no fear, because I'll love you no matter what."

"Ariadne," he breathed, eyes gleaming. He shook his head and pulled me into another long kiss, all tangling lips and sweet nibbling that hitched my breath. "You are..." He shook his head again. "You're beyond words."

We stood that way a long while, hands and gazes connected, chests rising and falling slowly, drinking each other up in the flickering candlelight.

I'd found the one who'd stand by my side for a lifetime... for *many* lifetimes, and he was as glorious and beautiful inside as outside.

He lifted our hands and his eyebrows. "Shall we?"

The ritual. Of course. Feeling this connected to him,

it was hard to believe we hadn't already completed it. I laughed at myself and nodded.

With gentle patience, he extricated his hands from the cord, then pulled it from around mine. A low sound of satisfaction came from him. "We didn't have to untie the knots to escape. That's a good omen."

"Oh?" I raised my eyebrows, looking up from his long fingers as he pulled the cord taut.

"Loose enough to allow us to go about our days, but still tied, symbolising that even as we do so, we're linked."

"I like that idea."

He grinned and kissed my forehead. "I thought you might. Now"—his grin faded to a smirk as he took a step back—"I have another idea I *know* you're going to like. Remove your clothes."

Just that look, so heated, made my skin flush and my body shiver at once in wonderful contradiction. Unhurried, I pulled the tie of my robe, the silk whispering as the bow slid loose.

Breaths a slow rise and fall, he watched my hands. He'd told me enough times that he loved them, so I slid the tie between my fingertips. The slipperiness of the silk sent another shiver through me as the sides of the robe fell apart, revealing a column of flesh from throat to toe.

Ly's gaze trailed down my neck, between my breasts, over my belly, and I spotted the moment he took in what Sylvie had done to the hair between my legs, because his lips parted on a silent *O*. She'd shown me a lotion that removed hair and mentioned that some fae liked to go hairless or leave only a strip as it increased sensation.

Ariadne of Briarbridge really had disappeared because the idea of trying something new had thrilled rather than frightened me, so we'd taken away all but a narrow strip of dark hair.

And now Ly's gaze was knotted there as he absently pulled the red cord between his fingers.

"My, my, Ari." He exhaled, the edge of a smile playing on his lips, begging me to kiss them. "Just when I think you can't surprise me further."

For once, it was *me* wearing the wolfish grin.

With a long breath and a bite of his lip, Ly's gaze continued down that opening in my robe—along my thighs, my knees, shins, and feet.

At last he gave a slow blink and returned to my face. He raised his eyebrows as if to ask why I was still wearing the anything at all, and suddenly even the silk's light weight was too hot upon my skin.

A roll of my shoulders and the satin slid away, rippling over me like it really was water

It landed in a pool around my feet, and Lysander's eyes were just as dark, just as glinting. He took in every inch of me and nodded once. "My evening star, you are beyond beautiful. You're divine." His knuckles whitened as he squeezed the red cord as though keeping himself from reaching for me.

"You're not so hard on the eye yourself." I arched one eyebrow and cocked my head. "Although you're wearing far too many clothes."

His canines flashed into view as he grinned. "No, I'm wearing exactly the right amount of clothes. Patience, Ariadne." He clicked his tongue and deposited the cord on the bedside table before retrieving a cobalt blue bottle. He spread its contents on his fingertips and the pads of his thumbs.

He prowled towards me, fingers and thumbs glistening as a woody, masculine scent reached me. It was some sort of oil and the scent was all him, without the sweet notes of rhubarb, and it made my head spin.

"My love," he murmured, stopping a foot away, "my wife, my evening star, I anoint you." He smeared the oil on my forehead, the tips of my ears, and along my collarbones.

I swallowed, fighting to keep my breaths deep and even as he moved lower. He ran that slick touch over my nipples, a softness in his gaze as he watched them pebble in response.

"My sweet love, my darling wife." His voice took on a soft, lilting quality, like he was speaking from somewhere far away as he drew a line down from my belly button.

The muscles of my stomach tensed and my breath caught in anticipation, but he stopped at the strip of hair Sylvie had left.

So far, he'd remained intent on his fingers' progress over my skin, but now he met my gaze and lowered to his knees. Something about the gesture jumbled my insides. I was bare and he still clothed, yet he was the one kneeling.

More oil circled on the curve of my hip bones, dotted on my knees, traced over the tops of my feet.

Graceful as a sabrecat, he rolled to his feet and produced the bottle of oil from his pocket. "Your turn." He peeled off his shirt and unbuttoned his breeches, letting them fall before kicking them away.

The candlelight's constant movement toyed with the lines of his body, highlighting this muscle, shadowing that one, before shifting and gilding an entirely different stretch of tanned skin.

I bit my lip and unscrewed the bottle, dripping the oil on my fingers and thumbs. "What do I say?"

"Anything you want. You can't go wrong." He gave a half smile. "This is for us, no one else."

When I tiptoed and reached for his forehead, he bowed to help. "My beloved." I couldn't help but flash a grin as I slid my fingertips along the edge of his ears making every one of his muscles ripple. "My fae." It felt appropriate with the points of his ears digging into the pads of my index fingers. "My husband."

Collarbones next, then nipples. Maybe it was the first chill of night in the air, but they were stiff under my touch. When I drew a line down from his bellybutton, I didn't stop at his hair—my fingertip ventured through it until it reached his cock, half-hard, and continued along it, only stopping at the very tip.

His jaw flexed, and a low sound, not quite a groan, came from low in his chest.

I knelt, looking up at him as he had me, and it was a surrender. I would let him do whatever he wanted. He'd shown me he knew far more of sex than I did, and every time we came together, he saw to my needs many times over before he took his own pleasure.

He wasn't a slave to it and it wasn't his duty—those terms suggested he *had* to please me.

No, the way he plunged himself into it—it was his passion, his prayer... his art.

I anointed his hips, just above the line that pointed down to his length, which grew harder with each touch. "My wonder." His knees, the back of his feet. "My night."

He held out his hand and helped me to my feet. His smile was as gentle as his touch when he gathered me against his bare body, the oiled parts of us gliding together. "I always wonder when you say that... Is it night with a *K* or an *N*?"

Pressed against him, I rose to my tiptoes, revelling in the way the slick points of my nipples slid over his skin and his dick pressed into my belly.

"Can't it be both?" I lifted my eyebrows in question as his hands spread over my back. "It was nothing like the stories—you didn't ride in on a white sabrecat and you had no shining armour. But you rescued me all the same." I half shrugged. "Even if I didn't realise I needed rescuing."

With a shake of his head, he lifted me until our faces were level. "I didn't rescue you." He nuzzled my jaw, my nose, taking a long breath in as though he loved the mingled scent of the oil and the lilacs and *us* as much as I did. "This place just gave you space to breathe, that's all. If anything, *you* rescued *me*."

I toyed with the short hair behind his ears and he shivered, most likely at how close I was to such a sensitive area. "Again, can't both be true?"

He laughed, the sound reverberating through me. "Are you sure you're not fae?"

He captured my chuckle with his lips, pulling me into a slow kiss that grew deeper as he carried me to the bed. I wrapped around him, taking his tongue, sliding mine against it, skin burning as his hardness pressed against my softness, stoking sweet pleasure at my core.

Placing me on the bed, he kissed his way down my neck, following the path of my scars, down my chest, the side of my breast. My heart drove faster, pulse throbbing at my throat, my wrists, and deep inside.

My beloved. My fae. My husband. Mine to bond with.

Good gods, how was my heart still beating? Surely it was stuffed to bursting with this bright joy.

He glanced up at me and smiled like he knew what I felt and had that same brightness in him. I hoped he did.

Still kissing every bare inch of flesh, his long fingers slipped between my legs, stealing my breath as he traced my edges. He skirted past the knot of nerves that tightened in anticipation.

Tease. He loved to do that. And although it always led somewhere glorious, the withholding killed me every time.

Well, two could play that game. I ran my fingers through his silken hair and trailed the outline of his ears, coaxing a groan from his throat that hummed into me.

His eyes closed, a tight frown of focus between his

eyebrows, while his breaths came quicker. His touch slid to my pussy, not quite entering, and swept up that centre line, finally landing on the spot that throbbed for his attention.

"Ly," I breathed as my body arched, delicious tension seizing my back like a bow bent to the huntsman's will.

Chest heaving, he opened his eyes, that frown still in place. "Gods damn it, Ari." He surged up and claimed my mouth in a searing kiss. "You keep that up and I'm not going to last to take you."

I bit back a grin and stopped tormenting his ears. Instead I pulled him to my lips again. The way he drove his tongue inside my mouth said he didn't mind that at all.

His insistent touch, circling, gliding, pulled me more and more taut. I whimpered against his mouth, but that only made his kiss more urgent, his lips firm, his tongue invading, just as he dipped a finger inside me.

I came apart with a cry, every muscle thrumming like a bowstring released the second before it broke. Dark and light and consuming pleasure. The writhing tension of my body under his command. There was nothing else.

Then the world seeped back in, his slick touch in and on me, his mouth hovering just above mine, sharing the same air and letting me catch my breath as my lungs heaved like bellows at the forge. I must've crushed the flowers in my hair, spreading their scent on the sheets, because a wave of lilac broke over me.

"Lysander." It came out more as a whimper than a word, my body trembled so much.

"Ariadne," he murmured against my lips. "I am yours." He placed himself at my entrance, making me tight with want. "My body, my soul, my magic, all yours, for all time." He took my hand and pinned it to the bed as our fingers interlaced. He took the red cord and wrapped it around our wrists, capturing the end between our palms. "I bind myself to you." With that he trapped my other hand against the sheets and eased in, the exquisite stretch and his words stealing my breath anew.

"I am yours," I panted as he filled me. "My body"—my back arched as if in emphasis, though I didn't tell it to move—"my soul, my magic, all yours..." I angled to take him deeper and tried to catch my breath so I could speak. "For all time." Then his pelvis was pressed against me and he stopped there with his forehead on mine. "I bind myself to you."

He pressed a long kiss to my lips, squeezing my hands. "That's it. That's my good love." And the praise warmed me still further, bright in my chest. He took up a long, languorous stroke inside me, building pressure in my every fibre. "Don't think I forgot, just because it happened months ago."

Barely able to focus on his words, I blinked. "Forgot what?"

"Your body's response after your escape attempt when I threatened to tie you to my bed."

A thrill ran through me, and my mouth dried. "Oh?"

"Later." He grinned and nipped my lower lip before releasing my hands. He tied a knot around my wrist and another around his, tethering us but still giving us length to move, like he'd said about the omen.

I couldn't help but picture him tying me to the bedpost, leaving me at his glorious mercy.

With a smirk that said he knew exactly what I was picturing, he nudged his nose against mine. "And here I was thinking you such a good girl."

"I *did* try to escape, so I must be a bit... naughty."

He huffed, part panted breath, part laugh. "More like *very*. And I need to punish you for that... thoroughly." He said it slowly, coiling me tight. "*Repeatedly*."

Not missing a beat of his glorious rhythm, he pulled me to the edge of the bed and stood over me, splaying my thighs.

I'd always cursed this bed because it was so high, level with his hips, requiring some effort on my part to climb onto. Now the height seemed quite perfect as he rolled into me, making black spots bloom across my vision and my heartbeat roar.

Eyes dark as night, barely glinting in the candlelight, he watched me arch and grind against him, gaze alert and on my mouth as though he could *see* the soft sounds of pleasure I made.

"You take me so well." His hands planed up the insides of my thighs until they held my hips, guiding, pulling me onto him, angling me upward until he hit my front walls.

I couldn't have helped the sharp cry if my life had depended on it. It tore through me, chased by the intense joy he pushed into my core, my nerves, my veins.

"And you look so good doing it." A flicker of a smile that only drove me hotter, higher, then his gaze trailed to the spot where we joined.

His smile faded, replaced with something raw and animal, the darker side of his sweet nuzzling against my neck. Lips parted, his canines showed as his breaths rasped.

He *was* raw and animal and so damn beautiful with it. I loved this part of him as much as the teasing gentleman who read me stories by the fire. This was the man who killed sluagh to keep me safe, who called me *his* to protect me from Goren, who both teased and devoured me.

And, Stars above, I was utterly his.

Hand shifting, he swiped my exposed bud, and I fractured around him, hard and tight, nothing and everything.

Still he wasn't done with me.

"I think you're ready." He gathered me to him with aching gentleness as I came down.

"Ready?" I blinked, world spinning. He was still in me, but no longer thrusting, just holding me to his chest.

He huffed a laugh, which jerked inside me and made me groan. "To bond."

My eyes widened. "You mean that wasn't...?"

"That was just enjoyment." He gave a rakish smile, eyes bright, teeth brighter. "For the bonding, we both have to find our peak, and I wanted to see you come apart for me first."

I clung to him, arms around his neck, legs around his

hips, somehow still finding strength in my liquid muscles. "What did I do to deserve this?" I shook my head and kissed him, heart aching.

He nibbled at my lower lip. "Being you was quite enough."

My heart, for all its fullness, leapt in my chest, and I cupped his cheeks, tracing the contours of his face as I kissed and kissed and kissed him.

Wearing a glowing smile, he turned us so he sat on the bed with me in his lap, and produced the bottle of oil. His hips rolled into me, deep and delicious, and I responded, riding his waves as he built higher ones in my very being.

The cool wetness of the oil was welcome when he drizzled it over my back, my burning flesh, then over my chest, the scent heady and thick, filling me as surely as he did. Then he crushed me against him, chest to chest, hip upon hip, bellies together.

Not even the finest spidersilk thread could've come between us.

We rocked together, my breasts slick and slippery against his chest, the sensation of gliding unlike anything else I'd ever experienced. His hands swept over every inch of my back, moulding to my shape, kneading my flesh, drawing groans from deep inside us both.

I kissed his throat, and his moan vibrated through my lips. I licked and nipped and sucked upon his salty flesh, as animal as he was. His pulse leapt under my mouth, my tongue, spiking and fast as his muscles hummed beneath me, against me.

"I love you so much," I whispered against his skin, letting his stubble scrape my lips, sending fresh shivers of pleasure through me.

He buried his face in my hair and took a long inhale as though he could breathe me, breathe this moment in. "And I you." His hands slid under my backside as he kissed me over and over and lifted me higher and higher, so I rode his full length. He captured my moans, consumed them, just as his touch consumed me.

My body throbbed with it, shook with it, the unbearable tension rising, rising, rising, threatening to destroy me. Good gods, I wanted it to. Such sweet, sweet obliteration.

A finger slid to my back passage, massaging, and I arched with a whimper.

He released my lips and searched my gaze, pupils wide, eyes hooded, a tiny questioning frown between his eyebrows. "Do you want—?"

"Yes," I panted. "I want it, you."

Watching my face, his pace slowed as he pressed and so gently entered. That sensitivity he'd built in me when only touching the opening continued, heightened on the inside. It twitched through me, made the stretch of his thickness in me all the sweeter, made the rub of his pelvis against my tight bundle of nerves all the brighter.

I nodded when I realised his breaths were slower as though he were focusing on my response and absolutely alert to any sign of distress. "Don't stop."

He slid a little deeper and the tightness made my

mouth fall open and pushed a primal sound from my chest.

I was somewhere at the top of a mountain or a cliff or some other high and deadly place, ready to fall.

I rocked against him, front and back, and he timed his dual thrusts so one went in as the other drew out. He was everywhere, everything, around me, within me, a part of me.

"Ly... Lysander." I think I shouted it the second time. His name was a prayer, a thanks, maybe even the only thing holding me in the world.

His triumphant smile said I'd cried it out, just as he'd wanted, and seeing him so pleased lifted my own pleasure higher even though I'd have sworn that was impossible.

"Reach for your gift, my love." His voice came out ragged, half-breath, half-growl.

I gathered the parts of myself threatening to pull apart and whispered my True Name in my head. The silver web spread out from us, but it was brightest here, in this tight thread between his chest and mine.

Raspberry and rhubarb flooded my mouth, the sudden overpowering taste making me cry out, and then I fell.

Night and starlight, I was the threaded line between the stars, spelling out their constellations.

I fluttered, tight and loose, full and empty, but not alone.

That night darkness was Ly, falling with and through

me, shattering my being into the motes that floated on the breeze when he shadowstepped.

But tonight those motes flickered and glimmered between darkness and searing silver light. Bright and black strands threaded between each one, drawing them back together.

Once all those flecks met, I blinked and found myself back in my body. Ly's eyebrows were peaked, his lips parted, the perfect picture of wonder as we rode out the end of our shared completion.

A knot in my throat, I sagged against him, tears in the corners of my eyes as I kissed his lips, his cheeks, his chin.

"Ariadne." His voice cracked as he said it and kissed my brow.

"Are we...?" I sucked in long breaths, trying to remind my body how to work for anything other than pleasure.

With a lazy blink, he gave a slow, private smile. "We are." So tender I could've cried, he lay me on my side, still pressed against his chest. "Look inside, to your gift, and you'll see."

Around us, the web still radiated out to the world, but the brightest, strongest thread stretched between him and me. I smiled at that and stroked his cheek. When I followed the thread inward, to my chest, to my heart, I found it wasn't only silver. It braided night with starlight, him with me.

A soft gasp in my throat, hand over my heart, I blinked at him. It had worked. We were bonded. My eyes stung, but it was a sweet sting, and the tears brimming were joyous ones. "You're here."

He inclined his head, that wonderful, dawning smile on his face. "I am." He took my hand, kissed the fingertips, and trapped it between his palm and his chest. "And you're here."

I pressed against him, soaking up his heartbeat as it slowed to a calm, content beat. "Always."

He brushed his lips over mine. "Forever."

THE END

If you're not ready for Ari and Ly's story to be over, you can get access to bonus scenes from Lysander's point of view, as well as other fun freebies and behind-the-scenes secrets by joining my newsletter.
You can also see more of them in Rose's book, These Gentle Wolves.

A Note from the Author
Caution – Spoilers Within

There you have it – Ari and Ly's story.

If you're not ready to say goodbye to them quite yet, you can download some bonus scenes from Ly's POV by signing up here: www.claresager.com/stolennl

I hope you enjoyed reading Ari and Ly's story as much as I loved writing it. They kind of caught me by surprise...

When my author friend Sylvia Mercedes approached me about joining the Stolen Brides of the Fae (SBotF) project, I was interested but also hesitant – I didn't have a story in mind and I already had other projects planned for the year. I said maybe.

The fey must've visited me overnight, because when I took a shower the next morning, about 70% of the story came to me, scene by scene. Wrapped in a towel, I hurried to my laptop and sat and wrote... and wrote and wrote and wrote. When I looked up, I had several thousand words of notes and snippets of dialogue and, most importantly, a story idea.

I went back to Sylvia and told her, "I'm in!"

The rest, as they say, is history. And now, a year after that original release of *Stolen Threadwitch Bride*, I'm updating the author note to reflect this new revised edition – The Author's Cut, as I'm affectionately calling it. The original series was all fade to black, with no on-page sex. Obviously, you've read this new version, so you know that's no longer the case!

With the SBotF disbanding after that initial year, I've gone back over the book to update it, add in the steamy scenes that had previously only been available as bonuses, and add in mention of Annon.

Not saying she's going to be relevant in future, but... yeah, she's totally going to be relevant in future! ;) After all, with its re-release, STB starts its own series: *Bound by a Fae Bargain*.

I'm currently working on book two of the series, which will follow someone a little closer to home...

Since STB first came out a year ago, some of you have mentioned in your reviews that you're sad you didn't get to see Ari reunited with Rose.

See. The thing is… I couldn't do that. Because STB needed to be a standalone story, but Rose… Rose was already off starting her own adventure.

Later this year (as I write this in July 2022), you'll get to read all about Rose's adventure and how she ends up *Bound by a Fae Bargain*.

[Edit February 2023 – Keep reading for a sneak peek of Rose's Story, *These Gentle Wolves*, releasing this spring.]

But, back to Ari…

It shouldn't be a surprise that this story idea and the character of Ariadne came to me so easily. I'm a stitcher and qualified corsetière (you might've spotted photos on my Instagram – @claresager) and made my own wedding dress, so it was really special to get to write a heroine who can make magic with stitches.

I've never worked with 'spidersilk,' though. That was something I made up – something fantastical that felt very fey.

Although, weirdly enough, as I worked on the outline for the story, I came across some articles on the real thing. It turns out people have attempted to create fabric from spider silk to varying degrees of success. You can see an article about the largest piece of cloth made from *natural* spider silk (and talks a bit about the history) here: https://www.wired.com/2009/09/spider-silk/ (warning, photos of spiders on the page!). There are also companies making synthetic spider silk, which some are touting as the future of clothing. Clearly, the fey are ahead of their time! ;)

I have to admit, I was nervous about writing Ari. Normally my heroines are much more confident. They're trained swordswomen who swing into action with a blade and a grin that's almost as sharp. (Especially Vice, the snarky pirate of my *Beneath Black Sails series*, also set in the Sabreverse.)

But I wanted to write a different kind of heroine. One whose skills and magic had nothing to do with violence. Perhaps even one who was quieter.

I didn't intend to write about a character who struggles with anxiety as Ari does, but as I wrote the first couple of scenes and Skeeves showed up, she had that intense physical response, edging close to hyperventilating.

I gave my subconscious a healthy dose of side eye and said, "Oh, OK, we're doing this, are we?"

Because I've battled anxiety all my life. I never planned to put something so personal on the page, but Ari was pretty insistent and unlocking that facet of her character made everything else fall into place. So here we are.

If it helps just one person understand or empathise with someone they know who lives with anxiety (including themselves), then it was 100% worth it.

And if you're that person who read this story and related, know that I see you. I get it. You're not strange. You're not broken. There are more of us than you might think! ;)

As well as personal experience, this story and Albion are heavily inspired by British folklore, legend, mythology, history, and its native, pagan religions.

Fluffy, with her white fur and red points, is based on the Cŵn Annwn, supernatural hounds associated with the Otherworld.

Elements of the sluagh are from Scottish Gaelic folklore, but I added the 'young sluagh' idea myself, just to give you something to look forward to when they appear in future books with their wings. (You're welcome!)

Ly's home is based on Wollaton Hall, a local country house here in Nottingham. You can see photos of it and some tour videos including the back of the house and terrace and *that* balustrade on my Instagram highlights

(@claresager). If you're ever in the area, I definitely recommend a walk through its deer park (entry is free).

Albion and its beliefs, Calan Mai celebrations, and the human marriage ceremony appear in *Across Dark Seas*. This free full-length book is set in the same world as *Stolen Threadwitch Bride* and tells the story of Avice Ferrers. She's another young woman stifled by Albionic society, who escapes in a very different way. You can get your free copy (as well as the Lysander bonus scenes) as a gift when you sign up to my newsletter here: www.claresager.com/stolennl

I also couldn't resist putting in another real world reference. YUZU! It's probably my favourite flavour, and I've always said it tastes like sunshine. I first tried it on honeymoon in Japan and now I have yuzu tea as my treat drink. Whenever I see yuzu on a menu, I *must* have it. I've yet to try a yuzu macaron, but I'd probably sell my soul to have one. Including them in Ari and Ly's afternoon tea was the next best thing.

Again, I hope you enjoyed Ari and Ly's story. They have a special place in my heart, and I'm looking forward to them making appearances in future books set in the Sabreverse.

You can get in touch and let me know what you thought at clare@claresager.com or just reply to any emails from my newsletter when you sign up – I love hearing from readers! :)

Thank you so much for joining me on this adventure, especially if you're one of the wonderful backers of my Kickstarter campaign for the hardback edition of this book. I look forward to hearing from you someday, but for now I'll wish you **happy reading!**

All the very best,

Clare Sager, July 2022

    x

PS – Remember to grab your bonus scenes by signing up for my newsletter here: : www.claresager.com/stolennl

PPS – I'll leave you with the sneak peek I promised of Rose's story, *These Gentle Wolves*...

THESE GENTLE WOLVES
SNEAK PEEK

Across the Wall

When I reached the wall, I wondered if maybe—*probably*—this was a terrible idea. I squeezed the knife tucked into my belt. It wasn't a dagger—it was far too crude for that, but it was iron.

In a country where iron was illegal, and for a woman about to cross the wall into faerie, it was worth more than all the gold in the kingdom.

The wall itself didn't look like much, just craggy hewn rock some seven feet tall, grey and blotched with yellow and white lichen. The stories Ari's papa used to tell us said it was infused with iron to keep the fae from crossing over.

Bullshit.

It hadn't stopped that fae lord from coming and taking her, had it?

Last night, as he'd stood over us, ready to take her,

she'd looked up at me tears in her eyes together with desperation.

I knew she saw tall, strong Rose, her protector and friend. But I couldn't save her. All I'd had were words. I only hoped they weren't empty ones.

"I'll find you." I'd whispered it to her, and now I said it out loud.

This time the wall was the only audience to my promise.

I had the iron knife, a steel dagger, and food. On a whim, I'd grabbed a small sack of flour. Stories spoke of invisible creatures beyond the wall, and I figured a handful of flour would reveal any such beasts. I'd managed to scrounge an old tent from one of the market-sellers, and I'd pulled out the little pouch of coins that I was saving towards a second dagger.

Saving Ari was more important.

She had no one else. She needed me.

That thought circling, I squared my shoulders and placed my hands on the wall.

Cold. Hard. Rough grain under my fingers. It felt like any other stone wall. I wasn't sure exactly what I'd been expecting—a magical barrier pushing me back perhaps—but not *normality*.

This adventure was getting off to a good start.

Grinning, I dug my fingers into craggy handholds and climbed up. The wall was so old and the stones so rough with no mortar in between, I scaled it in moments and lifted my head for my first glimpse of faerie.

The sky over Alba—or Elfhame as the fae called it—

continued clear and blue, the sun edging towards noon. Scrubby grassland rolled away across the hills, and dark woodland pooled in a valley ahead, creeping up the slope beyond.

It didn't look so different from Albion. Maybe the stories were all exaggeration.

Admittedly, the fae lord who'd taken Ari had made her disappear in a puff of darkness, and I'd never heard of a human doing such a thing.

But I had iron.

I got the blade from the wise woman who lived on the edge of Briarbridge, the one whose house we always ran past as kids. I went to her at first light, and she understood why I wanted protection from the fae and didn't want to leave my friend at their mercy. She pulled up a wonky old floorboard and gave me the blade with the words, "Iron cuts through flesh. Iron cuts through fae. Iron cuts through lies."

Good luck to the fae who came between me and Ari.

Iron was hard, but my determination was harder. I wouldn't give up until she was safe.

Left and right, I cracked my neck, then patted the iron blade. "Here goes." I swung my leg over the top of the wall and jumped down.

I landed in Elfhame.

Sun overhead. Grass and mud underfoot. It didn't feel any different to home.

As I adjusted my pack and started north, no vines tried to grab my feet, no fae monsters leapt out to attack; there was only me and the spring day.

With each step, clouds gathered overhead. By twenty yards, snow began to fall, thick and white.

I pulled my cloak closer, fingering the oak leaves embroidered down the front. Ari had sewn it, whispering magic into the stitches. And as I walked on, huge flakes of snow flecking the green wool and melting in my strawberry blond hair, I didn't feel the cold. She'd spelled it with warmth.

"Bad luck, Elfhame. You're going to have to do better than a bit of snow to keep me out."

Honestly? I wasn't sure anything could keep me away. Not when Ari needed me.

I pulled up my hood, smiled into the breeze, and pretended the white dusting on the ground was flour, just like at home.

Ma and Pa would've realised I was gone hours ago, when I didn't show up to help finish the morning's loaves and cakes and open the shop. They'd struggle wrangling my twelve brothers and sisters without me; it left a bitter taste in my mouth as I crunched through the fresh snow.

But I'd let that fae bastard take Ari, and that was a far, far worse flavour on my tongue. Sour and acidic like bile, burning even when I took a sip of water from my canteen.

I was the strong one: I looked after *her*. But at the stone circle, she'd looked up at me, and I'd been the one crying while she'd held back, jaw tight as her eyes gleamed with unshed tears. She'd protected me, even as she'd been stolen from us.

And I'd let her down.

I squared my shoulders and lengthened my stride.

"I'm coming for you, Ari. Just hold on."

I walked.

And walked.

And walked.

I hummed and sang little songs to myself as the afternoon sun passed overhead. Truth be told, Elfhame didn't seem as frightening as the stories made out. Great trees stretched high above, and I used the moss on them to keep myself on track, always aiming north. No paths or roads cut through the land, so I was grateful for nature pointing the way.

Admittedly, "the way" suggested a more concrete plan than the one I actually had.

And maybe "plan" was overstating it.

Quickest would be finding Ari and the fae lord who'd taken her. He'd magicked her away, but for all I knew, he'd only taken her just the other side of the wall. But I hadn't found any tracks in the snow. Though the fresh fall would've covered any tracks anyway. Great.

Which left plan *B*. If I could find a town, I'd be able to ask the locals. There couldn't be *that* many humans in Elfhame nor fae lords who were bound to take the Tithe from one of our towns. Even if they didn't know, they'd be able to point me to their capital city somewhere in the north. The fae had said he'd come by order of the Night Queen, so they would know of him there.

Not much of a plan, but it was the only one I had.

Sunset splayed across the sky in such a glorious display of gold and pink, I almost forgot what it meant.

Night.

Although Elfhame in the daytime seemed pleasant enough, I wasn't fool enough to think it would be safe at night. Even the woods around Briarbridge were off limits after dark, with wolves and bears and, on the new moon, the Wild Hunt haunting the game trails.

I also wasn't fool enough to think a tent and fire would keep me safe from whatever dangers came out here after sunset. Most likely a fire would attract more attention that it scared off. So, I climbed a tree and fastened the tent between its branches to keep off any rain that might come in the night—or more snow. Nestled at an intersection of several boughs, I found a cosy spot and tied myself in place using one of the tent's lines. On the edge of a copse, my tree's position at the top of a hill gave me a view down into the valley, but its leaves shielded me from sight.

That was when I heard the howls.

Three, long and low and eerie against the rising moon and evening blackbird song.

Every hair on my body stood on end as goosebumps crept across my skin.

Although wolves never ventured into Briarbridge, they roamed the land around. When I was five, a little girl had been helping her ma and pa round up sheep, and she'd disappeared. The wolves had taken her. That night, Ari's pa had told us the story of Little Red Riding Hood.

What big teeth you have.

I shivered and pulled my cloak closer.

I was safe up here and warm. It would all be fine.

In fact, this warmth? It was that gorgeous carpenter who travelled through town each spring and always found his way to the tavern and to my table. I closed my eyes and hugged myself. These were his arms around me. I would say something funny and throw him a grin and a wink. We always found somewhere quiet for a bit of fun.

Something shrieked.

The cold trickling through me was nothing to do with the weather. It wasn't the kind of cold this cloak could save me from.

That sound.

Fuck. *That sound.*

It was like nothing in Briarbridge *or* the woods. It didn't sound human *or* animal. It was...

I screwed my eyes shut. They had sprung open at the noise without any instruction from me. I was up a tree: no animal could reach me. For anything less mundane, I had cold iron.

I squeezed the worn leather hilt.

But another shrill cry pierced the night, different from the earlier shriek. This one was sharp and brief. Not close, but still...

My heart pounded, and as much as I tried to keep my breaths quiet, they came that bit too fast and much too ragged, steaming before my face in the moonlight.

I abandoned all ideas of sleep.

A low keening drifted up from the valley. It was a sad sound that made my eyes sting.

Or maybe it was a realisation that made my eyes prickle. A stupid, useless realisation to have up a tree, but here I was.

For all the stories I'd heard from Ari's pa, I knew nothing about Elfhame and its dangers. All I had was an iron dagger and a pack full of supplies.

And it was not enough.

INTO THE FOREST

I must've eventually fallen asleep, because I woke with a start to dawn sun flooding the sky. No howls. No prowling shapes in the valley or the copse below. Only birdsong, trees, and the snowy hillside.

I huffed a sigh that I felt down to my bones and descended the gnarled oak. Considering I'd slept in a tree, I wasn't too stiff. That had to be thanks to my morning runs.

They were the only times I had quiet. No Peony demanding to be picked up or Rory complaining he was hungry. No child on my hip while I fed another. I loved my brothers and sisters dearly, all twelve of them, but they were a whirlwind of chaos and endless work.

Running was my only break, even if it brought a twinge of guilt. Between that and dagger training, I only needed a quick stretch before I felt ready for another day of walking. I'd known the exercise would come in handy, even if they would never let me join the town guard.

Stupid old men and their stupid ideas about what women could do.

With a *hmpf*, I dug the loaf from my bag. It was two days old now, so it took some effort to tear off a hunk, but it was edible.

Checking the moss on the trees, I started north again and ate as I went. What had looked like a copse of oaks huddled on the top of this hill actually trailed down the far side, joining the woods crowding a rocky valley.

Where was Ari now? Was she in the wilds or had that fae taken her to a town? Were there even towns like—?

A low howl crept through the trees to my left.

The iron knife was in my hand before I even thought about it. My breaths stilled as I searched from tree to tree, shadow to shadow. No movement. Or was that—?

Another ghostly howl, this time from the right.

I spun, breaths starting again, quick now where they'd been steady before.

Craggy brown bark. Green ferns. The occasional patch of snow that had broken through the canopy.

More howls came, this time joined by yips and something that sounded suspiciously like a laugh.

Blade before me, hand shaking, I turned. My eyes strained, my ears, too, but my thundering heart was so loud, I'd be lucky to hear any soft noises over it.

A silent shadow split from the shade of a thick tree trunk. Over six feet tall, it walked on two legs, but it was *not* human—not with that long, shaggy head, the large ears, the bent, clawed fingers. It had arms, yes, but they were coated in dark fur. It didn't even bother to hide as it drew closer, yellow eyes on me all the while.

My lungs twitched as I backed away. I worked my tongue around my mouth, longing to tell the creature to fuck off, but the stories Ari's papa had told us were clear: don't offend the fae. If there was one thing they loved more than a bargain, it was a rule, and if there was one set of rules they loved most of all, it was *good manners*.

"Good... good morning." I tried to smile. "I don't mean you any harm." My smile threatened to turn into a hysterical laugh. My little knife, the blade no more than six inches long, against this beast with a muzzle full of sharp teeth. Sure, he was *really* scared I might hurt him.

Tittering laughter and yips echoed from all sides. Clearly they found it just as ridiculous.

"Is that why you bring iron into our forest?" Behind me.

I gasped, whirled, and found a man less than two yards away, though there had been no rustle of leaves or crunch of twig.

Yellow eyes, a toothy smile, more claws. He didn't have the first one's wolf head, but his fingers were long and bent. Brown fur tipped his pointed ears, and more fur peeked over the collar of his shirt and darkened his bare forearms.

Beyond him, three more shapes slipped from the shadows. Bent and shaggy, they ranged from wolf to man and all the twisted forms between.

Throat tight, I blinked and it was as though that

brief, blank moment let my brain catch up with reality and serve up the word.

Werewolves.

As clever as people; as strong and vicious as beasts. I'd never found the wolf in *Little Red Riding Hood* that frightening—not when wolves were very much *out there*, beyond Briarbridge, while people could walk our streets and taverns and be far more cruel to each other.

But these wolfmen?

They had my heart in my throat, cold sweat trickling down my neck, stomach churning around the couple of mouthfuls of bread I'd eaten. At five foot ten, I was tall for a woman, but they were all over six foot and thick with muscle.

My mind coughed up another detail from the stories: they could only be hurt by poison, silver, or iron.

I kept my blade between myself and the one who'd spoken.

He'd asked a question, hadn't he? And I was only gaping in response.

Backing off a step, I swallowed down the tightness in my throat. "It's for defence, not attack."

His smile widened to a grin that showed off long, sharp canines. "You're going to need it, girl."

Screw politeness.

He took a step closer, but I was already gone, bolting into the trees.

"We only want to play," they called after me.

But I crashed through the undergrowth, bread forgotten somewhere in my flight, one hand shoving away branches, the other gripped around the iron knife.

My legs pumped. My lungs heaved like the bellows I used to stoke the fire for baking. My heart roared.

Not a single footstep sounded behind me, but their yipping laughs and snarls said they followed, some much too close.

From somewhere behind and to my right: "We need a new plaything, pretty girl."

"Girl touched by fire." A whisper so close, it made my hair stand on end.

Movement, even closer, then snapping jaws, inches from my right arm.

Squeal lodged in my throat, I slashed and darted left, around a huge old tree, fingertips grazing its rough bark. My blade only found thin air, but it was enough to make the beast back off.

No sooner had I huffed my relief than long fingers reached from the undergrowth. As I twisted away, claws scraped my arm.

Wherever I turned, another appeared. They leered and grinned and laughed like this was all a game.

Despite Ari's magic in my cloak, a cold weight dragged on my chest.

They were toying with me. This was easy for them.

Meanwhile, my legs burned as I sprinted as fast as I possibly could—so fast, I barely had time to register the ground until it was a step away.

Mud, snow, an iced puddle. Ferns whose tips swayed overhead. Fallen logs and crooked branches.

I passed between the ferns, trying not to shake their leaves. If I could just get out of sight and take a winding path, I might lose them.

Then, a step away, there was no ground.

I leapt, barely. For a second there was only air and a brook burbling below, cutting through the soil, winding around roots.

Then, with a jolt, I landed, half-stumbled, and dropped into a roll. My body knew what to do. It was like fighting, and I'd practised for that. A moment later, I swept to my feet and resumed my pounding sprint.

The howls and laughs came from behind and either side, almost level with me. Still on my tail. Shit.

Breaths sawing through my chest, I turned downhill and used gravity to lend me speed. I jumped as much as I ran—over logs and down banks.

But their calls overtook me. They were too fast. My stomach was a solid ball, weighing me down even as my muscles burned with adrenaline.

Somewhere ahead and to the left, a howl broke into a sharp yelp, then an ear-splitting squeal. My blood ran cold—that sound was pure pain. I veered away. Had one of them fallen and injured themselves? Or…?

I kept up my breakneck speed, chest about ready to explode.

A rustle in the bushes, a whine, and one of the beasts stumbled from the undergrowth, blocking my path. I skidded to a stop, barely two yards away, fighting for breath.

My eyes burned as I stared at it for long seconds

before truly registering what I was seeing. It clutched its arm. Or the bloody remains of one—there wasn't much attached to its shoulder other than torn flesh.

What the hells had done that?

Despite being so close, the wolfman barely gave me a glance. Its wide, yellow eyes flicked in all direction as crimson blood spilled between its bent fingers.

From the undergrowth came a low snarl.

With a yelp, it turned. Behind it, the ferns shook and I caught a glimpse of a dark shape.

What was bigger than a werewolf and bad enough to frighten one?

Did I even want to know?

My legs knew the answer before my head and sent me hurtling off to the right, downhill.

Another squealing shriek pierced the air.

What the fuck was that thing? Tears gathered in the corners of my eyes as I sprinted, pushing, pushing, pushing. Moments later, there was another yelp, answered by uncertain whines. But their pursuit continued.

Ahead, through the brown trees and green ferns, a different texture snagged my gaze—large, grey, worn smooth by time. Boulders and huge stones—maybe an old rockfall. They turned the valley's bottom into a maze, and I charged into its winding pathways.

No greenery here, only dirt and shade. Yipping cries bounced off the rock, sounding like they were coming from everywhere at once, but this place would also echo my steps and heaving breaths, making me harder to track. It was my best chance.

If these monsters killed me, Ari really would be on her own.

There were no more yelps of pain. Maybe that shape had just been a bigger member of the pack and it was all part of their brutal game to tear each other apart in order to be the first to reach me.

"Come play with us." The call echoed from all directions. "We promise not to be gentle."

Fuck you. Left, right, ahead, I moved as quickly as I could through the tight passages. Gods knew if I was heading north, south, east, or west—even the narrow glimpse of cloud-veiled sky above was no help.

It didn't matter what way I went, as long as I got away from—

Something clamped over my mouth.

Find out how Rose escapes these beasts in *These Gentle Wolves*, a fractured fairy tale reimagining of *Little Red Riding Hood*, featuring grumpy X sunshine, enemies-to-lovers, and a marriage of convenience to a gruff protector fans of Wolverine and Geralt will fall in love with.

ACKNOWLEDGMENTS

There are many people who helped make this book happen, but of course first needs to be my Stolen Brides of the Fae authors. Emma Hamm, Sylvia Mercedes, Tara Grayce, S.M. Gaither, Angela J. Ford, Kenley Davidson, and Sarah K.L. Wilson – thank you so much for your hard work and dedication throughout this project, and for being such inspiring women in the author world. I'm honoured to work with you on this series and so excited to see these books go out in the world. Thanks also to the amazing Dominique Wesson for her incredible cover art for this whole series.

Thanks behind the scenes to two people who had to put up with far too much of my whining during the writing of STB: Lasairiona McMaster and Carissa Broadbent. You two deserve some sort of medal, not only for the aforementioned whining, but also for reading my raw and not-so-raw drafts and helping me shape this story into something... well, something kinda beautiful. <3

Many thanks to my dear, dear romfan author friends for their support and encouragement, as well as answering my questions and helping me work out problems – you are all amazing and I love you to bits. Catharine Glen, Beth Okamoto, Jennifer R Frontera, Tameri Etherton, Jessica Fry, Miranda Honfleur, Anne-Mhairi Simpson, and JA Clement.

Thanks always to my ARC readers for picking up early copies and reviewing. Your support means the world to me and helps get these stories into the hands of many more readers. Thank you!

Big thanks to my sewing friends for various suggestions about Ari's workshop and its magical elements: Dee Lushious, Rachel Haggerty, Jennifer Garside, Jeri Rossiter, Alison Campbell, Karolina Zarzycka, Julia Bremble, Evgeniya Dragoeva, and Sandrine. Special thanks to Beth of Moody Corsetry & Alycia of Emiah Couture – for SO MANY amazing sewing space suggestions that had me pining after such a place and all the magical equipment!

And, of course, thanks to my husband for not complaining too much when I'm buried in books with my head in my laptop for so long that he can't remember what I look like. Thank you, my love.

Also by Clare Sager – Set in the Sabreverse

SHADOWS OF THE TENEBRIS COURT

Gut-wrenching romance full of deceit, desire, and dark secrets.

Book 1 – *A Kiss of Iron*

Book 2 – *A Touch of Poison* – Coming 2023, pre-order now.

(Just might contain an appearance by everyone's favourite threadwitch and fae couple...)

BOUND BY A FAE BARGAIN

Steamy fantasy romances featuring unwitting humans who make bargains with clever fae. Each book features a different couple, though the characters are linked.

Stolen Threadwitch Bride

These Gentle Wolves – Pre-order now for March 2023.

(Featuring Ari's friend, Rose, plus appearances from Ari and Ly and **that** reunion.)

BENEATH BLACK SAILS

An enemies-to-lovers tale of piracy, magic, and betrayal. Complete series.

Book 0 – *Across Dark Seas* – Free Book

Book 1 – *Beneath Black Sails*

Book 2 – *Against Dark Tides*

Book 3 – *Under Black Skies*

Book 4 – *Through Dark Storms*

Printed in Great Britain
by Amazon